the enchanted island

Also by Ellie O'Neill

Reluctantly Charmed

ellie O'NEILL

the enchanted island

SIMON & SCHUSTER

London · New York · Sydney · Toronto · New Delhi

A CBS COMPANY

THE ENCHANTED ISLAND
First published in Australia in 2015 by
Simon & Schuster (Australia) Pty Limited
Suite 19A, Level 1, 450 Miller Street, Cammeray, NSW 2062

10 9 8 7 6 5 4 3 2 1

A CBS Company
Sydney New York London Toronto New Delhi
Visit our website at www.simonandschuster.com.au

© Ellie O'Neill 2015

All rights reserved. No part of this publication may be reproduced, stored in a retrieval system, or transmitted in any form or by any means, electronic, mechanical, photocopying, recording or otherwise, without prior permission of the publisher.

National Library of Australia Cataloguing-in-Publication entry
Creator: O'Neill, Ellie, author.
Title: The enchanted island/Ellie O'Neill.
ISBN: 9781925030013 (paperback)
9781922052995 (ebook)
Subjects: Lawyers – Fiction.
Detective and mystery stories.
Ireland – Fiction.
Dewey Number: A823.4

Cover design: Christabella Designs
Cover image: Pinvinok, NorSob, Anna Paff/Shutterstock
Typeset by Midland Typesetters, Australia
Printed and bound in Australia by Griffin Press

The paper this book is printed on is certified against the Forest Stewardship Council® Standards. Griffin Press holds FSC chain of custody certification SGS-COC-005088. FSC promotes environmentally responsible, socially beneficial and economically viable management of the world's forests.

For Joe

the enchanted island

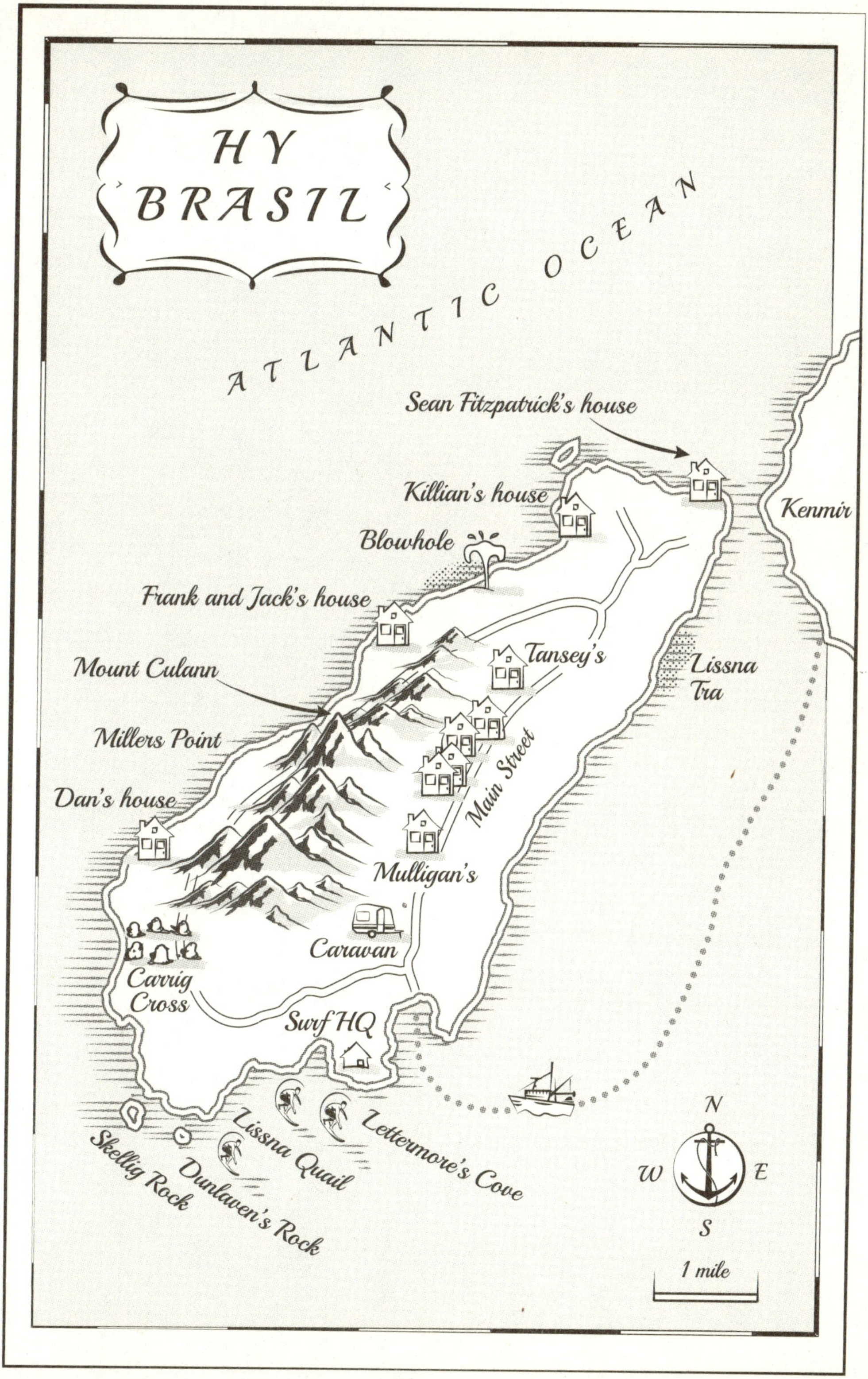

HY BRASIL
ATLANTIC OCEAN
Sean Fitzpatrick's house
Killian's house
Kenmir
Blowhole
Frank and Jack's house
Tansey's
Mount Culann
Lissna Tra
Millers Point
Main Street
Dan's house
Mulligan's
Caravan
Carrig Cross
Surf HQ
Lissna Quail
Lettermore's Cove
Skellig Rock
Dunlaven's Rock
N
W
E
S
1 mile

1

I had never been to Hy Brasil before. I had a vivid image of it as an island of green soggy fields, paddy caps and cigarette-rolling locals in diamond-patterned woolly jumpers who might sing you a song or punch you in the stomach if you looked sideways at them. I expected it to be insular and parochial, with violent, unforgiving weather. But still, I wanted to go. I wanted to leave Dublin. My carefully constructed life was crumbling, and I had been the one to start the avalanche. I needed to run away for a little while to straighten my 27-year-old head out.

When my boss suggested going to the western-most tip of Ireland on a job, I had practically high-kicked my way out of his glass office, cheering and waving pompoms. And here I was, three days later, wet and shivering and bouncing around in a tiny boat on a furious sea with inches of water at my feet.

The rain was black. It collapsed from the sky, building momentum, getting angrier, before it threw itself down in a temper. I tightened my grip on the edges of the wooden seat, the skin of my fingers welded into the grooves. I closed my eyes, giving in to the relentless seesawing of the boat. There wasn't much to see anyway – when we'd set off twenty minutes ago, the island had been a dark grey spot on a grey sea against a grey sky.

'It'll clear,' came the shout from the front of the boat. The owner of the fishing boat that was offering washing-machine experiences pointed to a tiny pinprick of light grey in the sky. 'It'll be a soft day.'

Blinded by the blankets of rain billowing at my face, I nodded and then straightened out the black plastic bag he'd given me to wear. At least it was waterproof.

'You from Dublin?'

I wasn't sure if it was the wind that was causing the whistle in his speech or the fact that he had no teeth. His chin and nose met in a perfect kiss. He pulled his tweed flat cap down further over his clear blue eyes and continued to swing the boat's rudder half-heartedly with his left hand.

'Yeah.'

'Not many Dublin folk come out this way.'

I nodded again. Hy Brasil was the smallest and remotest island off the coast of Clare; it was said that on a clear day you could see America. I doubted very much that there was ever a clear day. Google had taught me that Hy Brasil had a population of 534, many of whom were over fifty or under

The Enchanted Island

twelve, and spoke Irish as their second language. There were no cars, people got around on bikes and, if my imagination had taught me anything, probably donkeys. The main industries were fishing and knitting, as if knitting was an industry. It probably just meant there were a lot of sheep. One line on Wikipedia referred to the island as the Irish Bermuda Triangle, except it wasn't a triangle, it was more of a weird oblong shape, all seven by three miles of it. The seas around Hy Brasil were treacherous: for such a tiny coastline, it had clocked up more shipwrecks than anywhere else in Ireland. Strange static sounds came over the radio in the vicinity of the island, and compasses were known to go haywire. Larger vessels stayed miles away from it. There was one small fishing boat that travelled out and back from the mainland daily, and a larger one with supplies for the island once a week if the weather allowed.

I watched as a threatening shape with jagged edges appeared on the horizon, sheer cliffs stretching towards the sky as black velvet waves exploded with white foam against the rocks.

'What brings you to the island?' Boat Man peered inquisitively at me.

I shook my head briskly. 'Work,' I replied. I took a deep breath of salty air as the wind whipped around me. Heavy droplets of rain stalled on my long black eyelashes before plopping onto the plastic bag poncho like tears.

He swivelled his body to me, causing the boat's rudder to veer to the left, and me to swing awkwardly over the edge, close enough to the ocean's surface to feel the spray on my face like angry splinters. 'Work?' he repeated, shouting through the chasm of air between the wind and the waves. 'And you from Dublin?'

'Shouldn't you be . . . ?' I nervously pointed towards the island, attempting to direct the boat.

'She'd make it there on her own, believe you me.' He shrugged. 'What kind of work?'

'It's confidential.' I straightened myself up and deliberately turned my head to the horizon, channelling my inner beard-stroking, sea-faring captain.

He looked at me suspiciously. 'Right so, people mind their business here too. They like to stick to themselves. They won't take kindly to outside meddling – you'll learn that fast.'

'I won't be meddling.' After a pause, I couldn't resist asking, 'Are you from here so?'

'Do I look like a halfwit? Don't I've ten fingers and toes and me parents weren't brother and sister?'

I laughed.

'I'm a mainland man. Cosmopolitan, like yourself.' He pulled his tweed-jacket collar closer round his neck.

My shoulder-length black hair hung like a drenched shower curtain over my face. I was confident my work as a solicitor wouldn't remain confidential for long, all going according to plan. The trucks would be rolling in by the end of the month and Hy Brasil would be changed forever. I could deal with any islanders and their issues from the warmth and dry seclusion of my Dublin office. This would be flawless. My stomach lurched in nervous excitement. A bridge. A spectacular bridge.

The Enchanted Island

My dad had been an architect. He had built half of Dublin and his spirit whistled through the bridges, parks and corners of the city. Ever since I was old enough to click Lego blocks together, he had instilled in me his love of design and building. My university summers were spent working on building sites, not the norm for a middle-class Dublin girl, but I was a bit of a tomboy back then. I remember Dad smiling proudly at me when he'd pop on site in a hi-vis vest, a steaming mug of tea in his hand, joking that he was raising four boys, not three. It was nice to share his passion and the money was good – a lot more interesting than flipping burgers for minimum wage.

The guys on site didn't exactly warm to me, what with me being 'up her own arse' and a 'wanker stooooodent', not to mention 'gagging for it'. But they got bored of mocking me after a while and in spite of 'being on the blob' every day for four consecutive months for three years, I put in the hours like the rest of them, got covered in dust, lugged bricks, balanced on scaffolding, drank sugary tea and wiped my nose on my sleeve. While my peers went backpacking in Europe and kept thoughtful journals about one-night stands and views from lengthy train rides, I learned how to lay concrete, weave labyrinths of pipes, plaster walls so smoothly they felt like glass and decipher which grain of wood catches sunlight in a kitchen.

Dad died of cancer during my final year of college, six years ago. I didn't work on site that summer. I didn't want to feel like one of the boys anymore without Dad turning up to laugh at me in a hard hat. I didn't see the point. I took a job in a posh clothes boutique with a French name and dressed mannequins in silk fabrics with ornate gold-clasp belts. I kept my lipstick fresh, my skin dewy and skirts fashionably short. I smiled politely at perfume-drenched customers and oohed and aahed when they transformed in the change rooms. I tried not to think about how I would prefer to have calloused hands and itchy eyes filled with dust. I replaced my work boots with heels that summer, my hard hat with jewelled clips, I got manicures for the first time in my life and I shut the door on my tomboy self and all that it meant.

This trip to Hy Brasil had me so excited – I was going to be a part, albeit in a minor way, of a bridge build. It made me feel like I was doing something right. That I was still Dad's Miss Maevo, that he was still grinning proudly at me.

'Almost there now.' Boat Man looked straight ahead.

I couldn't see two inches in front of me with all the rain to know where we were. The constant motion had forced my stomach to lurch, and my head to spin. Nauseated and shivering, I wanted off this boat as quickly as possible before I passed out and landed head first in the black waves.

The bottom of the boat jolted, and we slid onto a ramp and came to a dramatic halt. The rain started to ease off slightly. I could have sworn the boat had stopped, but she was still rocking like a 1970s glam rocker at a revival concert. Boat Man leaped out with legs on springs and pulled the boat up along the cement slope so the front half was on dry land, then hooked a rope around a nearby pole. I went to stand, but my legs quivered and melted under me.

The Enchanted Island

'Whoa, watch yourself.' He held out a hand. I leaned my whole body into this tiny figure of a man and with great effort heaved myself over the edge and slowly clambered onto land.

While my wobbly legs adjusted themselves, he swiftly unloaded my luggage.

'Thanks very much,' I said, looking around, lost.

'Someone coming to pick you up?'

'Yeah, I think so.'

'No one's a good time keeper here. I'm sure they'll make it eventually.'

'Not to worry,' I said, worried.

I plonked myself down on my suitcase, trying to orientate myself. Water and earth. One fluid, one solid; I was now definitely on solid ground, even though it didn't feel like it: my legs trembled and my stomach still heaved ominously. I took a deep breath. It had stopped raining, and the grey clouds were magically dissolving, a whiter light illuminating my surroundings. It wasn't much of a harbour, more of a poor man's car park, anchored by two green fields, which was probably where the overwhelming smell of sheep shit was coming from. The road ran uphill, and two waist-high grey stone walls snaked alongside it. I couldn't see too far ahead, but there didn't seem to be any buildings at all, just a few bushes and some frizzy-haired sheep eyeballing each other in the distance. I braced myself for the great outdoors.

Boat Man was slowly easing the boat into the water again. He stopped and looked back at me. 'Be careful.'

'Will do.' I smiled, and nodded my head in a goodbye, cheerio fashion.

'No.' He turned around, one hand holding the boat. His face was flushed. 'This place is not how it seems. They keep secrets. It's dangerous. Don't stay long.' And with that he pushed off the boat, hopped into it and was away into the violent black sea.

2

As one of the only single people in the office, I was the most obvious choice for an assignment on a remote island. I'm sure non-singles could pack up and go at the twerk of a hip, but there were bound to be some protests, some squeaks about Portia's school play, anniversary dinners, head lice infestations. Not from me. The chance to get out of Dublin couldn't come at a better time. Things hadn't been going very well for me. And by things, I mean my life.

It was all my fault, I knew it was all my fault. I had done a bad thing and I wasn't sure I knew how to fix it.

I had had an emergency: an appointment with Dr Nash. You have to book months in advance to get time with him and it's not like you would cancel an appointment once you had one. I do believe anyone in my position would have done the same thing.

Dr Nash's surgery smelled of eucalyptus oil. I shimmied my shoulders back into the chair, but it was almost impossible to get more comfortable. Even with my eyes closed I could still see the white lights through my eyelids. I could hear the clinks and sounds of metal on glass as caps were being unscrewed. A rustle of latex gloves that I knew were caressing a sterile needle. Bliss. I waited for the familiar smell of alcohol as my forehead was wiped, cool and moist.

Dr Nash spoke calmly, 'You'll just feel a little prick now, Maeve.'

'Is that what you say to all the girls?' I sing-songed, then sniggered at my own joke and opened an eye at him, slightly raising my eyebrow. I could only slightly raise it, but I knew if I didn't tackle this movement now, in a few weeks' time I would be raising, furrowing and frowning, and my forehead would once again look like a garden rake had ploughed across it. You see, it *was* an emergency.

'Stop it, Maeve. You are terrible – you make me laugh. I need to concentrate.' He snorted and his whole body shook for a moment. He waved his gloved hands in the air. Hands with magic fingers that skip and dance along my face like it's an Etch A Sketch and wipe away all the lines. He smiled.

We have a nice relationship, Dr Nash and I. I see him about four times a year and have negotiated a fifteen per cent discount, which was tough to do. I needed to increase my procedures and try to get him down to about twenty-five per cent. A bit of Botox on my face is maintenance, but the future could involve more invasive procedures. I have to be ahead of the game. I'm twenty-seven now and preservation is key to successful ageing. I am a forward planner.

I closed my eyes and waited for the pinch, the glorious tight squeeze that will keep away those nasty laughter lines for another few months. The needle jabbed, the cotton balls wiped and I smiled wider with every little prick.

'You can open your eyes now, Maeve.' Dr Nash swung a mirror on a mechanical arm over me and hovered his little finger over the areas that he had treated. I looked exactly as I had fifteen minutes ago. My dark eyebrows were shaped to within an inch of their life, but still I thought the left one looked a bit wonky. My eyelashes, which had had a few extensions added to them the day before, accentuated my hazel eyes. I stared at the stubborn smattering of freckles across my nose that no amount of makeup seemed to be able to cover and I glared at a soft pocket of skin under my chin that I just knew would eventually morph into a double chin. I'm never happy. All the poking and prodding and preening and plucking I do seems to give me a momentary buzz, and then I find something else wrong, a chip, a chink, a blemish. It's a relentless battle, a never-ending treadmill, to look the way I want to look: polished and glamorous, almost untouchable, unbreakable.

The sheen wasn't there yet. The glossy reflective Botox shimmer would appear on my forehead in about a week. I felt a little shudder of excitement at the prospect. I love the shimmer. I don't understand people who talk about celebs who have it like it's a bad thing.

'You've done it again, Dr Nash,' I gushed.

'Well, it's easy, I have such a beautiful canvas to work with. You are stunning, Maeve, even without my help.' He returned the gush.

Susan the receptionist, with tremendously perky boobs for a woman in her fifties, rustled some papers and smiled up at me. Bubbles popped in my belly. I knew that a nervous rash was creeping up my neck, and my mouth was inching towards a rectangular shape, exposing all my teeth in a weird, fearful smile. There was a slight tremor in my hands as I rummaged through my cream leather Chloe handbag for my wallet. Why did I think I might throw up?

It wasn't like this was criminal behaviour, this was just a loan. But my conscience was wrestling with me, pulling me to the ground and kicking me in the belly. I know the difference between right and wrong. This was wrong. I was a bad person, doing a bad thing. My vision blurred and black dots speckled at the corner of my eyes.

I looked at Susan, who was tapping a pen.

'Do you think I could have some water?' Somehow the words came out.

She swung her chair about and wheeled over to the water cooler. I grabbed at the glass like I had trekked in a full woolly jumper and fleece tracksuit pants across the Sahara. I calmed down as I sipped. I took a breath.

This would be fine.

'What's the damage?' I said, trying to sound composed but aware that the strange scary square smile was dominating

The Enchanted Island

my face. Susan would be used to seeing weird faces in the surgery, and she didn't bat an eyelid. Maybe she can't.

'With your discount that's five hundred euros.'

I slid Sasha's shiny card across the desk.

Susan didn't look once at the card, ringing it all through with a swipe, a beep and a smile. Sasha's pin was the same number as the alarm code in the flat that we had shared for the last five years. And as we were best friends who pretty much shared everything, it was also the pin on my credit cards, only my cards were miserably maxed out. The problem – oh, and I know you're going to judge me harshly for this – was that I hadn't asked Sasha for her card. This was her emergency credit card that was literally only to be used in an emergency. If she found herself being kidnapped by balaclavaed baddies in a white van threatening to bind her feet for a ransom of a few hundred quid, then and only then would she justify using the card.

Unlike me, who genuinely sees a heart-palpitating emergency as getting my hands on a new shampoo that some celebrity is on TV promoting with their swooshy shiny hair. I once didn't sleep for three nights waiting on delivery of a very expensive pair of wonder knickers, which I had maxed my card out on. I had these visions of my well-sculpted bum drawing envious glances, and of myself strutting in a finger-clicking, you-can't-handle-this-much-booty way. I was giddy and sick with how dazzling my life would look with these knickers in them, and when they arrived, those chicken fillets for the arse just made me look fat and dowdy.

Sometimes the real thrill of shopping is that moment before the purchase, when I can feel euphoric with the potential of where whatever I'm buying can take me. It's exciting. Sparkly lights are about to twinkle. And nothing, like money or credit cards, or a little bit of debt, can stand in my way.

But this was different, this was a new low for a shopping high. Even I could see that. I was slipping into a very big black hole. I was using my best friend, taking advantage of our trust and friendship, and for what? A bit of Botox. I knew this, yet it didn't stop me. Whatever blackness was inside of me, whatever it was that had to be coated over with products and procedures – vanity, selfishness, ego – at that moment, that blackness, those voices that demand I look a certain way, was louder than my conscience, and I gave in to it.

Sasha is six-foot-one, as opposed to my five-five, has long chocolate brown hair, laughing blue eyes and a wide mouth that is permanently fixed in a smile. This has been known to cause her some problems at work. She's an apprentice solicitor, same as me, but she specialises in divorce – not exactly a smiling matter. We have been an inseparable duo like Dolce & Gabbana or Bananas in Pyjamas ever since we met at college at seventeen. She is my keeper of secrets, my common sense, owner of my second wardrobe, my stylist, my book and movie adviser, and my-dancing-on-tables partner. Sasha has savings, doesn't believe in credit cards and is planning on buying a flat next year with her boyfriend, Boring George. Obviously she doesn't call him that, and neither do I – to his face. Even though we're the same age, I always feel like she's the grown-up, and I'm the pretend grown-up. I wear cartoon characters on my T-shirts. My friends call me Twisty Arm Maeve, because I will literally go to any party, anywhere, at any time. Mam slips me fifty euro every time I see her. I still use my student card to get a twenty per cent discount at Top Shop (sales assistants never check expiry dates, but if they did, they'd see my card was seven years out). But I am kind of a grown-up, I do have a job, a good one, where I make noises like a grown-up would in an authoritative, adult-style voice, things like 'moving forward' and 'let's draw a line under that'. And very importantly, my job as an apprentice solicitor gives me a credit history that allows me to get credit cards, and right now a shiny new one was winging its way to me, and Sasha would be paid back before she even knew the money was gone. We'll have a good laugh about it and slosh back some wine and admire my wrinkle-free forehead. This would all be fine.

A receipt curled out of the machine, which Susan ripped off and handed over to me.

My shoulders relaxed.

'Will I put you in the diary for three months' time?'

'Absolutely, I'll see you then.' And out I skipped into a sunny spring evening, a shiny forehead awaiting me and not a care in the world.

'You slept with Carl again, didn't you?'

I nodded.

'Oh my God, Maeve, what are you like? You always hate yourself after you sleep with him.' Hazel took a bite of her chicken salad. We had snuck out for lunch – no one lunches in our office. It was more acceptable to leave the office to do a cross-fit training session than eat a salad. Hazel was five years older than me and worked as a legal secretary. We had bonded over a mutual dislike of Antonia, another apprentice, who was effortlessly beautiful and intoxicatingly lazy. She gave off an aura of casually flicking the sand of sunny South-East Asian beaches from her manicured toenails, wondering what time her massage was, while the rest of us scurried around, slamming down case files on desks and pounding at keyboards.

'I know, but he's cute and we have a thing.' We were in a cafe on the quays, perched on the river Liffey, overlooking the Samuel Beckett Bridge, which looks like a giant musical harp rotating in the air, in tune with the edgy historic Docklands environment. The cafe had been christened the anti-cafe, and had charcoal walls, steel chairs, industrial tables and a slate floor. The barista was a handlebar-moustached hipster who, through a series of eye rolls and ironic tuts, served fantastic coffee. There were no pictures, no dainty flowers in milk bottles, no homey ma and pa feel. There was an overall lick of communism about it. People happily queued out the door every morning.

'Of course he called you, you are such a catch, but he makes you feel like shit. Why do you hook up with him?'

Because he calls, we have fun together and he has a nice apartment and – I don't know. 'He's cute.'

The Enchanted Island

She rolled her eyes at me. 'He might be cute but he's an arsehole. He told you to get a haircut.'

I ran my fingers through my shoulder-length poker-straight hair and laughed. 'I did kind of need a trim.'

Carl was my friend with benefits without actually being my friend. We'd met a few months before at Twisted Pepper, a nightclub that had sprung up in Dublin and was the place to be for a good eight weeks before the crowd moved on. But I already knew who Carl was. He was an It boy around town, a complete horndog with a charming grin who shagged every model in Dublin. His face was plastered all over gossip blogs for being in love triangles. He was a total metrosexual and gave off very effeminate vibes, he curled his eyelashes and got facials, so the horndog thing kind of came out of nowhere. He wrote a social butterfly column in one of the Sunday newspapers, and owned a high fashion men's shop on South Anne Street. And on weekends, he was a DJ.

That Saturday night he had been like a messiah in the DJ box, ten feet above the dance floor, arms outstretched, grinning like a euphoric monkey, probably high I think now but I didn't know it at the time. He commanded the crowd like a puppeteer. The pulsating dance floor was under his control. The rhythm was like an exploding heartbeat. He was mesmerising. I was one of the masses throwing my shoulders around to the music, dancing towards the DJ box with singular devotion. It was religious, the clapping, the dancing, the connections with the other dancers, the smiles. If music was our God, that night Carl was our saviour on earth.

Heart still racing, residual beats still pumping through me, at the end of the night I went looking for Sasha. She'd gone off seeking a house party while I remained on the dance floor. Searching for her, I literally bumped into Carl: he was spinning round from the bar, the obligatory water bottle in hand, which simultaneously grazed my breast and spilled on me.

I jumped backwards. 'At least buy me a drink first.'

'God, I'm so sorry.' He blushed beetroot red and started grasping for napkins. On only finding two Heineken beer mats, he waved them sheepishly at me. 'These won't really do, will they?'

He was tall, lanky tall, like his legs and arms didn't quite belong to his torso. His light brown hair was combed forwards and he wore a hang-dog look.

We had six official dates, two dinners, two drinks nights and two sleepovers.

Then one morning we were lying in bed, a little hungover from the night before. I had been weighing up scrambled versus poached eggs for breakfast when he blurted it out.

'I like you, but I think we should see other people.'

'Really?' Suddenly feeling very naked, I'd rolled over and propped myself on my elbow, clutching the duvet to my throat and trying not to look like a sledgehammer had just hit me on the head.

'Yeah, you're wicked.'

I cringed, of all times for him to choose to be a character from *EastEnders*.

The Enchanted Island

'But you know, let's not make this a thing.' He formed his fingers into quotation marks to emphasise his point. I hate people who do that.

Immediately I started to scan back through our very recent and brief dating past. Had I at any point limpeted myself to him? I didn't think we'd even held hands in public. He had asked me out, and I had prided myself on barely responding to his text messages. Was he joking? This had to be a joke.

I threw my head back onto the pillow and laughed. 'Right, a *thing*.' I made giant quotation marks too.

'That's cool. I knew you'd be cool.' And he rolled on top of me and started kissing my neck, softly nuzzling into me.

'Like this isn't a thing, what's about to happen isn't a thing,' I said, before I squealed in delight as he delicately brushed my belly with kisses and positioned himself between my thighs.

He grinned and I melted as he slowly drawled, 'Oh, this is a thing. This is definitely a thing.'

Sex with Carl was exciting and passionate. Not the kind of sex that you could put on if you weren't that into a person, or so I told myself again and again.

Turns out Carl hadn't been joking. The texts dried up. What had been a waterfall of emoticons became a slow drip of half-hearted XXXs, which eventually came to a full stop. I was 'wicked' but apparently so was Natasha Kadyan, the only Irish girl I knew of who could pull off white shorts and flat shoes. She was spotted hanging at the DJ box at one of Carl's gigs, dancing and jiggling her perfect bum in his direction.

I growled when I heard about that. It obviously didn't last too long, because a few weeks later he called me and I trotted over to his apartment and then it happened again and again and again. And somehow over the last three months, I had become a booty call, and I wasn't really sure how I felt about it at all.

But then I reminded myself that this was exactly the kind of fun, non-committal relationship I should have in my twenties. After all, I didn't need a serious boyfriend, I was part of the generation that could do everything: have a big career, freeze my eggs, develop a modern family with fabulous female friends and an army of gays, and have sex on the side. I could catch my own spiders and, with some contorting, massage my own feet. I didn't need anyone to complete me. I knew the line from magazines, that I was the sum of my parts. I didn't crave marriage and romance, or at least I didn't think I did. I was confident it wasn't for me. What was the point of it anyway? Marriages ended in divorce or death, with heartbreak and grief, I'd seen it with my mam and dad after he died. It was better to construct your own life, one that no one else could break.

Sasha, the armchair psychologist, thinks that I'm attracted to Carl because he's so unattainable, that he isn't boyfriend material, so we'll never fall in love and he'll never leave me like Dad left Mam. That way, I'll never be heartbroken like I've seen my mam be. Sasha thinks my attraction to Carl is all a defence mechanism, as is my aversion to serious relationships. I think she's going way too deep into her self-help analogies and, really, I just fancy Carl because he's cute. And to be fair, my romantic history has always been abysmal, way before Dad passed away. I didn't kiss a boy until I was fifteen – it felt like other girls my age were onto their second divorce and third baby by then. I hadn't particularly liked Steven Martin, his school trousers were too short for him and his hair was always greasy, but he seemed to like me, and I remember feeling like if I didn't kiss someone, anyone, soon, I would have to sign up for the convent and be done with it. I had lied outright to my friends, and told them that I had had a French boyfriend on an exchange the previous summer and we'd had sex. They had nodded approvingly and asked for all the details. I was big into romantic novels at the time, bodice ripping and heroes on horses, so I described his purple member thrusting into my love cave. Jackie Murphy was the only one who looked at me suspiciously. She had a boyfriend in college (which when you think about it is ridiculous, a fifteen-year-old school girl dating a second year in college) so chances are she probably had at least seen a penis by then. And I don't think she would have referred to it as a throbbing warrior.

I pinned Steven Martin to a wall in the bowling alley. I pushed my body up against his and planted my open mouth on top of his angst-ridden face. I can still see his eyeballs popping like a Pringles box. My big brother Johnny saw us – there wasn't anything secretive about the kiss, we were in full view of the score board – and collared Steven Martin and decked him. Poor guy, he probably just wanted to bowl a bit, maybe have some cheesy nachos. Instead he got a tongue shoved down his throat and a black eye. Anyway, word got out on the teenage grapevine of North County Dublin not to mess with Maeve O'Brien.

And so I started college with my virginity intact. Not for long though: Phillip Cummins saw to that for me, and for quite a number of other first-year students. I scratched up a few notches on my bed post, but the big stuff, the lasting stuff, for whatever reasons, has eluded me.

I swirled my tuna salad around my plate. The hipster had poured vinaigrette all over it and I could do without the calories. I had just come off the Atkins diet and had successfully lost a stubborn four pounds that had been nagging me for an age. I didn't need them creeping back. I liked that my size ten jeans were a little bit baggy at the waist.

'How are the boys?'

Hazel had five-year-old twins. I loved them. I babysat whenever she asked and let them run riot. They could dress up as superheroes or run around in their underpants, eating sweets and waving sticks; there were no rules when I was in charge. I'm convinced I enjoyed it more than them.

'Good. Wild. We may call you in for a night soon, Brian and I are overdue a fight in a public place.' She smiled.

'Any time.'

'You looked great in that picture on Instagram the other night.'

I felt a mini surge of pride. It was my best selfie yet. I had pouted, stretched, preened and contorted myself like a trapeze artist to get that photo right. There's a feeling I get when I post, an adrenalin rush, like dropping a coin into a slot machine waiting to win big, waiting for the likes to pop up. *You win. I choose you.* Now, now, now. I picked up my phone and scrolled down to it, flashing the screen at Hazel.

'I'm polling very well – 237 likes,' I said with as much mock irony in my voice as I could muster.

Hazel laughed. 'With numbers like those you should go into politics.'

'I'd campaign on fifty per cent discounts on designer clothing, free microdermabrasion facials and waxing for everyone.'

'You'd be in in a week.'

'It's the important stuff. This is what matters to people, not potholes in the road and electricity bills.'

Hazel laughed, not realising that I was only half joking.

3

A few days later, I picked up some biscuits on my way home from work. I was looking forward to an evening on the couch with the usual 'I've never felt a connection like this before' women on *The Bachelor*. There would be cups of tea and non-stop chat with Sasha. We had recently discovered to our equal delight that the couch had moulded to our shapes: Sasha sprawled on the right-hand side, all legs and arms, while I curled up like a cat on the left.

When I got in, Sasha was in the kitchen chopping up some cabbage. She was on day two of the cabbage diet and the smell of noxious gases in the flat was inhuman. Kicking off my wedges, I went straight to the window and heaved it open without even saying hi. She bit her lip and squished up her nose in apology. I was happy to see that Boring George wasn't there. Our open-plan flat turned a little too cosy when George was around. I guess he didn't know that it was my side of the couch that he seemed to gravitate to – it's not like there was a sign there or anything, but still. I hated coming home from work and meeting him here. He'd pop up like a jack-in-the-box, all stuffed and waxy, coughing and nervously thrusting a hand at me, 'Hello, Maeve.' I mean, hello! Who says 'hello'? Surely it's 'hi', isn't it? He made awkward conversation about politics and current affairs. I haven't read a non-style section of a newspaper in years. I don't know or really care about what's going on in the world. But George, George could bang on about the Middle East and water shortages in central Africa all night.

'There's a letter for you on the coffee table.' Sasha tipped her head towards the lounge.

It was the letter from the bank I'd been expecting. The familiar gold logo winked at me from the envelope, but something was wrong. There was no card outline. This was supposed to hold my new credit card. I ripped it open and quickly scanned down for a date as to when they would be delivering the card, only it didn't say that. It did say, *Your application has been denied.*

Oh, that sinking feeling. I froze. This had never happened before. There were always cards. There was always money. Not my money, granted, but access to money.

I heard my heart pumping in my ears. My breathing was wheezy and raspy. I noticed my hands were shaking, the letter quivering in the air. The knot in my stomach that had been there every morning since borrowing Sasha's card suddenly doubled in size. And then it travelled, it crawled up across my shoulders and forced them to freeze into a rigid block. It cracked into my head and banged hammers behind my eyes. It made my mouth dry. It released a hive of bees into my ears. I placed my hands flat on the table and forced myself to breathe in and out slowly.

Do not think about this now, I told myself. *This will all be under control eventually. Do not sweat the small stuff. Remember this is small stuff.* But could €13,000 in debt be called small stuff?

'. . . we can do back-to-back *Bachelor* and then there's a *Grey's Anatomy* or *Orange*. But I'm thinking *Grey's*.' Sasha's conversation streamed across the room as she slid on her slippered feet towards the couch, and collapsed onto it.

'Sash.'

'You look weird, Maeve, you okay? I should have gotten wine, shouldn't I?'

We'll laugh about this later.

I smiled at her, a gritted-teeth, slightly pleading smile. 'Sasha, I may have done something.'

She stopped talking immediately and I watched her jaw clench. Her face froze.

'Obviously there's been a mix-up at the bank, so I'll have to get on to them, but . . .' *Just say it fast, just blurt it out, you've been friends for years; this is nothing in the grander scheme of things.* 'I borrowed your emergency credit card to go to Dr Nash, and I was going to pay you back with my new card, but the bank haven't sent me a new card, but I'll sort it out, and I'll pay you back. Of course I'll pay you back. It just might take me a bit longer.'

The Enchanted Island

She sat up and moved to the edge of the couch, her face getting paler with every inch she crossed. Very quietly, she spoke, 'You stole my credit card.'

I felt my eyes widen. 'No. Sasha, I borrowed it.'

She shook her head. 'You took it, without my permission and you used it. That's stealing.'

'I'm sorry, Sasha, I just . . .' I borrowed stuff off Sasha all the time. Although I knew this was different. This was probably a much bigger deal than even I was willing to admit. Why had I done it? Why couldn't I have just waited until I could afford it? Did I really need it that badly? What was wrong with me?

'Do you know how much money you already owe me? How many times I've covered your bills, your rent? And now you do this? It's not just the money, like, Jesus, Maeve, I can't even trust you. Like, who the hell are you?' She put her face in her hands.

I don't know. I don't know. And I don't know why I did something like that. I didn't think – I wanted to do it so I just did it. I never stopped to think about what it meant. I felt terrible about it.

But maybe she was going a bit overboard. It's not like I didn't feel bad. I had made a mistake. It didn't deserve a complete re-examination of our friendship.

In a quiet voice, I mumbled, 'It was for Dr Nash. You would have done the same thing.' Except she wouldn't: Sasha didn't get Botox. But Sasha didn't have the pressures I had. She worked in a tiny office with four grandad types. If she came into work in a low-cut blouse they'd send her home in case she got a chest cold. My office was about tight skirts and boobs pushed so high they'd pop out your eye sockets. And yes, while I liked getting Botox and looking good, there was a corporate game to be played out. Most of the senior partners were gay men and they out-Botoxed, out-massaged and out-marathon-ran any junior trying to climb up the ladder. You needed to have them onside, and they were like magnets to a Barbie doll with a flawless complexion who enjoyed discreet conversations about a hectic social life involving club openings and cocktails with ironic umbrellas in them.

I threw my hands in the air. 'I'm sorry, Sasha, I didn't think, I thought it would be okay. We borrow stuff all the time from each other.'

'No, Maeve, you *take* stuff all the time from me, but this, this is really it.'

'It's not the same for you.' Sasha earned more money than me and got bonuses even though she was an apprentice too. It was really disappointing that my salary was genuinely in the negative count. Sometimes I wondered if I'd be better off paying them to work there.

'Not this conversation again!' Sasha shouted. 'You *don't* have to go to work in designer clothes. You were hired because you're good at your job. No one expects an apprentice to have money for clothes.'

'That's what you think.'

'No, I know.' She put her hands to her face again. 'You're good at your job, Maeve, really good. You would never have been hired by Holmes and Friedman if you weren't top of the pool. It doesn't matter what you wear. You don't need to be so insecure.'

I stayed silent.

She sighed heavily. 'You've lost yourself, Maeve, in all this stuff.'

'What are you talking about?'

'Maeve, the selfies? The shopping? The Botox? You never used to care about this stuff, but now you just obsess over it. Who cares about the number of likes you get on a photo? None of it matters, and you *know* none of it matters. You're smarter than this, Maeve.'

'Everyone takes selfies,' I muttered to myself.

'You've just built up this wall of crap. You're in there. I know you are, and I know you've been through a lot . . .' Her eyes were filling with tears. I didn't understand why she was getting so upset. She shook her head briskly, composing herself. 'When I met you in college you were wearing your brother's jeans and no makeup and you looked hot and you didn't care what anybody thought of you. You were fearless. And then after your dad . . .' She trailed off, and I wondered where she was going with this. Why was she talking about Dad?

She took a deep breath. 'Not everyone is going to die on you, Maeve, you don't need to push everyone away by building up this wall of protection around yourself. You just need to get back to you.'

'I know that, I know everyone isn't going to die.' I rolled my eyes at her. 'You don't need to psychoanalyse me, Sasha, sometimes I just mess up.'

'Sometimes . . .' She released a groan. 'I'm sick of it. You need to start by sorting out your money. Take control of your life, not just your appearance.'

'For God's sake, Sash, what do you want me to do, stop living? Stop going out, stop dressing up, stop putting my best self forward?'

'Maeve!' She was shouting again. 'Your best self isn't your Botox self, it's just *yourself.*'

'Whatever. Do you think Carl would look at me twice if I had wrinkles?'

'Maeve, listen to yourself. And I mean, come on, *Carl*? You know he's just a time waster.'

'I have time. I'm twenty-seven.'

'Exactly, Maeve, you're twenty-seven, you're nearly thirty. You need to stop living like a nineteen-year-old. Sort your life out.'

She was going to get personal, was she? Right. I could feel the embers of my temper starting to ignite.

'Is this you talking or George?'

'What's that supposed to mean?'

I made a face. 'You know, sensible, maximum-of-four-drinks-on-a-Saturday-night George.'

'You know nothing about him, Maeve. You've never given him a chance.'

'So, what, am I jealous now? Jealous on top of everything else?'

'You said it.'

'Bitch.'

The Enchanted Island

Sasha stood up and waved her hands in the air like she was slicing through it. 'That's it, no more.' She walked into her room, slamming the door behind her.

I shouldn't have said that about George. Me and my big mouth. George was nice, he treated Sasha well. Why was I so hateful about him? God, was I jealous on top of everything else? This was a mess.

I slumped on the couch. It wasn't the first fight Sasha and I had ever had, there'd been a few over the years, but this felt different. We felt different. But it was stupid. I didn't want to fight with her. I probably should have gone and knocked on her door. I should have been a better person, like Gandhi; I should have ripped the sheet off my bed, made a toga and clasped my hands in prayer. Then we'd both laugh and this weirdness would be over. But I didn't, because I didn't feel Gandhi-like, I felt Genghis-Khan-like: angry and more than a little bit wild.

Things went downhill from there.

Sasha said she thought it would be better for everyone if I moved out. I could move back in with my mam and get on top of my finances.

Honestly, I thought she was joking. That's the type of thing someone on TV says, *Get on top of your finances*. Real people don't talk like that, all weird and preachy. But she was so distant. She said I'd crossed a line, like every friendship has an imaginary line. I didn't get that. Friendship, I told her, was more of a circle.

She wasn't joking. I was out and George was in. Sasha's dad owned the flat. He'd bought it as a little investment property when that was the done thing, when everyone in Ireland was a property mogul. The best part about the arrangement was that our rent had remained the same for five years. That's how I could manage my bills and my shopping habits, and while my debt had spiralled, I still had control of it, or at least I thought I had control of it.

I was devastated. I didn't want to leave. I wanted to shake Sasha, shake myself, stop this, but something – pride, stupidity, stubbornness – jumped up and down in front of me like a seven-foot-tall quarterback with a helmet and knee pads on.

I left immediately.

'I feel terrible about this, Maeve, but I don't know what else to do, you just have to cop on to yourself,' Sasha cried, her face red raw.

I'd watched enough *Oprah* to know what she was trying to do, she was trying to tough love me into being a grown-up. I stuck my tongue out at her (behind her back).

'If *you* feel so terrible, why am I the one moving out? I'm the one who is going back home, I'm going to have to listen to Mam telling me my skirts are too short and watching how many potatoes I eat at dinner. Seriously, Sasha, can we not work this out?' I was begging, I could hear it in my voice, I was pleading with her.

The Enchanted Island

'You have to change, Maeve. You owe it to yourself, to the real you. Anyway, you're turning me into an enabler.'

Sasha always had a way with the dramatics, it was one of the things I loved about her, her flair. I loved a lot of things about Sasha: the way she can always find the best camping spot at a festival; her addiction to reality TV; the fact that she knows the words to every Nicki Minaj song. Aside from all that fun stuff, she's always been such a good friend to me.

'This is a massive overreaction. How many times do I have to say I'm sorry?'

I was really angry with her, and now I was furious that she wouldn't give me the benefit of the doubt. It was only a couple of hundred euros, for God's sake. Was it really worth losing our ten-year friendship over?

'Sorry's not going to cut it, Maeve. Anyway, you don't even sound like you mean it when you say it.'

'I do mean it. I made a mistake.'

'Another one.' She looked at me deadpan. 'Another mistake like the time you never told me you borrowed my grandmother's necklace and lost it in some pub in Temple Bar, or the night you threw an impromptu party in the flat when you knew I was in court the next day, or what about the time you stood me up for dinner because Carl had called looking for action? I ate two baskets of bread waiting for you.'

'Sorry, I said *sorry*,' I spat back at her, 'you don't need to go dredging up everything.' It sounded bad when she turned my mistakes into a list. But I'd never pretended to be perfect. Everyone messes up.

I ran around the flat furiously squishing everything into bags. As I left in a taxi rammed with my packaged life, my gut lurched. Gone. Just like that. I was gone from Hope Street. I stared out the window at the street that I was so familiar with. The kebab shop where I had sampled every item off the menu; the weird newsagent's with the paranoid shopkeeper who kept his hands under the counter at all times, possibly holding a gun, but more likely a rolled-up *Hello* magazine; the street light that had never worked in five years; the one house that kept a pristine garden that grew the most beautiful-smelling roses every spring. Oh God, this was hard. This was much harder than I imagined.

I could see Mam's mouth scrunch into a million little wrinkles as the taxi pulled in to the four-bedroom semi-detached in Clontarf where I'd grown up. She had tut-tutted, sighed and crossed and recrossed her arms a hundred times before I'd even gotten out of the car.

'It's only temporary, Mam. I'm not going to be here for long.'

In the kitchen I pulled out the teapot and a couple of mugs, then reconsidered and took out the teacups. Mam likes things done properly, teacups with saucers, high heels with skirts, no shoes indoors and thank-you cards are just some of her house rules. Mam keeps a tight rein on her house. She likes to clean. She's obsessively tidy, and never sits down. She is always walking around spritzing some chemical in the air and re-wiping an already spotless surface. Her aversion to dirt and disorder only developed after Dad died. I grew up

The Enchanted Island

in a messy, higgledy-piggledy house; a happy home, with a happy mother. Nothing like the sad echo of who Mam is now, with a pinched face and a constant shadow enveloping her.

'You know you're welcome here any time. Sasha is moving on, she's got a boyfriend.'

My relationship with Mam is all based on the pauses. She fills a room when she says nothing. She can write chapters on disappointment in one fleeting glance. I fill her pauses with half-truths most of the time. I let her assume that I made plenty of money because I was a professional. She seemed to like the way it rolled off her tongue, 'My daughter the solicitor.' It sounded a lot better than 'My daughter the debt-riddled spinster.'

I felt my hand grip the handle of the teapot. 'Mam, loads of people aren't married at twenty-seven, none of the boys are.'

She replied with her mantra from my childhood: 'It's different for your brothers.' The three of them were all in long-term relationships, none in any rush to march up the aisle.

I sat down, putting the teapot on the table, and reached for a plate of biscuits (always on a plate, never served in a packet). She glared at my hand and I snatched it away, biscuit free. I knew what she was thinking: *Biscuits won't catch you a husband.*

She hovered over me. '*The Terminal* is on later, Tom Hanks is in it, he's stuck in an airport. He's a marvellous actor, it'll be great. We'll watch it.'

I would love to have a conversation with Mam that I imagine other daughters had, or at least the ones I see on the telly did, about life, sex, men that never phone back, friends that fall out. Instead this evening we'll talk about Tom Hanks, how he seems like a lovely man and whether or not he dyes his hair.

That night, with my Spice Girls duvet cover tucked under my chin, whirling like a dervish in my single bed, with my under-12s Leinster shot-put bronze medal above my head, I thought long and hard about how I would fix this. How I could straighten things out between me and Sasha. A couple of weeks of living with Mam, then I would be able to pay Sasha back every last penny and *then* we'd be able to laugh about it all. I might even buy her a present as an extra thank you, maybe a Mulberry handbag or something absolutely gorgeous that smelled mega expensive. Then we'd talk about 'Remember that time you kicked me out, ha ha ha.' It would be LOL central. This would be fine.

4

My job is very important to me. I love it. I like that the law gives society a structure, that there is a hierarchy, that people have to adhere to guidelines for the better of everyone else. That there is a greater good. I like that. And I know that this sounds completely at odds with who I am, a current law breaker, but that's a blip on the radar. That's not what I'm really about. I have great plans for really helping people and working pro bono after I qualify. Being the good person that I know I am deep down. That will happen as soon as I get out of debt and I'm done partying – sometime in my mid-thirties, I suspect. That'll be when I manage to start the wheels turning on the life I'm supposed to have.

Holmes and Friedman was one of the few independent legal firms that was seeing out the Irish recession – just. We were a team of eighty people in an old mill house on Grand Canal Dock in Dublin's financial district. It was a great place to work, coffee shops and bars shoulder-bumped each other for attention in this buzzy area stuffed with technology companies, and foreign accents complaining about espressos. I felt lucky to have been hired as an apprentice solicitor along with two others straight after our FE-1s, the dreaded law entry exams. For an entire year we were referred to as The Apprentices. No one knew or cared what our actual names were. We chased the shouts, 'Get an apprentice to do it!', like expectant puppies, waiting for some three-piece suit to throw us a case. We were fiercely competitive, always trying to outshine, out-strut, out-fox each other with smiles on.

There was Padraig, or Pigface Padraig as I called him, on account of him coming from a family of pig farmers and having a snouty nose. He came across as a bit of a gormless eejit, all shoulder shrugs and 'Ah, sure, that's for you big city folks'; he was only twenty-five but spoke like an auld fella. Turns out it was a cunning ruse, and he was a good old-fashioned cute whore. Padraig attacked every case in the office, even the ones he wasn't asked to work on, and he occasionally slept under his desk, I think just hoping to absorb the files in the office by osmosis. Then there was Antonia, the hated Antonia, all legs, tight skirts and glossy mane. She was slippery. She let us know very quickly that she wasn't one of us: 'Daddy is a major player in the construction industry in London and is considering moving his business to Dublin.' Antonia was a trust-fund baby. I thought only Marys from the four Marys had trust funds, but apparently not. She oozed money, she wore Stella McCartney dresses teamed with Louboutin wedges. The gay mafia in the office hovered around her adoringly. They actually handed her work without waterboarding her first.

My grades had always been good through college and I worked hard, but I didn't feel like I belonged at Holmes and Friedman. (Sasha has given me many kick-your-insecurities-up-the-arse pep talks over my attitude at work.) I have always tried my best to fit in, to look the way I was supposed to look, confident and together. I work late most days. I put in the hours. It was the culture in the office, it was *understood*, that you would clock up a seventy-hour work week, especially if you were single. And I was so hungry to prove myself, I was like a rabid dog waiting for a bloody steak. I was desperate to outshine the other two and to finally qualify.

Working in such a vibrant area, it was hard to believe that Ireland had a clammy hand over her windpipe. The recession was crippling. The news reported daily on the explosion of the Irish property bubble as if the country had been dependent on semidetached conservatories and garage conversions to stay afloat. At the airport there was a conveyor belt of young, educated people emigrating for work; the brain drain they called it. I knew I didn't want to be one of them. Recessionary Ireland was all I had known as a working adult. Much to my disappointment, I had never quaffed champagne in smooth-marbled Dublin bars or booked in for stone massages. I had missed that legendary time in Irish history. I had been knee-deep in books, studying at university, four years for a bachelor's and a two-year master's, followed by a year to study for my law exams, and now I was in the second year of my two-year apprenticeship. I worked really hard, and got good results. But it was a competitive market place, the recession had forced a lot of people back to study. Ireland had some of the most educated dole lines in Europe.

Recently things had taken a turn. I had thought, naively perhaps, that our company was somehow in a bubble. The recession had been running at full pelt for years, but our company still hired and still gave occasional pay rises. Then the whispers started, the rumours, conversations laced with anxiety. *Redundancies*. The word appeared like a shadow on a lung. *Imminent.* And then the numbers? Plucked from outer space, or from our very blonde receptionist's chosen bottle of hair dye: fifteen per cent, twenty per cent, twenty-five per cent. Everyone became an economist overnight. The cuts had to be made to stay afloat. And there was no conceivable way that the company could afford three apprentices. We were clinging to the last rung of the ladder and according to the rumour mill, only one of us would survive the cut.

Management remained mute and poker-faced. They never addressed the rumours and were never directly asked about them. We all turned into nervous mice, determined to stay under the radar as though standing in front of them and asking, 'So, what's the story with redundancies?' would cause them to raise an eyebrow, shake your hand firmly and say, 'Well, we weren't going to make anyone redundant but since you asked, we've decided on you. Sayonara.'

What would I do without a job? Especially since I wasn't fully qualified. I couldn't get one anywhere else. I'd be forced

The Enchanted Island

to emigrate and build sandcastles in Dubai. I didn't want to do that. I liked Dublin. It was home. I wanted to stay at home. And more importantly, how would I make minimum payments on my credit-card debts without a job? The thought of not having a salary even for a month made me feel anxious.

It was a Friday when Harry Holmes, one of the two managing partners, summoned me into the office. Harry called all us apprentices in on occasion, to see if we had any new business leads. I never did – I didn't have a rich daddy to dangle suggestively. I didn't like him calling me in now though, not now with all the redundancy rumours. What if I was going to be the first head on the block?

I had just been discreetly googling Antonia's pink cashmere cardigan on my phone to see how much it cost. I recognised it as Ted Baker. It was magnificent, and I wasn't just green with envy, I was a septic, putrid, acid green colour. I wondered how stretched my cards really were – could I afford to get it in a baby blue? I IMd it to Hazel.

She confirmed my suspicions.

Stunning. That colour would look amazing on you

I wondered if Mam would buy it for me as an early Christmas present. Perhaps May was a bit too early. I'd need to think this one through.

Harry was handsome, permatanned, suspected face lift, trim and early fifties not forties, as he emphatically pronounced. In the good old days he had writhed on marble floors and scoffed quail eggs in the south of France while writing legal briefs. And if only this damned recession would end he knew he'd be back to doing bags of coke off chandeliers in the VIP suite of the Elephant and Castle with models wearing only Jimmy Choos.

He smiled. His white teeth were blinding. He ran his finger across the neckline of his tight wool charcoal-grey jumper, stretching it for air. He signalled towards a 1960s moon bucket–style seat, white plastic, red cushions, massively uncomfortable and worth a small fortune.

I sat down and pulled my skirt over my knees, feeling a bit nervous. *Not me, not me, please not me.* I knew I looked tired. I hadn't slept all week, worried about how to make things right with Sasha. My normal peaches-and-cream complexion was pasty and my dark eyes were shadowed. I'd just had time to run a brush through my hair and apply some rose-tinted lip gloss before entering. The whole office knew Harry liked his female staff attractive. It was all playing to his ego, and I was happy to dial myself up a notch to get noticed. It wasn't a gender war if you were winning it.

'I've got something for you. A job. A good one. I know you're keen, so this might work for you. What have you got on at the moment?'

I could feel my colour rise. This wasn't a redundancy chat. I might even be getting the break I'd been waiting for.

I quickly listed my current assignments: a company merger, a number of wills, a large family financial dispute and a technology company start-up, among other things.

The Enchanted Island

'This is a conveyance file. It's for Hy Brasil.' The way he delayed over the name, the way it slowly spilled out of him and lingered menacingly in the air between us raised my suspicions immediately. It didn't sound familiar, I didn't think. He raised his eyebrow at me inquisitively.

I nodded. 'For Hy Brasil.'

'You haven't heard of it?' Again, that look. Frozen with intent, but yet completely innocent.

'Nothing other than it being an island. It's in the west, isn't it?'

'Good. No . . . no.' He paused and pulled at his jumper again. 'That's good, right. We won't worry about it.' He straightened up in his seat. 'An old friend of mine wants to commission a bridge to connect the island to the mainland. There's a three-acre site. It's all in this file.' He pushed a dog-eared manila folder across his pristine glass desk.

I nodded, feeling my cheeks turn pink and hoping my eyes wouldn't betray me. I leaned forwards and drew the file to me greedily with both hands.

'Thank you, Harry, I can't tell you what this means to me.' I bit my lip, terrified that I might lose it and explode with emotion, a festival of snot and coughs.

'So you'll need to go to Hy Brasil and get a signature from a Sean Fitzpatrick. The land owner. I'd, eh . . . pack, it could take a while, but I'd like you to move things along as quickly as you can.'

I was hardly listening to him, I was so flooded with excitement. 'I've wanted an assignment like this since starting here.

A bridge, a monumental bridge, that can change the landscape, alter people's lives, it's just . . .' I could see Dad, I could see his smiling face. I could hear him: *That's it, Maevo, grab it.*

Oh please don't lose it, I thought, *just try to be cool and a pretend professional.*

'Yeah, I get it, but this might be slightly different. Look, just stick to the rules, stick to what you know. You're going to be stepping on toes.' He paused and looked quizzically at me. 'You've never heard of it?'

I shook my head.

'It's got a reputation as being . . . protected.' He rubbed anxiously at his neck, his tan slipping somehow, his complexion growing pale.

'Protected? Like the Mafia protected?'

'Maybe. In a way. Look it's all old wives' tales, I'm sure.' He shuddered slightly, then sat up straight, shaking off his look of anxiety. 'Well, you know, bottom line is there's a job to be done and I don't need to tell you how important any job is in this office in this current economic climate.' The recession. The bloody recession. 'Also, Maeve, it's a highly confidential job. Until the construction starts, no one there needs to know what you're doing.'

'I am so honoured and flattered to take this on, and I will not let you down.' I beamed from ear to ear, my emotions having flicked from the verge of hysterical tears to just plain hysterical. I wanted to clamber out of this uncomfortable seat and hug him, to feel his bony rib cage in my hands, to kiss the top of his forehead and sucker punch his shoulder.

'Fine, fine.' He looked decidedly uninterested. 'I'm giving you this job because I know you are thorough, you're good at what you do and you get things done.'

I'm also available to drop everything at a moment's notice on a request from the managing partner. Antonia would never get asked to do this, in case it upset Daddy, and Padraig was almost working exclusively for the other managing partner, Paddy Friedman, these days. I also knew full well that none of the qualified solicitors would be able to leave their posts indefinitely. It was a job for an apprentice, and I was delighted that it would be my job.

'On completion there will be a guarantee that you'll stay on after your apprenticeship. I don't need to tell you how important a job like this is to your position in the company.'

I gulped nervously. Job security. Surely job security might come with a pay rise? I know a better person than me would immediately see their giant credit-card debt erased but not me, I thought Ted Baker cardigan. And I'd be able to pay Sasha back, and maybe move back in with her and George – no, that might be weird. But I would definitely be able to straighten things out, and get out of Mam's house. I felt my mouth go dry. I nodded back.

'Okay, okay.' He signalled towards the door. 'It's Friday. Can you get out there for Monday?'

'Absolutely.'

'I'll get Dan to meet you there. He's the . . .' He pointed at the file. 'The client.' We both nodded, knowing what 'the client' meant: the money. He who must be pleased, collaborated with, appeased at all costs, and most of all kept happy. 'He could bring a lot of business our way in the future. This is one of –' he paused, *'those* jobs.'

I swallowed loudly. A career job. I blinked hard. This was it. I may vomit. At last things were taking shape, at last I was going to get up and get going. Bring on Hy Brasil, I was ready for it.

5

The brakes screeched as he came careening down the hill towards the sea, a real-life Humpty Dumpty precariously balancing on a bike, freewheeling towards me with rigid legs and the largest belly and the reddest face known to man. His feet skidded and skipped along the road, acting as a secondary set of brakes as he swiftly angled the bike to the left and up a narrow ramp, coming to a slow, controlled stop. Dan? Could it be Dan?

'Maeve?' he shouted, awkwardly dismounting and tucking his shirt into his waistband at the same time. He nervously kicked the bike's stand to the ground.

I ripped the black plastic bag off, happy to see my navy fitted pencil trouser suit had somehow remained dry. 'Yes, Dan. How are you?' I thrust my hand forwards, self-assured. I knew the drill: at all costs he must trust and respect my decisions. I would play this game.

'Great. Welcome to Hy Brasil.' He enthusiastically shook my hand and held eye contact for just a second too long, and that extra moment made me start to sweat. I knew – the way any girl who has ever carried a vodka and Coke from the bar in a nightclub knew – that there were men who will politely stand out of your way and who deserved a thankful smile, and there were men who will use the anonymity of the crowd to pinch your bum and need to be slapped. Standing in front of me was a man in need of a slap. His eyes scanned me – he didn't even try to hide it. He didn't even have the manners to wait until I looked away to check out my rack. Nope, there he was, head dipped, eyes firmly fixed on my mammary glands. I quickly folded my arms and waited for his eyes to find mine. *How's the peeping, Tommy?* He smiled at me, clearly delighted. 'You got here in one piece, hey? You didn't get scared off?'

I hadn't expected an American accent. 'Scared off? By a bit of sea?' I laughed, hoping to sound fearless while swallowing back a bit of vomit.

'You might be a little foolish not to be scared of the sea, especially around here.' He self-consciously sucked in his belly and hitched his jeans up high.

'Thanks for letting me know.'

'Well, thanks for coming. And I have to say I had no idea Harry was sending down such a beautiful girl. You look like a young Sophia Loren. I'm sure you hear that all the time.'

I had heard it before, but all Dan was doing was making me feel awkward and uncomfortable, so I clapped my hands together, hoping to put an end to his inappropriate compliments. 'I'm delighted to be here.'

'Good, good.' He looked around and pointed at my suitcase. 'Is that it?'

'I've packed well,' I said proudly.

'But you're here for a while?' His grey eyes narrowed slightly, cheeks puffed out, and his top lip curled a fraction.

I nodded. 'Of course. Whatever it takes.'

'Do you want to wheel the bike or the bag?' He grinned.

'Bag is just fine by me.' I expertly kicked out the handle and manoeuvred it behind me.

He wheeled the bike at his side as we ambled slowly up the hill. 'I haven't been on one of these for years, used to go everywhere as a kid – that's a while ago now.'

'Will we get out to the site today? I'm anxious to get a look at the land, to make sure the estate matches up to the contracts.'

'I think that might be better tomorrow. Let's get you to your accommodation and I'll fill you in on the project. I'm not sure how much Harry has told you.' His American accent dragged, elongating the vowels.

'Yes, great, I'm keen to move as swiftly as possible.'

'Hmm.' He nodded. 'And the, eh, accommodation is pretty basic, again not sure what Harry told you.'

Nothing, I thought, *Harry really has told me nothing*. 'I'm sure it's fine, it's a short stay. I'm here for work.'

'It can't be all work,' he said in a lilting tone. 'I'll fill you in on the job over a glass of wine.'

The road was like a centre parting, with lustrous shiny green fields curling on either side. The air tasted clear and peculiarly salty and bit into my lungs sharply. The wind whipped around me and stung my eyes. I blinked fiercely – clean country living. Eugh. I knew immediately I wasn't going to be a fan of this. I much prefer my air recycled and heated. I can't stand those women who march about in hiking boots and Gore-Tex jackets with rosy cheeks and broken veins shouting about how great it is to get out into the fresh air. Like that's a thing.

We walked for about twenty minutes from the jetty. Dan hadn't been lying about basic accommodation.

I looked on in disbelief. 'You're serious? This is it? A caravan?'

Home for the next while looked like a giant green bowling ball made out of tin. The mud levels in the field were so high that only the tops of the wheels were visible at the base of the bowling ball. There were cement block steps up to the doorway, but the first two would have to be jumped.

Dan nodded. 'Like I said, pretty basic, but we don't get tourists here. There's no B and B, no hotel. The pub down the road, Mulligan's, owns this place. I think they use it now and again for any drunks who can't make it home. It's grand like, it's all paid up, Harry's getting the bill. It's this or my place, I suppose, but my place isn't –'

'Fine, this is fine,' I swiftly interrupted.

'Look it's dry, there's a cooker, a bed, a kettle, everything.'

I nodded. Dry. When had dry been a box to click on Airbnb while browsing holiday accommodation?

The Enchanted Island

He handed me a key that had a little plastic dog attached to it. 'He can be your guard dog,' he said and sniggered, and I contemplated violence. 'I'll leave you to settle in and I'll see you in Mulligan's in an hour or so. Say seven o'clock?' Dan shifted uncomfortably. 'It's just over the hill there, before Main Street.' Sheepishly he shuffled off, before delicately hopping over the mud hills and mounting his bike, which sighed heavily under his weight.

Here we go. I heaved the suitcase up the steps and balanced on my toes to avoid the mud, while jiggling the key in the lock. I burst through the door.

It smelled like a wet sock that had been rammed into a welly for a whole summer and forgotten about. But it looked clean. Cleanliness must have been big in the 1970s, which was clearly the last time anyone had set foot in here. There was a bedroom, a couch that ran the length of the wall, a pull-out kitchen table, a bathroom stolen from a doll's house, a small radio, and a TV set from the 1960s that would probably cost a fortune in a vintage store.

I felt a twinge of nostalgia. As kids, we used to spend our summer holidays in Courtown, in a caravan by the beach. Those were the days when a game of Monopoly could stretch for weeks and 20p bought a packet of Tayto crisps, and we were only ever allowed watch TV when it was pouring rain. This was all before video games and zombie exterminations crept into our lives. My three brothers and I ran wild on the beach, freezing in the Irish sun. We'd huddle around a windbreaker after feasting on mayonnaise and tomato sandwiches dipped in sand, fighting over who would be next to be buried alive. Invariably it was me. You'd think being the only girl, and the youngest at that, that I'd have been treated like a princess, but I was regularly used to make up the scrum, or as a punching bag, even when I was getting too old to be at those games; I wasn't the goalie when we played football, I was the goal. We'd collapse, exhausted, every night into our bunk beds, racing through the day in our heads, planning the next one. We'd listen to Mam and Dad chatting and sipping on rum and Cokes in the main part of the caravan. That's one of my enduring memories of them as a couple – talking. They were always talking to each other. It was a never-ending conversation. They were happy days, and lovely memories to have of our childhood and long before Dad died, and before Mam slipped into this weird controlling state and became a ghost of who she used to be. She used to smile all the time, she used to kiss us on the top of the head and call us her little terrors. I remember the sound of her giggling as herself and Dad danced around the kitchen. She'd twirl into his arms and he'd rest his cheek on hers. In my memory, twinkly lights would appear and everything swirled around them, a perfect whole. Now she's shrouded in overwhelming grief and misery that six years on isn't any closer to shaking, a shattered person verging on incomplete. I felt an uncomfortable pinch when I thought about Dad. I couldn't think of him now – maybe another time.

    I managed to unstick a window. I stripped off my suit jacket and unzipped my suitcase. I had packed for every eventuality, as I wasn't sure what island attire might be. I had brought casual boyfriend style, low-slung jeans; slightly more formal skinny jeans; a few rich cotton shirts, good for formal or casual looks; some sports gear; an expensive black dress; a sparkly top, just in case; a selection of light jumpers; a few pairs of shoes; some formal trousers; and a giant bag of cosmetics, lotions and creams to put on and creams to take off.

With a sigh I texted Mam, she'd be coming in from her Pilates class round about now. In the week since I'd moved back home she'd become militant about where I was and who I was with. Would I be home in time for *Fair City*? Should she tape it? Did I know how to work the DVD player to tape it?

I left Sasha another voicemail. I really felt she should be picking up by now. Who leaves voicemails anymore? She was probably just deleting and not even listening.

'Sash, you won't believe where I am? This island off the west coast, it's mental, and I'm in a caravan. I'm on a case. *Ha!* That sounds like I'm on *CSI*. Anyway, I think we should talk. Was thinking I could book for dinner for us in L'Ecrivain when I get back, my treat. Let me know and I'll make the booking. Bye.'

I hopped around under a cold shower, performing more of a whore's wash than a deep cleanse. Feeling decidedly fresher but probably not much cleaner, I put on the dark denim skinny jeans, a crisp white shirt, navy blazer, and flats. I looked longingly at my heels but I wasn't stupid enough to try to hop across that field in three-inchers.

I quickly scrolled through Facebook on my phone to see what was happening in the real world. The connection was surprisingly speedy, and everything pinged up immediately.

> **Alma Finnerty** *Just now*
> *Moya – finally in a big bed*
> **Claire Taaffe** *11 mins*
> *Exhausted after a mega weekend*
> **Patrick O'Brien** *28 mins*
> *Morocco here we come*

I gave my brother Patrick a like. Himself and his girlfriend, Amy, were off on a two-week holiday. I snapped a quick selfie, including the caravan decor in the background and posted it on Instagram, tagging it #islandlife. I'd make a few witty and ironic comments later about coconut bikinis and grass skirts by bonfires. Sometimes it can take up to half an hour to get a good selfie, but this one I nailed first go. I was getting better at angles and head tilts. I watched the post for a few seconds, and bingo, two likes. I hoped Carl would see it.

6

It was positively warm when I stepped outside. Maybe even balmy. Uncharacteristically warm for a spring evening. I danced through the muddy field as best as possible and, following Dan's directions, headed over the hill. Mulligan's was only a short hop from the caravan. It was a lonely two-storey house at the side of the road, clearly the beginning or the end of the town. I could see more shops and what looked like a village further down the street.

A loud grunting noise crawled up my spine and exploded in my eardrums. It was like an animal moaning, being strung from the heavens. I jumped and looked down the street to see where it was coming from. A heavily pregnant woman was crouched over the side of a wall, her belly so ginormous and swollen it looked fake. A man holding a bag hopped from foot to foot beside her like his shoes were on fire. She moaned again, and then stopped, stood upright, rubbed her back and, with a gait borrowed from Donald Duck, started to waddle down the street. The man circled her like a race car at the Grand Prix, zooming frantically around her. They were walking towards the jetty. I knew from earlier that there was absolutely nothing there except some boats. There was no mini hospital or even a doctor's surgery. If TV hospital dramas have taught me anything, I could see that she was in labour. Were they going for a row? Surely now was not the time for fishing or sightseeing.

I took a few steps towards them. 'Are you okay?' I shouted. 'Can I help?'

The man waved back to me, the woman clearly preoccupied.

'Grand thanks, heading to the mainland, the baby's coming.' He jumped excitedly.

'On a boat? But why?' My voice fell soft in the wind. They didn't hear me, already proceeding down the hill.

I didn't think that seesaw boat trip would be much to get excited about at the best of times, and especially not if you were in labour. Why wouldn't she just have the baby here? Surely there's some lovely birthing suite with pictures of chubby-cheeked babies on the walls, fresh lilies bursting into bloom in vases and crisp cotton sheets and a matter-of-fact but caring country doctor? Isn't that how everyone had babies these days, to the sound of Mozart in a heated pool of rose petals? But maybe she had some strange birth plan that couldn't be accommodated on the island. Seemed like a lot of hassle to get into a boat, though, to get to the mainland to find a hospital, all for the sake of having some Buddhist monks or Hare Krishnas or whatever it was she was after at the birth.

I turned back to the pub, feeling a bit confused. Mulligan's was painted a dark shade of purple and a Guinness sign swayed jauntily from the eaves. The flower boxes out front were in full bloom. It looked inviting, which turned out to be terribly misleading. I pushed open a dark mahogany door and walked into a room that felt like a heavy storm cloud, gloomy and depressing and dark. I squinted to allow my eyes to adjust. Heavily patterned carpet clashed with heavily patterned wallpaper that was stained with cigarette smoke, even though smoking had been banned years ago. Knee-high dark wood tables were littered with beer mats, and stools so small a leprechaun would trip over them were scattered randomly around. It felt uncomfortable and unwelcoming.

A skinny old man with a long nose and delicate fingers stood behind the bar in front of a wall of well-positioned spirits, transfixed by the TV. The horses were on. He wore a blue Argyle jumper that looked well lived in. He didn't turn towards me, no nod hello, no half-hearted wave, no interest, no welcome.

Dan was already perched at the bar, his stool awkwardly pulled out to allow room for his ample belly, his feet dangling. He was wearing the same red-checked shirt as earlier, but his cheeks were now more of a glossy pink. His spiked brown hair had been combed higher for a few more inches of height. He was swooshing a large wine glass in a circular motion, staring at it. He looked relaxed.

'I'll have whatever you're having.' I slid onto a stool to the right of him and crossed my legs. I pulled a notebook and pen out of my bag and placed them on the counter; business, this was strictly business. There were three older men at the far side of the bar, hunched over pints of Guinness with eyes locked on the TV. None of them looked over.

A shout cracked like a whip through the room: 'Git off me stool.'

I spun around.

An old woman cloaked in a black shawl marched through the door like a storm cloud, her white hair scraped back from her pale face. She viciously pointed her finger at me, shouting louder this time. 'Git off me stool!'

Me? She was shouting at me?

She was on me in seconds. I could see the spittle at the corner of her mouth as her finger jabbed my shoulder with surprising strength. Immediately, and in complete shock, I jumped up.

'Sorry, I didn't realise.' I scurried backwards.

'Ya shite, ya,' she hollered after me, and hopped up onto her throne. She disrobed to reveal a black dress, and a pint of Guinness appeared majestically before her, the creamy head settling. She crouched over it, spitting venom. 'Shites, why do ye let shites like that in here?'

The barman shrugged apologetically. 'I didn't see her, Maggie. I'd never have let that happen, she must have just come in before ya.'

She sniffed at the air and wiggled herself around, grunting what I thought might have been a forgiving gesture. 'Load a shites.'

The Enchanted Island

As invisibly as possible, I sat on the other side of Dan, hunching my shoulders over, trying to disappear, terrified of the wrath of the aged.

'What a lovely welcome,' I whispered.

Dan shrugged. Then he nodded at his drink, at the barman and then at me. Gestures fully understood, a wine appeared before me.

'Let's, eh, move down to a table, away from . . .' He dipped his head in the direction of the other drinkers. We hopped off our stools and sat on opposite sides of a small circular table.

I flipped through my notebook, looking my most efficient and professional. 'I have some questions, if that's all right with you? I've inherited this file and I'd like to get your input on everything, to make sure we haven't missed a beat.'

He took a long sip of his wine. 'Make sure you stay on track.' His eyes looked coldly at me.

I nodded slowly, hearing the threatening tone in his voice. He was all business now, I noticed, nowhere near as jovial as earlier.

'I've a job to do, Dan. I intend to do it and do it well,' said alter ego Maeve the grown-up, while the real Maeve saw that her nail polish was chipped and wondered if there was a beautician's nearby.

Dan tapped his fingers rhythmically at the edge of his glass, uneasy somehow.

I chanced a peep at Maggie, who had struck up a conversation with the barman. She was leaning into him and talking quietly. She brought a small black pipe to her mouth and chewed on it, her jaw jutting defiantly. I didn't think I'd ever seen a woman smoke a pipe, or chew a pipe even. I'd heard of it happening but I guess it hadn't quite taken off in Dublin bars just yet. She looked agitated and even scarier up close than when she'd swirled in in her cape. Absentmindedly, I rubbed my shoulder, wondering if that little old woman might cause a bruise.

I scanned my notes. 'So, we're awaiting a signature from a Sean Fitzpatrick, the landowner where the bridge will be built. I have all the documentation ready – he'll be my first call tomorrow morning, I have all his details here. Once I have that, I can survey the site and make sure that plans are on track. Then we'll put the wheels in motion and there's no reason why building won't start by the end of the month.'

He shook his head slowly. 'You know, I'm paying five times what that site is worth. A three-acre field of sheep shit, that's all it is. He's making a fortune out of me. He has me over a barrel. It's the closest point to the mainland, you see, anywhere else would involve millions and millions of euros in construction fees. I wouldn't be able to do it, not without major independent funding. He knows it too. I mean, don't get me wrong, I have money.' He puffed out his chest and looked at me for an approving nod. Not getting it, he continued, 'A lot of money.' He paused and pretended to nonchalantly flick his fingernails clean. 'Let's just say I'm very wealthy.' He raised his eyebrows suggestively.

The Enchanted Island

I got it: bank balance up, knickers down. I remained stony-faced. I was not playing this game with a man who had fingers that looked like cocktail sausages.

'Sean Fitzpatrick needs the money. He has some debts to some angry casino owners on the mainland. If he didn't, I don't know if he'd sign over to me, since he's no real motivation to change things. I've known him years.'

I cocked an eyebrow at him inquisitively. This was interesting. 'You? Are you from here?' His American accent never betrayed a hint of his ancestry.

He smiled. 'This wonderful shit hole is where I was born and bred. I catapulted myself out of here at the age of eighteen, couldn't wait to get out of the wind and rain and the bloody isolation of it all. I couldn't wait to get *into* it all.' He looked angry somehow, his brow furrowed, and his fists started to clench. 'This bloody place, it gets to you, it's hard to leave. That's the problem.'

'And yet you're funding this bridge that will open the island to the mainland, it will allow local children easier access to better education and there'll be open trade, I'm guessing. I haven't seen much of the place, but it's a remote island, so you would think that life will improve a hundred times over for people here. It's admirable what you're doing, how you're giving back to the community.' I hoped I didn't sound like I was gushing, but I had done my homework and I was impressed by what seemed like a completely altruistic gesture.

He shifted uncomfortably on his stool. 'Yes and no. It's not quite as clear cut as that. Let's just say, I have my reasons.'

I nodded. Even if he did have other reasons, I felt, really felt, that there wasn't one negative aspect to building a bridge to the mainland.

We ordered some dinner, fish and chips, and it was hands down the best fish and chips I had ever eaten. I wouldn't normally order anything so obviously fattening but there was nothing else on the menu and I was starving. There I was sitting in the dingiest of pubs, at a sticky table, on an island that God took his eye off an eternity ago, and the fish and chips would rival anything I'd ever eaten in a fancy restaurant in Dublin – and I mean a restaurant with linen tablecloths, and those little towels to dry your hands in the bathroom and then throw away (after only one wipe!). The meal was incredible. I inhaled it, and while I didn't lick the plate, I did discreetly trace the tip of my finger repeatedly around it, trying to soak up the last of the flavour. Yum.

Dan and I chatted away easily enough. The conversation was fine. He was knocking back the wine, he had eaten his fish and chips just as lovingly as I had, and had started to explain his 'relationship with food'. So American, I thought, to have a relationship with it.

'I was spending all this money on a nutritionist and a trainer, had tiny parcels of food delivered to my apartment, apples and no fat, no dairy, salads with cucumber dressing, steamed fish no meatier than my little finger with cauliflower mash. All wrapped in eco-friendly recycled packaging. And then I'd hoover it all down in a mouthful. Breakfast, lunch, dinner and snacks disappeared before they had a chance to

The Enchanted Island

get onto a plate.' He smiled. 'I don't know why I do it. An hour later I could be in a diner across the street ordering double fries and a six-egg omelette. It's always the same: I'd lose thirty pounds and put on forty. It frustrates the hell out of me. Maybe I'll sort it out when I get back to LA.'

I didn't really know what to say to him, except that I could probably eat another plate of fish and chips, but I didn't think that would be appropriate to mention to someone in a relationship with my dinner.

I looked over at Maggie, who I noticed had whipped out a phone from a pocket of her dress. It was a sleek iPhone, and I was more than a little put out to see that it was the model up from mine. She tapped away on it like an accomplished pianist, never bending down to peer at the screen or squinting to register typos. I wondered who she was texting, or maybe she was playing Candy Crush. It was kind of funny seeing an old woman with a pipe and an iPhone. And then, as if she'd been stung by a bee, she leaped up, drained her Guinness, swung her cape around herself and scampered out the front door.

Dan was warbling on. 'I'm not trying to save this place, this place doesn't want to be saved.' He laughed into his drink. 'If you knew . . .' He looked at me, giddy. 'They . . . this island, well, let's just say she thinks she's better than you, than all of us.'

I frowned at him.

'We might travel the world, live full lives, make money, find diamonds, you name it, but she's still got the edge, she's still got us all here.' He held his hands up in the air, and cocked his neck to the side, and let his tongue hang out, like he was in a hangman's noose.

I shook my head, puzzled. 'I don't . . .'

He snorted, half laughing. 'Call it island humour.'

'Okay.' Note to self: stay away from the particularly unfunny form of island humour.

The lights in the pub flashed on and off. The three barflies stood up hastily and finished their pints. They placed flat caps on their heads and started rummaging for jackets. The barman looked over to us and leaned across the counter. He eyeballed Dan.

'You've about thirty seconds.'

Dan looked at me. 'Drink up fast.'

I shook my head, not knowing what was going on.

'Right so.' The barman swooped over and grabbed my half-full glass of wine. 'We're closed.'

Dan drained his glass and stood up quickly.

'Out.' The barman raised his voice this time. 'Everyone out.'

I looked at my watch. It was nine o'clock. 'It's so early, why are you shutting?'

'Time for you to leave.' The lights flicked again. 'Everyone out.' He waved his arms.

Dan was already at the door. He signalled for me to get a move on.

'I'd a glass half full,' I moaned as I put my coat on and moved outside. 'That's ridiculous! He takes a notion and everyone has to jump. What is it? Is *Coronation Street* on the telly?'

The Enchanted Island

Dan's ruddy complexion had paled. His eyes shifted nervously, searching for something in the distance. 'I'll walk you back to the caravan. There's still time before the patrol starts.'

'What? Did you just say patrol?' I looked up at him but it was like he couldn't hear me. 'Is it the Garda patrol?' Why would the guards patrol this place? Nothing would ever happen here. I glanced up the main street towards where I assumed the village was and saw a few shadows disappearing indoors.

'Come on.' Dan put his hand on my shoulder, deliberately trying to hurry me up.

'Okay, okay.' I don't know if I was more annoyed about having half a glass of wine snatched away or being hurried along like a lazy child. And then I heard something. It was unearthly. A cry from something unimaginable. A shriek that hollowed out my core. I froze, terrified.

'Hurry.' Dan pushed my back.

The noise seemed to fall from the sky. It was everywhere. I'd never heard anything like it.

Somehow my legs were moving. Somehow we crossed the field and were at the caravan door.

The noise stopped.

'What? What was that?' The words clumsily fell from my mouth.

Dan looked at me straightfaced. 'The wind. Just the wind.'

I shook my head. 'That wasn't the wind. That sounded nothing like wind. Wind blows.' I pursed my lips and started exhaling, making my best wind noise.

'Trust me. It was the wind.' Dan was white-faced and serious. His eyes shifted nervously. 'I have to go. I have to get home quickly.'

I fumbled for my guard dog and unlocked the door. I noticed my hands were shaking.

'Don't leave here tonight. You've no reason to go outside. Don't.'

I stood in the doorway and looked back at him. 'What the hell is going on?'

He bit hard down on his lip and shook his head slowly.

'I'll lock the door.'

He sniggered slightly. 'There's no need for locks. I should go.' He turned to leave and then hesitated. 'The old duck in the pub, Maggie.' He pointed back towards Mulligan's. 'If you see her again just, eh . . . steer clear.'

'Like, ignore her? Well, I don't think I'll be rushing up and giving her a hug, we're hardly bosom buddies.'

'No, just, eh . . .' He pulled on his nose. 'I mean, she's seen you now, but just do your best to keep away from her, and the others like her.'

'Old people drinking Guinness?' I raised my eyebrows incredulously at him.

'Yeah. They're not what you'd expect. Best to avoid them at all costs. There's a lot of them on the island – you won't have met people like them before, just try and stay out of their way. I mean it.' He grinned slightly and waved a finger in the air. 'Night, Maeve. Don't worry about this stuff. It's just island stuff. It'll be over in a few hours.'

The Enchanted Island

My head was still ringing from that noise, that terrible noise. I shut the door behind me and locked it, in spite of what Dan had said. I felt safer with it locked. I turned on the TV and sat on the edge of the couch watching the screen flicker. I was shaking a little bit, creeped out, so I wrapped my arms around myself. I'd never heard anything like it before, it was a biblical wail, like something the Banshee would produce, combing her hair into the wind, with hollowed cheeks and mystical eyes, screaming about death. Thank God I didn't believe in any of that kind of thing or I'd have been really freaked out.

7

'Don't even think about coming back here without that signature.'

'He got onto that boat and sailed away, Harry, there was nothing I could do.'

'How did he know you were coming?'

'How could he have? He didn't know.' It had to have been the bearded woman in the coffee shop.

'I gave you this job, Maeve, because you are thorough. You cross your t's and dot your i's. Be thorough, get that signature.'

What? Should I go fishing? 'Absolutely, not a problem, I'll track him down as soon as I can,' I said politely, exactly what he wanted to hear.

Harry hung up.

Overall it had been a bad day, and it had started early.

Surprisingly, considering the ruckus when I went to bed, I'd slept like a baby should. I woke up full of plans, mapping out my day, making returning to Dublin the main focus. Signature in hand, by nine o'clock I'd be sipping from a glass of wine and indulging in some runny cheese in that over-priced French wine bar near Trinity that weirdly enough smelled slightly of curry. Except it didn't play out like that, not at all.

The rain was falling heavily as I headed for Main Street. Mulligan's was just at the foot of it, so only a five-minute walk from the caravan. Main Street ran on a perfectly straight line, like a railway track. It was nestled inland, protected from the elements, and cut right through the centre of the island. It fell into a sheltered crevice as the road dipped slightly downhill. There were probably twenty buildings on Main Street, mainly single-storey cottages converted into shop fronts. I saw a butcher's and a baker's, so I eagerly awaited the candlestick maker's. A wool shop and a shop that had a display of wellies in the window that predated music-festival chic, which demanded they be worn with short shorts and floral head bands. There were white-washed houses on either side of the shops, with the occasional thatched roof. Bright and freshly painted doors – yellow, blue and pink – proudly punctuated the white walls, complementing the flower boxes that some of the houses had. I supposed it was picturesque if you were into that sort of thing, that quaint, twee, picture-book Ireland. I smiled to myself, thinking how, if I was let, I'd probably level the cottages to make way for duplex townhouses. I'd definitely create more living space; those cottages must be tiny inside, even the door frames looked small, a tall person would have to face decapitation to get through. Maybe this was an island of certified midgets.

Main Street was bordered on either side by a patchwork of fields, a number of paths snaking off through them. At certain points on the western side of the island the terrain seemed to rise upwards, and hilly mounds appeared. In contrast, the east looked to be as flat as a putting green on a golf course. With no cars and only the sounds of birds chirping, the place felt otherworldly, like I'd jumped a hundred years into the past.

I tried to peep inconspicuously through windows as I walked by, slowly angling my head and straining my eyes to the side. What I really wanted to do was stop at a window and hold my hands to the glass, cupping my face to see indoors. What happened in these little houses? What did people do? Did you spend your day going from the coffee shop to the pub? Wouldn't you just die of boredom? Where was the fun? The high heels and champagne? Where was *life*?

I pulled my jacket close. God it was wet; rain-spraying-everywhere wet. The few people I passed stared at me like their eyeballs were going to roll down their cheeks. They really must be short on visitors here. It was like a scene from a wild west movie, me clip-clopping into the town, tumbleweeds flying and locals anxiously watching, hands hovering over pistols in holsters: 'Here she comes now with her big-city ways'. I smiled politely at anyone within a few feet of me, but no one returned my cheery greeting.

Main Street was anchored by a small grey building that might be a community centre or a town hall, with oak doors

The Enchanted Island

that looked somehow apologetic. It was directly across the street from Tansey's pub, which was not quite as modest. A chalkboard hung out the front: TODAY'S SOUP . . . WHISKY. A Guinness sign creaked back and forth.

There were two old men perched on a grey wall, sheltered from the drizzle by a large oak tree. They wore similar tweed jackets, one a speckled blue–grey, the other a dirty brown. Both had black armbands on. Their flat caps slid down their noses. I could see the deep lines of old age chiselled into their faces. They looked to be in an easy conversation, leaning into each other and nodding amiably, a forty-year-old conversation, with no beginning, middle or end. Not exactly *Waiting for Godot*, so much as just waiting. Instinctively I waved to them. I was the only other person on the street, of course they'd seen me. 'Good morning,' I shouted, continuing on my cheerful way.

Grey Jacket turned his shoulder inwards, inching closer to his friend, and pulled his cap even further down. Brown Jacket jumped slightly and went to raise a hand but as he did so I noticed it wasn't an open wave, more of a closed fist, a shooing motion. Neither of them even glanced in my direction.

So rude. Those poor tourists who come to the west of Ireland to walk these cobbled streets don't pay thousands of euros to be greeted by closed fists and sneers. All they want is a bit of chat, a pint of Guinness and a jumper with *Ireland* written across it in that loud Celtic script that no Irish person would be seen dead in. I should really write a letter to the Irish Tourism Board, tell them they need to give these islanders lessons in hospitality. I love a good complaint letter with a lot of *I was outraged* exclamation points. Sasha had once bought a Twix with only one in the packet instead of two and she was going to do nothing about it, so I wrote an outraged letter and got a full box of Twixes for us. They lasted about a month – it was great.

Waist-high stone walls lined every field and pathway. I could see miles and miles of stone walls in every direction interlacing over the whole of the island like a crocheted doily. Large flat stones had been cleared out of the fields and piled on top of each other, big stones at the bottom, getting smaller at the top, although they all look roughly the same size. I knew these were famine walls and had been built all over the west of Ireland during the Irish famine in the mid-eighteenth century. Fields were cleared to allow for farming, and more importantly to create employment, to give people something to do. Rural communities, particularly in the west, had been devastated by the famine. The grey stones piled on top of each other always made me think of the phrase, 'If these walls could talk'. There must be an imprinted memory of the hand that first moved the stone from the field almost one hundred and seventy years before, and what would have been going through his head during that time of hunger, disease and emigration. I patted my hand along one of the stones respectfully, understanding that I was just walking in the footsteps of the wall builders who had gone before me.

The coffee shop was painted a pale blue, and through the window I could see yellow daisies in milk bottles on plastic tablecloths. It looked warm and inviting. Delighted and suddenly ravenous, I burst through the door, which tinkled, announcing my arrival, and I shook myself off like a golden retriever after a muddy swim. A thin elderly woman in a navy woollen jumper with a dishcloth between her hands stood behind the counter. Wiry white hairs sprang out of her chin. She was chatting amiably to a rotund middle-aged man in a dark green waxed jacket. I could feel the rumbles of his deep belly laugh as I entered.

I found a seat near the window and peeled my wet jacket off, swinging it onto the back of a chair. The door tinkled again, announcing the arrival of a pixie-sized old woman, who daintily stepped indoors like a ballet dancer. She tiptoed up to the counter, and I watched as Waxed Jacket immediately went quiet and a serious expression washed over his face. He took a step backwards and, practically bowing down to the ground, spoke to the little old thing.

'Honora, what a pleasure to see you. Please, please take my place. We can't have you queueing.'

I watched, a little delighted at first to see such chivalry alive and well. And then it creeped me out. He was being so reverential and over the top towards her, his nose was nearly touching the tiled floor. It was almost as if he was scared of her. But why would he be scared of a geriatric ballerina?

I let their little dance play out and watched a bit confused as they were served, Honora first, naturally, and then retired to their respective seating.

The woman with the beard smiled hello, and her teeth started to slip out of her mouth, but she quickly caught them with her lips, pushed them back in as she giggled to herself.

'*Dia Dhuit.*'

I stumbled immediately when she used an Irish greeting. I knew the island, like a lot of spots in the west of Ireland, was bilingual, I just wasn't sure if I'd have to pull out my remedial language abilities. I smiled back at her, and it seemed to work. Phew.

'What's it to be?' She straightened her face up, thankfully responding in English, rubbing circles into the counter with her dishcloth.

'I might get some eggs? Poached eggs?'

'Kitchen's closed. We're shutting early – there's a wake.' She smiled happily.

'A wake?' A wake is sad surely? Why the big smile? 'I'm sorry.'

'Don't be. Jimmy the Yinkee was well past his sell-by date, he went early morning. He should have jumped ship a long time ago. He was an auld fart.'

The black armbands, I thought, that's why the two old codgers were wearing them. They were in mourning.

'Okay.' I wasn't sure how to react to her matter of factness.

'Coffee?'

I nodded. I wondered about asking her about the noise last night, that unholy shriek. Surely she'd heard it too? Was it the wind? I laughed at myself at how thoughts of the Banshee had popped into my head. One night on the island and I was already losing my marbles. Although wasn't that the

The Enchanted Island

Banshee's thing? A shriek warning people about an imminent death? I reached back to the very far corners of my memory to what I'd heard in school. I came up blank; she was lost among fairytales of the Children of Lir being turned into swans and giants pretending to be babies.

The Beard interrupted my train of thought. 'Have one of them scones.'

I eyed a stack of crumbly scones oozing sultanas and raisins. A small sign hung over them: FRESH TODAY.

'No, it's okay,' I said, thinking of the calorie-loaded fish and chips I'd eaten the previous night. 'Just coffee.'

'Nonsense, look at you, you're skin and bones.'

I felt a momentary flash of pride, and wanted to put my hands on my waist to cinch it in and twirl in front of her, but her face looked so disgusted the moment didn't last long.

'Well, I guess I could.'

'Absolutely, you need some meat on you, girl, you're skinny as,' she sneered.

She busied herself with a plate and butter, not waiting for my response.

'The old have to move over and make way for the new. That's the way it is. That's life.'

A fruit scone and coffee slid onto the table. Just as I was about to broach the subject of the creepy noise, the old woman bent down over me, her wrinkly skin folding in on itself like pleats on a curtain. She pointed a knobbly finger towards a page that had slipped out of my file onto the table. I wished I could have slapped my hand over it.

'Are you looking for Sean Fitzpatrick?'

I plastered on a friendly smile, which must have looked completely fake. 'I have to look him up. Do you know him?'

The woman immediately shook her head, her face shut like an automatic garage door. 'No. Never heard of him.'

Well, that's a flat-out lie, I thought. *This is a tiny island, of course she knows him, they may not be bedfellows but she's definitely heard of him.*

'Why would you want him?'

'Just, you know . . .' I panicked, I felt my skin go pink as my brain scanned through possible lies I could tell. I settled on a heavy sigh, shrugging and making a weird noise that could have been mistaken for a stomach growling.

'We'll be shutting up soon, you'll need to leave.' She clenched her jaw and raised her eyebrows. The island or the coffee shop?

I smiled politely at her, a passive-aggressive protest. I picked up a knife and sliced into a fruit scone, which crumbled and then exploded with delicious aromas.

She made her way back to the kitchen and through a crack in the door I watched her pull a mobile phone out of her pocket. I wondered which model of iPhone it was. Her back hunched and her hand covered the receiver, secretively and gently stroking her beard as she whispered and then moved out of view.

Not being a private investigator, my intuition wasn't always correct, but I was pretty sure that this old woman – and this phone call – wasn't a good sign.

The Enchanted Island

On the plus side, the fruit scone was delicious.

The forty-minute walk to Sean Fitzpatrick's house turned into fifty and I felt the rain seeping through my canvas shoes and into my socks. The air tasted salty. There was a chill in my bones that I didn't think would ever come right. Main Street had turned into Main Road, and the houses became scattered freckles on the landscape. The fields on either side of the road were an emerald green, divided by famine walls that looked as if they'd wobble with a gust of wind, but I knew they'd been there so long it would take more than some wind to blow them over. I was a few fields from the foot of what looked like a giant hill, maybe even a mountain. My map referred to it as Mount Culann, and it loomed ominously. Grey slate rock clung to its sides like ivy, mossy green patches further uphill caught the sunlight and emanated a luminous glow that was quite spectacular. Natural beauty aside, I was delighted to see that the path to Sean Fitzpatrick's house did not involve scaling it.

There was a distinct smell of lavender in the air, but I couldn't see the flower anywhere. I didn't know where the scent was coming from. There was an array of yellow and white flowers sprayed through some fields. On a sunny day, if the mood took you, you could have had a Julie Andrews moment and skipped through them, although you'd have to watch out for the sheep that seemed to be everywhere, glassy-eyed, staring and bleating.

The road forked. Sean Fitzpatrick's house was at the end of the road on the right, I knew that, but looking along the road I could see figures, a small crowd of maybe fifteen people. The road sloped downwards to a beach about half a mile away and they were perched anxiously on the shoreline. I knew from my map that the beach was called Lissna Tra. I hadn't seen one other person on this walk, and now here was this group huddled together. My curiosity got the better of me. I picked up my pace and detoured towards them. As I approached I heard a low murmur from the crowd – they were chatting softly. I was only a few feet away, but I hung back, as there was something intimate about them. Even though I was only looking at the back of their heads, it felt like they were having a shared experience. I heard some very gentle sobbing.

'He's gone now,' a soft voice whispered.

They kept looking out to sea, watching the waves lick the sand, shuffling closer to the edge expectantly. What were they waiting for?

'It'll be Mulligan's so, for the wake?' An elderly man nodded to another white-haired man beside him. I stood just to the left of them, slightly behind; I don't think they saw me.

'Ah sure, I suppose it'll be a bit of craic.'

They both nodded enthusiastically.

'Did you get in before the wailing?'

'I did. Couldn't hear the telly though, so I missed *EastEnders*.'

'You'll get it in the omnibus.'

More nodding.

The sobbing from the front of the beach got louder. I heard a name. 'Jimmy, Jimmy, Jimmy!'

It felt eerie, and I felt like I was intruding on something that was invite only. I backed away.

'There it is.' Fingers pointed out onto the horizon, where an empty rowboat was bobbing.

'Well done, Jimmy.' The old men turned to another. 'Will you let Annie know? Go on sure, you can race back?'

The messenger straightened his cap, and I knew to turn around and move away before I was spotted. I retreated back to the road and continued on towards Sean Fitzpatrick's house. I really wasn't sure what I'd stumbled across, but I didn't like it.

Sean Fitzpatrick's house was a small white-washed cottage that looked neglected and sad, hidden among long grasses and overgrown fields. There was smoke coming out of the chimney. I knocked on the front door, and again, even heavier the second time. No answer. I moved to a window at the side of the house, and like the nosey parker I am, peered inside: a kitchen table with cups and what looked like breakfast plates on it and a fire burning in the hearth. Feeling like Jessica Fletcher, I kept moving, and bellowed my hellos. The garden was very overgrown. I hopped over long grasses and briars, and came to the back of the house. This must be it – the site.

There were fields, three I knew, from the files I was clutching. I squinted and could see the three-acre field, the one we needed, with access to the road through the first two, spilling up to the island's edge. The fields were on a dramatic slant, a steep hill, with the final field meeting with the slimmest sliver of sand, cupped by cliffs on either side, sheltering it from the weather. There were clouds hanging on the horizon but the faint outline of the mainland was clear to see, it was only six hundred yards away. I could see instantly why this was an ideal site to build the bridge. It was calm. The area was cocooned; the earth met the ocean in a smooth transition. It was perfect. I started downwards, careful not to twist an ankle on the steep descent.

There were figures on the beach, I was sure of it: two, maybe three, men and a boat. I quickened my pace. I was getting closer and I could see that they were pushing the boat out onto the water. A small fishing boat, with a noisy engine that was spluttering so loudly it could be heard over the wind. I jumped through the sand dunes and pampas grasses and slipped onto the golden sand. Complete shelter. The wind stopped, the sea licked the shoreline lazily, and there was even heat in the morning sun.

'Hello,' I shouted to the three men, one of whom had a leg in the boat, and a knee deep in the sea, trousers rolled up. He popped his full body into the boat as I spoke.

'Hello,' I said again, maybe ten feet from them. 'I'm looking for Sean Fitzpatrick.'

One of the men on the shore turned, he was wearing a navy jacket with the collar turned up, his face mapped with wrinkles and lines. His upper lip moved in a sneer. 'Are you now? And who might you be?'

'Maeve O'Brien. I have some papers for Mr Fitzpatrick to sign.'

'Did you hear that, Tommy?' he shouted to the equally wrinkled man nearby, who had one hand on the fishing boat.

'Papers? What kind of papers?'

They could bat this back and forth all day, leaving me a hapless pawn. Meanwhile, who was that man on the boat, could that be Sean Fitzpatrick? He had his back to the shore, busy picking away at the engine.

'That's confidential. Do you know where I can find him?'

'Confidential she says, Tommy.'

'Excuse me, sir? Sir? Are you Sean Fitzpatrick?'

The engine let out a roar, and a smell of gasoline washed onto the beach. The figure on the boat turned around. It would be hard to put an age on him, but he seemed very old, bordering on ancient. There were deep crevices on his face, and wonderful sparkly blue eyes. Like the other two, he was a wizened figure from an old Irish fable. He had a rolled-up, unlit cigarette in his mouth. He frowned at me nervously, half nodding. It was him. The other man hopped onto the boat with the grace of a man forty years younger.

The one called Tommy pointed a long finger in my direction, shouting loudly over the sound of the engine: 'You can tell that Yankee bollocks that there'll be no signing nothing.' He turned to the two other wizened characters. 'Lads, are we off or what?'

There was a flash of something in Sean Fitzpatrick's eyes – he looked scared.

'But where are you going? When will you be back?' The panic rose in my voice.

'Fishing,' the navy jacket answered. 'Depends if they're jumping. Could be gone a day, could be six months.' He cackled, and the boat zipped off, leaving a shiny trail of oil and me, stunned, on the shore.

8

I hung up the phone from Harry. So that was it, was it? I was just supposed to sit around and wait for Sean Fitzpatrick and his cranky cronies to come back? I was supposed to patiently twiddle my thumbs and file my nails until the fish jumped into the net?

Grand so.

No problems.

Except for a huge problem – like, what the hell was I supposed to do with myself? How long would I be here?

After twenty-four hours the curved walls of my tin caravan were already closing in on me. I wondered if this was like prison when you get thrown down the hole and you don't know how long for, though at least there I'd get to whisper to other inmates through a grate, comparing maggots in food. Here, I had no one to share this terrible experience with.

So, here's a confession: I have never been on my own. I've never spent time with me, myself and I. I say things like, 'I would love to just lie on a beach by myself for a week and do nothing,' or 'Wouldn't it be amazing to just walk across Spain on a pilgrimage in silence, so Zen, yah.' But I don't mean it. What would I do on my own? I would be so bored with my own company. Silence doesn't do my already drifting mind any favours. My head would be wrecked with the imaginary conversations I'd be getting myself into knots over. I'd replay something from years ago, except I'd change the ending so instead of smiling politely when I got dumped I'd do a Miss Piggy hi-ya and then, like magic, a new and better-haired version of me would appear, featuring mahogany-coloured boyfriends and an array of tapas.

I choose to lead a busy life. I go from work to friends, to the gym to the pub. It's a constant chatter. I don't even go for walks on my own, I'm always marching with a friend, gossiping as we pound the pavement, or I plug into a podcast. I've never lived on my own, I went from a noisy, busy family home with three smelly brothers to a packed-out student house with even smellier occupants, to a flat with Sasha. My whole life, every night, I've gone to sleep to the sound of cars whirring past, occasional shouts from revellers, doors banging. My head has always been filled with the noise of other people, that's why I like cities – you can never be lonely in the city, you don't have time.

But here there was only green field after green field. There were no cars, no chatter, no ambulance wailing in the distance,

The Enchanted Island

no kebab shop smells or drunk teenagers collapsing on their heels. No cinema, no nightclubs, no busy train journeys to make eye contact with handsome strangers, no fashion. Nothing. There was nothing but ear-shattering silence and an emptiness and a vastness that I found terrifying. The prospect of being on my own indefinitely was such uncharted territory that I genuinely didn't know how I would cope.

I know people did this all the time, they go off on yoga retreats, they even go on silent retreats. Who knows why? But I would never choose to be on my own, ever. My head was already spinning with thoughts. The nothingness in front of me, stretching day after day, was filling me with an icy-cold panic.

I was ridiculously thankful for the internet and social media. I'd kiss it if I could. The internet signal was surprisingly strong here. Fast, no flickers and hadn't dropped out yet. My little dongle plugged into my laptop was happily dongling away. I could still feel part of something even though I wasn't. I could lose myself in other people's social lives while not having one myself. I could take this time to better myself, to read up on current affairs, find out what really is happening to the environment, that kind of thing. Or I could just do some online shopping and Google celebrities. Either way, the internet would be my constant companion and new chattering best friend. I would also have the radio, I decided. I would keep the radio on. I would sing along to Beyoncé. Focusing on the lyrics, shouting them out, loud and proud. Maybe Beyoncé would get me through this.

On the other hand, there might have been other benefits if my phone wasn't working quite so well. Harry seemed very interested in my progress, which was a bit strange. I know he'd given me the job, but it was small fry compared to most of the deals in the office. There had been an edginess to his tone that I didn't like. It made me suspicious, and I didn't know why. But I needed to put that out of my head; I should be grateful for the opportunity that I'd practically leaped into his arms over just a few days ago.

There was something else bothering me and if I was honest – obviously I'd only admit this to myself – it was that I was worried about putting my social life on hold. And my real concern, as reluctant as I was to own it, was Carl. If I wasn't around, who else was?

I didn't have to look too far. I glanced at Twitter and there was a picture of him with his arm draped around Rebecca Sheils, renowned in Dublin circles: she had slept with the entire Leinster rugby team, including subs. I zoomed in on his face, magnifying it to see if there were any signs that he was sleeping with her. I searched for that glint of glad eye that he had given me many a time before. I couldn't see anything, but that didn't mean much.

I felt a sudden sense of overpowering rage. I looked around the musty caravan and wanted to throw a temper tantrum and scream and shout. I hated this. I didn't want to be here. It had only been one day but already I felt like I might go mad. And I did. I picked up a plate and I threw it across the room. It bounced onto the wall and fell to the ground, where it smashed in two with a satisfying crack. Relief washed over me. I felt better already. I had released my anger, and was calmer for it.

Picking up the pieces, I realised that I would have to grin and bear it. I would have to find an inner calm or just keep smashing plates. Remember the goal, remember what I was here for. And in the meantime there was Beyoncé.

9

'Those pricks.'

At last, there's the Irish accent.

'Those scuttering pricks.' Dan's fuchsia complexion went seventy-five shades deeper with rage. His chest puffed out and he started to pace.

We were at Dan's house – well actually, as I learned, it had been his parents' house, where he had lived until he was eighteen. He'd inherited it when they'd passed. It was situated at the far side of the island, the most westerly tip. A white-washed two-bedroom cottage, it was overgrown and rundown. The house was surrounded by a number of fields that must have been part of the estate, one of which dramatically and abruptly ended as it hit the sheer cliff face of Hy Brasil. There was nothing to see for miles other than a flat green blanket of grass. It felt lonely.

He was pacing the kitchen, or what could be assumed to be the kitchen: a darkened room at the back of the house.

The Enchanted Island

It had unplastered stone walls, sticky lino flooring, a small gas oven and a sink with a cupboard over it containing a collection of tinned peas and baked beans. There were no signs of a dishwasher or a fridge-freezer. It all felt very old-fashioned. Dan couldn't live here. It didn't look as if he'd put any money into the house, though maybe he planned to; maybe that was part of the bridge build? It seemed strange to want to invest all that money in a bridge and live in a house without – well, without a lot of mod cons. I spied some damp on the corner of the walls and thought there probably wasn't ever 'dryness' here.

I pulled up a stool. 'Look, he'll be back. I'll get him on his return. Like you said, he needs to sign this, he needs the money, we've no reason to think he's pulling out of the deal.'

Dan's mouth formed a straight line. 'Maybe I'll offer him more.'

'Your offer is overly generous as it stands.' I was confused. Clients were never so keen to throw their money away without a fight.

'Mmm, that might get him.' He was speaking to himself. He rubbed at his chest and sat on a red-cushioned stool. 'More money, it's really all I can do. Although he'll know then, he'll know I'm desperate to get it.' He took a deep breath. 'Was he alone?'

'No, there were two other elderly men with him.'

'Those two gobshites. I know who they are . . . Elderly, huh?' He laughed. 'They're all elderly here, or haven't you noticed?' Dan looked at me deadpan. 'That's part of our problem.'

'I don't understand.'

He shook his head. 'No, you wouldn't.' He stood up again and stretched his arms to the ceiling, his fingertips touching it, then swivelled around. 'You've got to think about the islanders as being split in two, with the elders – anyone over seventy – on one side, and everyone who isn't on the other. Those elders unofficially rule this place. And they will stop at nothing, *nothing*, to keep the island just so.' He wagged his finger from side to side like a pendulum on a grandfather clock. 'But you don't need to concern yourself with them. Ignore them – you just need to focus on getting that signature, and fast. I have deadlines. I have investors in the US. There are appointments made for six months from now. This bridge *has* to go up.' He slammed his fists on the table.

I jumped and he immediately went pale. 'Sorry, I didn't mean to. I'm under a lot of pressure.'

I braced myself, not sure if I would need to make a speedy exit at any minute if Dan the pressure pot actually boiled over.

'Look, can we speak confidentially?'

'Of course.' I nodded and tried to adopt an agony aunt-style face, kind, compassionate and discreet.

He looked at me, unsure, then said, 'Come with me.'

Pulling my jacket on, I followed him out the back door. He tramped down a cleared pathway towards the back field, in the direction of the sea. The closer we got, the louder and harder the wind howled. Dan seemed oblivious, he walked at a furious pace to the edge of the field, where nothing stood between him and America. He rocked back and forth on the balls of his feet, and without looking back stepped off the edge. I watched in horror as he disappeared. I ran towards the precipice, terrified. 'Dan, Dan! What are you doing?' I screamed. My words caught in the wind and floated across the Atlantic.

He had dropped to a ledge and turned around, his belly sandwiched onto the rock face, his hands clawing at it.

'Are you okay?' I shouted at the top of his head. He ignored me, busily foraging for something.

I watched as his right hand came flying upwards onto the ledge, and then his left, both clutching what looked like clumps of mud. He heaved his body upwards, I grabbed the back of his jacket attempting to pull him towards me, and he swung himself forward, rolling into the field to safety. Covered in grass stains but smiling triumphantly, he waved at me. 'This is it. *This is it.*'

I crouched down to him, peering into his hands.

'Seaweed. This stuff is going to make me super rich.' He gave a belly laugh. 'You'll never guess what it does.'

I shook my head, perplexed.

'Cures cellulite.' He grinned at me expectantly, perching on his knees. 'Wipes out all those little lumps and bumps. Gone. One session and not a dimple to be seen.'

'Seriously?'

He nodded and slowly got to his feet. 'Gone. It's the stuff of magic. You can't believe it until you see it.'

'This?' I reached out and touched it, the slimy, dark green, almost black seaweed, with little bubbles that gave it a lizard-skin surface. 'This cures cellulite?'

'And it's only on my corner of the island.' He waved his seaweed-filled hands in the air.

'How is that even possible?' I rubbed my fingertips, which were coated with slime.

Dan stepped towards me excitedly, his face so close to mine I could feel his breath. 'It's this place. This island. It has something.'

I had not been expecting this.

He continued, almost dream-like: 'I've had this stuff tested by some of the top cosmetic scientists in LA, and they can't explain it. They can break down the molecules and tell you about the vitamins and the nutrients and how good they are for the body, but we knew that anyway. People have been eating and bathing in this stuff for years, but how it works on cellulite, how it works like an eraser rubbing out the creases, they don't know.' He grinned from ear to ear. 'It's magic.' He shook his head, as if he didn't really believe himself. 'The seaweed and sand create a soil here on the bare limestone rock that the crops grow in. You'll see the farmers dragging up the seaweed from the shoreline and spilling out the sand. Seaweed has been used here for all kinds of things for thousands of years. But this is different. This is the *big* money. I'll be moving into a different league.'

Quieter now, he said, 'I have five of the top plastic surgeons in LA literally begging me for this. I can name my price. They're waiting.' Then his face went cold and he stepped away. 'I won't let this opportunity slip by. I won't let the island get one over on me.'

The Enchanted Island

I shook my head in disbelief. Was he waging a one-man battle against an island? What was this vendetta he had, which made him so angry? And magic? Why did he talk of magic when it was science at play?

'If this is true and it works, this is revolutionary.' Images of celebrities popped into my mind, proudly flashing their nether regions, nothing to hide now that the embarrassment of cellulite was gone. It would be open season on hot pants. Spanx would be a thing of the past; pale skin wouldn't need to be spray tanned. When this hit the high street, women would literally go crazy for it. There would be fist fights at chemists for the last bottle. They'd never be able to satisfy the demand. Hysteria and riots would ensue.

'Yes.' He punched the air. 'Revolutionary.'

'So the bridge . . . ?'

'Supply and demand. It's the only way I can get it off the island in bulk – the boats crash here, there's no guarantee of a safe arrival.'

I nodded, understanding now, understanding the urgency, understanding the implications. This was a business transaction after all.

'And it's only here?'

'I think it's to do with the fish and the birds on this part of the island, they only pop up here, the gull and the codfish. I think they might have something to do with it, that and the North Atlantic Drift. But I can't be sure. There's tonnes of the stuff though, tonnes and tonnes, and we can dig deep into the ocean bed to get more.'

'It'll run out eventually, though?'

He grinned mischievously. 'Not before I've made my fortune. I'll make at least four times what I spend here.'

There was no doubt there was a fortune to be made. I was dumbstruck. I never would have predicted this. All my grand altruistic ideas about the bridge being built for the good of the island were shattered. It was for one man's profit, and yet, I still felt that the bridge would benefit everyone. That, yes, Dan would grow very, very rich from it, richer than he had implied he already was, but that the island could grow rich and prosper too. That the island could be the kid who finally left home, could go overseas, backpack, listen to rap music, broaden horizons and return with different skills and knowledge.

The bridge build was positive for everyone. The island was such a backwater. It needed life. It needed lip gloss, hair dye and hip-shaking rock 'n' roll. It needed cars and traffic lights, for God's sake.

And let's not forget the little matter in front of me. I could in some small way help bring a cure for cellulite to the world. All of a sudden I was on a mission for womankind, for the sisterhood. For anyone who has ever rolled and squeezed their dimpled thighs into a swimsuit, who has tried to urgently wriggle out of Spanx in a nightclub toilet with four vodka and Cokes in their belly. Smooth-skinned women would no longer be able to smugly shake their behinds at the swimming pool. Beach holidays wouldn't have to be met with fear and anxiety attacks. Cottage-cheese thighs of the world could unite firmly together. The war against cellulite was about to be won.

The Enchanted Island

At that moment I knew that the only thing blocking my path, standing in the way of me assisting the women's movement in a small way and maybe becoming a modern Joan of Arc and liberating women's thighs everywhere, was that signature from the missing Sean Fitzpatrick. I was more determined than ever to get his wrinkly hands around a pen.

10

There was one hairdresser's on the island: Maura's. After walking back from Dan's, I decided to call in for a deep-conditioning treatment and a blow-dry. The wind was turning my poker-straight hair into a candy-floss experiment.

I opened the door, stepped in and spun right back out again.

A woman in her fifties – Maura, I assumed – stuck her head out the door after me. 'Where are you going?'

'I thought this was a hairdresser's?'

'Well, what do you think these are for?' she said, waving what looked like garden shears.

'So you are?' I asked, confused. 'But I saw a horse?' I had seen the rear end of a horse at the back of the shop, and more importantly, I had smelled him.

'Aye. That's Brendan's horse, he comes in to use the serums and braid the horse's tail.' She laughed and her blue eye shadow creased into her eyelids. 'Ah no, my husband shoes the horses out the back, and sometimes we make them look pretty. Only the good-looking ones, mind.'

Oh, well, that made sense.

'Are you coming in or what?'

I shrugged and stepped inside.

Maura shouted to the back of the shop, 'Don't come near me now for the next hour, Brendan, I have a lady with me.'

I looked over my shoulder. Lady? There must be someone else here, someone much older and frumpier. Then slowly it dawned on me. Oh sweet Jesus, she meant me. I am the lady. I. Am. The. Lady. A lady? Is that how people see me? Why was I spending all that money (albeit not always my money) with Dr Nash if all that was happening was Ladydom? I wanted to shake it off. A lady has a really wide arse, a crinkle in the centre of her forehead, a doughy tummy, weird blue veins and watches political debates on TV while sucking on a carafe of wine in a depressed state. I am not a *lady*.

I flashed a very cross look at Maura, hoping she could read minds. 'Do you call all your customers ladies, like, of any age? Like, if I was fourteen I'd still be a lady?'

'But sure you're not fourteen, are you?' She smiled back at me.

I wasn't happy, not one bit. What would she know, though? This wasn't like going to my beautician, Camilla, who also did a few A-listers' eyebrows and once dyed Gabriel Byrne's hair for a movie role. She was the real deal. Maura with her pearl-coloured nail varnish and floral shirt was clearly a beauty novice.

She picked my hair up and waved it around like bird's wings. She shook her head. 'Do you use conditioner?'

'Of course, I use a number of specialist products, and an oil that you can only get from northern Africa, it comes from digested pecans,' I said, delighted with myself and my clearly superior knowledge of hair products.

'You wouldn't know, it's half dead.'

I felt my face slip into a stony expression. 'Just a wash and blow-dry.'

She smiled in a slightly exhausted I've-heard-it-all-before way and ushered me towards a basin. As I put my head into it, I nervously scanned every shampoo and conditioner bottle I could see. I wasn't one hundred per cent confident that there wouldn't be some crossover horse product being thrown in for good measure.

'You're in the caravan, aren't you?'

Nowhere to run, nowhere to hide.

'Will you be staying long? We don't seem to get many tourists here, they don't bother me, mind, I'm happy. Money's money; if it comes from an islander or a tourist, it's fine by me. It's a great time of the year to be on Hy Brasil. It's the sunniest time of the year, the flowers are blooming. We've all kinds of Arctic and Mediterranean plants here if you're interested.'

Plants? Are you kidding me? I watched my nostrils flare in the mirror and rolled my eyes while she wasn't looking.

The Enchanted Island

'The puffins come in to rest, if you like wildlife, the gannets too. This is their breeding season.'

Right? And will I stick needles into my eyes while I'm at it?

'You're lucky I had a free spot. For some reason the women on the island like to get their hair done when there's a birth. Who knows why, it's not like the baby knows an up-style from a blow-dry, but it suits me something grand. Annie Carrig had a little boy. Had him at home, easy birth I heard. I haven't seen him myself yet but I've heard he's a strong healthy fella. Beautiful. Love a boy. I have two, teenagers. They're off at school on the mainland, probably up to no good.'

It must have been a different woman to the one I saw waddling down to the jetty.

'Do you go to the mainland much yourself?' I was zoning out with the noise of the water.

'No. No need. The boys will come back for holidays.'

I wasn't asking about her boys – I was more concerned about my hair. 'You don't try to keep up with mainland fashions, for you know hair styles and . . .'

She didn't hear me. The hose was drowning me out.

An hour later I had my answer and a large Dolly Parton–style bouffant hairstyle.

Maura also did makeup. She proudly showed me an array of forest-green eye shadows and orange-tinted lipsticks. I told her I'd keep her in mind.

I raced back towards the caravan hoping that no one would see me, snap a picture and post it online. Which is ridiculous – this wasn't Dublin, no one was going to name and shame my bad hair: one of the reasons I would never leave the house without looking camera-ready. You never know when a camera phone is nearby, and one bad photo can cling to you like a dolphin tattoo on your hipbone. Here I didn't need to duck or dive. But I still did, a habit I suppose.

As I neared Mulligan's pub I heard someone giggle in the liveliest way that would melt the coldest of hearts. It stopped me in my tracks and I twirled on my heels to find who was making the jolly noise. I looked down a cobblestone lane by the side of the pub, where kegs rested on top of each other like building blocks. There were figures at the end of it. I snuck down, safely hidden by the kegs. There was a humming in the air that turned into a little tune. Five kids were playing hopscotch, and next in line to take her go was Maggie, the ancient battleaxe from the pub the first night I arrived. She was giggling away to herself, and spinning around excitedly like a whirligig. The kids were jumping around her, singing. She threw her stone, hitched her skirts up around her knees, and hopped like a surefooted gazelle up and down the lane, her face a picture of giddiness. I don't think I'd ever seen an old person play hopscotch before. There was something really lovely and quite charming about it.

I rang Hazel when I got back. She was keeping me posted on all the office gossip and it was non-stop redundancy chatter. She had even gone and calculated her redundancy package.

'Shite, absolutely shite,' she informed me, whispering down the line. 'If I'm lucky, I'll get seven grand.'

'Sure that wouldn't even keep Antonia in knickers for the year.'

'That one,' she spat down the phone, 'she swanned out of here yesterday at five, not a care in the world, off to meet Dah-ddy for suppah, the rest of us slipping a noose around our necks on the hamster wheel trying to keep our jobs.'

'Nobody's seriously talking redundancies, though, are they?' There was panic in my voice.

'Everyone is, but not a word from the big boys.' Her voice started to shake. 'My boys won't survive public school – Cian wants to be a pastry chef when he grows up. He's five and he knows the ingredients in a Victoria sponge. He'll be annihilated in the public system.'

'Oh no,' I wailed, 'I'll never qualify. I'll have to emigrate! I don't want to emigrate.' I gulped loudly. 'Maybe I'll be forced to do a social welfare course, I'll be weaving baskets and making my own honey.'

'Ah, things will never get that bad, McDonald's will always need someone to clean their jacks.' She laughed at her own joke. 'I tell you, Harry is looking very jumpy this week too. His tan is even a bit pale.'

'He's been in contact with me since I got here, a phone call, a few texts. He seems really keen to sort out this deal.'

She paused. 'That's weird, isn't it? Why does he care about an apprentice getting a signature? No offence, Maeve, but has he ever had any interest in your work before?'

'No, never.'

'Oh God, what if this deal is going to keep the office afloat?'

'It's not that big a deal. The site is only selling for sixty thousand euro.'

'That doesn't make sense then. Why is he interested?'

She was right, it wasn't a major deal. It was quite a small one. Why did he care about a bridge being built on Hy Brasil?

'Shall I snoop? I'd love an excuse to snoop. I should have been a private investigator.'

'In a Burberry trench.'

'Obviously.'

'Get snooping, Snoopy.'

She snorted. 'You're one of the best workers in here, Maeve, apprentice or not. He knows you'll do your job. He'd have absolute confidence in you. He should be able to just let you roll with it. I wonder why he's micro-managing?'

'Thanks, Hazel, that's nice of you.' It felt a bit strange getting such a straight-up compliment about my work, especially since I constantly doubted my own ability.

'It's the truth and he knows it, which is why it doesn't make sense that he's getting involved.'

I hummed in agreement.

'Come back soon anyway, I miss you around the office. Padraig washed Paddy Friedman's car on his lunch break yesterday. Imagine washing the managing partner's car in this day and age? It was like something out of a comedy. Such a lick arse. Ridiculous carry on.'

'I swear if he keeps his job over me because he's car washing, I'll go mental.'

'Get that signature then, and it's all in the bag.'

'I know.'

11

Every day for three days I went back to Sean Fitzpatrick's house. Sometimes twice a day. Loitering, I suppose, with intent. He was never there. I tapped on the window, rang the bell, and posted a note through the letter box. And every time I walked there I felt like someone was watching me. Or many people, many pairs of eyes burning holes into my back. Lace curtains twitched as I passed cottages, shadows jumped behind me, sending shivers across my shoulders.

I continued to cheerfully greet anyone I met, but I wasn't getting anywhere. If I got a sneer, it was a bonus – at least I'd been acknowledged. Most of the time they flicked their eyes to look away when I caught them peeping, which just signalled how hard they'd been studying me. On the odd occasion where I spotted an islander first, at ease in their natural habitat so to speak, I did witness something unusual, something that I was very unfamiliar with. Dare I say it, they looked blissfully happy, just going about their daily business, traipsing around a field, not even remotely bothered by the smell of sheep shit, or pottering down Main Street, oblivious to the fact that there was no Marks & Spencer on the island and where would you buy a decent pair of tights? They held a look of inner peace and calm, of absolute serenity.

Harry had allotted me forty euros a day, which is a ridiculously small amount of money, but I literally couldn't spend it. In six days all I'd bought was a pair of wellies and that in itself had been an ordeal. Normally when I shop, I'm giddy. I feel like the coat I'm about to buy will change everything, will turn me into a better *me*. That moment of transaction is like giving birth, metaphorically speaking, all that potential, the future feels exciting and up for grabs. I hadn't felt like that when I bought my new wellies. Fallon's sold furniture, baby clothes, picture frames and wellies. They came in green, just green. The only size available was half a size too big for me but I was told to wear thick socks and I'd be grand. There was no shop assistant fawning over me, no tinkly music to make my heart race. There was also no anxiety or sweaty palms at the register. I just paid my eight euros and left. Easy.

For lack of anything better to do I became familiar with the island. I took a lot of photographs. I noted how the sun rose on the shore of Lissna Tra and how, on a cloudy day, the shadows made the sand shift, like there were creatures coming to life underneath. On a dark day the sun didn't appear at all and the black clouds bashed against each other and formed shapes like horsemen angrily racing across the skies. Those were days I wanted to stay indoors. The very air I was breathing was frightening, and my chest would grow tight with anxiety as the day went on. But then they would pass and peace and calm would be restored. The wetness was incessant; if it wasn't raining it was about to or it had just stopped.

On my fourth day on the island, I buttoned up my jacket and decided to dive headfirst into the wind and climb up Mount Culann. You could call it curiosity, but I think I was just bored, and I thought there might be a nice view from the top. I was right. There was. It took me over an hour to heave myself up it. No amount of Stairmaster action in the gym could have prepared my calves for the beating they got. There was a pathway that was home to many goats and sheep, who looked at me with dead eyes. As I neared the peak, most unexpectedly, I saw a house. It looked like a modern conversion that had been made of an ancient lookout. Stark grey fortress-style walls loomed threateningly on the otherwise soft and misty landscape. It had a name plaque on the gate: ABHAILE, the Irish word for home; a comforting word for something that looked the complete opposite. There was a crack at the side of the gate that I peeked through. There were gardens inside, and in complete contrast to the surrounds, they were beautifully manicured. I could see roses and trees that had been primped and pruned. I wondered who lived there, and if they'd object to me having a poke around some time.

The view from the top of Mount Culann caused me, the unbendable city lover, to freeze in sheer intimidation. The entire island was mapped out and I could see everything, every little nook and cranny, every tin roof and winding pathway, the island's coastline and the sea biting into it, the immense vast world of the ocean surrounding this tiny place. It shook me, I'll admit it. The starkness, the beauty; I would never have expected nature to pull at me. But it did. I was impressed.

Equally impressive but in a different way was the beach, the proposed site of the bridge build, at Sean's house. That Saturday I strolled down towards it as I had done a few times before. Again I marvelled at how the weather subsided magically, the rain stopped and all was calm on this sliver of sand. It was maybe half a mile long, and really beautiful. This little spot, this was special. The waves trickled into shore and I gazed upon the silhouette of mainland Ireland, so close but so far away.

I sat down on the sand for a moment to take it all in. Here the silence of the island that could drive me insane in the caravan, the sheer nothingness of it, didn't feel so loud. It felt peaceful and, I had to admit, nice. I hugged my knees to my chest and took a mental photo before taking an actual photo. This was lovely.

I heard it before I felt it: a loud crack. I was hit on the head. A blow right to the back of my head. And just as everything was going black there was a shout: 'Get off our island!' Before I could scream out myriad curses, I'd crumpled into the sand.

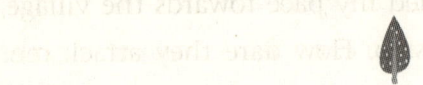

The Enchanted Island

There was sand up my nose when I came to. My cheek was firmly implanted on the beach. I opened my eyes and brought my hand to the back of my head. The ache across my forehead was overwhelming. There was a large bump about the size of a mandarin at the base of my skull.

Ow ow ow.

I straightened up, feeling incredibly dizzy. And then I remembered. I had been hit over the head. Someone had hit me over the head. Slowly I turned around. Were they still here? Were they going to hit me again? But the beach was empty, once again an oasis of calm. There was a very large stone behind me, about the size of a peach. I leaned backwards and grabbed it. It was as smooth as glass. I was pretty sure this was the weapon. I put it in my pocket. Thrown from where, though? It could have been anywhere for anyone with a good aim.

Carefully I got to my feet. I felt okay, but I was sure I'd have a giant headache sooner rather than later. I'd had worse knocks. I guess it was more the shock that had me trembling. I needed to get back and take a long shower. I felt so cold.

I walked heavily through the fields, looking anxiously from side to side; was I being watched? Was the rock thrower still here? *Get off our island!* What kind of stupid intimidation technique was that? I couldn't see anyone. I was happy to reach the road, and quickened my pace towards the village, getting angrier with every step. How dare they attack me? How *dare* they?

I was furious by the time I reached the shop on Main Street called The Shop. I felt cold and a bit shaken up and the smell of tuna mayonnaise from the deli didn't help much. I grabbed a few supplies, but really what I was looking for was headache pills. And while I was at it I should stock up on some vitamin C, I was bound to catch the flu with this weather. But there was nothing. The neatly organised shelves stocked lasagne sheets and tampons but no Panadol. I got to the counter with a basket full of groceries.

'Headache pills? Where are your headache pills?' I barked at the old man with red eyes and a bulbous nose behind the counter.

He shook his head at me, scoffing slightly. 'We don't have any.'

'What? Really?' I sighed. 'Well, where's the chemist then?'

'There's no chemist on the island.' He started running the groceries through the scanner.

'What?' I sobered up and snapped into reality. 'How can there be no chemist? Where do you go then? Where do you get headache pills and antibiotics and creams?'

'No need for them here.' He shrugged while scanning the milk.

'What?' I scrunched my face up. 'That doesn't make any sense. I have a need for them.'

He paused for a second, studying my scrunchy face. 'What's wrong with you?'

'I have a headache. Well, I don't have a headache now, but I'm pretty sure I'm going to get a headache.' I said this with so much dramatic flair it could easily have been mistaken for a daytime soap opera confession of an affair with a priest.

He made a dismissive sound. 'You can predict the future, can you? Why don't you get some fresh air into you, and have a bowl of soup in Tansey's, and you'll be fine.'

Well, thank you, Doctor The Shop. Thank you for your medical opinion. In a complete huff for the lack of sympathy, I paid up and, swinging my brown paper bag, I turned on my heel. How can there be no need for medicine? This was the modern world. I hadn't gone back in time. There had been a cure for smallpox. Modern medicine is a necessity, not a luxury. What did islanders do when they got the flu or sprained an ankle, or got really sick? This didn't make any sense. How did people fill prescriptions? Or deliver a baby? I remembered the woman I saw in labour heading down to the jetty – was it possible that she wasn't looking for an alternative birth? Was it possible that there wasn't a doctor on the island? No, that didn't make sense. There must be. I hadn't seen one, but that didn't mean anything. Of course people got sick. Illness was an inevitable part of life. The Shop guy didn't know what he was talking about.

Back at the caravan I took a hot shower and dried myself off. The bump on my head was still there. I felt a bit tired and weirded out but the ache was definitely gone.

I sprawled as best as I could on the hard couch-cum-thirty-years-of-dust-collector in the caravan. The smell was really getting to me – it was foul. I had spritzed some perfume around the place, which was really just a waste of money because nothing could shift the lingering odours. I'd have to hunt down a scented candle, a truckload of them.

I checked Snapchat and Instagram, delighted to see that my last selfie had gotten tonnes of likes and lots of 'gorgeous' comments. Although some people said everyone looked 'gorgeous' when clearly they didn't. And if I was honest I wasn't looking particularly gorgeous: my hair had entered into some kind of Medusa fashion all by itself. But there was a like from Carl that gave me a flutter – three little cherries had just popped up on the one-armed bandit. Brilliant, I was still in the game then.

I was going to ring Harry, to update him on nothing much, when there was a loud knock on the caravan door. The whole place shook slightly.

I flung the door open. A very large man stood in front of me, his square jaw set in a stubborn line. His blue eyes met mine with a menacing glare. He was wearing a suit jacket, tweed, he had a full head of white bristly hair; he looked old, but it's hard to put an age on people when they reach that white-face, white-hair period of life. I'd guess he was in his eighties. I wondered if he was one of the elders Dan had mentioned. The ones I was supposed to ignore.

He rocked back on his heels and thrust his hand out to me. 'Maeve O'Brien?'

I shook his shovel-like hand, amazed at the roughness of it.

'Ed O'Donnell.'

The Enchanted Island

I nodded, confused as to what Ed O'Donnell was doing on my doorstep. His voice was heavy, his accent hampered by a thick tongue.

'*Sergeant* O'Donnell.'

'You're a guard?' I looked him up and down, his tweed jacket not portraying any particular sense of law and order.

'A sergeant.' He nodded gruffly. 'I am the law enforcer on Hy Brasil.'

Well, there can't be too much that needs enforcing on the island, I thought, *if they have a guy in his mid-eighties in a tweed jacket holding up the law.*

'How can I help you, sergeant?' I asked, in what I felt was a very mature, grown-up fashion, so that he might understand that I was one of them: a goodie, fighting the battle against the baddies of this world, united in our desire to eliminate anti-social behaviour like dodging bus fares and jaywalking.

He reached behind him and produced a small notebook; it may have been a large notebook but in his hands it looked positively miniature. He brought his index finger to his mouth and licked the tip of it. I looked away. I can't stand the way people are so liberal with their saliva. What is it with the licking of things? Keep it in your own mouths, people. Leafing through, he stopped on a page. I strained my eyes to see what was written, but the inky scrawl was illegible.

'I have had a complaint about your whereabouts today.'

A complaint about me? There must be some misunderstanding.

'A complaint of trespassing.' He raised his left eyebrow and peered at me.

Ah, well a spot of trespassing might be different? I did my best to remain stony-faced.

'On the property of a Mr Sean Fitzpatrick. Were you there?'

I bit my lip, attempting to remain composed. Inside I could feel my temper begin to rise. I was the victim here, after all. I had had a rock thrown at me. I took a breath.

'I was, sergeant, yes.'

'And?'

He already knew the answer, he was just going to make me say it. 'I went to the rear of the property to see if he was out the back.' A small white lie.

'You were taking photographs?'

'Yes. I was. I've been commissioned on a project.' I hoped I sounded vague. I didn't want to give away anything confidential.

He tutted at me. 'Island matters are for island people.' He gave me a thin, disingenuous smile. 'There's no need for you to be working on any kind of project here.'

'I have a job to do.'

'We all do.' He closed his notebook and slowly shook his head at me like I was a naughty child in need of a scolding. 'We'll let this offence of trespassing go with a warning, but there's nothing here for you now, Maeve, be a good girl and go back to Dublin.'

A good girl? I wanted to lash out and pull his hair, then stamp loudly on the ground and scream at him. I straightened my back. 'I'm here to do a job, Sergeant O'Donnell. I don't quit.'

'Like I said, there's nothing here for you. And if you step on the wrong toes, well let's just say there are higher forces at work here.' He took a step backwards.

I felt panic bubble up inside me. 'Somebody threw a rock at me on the beach. It hit my head. I could have been killed. Well, probably not killed, but, you know, hurt.'

He dropped his eyelids to half-mast and feigned a look of boredom. 'You should think twice before you go around making accusations about island people.'

I crossed my arms defiantly. 'It's not an accusation, it happened. You're the guard, sorry – *sergeant*. I want to file a complaint or a something.'

'Well, I'll take note of it.' He scribbled in his book what could have been a drawing of a Tellytubby.

'Do you want me to make a statement?'

'You just did.'

'That wasn't official.'

'It was. I've got it all here. Somebody threw a rock at you while you were trespassing on Sean Fitzpatrick's property.'

I clenched my teeth, silently releasing a battle cry.

'I'll be off, so. Like I said, Miss O'Brien, it might be worth thinking about going back to Dublin, the weather is shocking bad here, and there's not much to do really.'

Get off our island.

'Thanks for the advice.' I summoned up my best sarcastic tone, sounding like my thirteen-year-old hormonal and spotty self used to when fighting with my brothers.

'You're welcome.'

He turned and ploughed through the field towards a bike leaning against a stone wall.

I slammed the door shut and thought I'd spontaneously combust with frustration. This place could drive me mad, so I was going to have to work very hard at keeping my cool.

12

I was slurping my soup, giant licks and gulps and I didn't care who heard. It was delicious. Potato and leek, creamy and salty but with a surprising sweetness to it. I couldn't shovel enough of it into me. I had reluctantly taken The Shop man's advice and gone to Tansey's for a bowl of soup. My headache had never transpired, but after the whole shady event and the visit from Sergeant O'Donnell, the soup was giving me tremendous comfort. Tansey's was a livelier pub then Mulligan's, busier. The decor wasn't much more spectacular than Mulligan's but Tansey's was friendlier, and there was chat and laughter bouncing off the walls. It felt happier, even though the elderly barman, busy changing kegs at the bar, was wearing a black armband. That had to be for the guy who died, Jimmy. Although, like the bearded lady at the coffee shop, the barman seemed happy. The local radio station was playing, and the warm-hearted laughter of the elderly DJ was a gentle melodic background noise. And there was a gorgeous glossy-coated sheep dog asleep under the bar, who occasionally popped open an eye and scanned the room to make sure everything was correct and accounted for before falling back to sleep again.

A keg somehow broke free from the bar and rolled into the lounge area. An old man in a khaki green raincoat, who looked as skinny and frail as a baby bird, hopped up and firmly placed a hand on the renegade keg.

'I got it, Stevo, not a bother.'

I hovered over my seat, about to offer to help him roll the keg back to the bar. He looked like it would flatten him. And then I watched as he bent his knees, flipped the keg upright, hugged it to his chest and carried it the twenty steps to the bar, as if it was as light as a newborn baby. The barman didn't even flinch, didn't even offer to help, he just pointed to the Guinness tap.

'Lay it down over there, Marty, that'd be grand.'

Now even if that were an empty keg – which I didn't think it could be, because why would he be hooking the Guinness tap to it – how could bird man Marty with his legs as skinny as needles lift that? And why was I the only one in the place staring at him? Had nobody else witnessed this man of iron?

My phone buzzed. A Harry text.

> *Any progress?*
> *No news yet, Harry. I'll call you later.*

No news, except maybe Superman's granddad is here.

'Well, hellooooooo!'

The Enchanted Island

I turned my head in shock. A slim-waisted fifty-ish man, in denim shirt and trousers, stood in front of me. He had a short haircut, luminous skin and dark brown eyes. He fanned the fingers of his right hand at me, his left hand balancing a meringue pie. 'Who is this?'

He was speaking to me, in fact, not only was he speaking, he was smiling at me. He grabbed a stool opposite and straddled it, then leaned across the table and gently slapped my hand. 'Well now, where have you come from?'

'Dublin. I'm Maeve, Maeve O'Brien.'

'Dublin.' He sighed heavily. 'Ahh, the real world, not like this little fairytale place.'

I nearly exploded with laughter. Fairytale place. Is he mad? Isolated, wet, bleak, unfriendly; I don't remember any Hans Christian Andersen tales starting with *Once upon a time it rained and it never stopped raining*. But I grinned politely, not wanting to seem rude to someone who was actually being nice to me.

'Well, I am delighted to meet you, Maeve, Maeve O'Brien. I'm Jack.' He held his hand across the table and I shook it, smiling.

'Are you staying long? How did you find us here? What brings someone from Dublin to our little paradise? We don't get many visitors.'

'Work.' I eyed him cautiously, not willing to give too much away. 'I've been here six days already and I might be here for a little while, I'm not quite sure yet.'

'It's so nice to have you here. I'm not one of those islanders –' he looked up to the sky, '– who doesn't want visitors here. We can't be the only lucky ones.'

'It's definitely an interesting place,' I said, though I doubted very much that I'd be describing myself as lucky if I lived here. And then I remembered some of the beautiful natural sights I'd seen: the sun glistening on the rocky side of Mount Culann so it looked like the surface of a shimmering lake, or the passionate ocean biting the coastline like a lion gnashing its teeth, or the intricate weaving of delicate white flowers tangled up in the breeze. There was great beauty here. Maybe I had been a tad snappy in my judgement.

'It's just about the most gloriously isolated little enclave on earth.'

'It is definitely isolated. And it is beautiful.'

He grinned widely. 'Yes, but it can't be all work and no play. Frank and I will have you for dinner. You can fill us in on big-city life. It'll give me an excuse to share this lemon meringue pie. Otherwise I'd probably just eat it all on my own. I'm fighting to hold on to this thirty-two-inch waist as it is. But you don't look like you've any problems in that department.'

'That'd be lovely,' I said, slightly bamboozled by Jack's generosity. 'I saw those pies, they look great.'

'Magic.' He closed his eyes dreamily, then opened them suddenly. 'Tomorrow, it's Sunday. Do you have plans?'

I laughed. 'My social life hasn't really taken off here yet.'

'Give it time, darling, give it time. It's all about who you know in Hy Brasil, and she wants you to be happy – she'll point you in the right direction. Whatever the heart desires, she'll give you.'

'She?' I crinkled my nose at him.

'The island. And look, she's brought me to you. She knows what she's doing.' He winked and stood up. 'Say half-seven?'

I nodded.

'We're on the northwest of the island, this side of Mount Culann. Just ask anyone where the big old queens Frank and Jack are, they'll point you in our direction.'

'Thanks so much, I am really looking forward to it.'

He smiled and walked out, expertly balancing the pie on his upturned hand.

What a pleasant surprise. He seemed like a lot of fun. Maybe I might enjoy myself if there were more people like Jack here. Although I doubted that a fun evening would take away the anxious feeling gnawing in the pit of my stomach. Sean Fitzpatrick. Where was he and how could I find him?

※

'Slap it on your arse.'

'That's the medical advice?'

He smirked. 'I could always help you.'

Dan's Irish accent had gotten thicker somehow and his face redder. Something in the water? I needed to have a conversation with him, a proper one. I was frustrated beyond belief. I was seven days in and none the wiser. Where was Sean Fitzpatrick? Why was he avoiding this deal? What was Dan holding back from me? But more importantly, I really wanted to get my greedy little hands on some of that seaweed. I needed to test it out – for womankind, you understand.

I had an aching desire to wear shorts this summer and acres of cellulite that needed to be farmed before I could even consider wriggling into them.

'I literally just put the seaweed on the problem areas?' I said, avoiding the words *arse, thighs, butt cheeks*, anything that might give Dan an excuse to perv.

'That's it.' He took a big slurp of milky tea. We were sitting in his kitchen. My creaky wooden chair was stuck to the lino floor. The kitchen table was filthy and my mug took that second too long to detach itself from it. Dan looked clean though, the plumbing must work. He had two laptops and a tablet on the table, and his eyes darted from me to them like a bee trying to decide which flower to pollinate. 'You, eh . . . you can wrap a plastic bag or something around it to hold it all in, the heat helps. Leave it on for an hour.'

'And that's it? One treatment?'

'Poof!' He splayed his fingers in the air. 'Gone. Like magic.'

I felt a shiver of nervous excitement and wanted to run back at top speed to the caravan and dose myself in seaweed. It was all a little bit too much. I am a big fan of beauty products. I lather, cream, exfoliate, tone, cleanse, detox, steam, pluck, wax, file, smear, pop, smooth and then I do it all again, deeply. I can lose myself in foams and creams, their rich sensations, the smells that make my nose tingle. I read beauty blogs. I subscribe for free samples. I bow down at cosmetics counters and shamelessly ogle the beauticians, who are so immaculately put together. I question their eyebrow techniques, their lip liner secrets, and always confess my lifelong quest for dewy skin, you know the type: the kind that's nearly reflective. Beauticians have it. And probably movie stars, but I've never seen one of them in the flesh. Skin that's beyond flawless because it has a sheen to it, like a healthy fruit, plump and fresh. I want that.

'You'll have to show me a before and after shot.' And he did that thing that really pervy men do – they've turned it into an art form – he turned the disgusting, sleazy statement into a joke. He leaned back in his chair and winked at me, forcing out a wheezy laugh. 'For research purposes. Sure, we could even use your arse in the advertising.'

I let his sexual harassment lawsuit hang between us for a few moments too long. Then I gave him my death stare. My do-not-mess-with-me stare. I said firmly, with my words clipped but still trying to remain professional and keep this job, 'That would be highly inappropriate, Dan.'

'Ah, would you stop.' He pushed himself away from the table. 'I'm only messing. Jesus, can you not take a joke?'

You see? You see how the perverts do it? He flipped it onto me. *I'm* the one who is flawed. *I'm* the one with no sense of humour.

'That was a bad joke.' I dialled down my death stare a notch. It is very powerful.

'Jesus.' He reshuffled himself on his chair and started to play his laptop like a piano, pushing heavily on the keyboard. *Click click click.* I waited for the moment to pass and sipped on my tea.

'I need to give my contacts dates . . . what are we looking at?'

I wanted to grab my seaweed, shrug and run away. But no, I was Maeve the grown-up. I could handle this.

'I'm confused, Dan. I don't believe Sean Fitzpatrick has disappeared off the island to go fishing, but I can't find him.' I hadn't actually expected to say this but it had just fallen out of my mouth. 'I think there's something else going on. There's another reason why Sean won't sign.'

'Ah, he's a brazen thick. Just give him the document to sign and don't take any crap from him.'

I nodded. But if it was that simple, why hadn't he signed it ages ago? What was holding him back?

'But what if I can't find him to give him the document? I don't know where he is. Is there anything I need to know, Dan?'

He squeezed his eyes tightly shut and put his face in his hands. He took a deep breath. 'I'd imagine that the elders on the island are putting him under a bit of pressure.'

These guys again. 'The elders?'

He cocked an eyebrow at me and chewed his lip, deliberating. 'Like I said before, the island is split in two. There are about thirty or forty families that have been here since billy-o. That crowd, the old ones in those families, they make up the elders and they don't want any change. They're protecting a way of life from hundreds of years ago – their way of life. They're protecting themselves.'

'They'll need to move with the times. Everyone is nervous of change at first.'

'Hmm.' He clenched his jaw, deciding on whether or not to tell me something. 'It's not just a way of life, it's the island.'

The Enchanted Island

I nodded, not seeing much of a muchness.

'They believe, and Jesus, who knows, maybe there's something in it, that the island is special.'

'The views are nice.'

'No. Maeve, they believe that there's something different about this place, this ecosystem. It's unique. They'll do whatever they can to keep it secret, and to keep the secrets of the island secret.'

'I guess the seaweed is a pretty interesting concoction, though I'm sure there's a scientific explanation for it.'

'Absolutely, and you and I would both agree on that because we're worldly people, and to be honest I don't know how or why this seaweed works. I just care that it does.' He shook his head. 'But the old people here, they're backward. Some of them have never even left this place. They're not interested in the outside world. Their world starts and stops on the four corners of this island. And they don't want any interference with that life. They're happy with things just the way they are.'

I rubbed the back of my head, wondering about how far they'd go to keep things just the way they are. 'Time moves on, everyone has to change.'

He paused for a moment. 'Not this place. Why would they change when they've already found paradise?'

'Paradise?' I scoffed. 'It's so wet here. Everyone is so grumpy, especially the old people, these elders.'

'To you maybe, Maeve, they don't want you here, but these are the happiest, healthiest people you'll ever meet.'

'And the bridge – the bridge will change that?'

'I don't know, and they don't know. Why would they risk it?'

'Their happiness can't be based on isolation?'

'They don't feel isolated. They feel protected.'

Protected. Harry had used the exact same word to describe the island.

'By what?'

'What? Who?' He raised his eyebrows. 'Does it really matter?'

'Well, maybe if I could speak to the elders.' I had a vision of me approaching a naked man with paint on his face standing outside his wigwam, smoking from a giant didgeridoo-style bong, bowing my head and presenting him with an iPod, so sleek and filled with music that was not just bongo-based.

Dan rolled his eyes at me. 'Don't bother. You wouldn't even get close to them.'

'Who are they?'

Dan shook his head. 'This is not the route to take, Maeve. Just get hold of Sean.'

Easier said than done.

He gulped back his tea. 'In fact, I need to leave the island. I have to go to Dublin for a bit. I'll call in to see Harry.'

'You're leaving?'

'Yeah, work.' He closed down one of his laptops as if he was leaving this very second. 'Thanks, Maeve, I'll tell Harry you're doing a great job.'

I liked the sound of that. Maybe Harry might increase my day allowance. I could splash out on a second pair of wellies.

'Just keep going, Maeve. You can do this.' He gave a little fist pump. 'You have to do this. This is all I've ever wanted. This will make us all rich.' He spoke dreamily, as if he was conjuring up gold bars and sports cars in his imagination.

I left Dan in his kitchen with his blinking laptops and a phone glued to his ear. I had two plastic bags stuffed to the brim with seaweed. Dan had said I didn't need that much, but thankfully he hadn't seen my arse.

I am experienced in the ways of products, but this seaweed venture was definitely new. I stood on some newspaper, because God forbid I'd stain the lino. I was in my bra and a pair of socks, a treat for any peeping Toms. I wrapped long strands of seaweed around my bum. It kind of stuck to my skin and sealed itself to me. I didn't experience any burning, it was just slimy and gooey and felt a bit gross, if I'm honest. I tried to cover all angles but it was tricky, and I understood why you would get a beautician to put it on for you. Clumps of ooze fell through my fingers and onto my legs. The plastic bags. I rummaged through the drawers and found some Sellotape and used it to tape the bags to my legs. I had created a seaweed nappy. I threw a blanket on the couch in case of leakage and turned on the TV. An *OC* rerun, sure, what else would I be doing of an afternoon other than watching good-looking American teenagers in the Californian sun while wearing a seaweed nappy?

I had taken a before photo, a never-to-be-shared photo of my rear end and dimpled thighs. That was the scientist in me, planning on comparing and contrasting the amazing results (please God let there be amazing results). Also it was pretty hard to see with just a pocket mirror and a sink mirror; all my jumping and angling weren't really giving a true reflection of the dire state of affairs that was my cellulite.

An hour later, after I'd rekindled my love for Adam Brody and his teen angst ways on *The OC*, I peeled the plastic bags off my nether regions and hopped into the shower, rubbing vigorously. Big clumps of dried seaweed, giving off a slightly sulphuric, stale smell, fell at my feet and started to block up the drain. I wanted it to work. I knew I wanted it to work. I wanted a dimple-free bum as much as the next non-model woman. But surely this wouldn't be the miracle Dan had promised – as much as I'd love to believe the island magic story, it just seemed too far-fetched. Realistically, there was no way this tiny island in the middle of nowhere held the cure for cellulite. The cure for cellulite, if there would ever be a cure, would come from some laboratory, some guy in a white coat with test tubes and Bunsen burners would accidentally stumble across it over a cheese sandwich on his lunch break and stick a multimillion-dollar price tag on it. The cure wasn't just growing in the wild off the west coast of Ireland. And the cure most definitely wasn't currently in my hands.

With much contorting and bending, I snapped a photo. I braced myself for disappointment, knowing that I should be concerned about my job and the bridge build, but really at that moment my main concern was my upper thighs.

But lo and behold, oh joy, oh rapturous day! I could hardly believe it. The after photo was such a thing of beauty that even Michelangelo would want to travel in a time machine to capture it for some ceiling art. A smooth, positively radiant-skinned arse. It was bloody perfect. It worked. The seaweed worked. Dan was right. It was magic. There was something incredible going on here. I had tried so many potions and lotions, I had spent a fortune particularly before any holiday that would involve a swimsuit, and nothing had come close to this. Nothing.

I had a sobering moment. I didn't know what was happening on this island, what strange chemistry or magic was at work, but I knew the bridge had to happen. I owed it to women everywhere.

13

I was early. I thought about walking back down the road for a bit and maybe sitting on a wall for fifteen minutes, but I wasn't sure if I had been spotted on approach. The invite had been for an Irish seven thirty, which meant eight, and here I was like an enthusiastic groupie at the doorstep at seven fifteen. I sighed. I'd have to knock. If I had been spotted, I'd look like an even bigger gombeen just hanging out at the front door. God. I was trying to make friends, not scare them. I knocked loudly and two seconds later the door swung open. Jack. He must have seen me walk up. Otherwise he had just been standing on the other side of the door ready to pounce, like a skeleton on a ghost train.

'I'm so sorry I'm early!' I heard myself shout at him.

'I was just passing the front door! I wasn't standing behind it! I don't just stand behind hall doors!' Jack shouted back at me, flustered.

The Enchanted Island

We simultaneously burst out laughing.

'You're early and I'm a stalker. Come on in.' He swept open the door and stood back.

I thrust some wine and a chocolate cake into his hands as I stepped through. 'I know you have cake, but they didn't have any chocolates in The Shop, which is pretty weird isn't it, no chocolates? So I saw this, it's store bought but homemade, it'll keep for a few days if you don't want to eat it tonight.'

'Deeelicious.' He dramatically stuck his nose over it and inhaled deeply.

'Oh, this house, you wouldn't expect this from outside.' My mouth hung open as I admired the sweeping expanse of traditional wooden beams leading to a sun-lit, open-plan house. From outside, it had looked like all the other cottages on Hy Brasil: small, poky, two-windowed, cute but uninviting. But inside, this house was straight out of *Architectural Digest*. I ran my fingers along the walls and paused to admire the floors, the ceilings, the door knobs. It was sheer and modern. I felt like I should be wearing a minimalist white linen trouser suit and raspberry-toned lipstick to fit in with the decor, my hair slicked back in a bob.

'What a house. This is spectacular.'

He waved me away. 'This place, this is Frank's baby. I probably would have kept it dark and dingy but Frank had a dream.' Jack splayed his arms out to indicate Frank's big dream. 'Come down to the kitchen and meet the dreamer and let's crack into some wine.'

The kitchen was downstairs. The entire back wall was a giant window that looked onto the sea, that dark, threatening, vibrant and dangerous sea. The kitchen itself was a stainless-steel explosion, neat clean lines, immaculate and modern. Frank – it had to be Frank – had his head in the oven and a very large posterior pointed towards us.

'That's my boy.' Jack winked at me and slapped Frank hard and fast on the bum.

'I knew you'd do that.' A grinning face swung out of the oven. Frank straightened, tucked his white shirt over a perfectly round belly into his chino pants, and stretched a long arm towards me. 'Lovely to meet you, Maeve, I'm Frank.'

I normally think moustaches are possibly the most offensive facial feature that could willingly be inflicted on people, but there was something about Frank's moustache that made me reconsider my stance. He had floppy brown hair that belonged to a 1990s romcom hero. He had a welcoming happy smile, which overrode all fashion faux pas. He was definitely older than Jack, but I wasn't sure by how much.

'She's been admiring.' Jack grabbed a chip, dipped it in some hummus and popped it in his mouth.

I smiled over at Frank enthusiastically. 'This house is spectacular.'

'A labour of love.' He moved towards the wine bottle and pulled some glasses out of a cupboard. 'It's taken a while but we love it now.'

'American?' I blurted out. 'You're American too?'

'I am. Originally from Iowa, moved around a lot, but Iowa is where I grew up.'

'Well, that's another surprise for me. You must know Dan?'

'Dan the Man.' Jack raised his eyebrows. 'He's not that far from here. But he's Los Angeles, isn't he?'

'I think so, yes.'

'How do you know Dan?' Frank raised his bushy eyebrows at me.

'Oh, just . . .' I wondered what I should or shouldn't reveal. 'Work.' I sipped at the wine that had found its way into my hand.

Frank and Jack exchanged a quick glance.

'I'm here doing his will and organising his estate, I'm with a solicitors' firm in Dublin.' Should I ask them about Sean Fitzpatrick? They might know him, but then they might ask why I needed him, why Dan needed him. I couldn't tell them about the bridge. I'd have to consider another approach. I changed the subject quickly, impressed at my smooth lie but not too sure if I'd ace a talkshow lie detector test. 'So how does an American end up here?'

Frank smiled. 'I inherited the house, well, actually me and my siblings jointly inherited, but they weren't interested in it, so I bought them out for a few pennies –'

'Literally,' Jack interrupted.

'It had been my mother's, and her mother's and her mothers', generations back. I thought it would be a shame to lose it out of the family, to sell it off. So I bought them out about – what, Jack, fifteen?'

'About fifteen years ago, I'd say.'

'About that. I hadn't even seen the place, remember we had to get out a map to find out where the hell Hy Brasil was?'

Jack smiled wistfully. 'We were so young and handsome then.'

'We didn't make the move for a long time; we were never going to make the move really. We were living in Chicago, happy, out, and then . . . Ah, you know . . .' His mouth turned down and he smiled sadly, and I got the impression that there was a lot more to their story.

A plate of finger food appeared, cherry tomatoes with feta cheese, and mini bruschettas.

'Yum,' I exhaled hungrily. 'Is it just me or is the food here unbelievably good? I haven't had a bad meal yet. I'd never have thought Hy Brasil would be some gastronomic capital, but lo and behold.'

'Amazing, isn't it?' Jack laughed. 'Anything that's grown here has got that extra flavour, that something else. These tomatoes grew in our greenhouse out the back. Just taste them, they're as sweet as a sugar cube.' He kissed the tips of his fingers. 'Sorry, that's the Italian in me.'

'But you're American too?' I popped a truly delicious tomato into my mouth.

He nodded. 'Wisconsin originally, although I have seriously picked up the Irish accent, but there's an Italian sailor generations back. I'm too good a cook and I have too much passion not to be Italian.'

The doorbell rang.

'The guests, the guests.' He flapped his arms pretending to be massively flustered as he hopped off his stool and raced towards the hallway.

The Enchanted Island

'There's a few others coming,' Frank said, 'we thought we'd make a night of it. Jack is the real cook, I'm only the sous chef really, but we do like to entertain.'

'So, there's life on the island.' I nodded appreciatively.

'Yes, there is. Quite a lot of it. Hy Brasil is a bit like our greenhouse out the back, we are all growing together intertwined, under the same sun, sealed off from the rest of the world, probably growing inwards. We may be too dependent on each other, but there's brilliance in it really, brilliance in all our eccentricities.' He beamed.

'You love it here?'

'Oh, I do, I do. Wouldn't change it for the world. It's strange at first. Different. Not everyone warms to it, but you will, you'll see.'

I nodded politely, but really I thought how unlikely it ever could be that I might like this place. It was unfriendly, unfashionable, remote, not to mention the terrible weather. And there was something else, something more sinister and threatening about the place; I didn't think I could ever feel comfortable here. That said, I could recognise the staggering beauty – there were parts of the island that I had found to be terrifyingly awesome.

'To be honest, Frank, I haven't found the place very hospitable. In fact, I've found a lot of the islanders to be quite rude, present company excepted.'

He smiled. 'Of course. The older contingent?'

I nodded in agreement, thinking that by far the narkiest people I'd met had all been older.

'They are very protective of the place, I mean I suppose we all are, but they are pretty militant about it.'

Militant, what an odd word to use. 'You mean . . . ?'

He waved his hands in the air, as though brushing the conversation aside. 'Oh, it's just, they're protecting another way of life, something that they think still exists. I don't know. The only reason Jack and I are accepted here is because of my mother, some of them remembered her.'

'Really? But she must have left here such a long time ago?'

'I know, and I'm not as young as I look.'

'And the islanders, they don't mind you and Jack being together?'

Frank sighed heavily. 'Do you know, we have lived all over the world, and encountered all kinds of prejudices and been in some horrible situations, but nothing, absolutely nothing here. We couldn't believe it, we thought we'd have all kinds of trouble in rural Ireland, but we were wrong. We wondered at first if people didn't know we were gay, if they just thought we were brothers or friends or something, that they hadn't quite figured us out, that's why we got no trouble at all. But then we realised they knew and they just didn't care. Couldn't care less. They were happy to take us as we are. And we liked that attitude, Maeve, we liked it a lot. It kind of sums up the mentality of the islanders. There's great acceptance here, a real type of peace.'

I was very surprised at that. I had this place down as backwards, fire and brimstone backwards.

'Maeve, meet Niamh.'

The Enchanted Island

I spun around to see a curvaceous woman in a red dress, acres of cleavage spilling out, blonde hair tumbling across her shoulders and a bright red lipsticked smile. She was late forties, I guessed, and vivacious. A floral scent lingered as she moved in to give me a kiss on the cheek hello.

'And Killian and Tim.'

As Niamh shuffled towards Frank, I dipped my head sideways to say hello to Killian and Tim. A tall blond-haired guy with a scattering of spots across his chin offered his hand and used his other to awkwardly pull on his ear. He had a freshly ironed blue shirt on, jeans and a well-worn pair of runners; he would have looked at home on any university campus in Ireland.

'Tim, nice to meet you,' I said, watching as he blushed slightly. I moved in my seat to face the curly-haired man behind Tim. 'And Killian . . .'

And there he was. Killian. I locked eyes with him and fizzed. Had we met before? His face, his open smile, his twinkly green eyes with amber flecks peeping through, his wavy copper-coloured hair, it was all so familiar. Who was he?

'Maeve.' He held out his hand, which had a light dusting of freckles across it, and I thought I would fall off my stool.

'Do we . . . ? Do I know you?' Was it just that he was handsome? No, it couldn't be, he was handsome but that wasn't it. I liked him. But how could I like him? I didn't know him. But I knew him – I *knew* him – and I liked him.

He grinned. 'No, I don't think so.'

'You're so familiar, are you on telly?'

'No.' He chuckled.

'It'll come to me.' I stared hard at him. Had he been a drunken snog in some sticky nightclub in Dublin? I snatched my hand back and looked at the floor. I wanted to grab my phone and run to the loo and google him, see if we had people in common.

He stepped back and admired the view of the ocean from the kitchen. 'I never get tired of this.' He walked over to Frank, shook his hand and took a full wine glass, clearly at ease in their kitchen. I tried not to look at him, I couldn't trust myself, but I had taken him in, drunk in every inch of him.

He moved comfortably, assured and relaxed. He wore a soft grey V-necked jumper, a white collar, and dark denim jeans. He had a strong build, was muscular and tall, but not overly so. He was undeniably sexy. I strained my neck as subtly as I could, hoping I wasn't having too much of an overt ogle. I watched his every move and sighed approvingly as he turned around. He had a gorgeous bum – I knew it! I could have a go of that. I really could. Maybe I could have an island fling and then Carl would hear about it and be consumed with jealousy and come to the island and beat Killian up in a *so macho* way. That would be great.

And then I looked at Killian's cute face and thought it probably wouldn't be fair to give him a black eye, even an imaginary one. Maybe instead we'd just hold hands and stare lovingly at each other, in a *Romeo and Juliet* way, after all, he lives on a weird island in the middle of nowhere and I like my

The Enchanted Island

high street packed with sale signs and my roads with traffic on them. Call me crazy.

I snapped back to reality and saw he had entered into a private conversation with Frank. His voice was deep and gentle. I swallowed hard. These heightened senses had thrown me off guard. I took a long breath and a large gulp of wine to settle myself.

'And what about you, Maeve?'

'Sorry?' I tuned into the conversation.

'Do you surf?' Tim asked.

'No. I've never even tried it. Do people surf here?'

Tim nodded happily. 'Yes, all the time. There are some sheltered bays along the island and all you need to do is stick the nose of the board out, and the waves are majestic. You don't need to go out too far to catch them – it's like they're waiting for you.'

'Well, you won't get me out there.' Niamh shook her head, her blonde curls trembling gently. 'I wouldn't even fit in a wet suit, ugh, the thought of it, I'd be like a massive eel. Any more vino, Jack?' She passed her empty glass to him. 'I've an awful thirst on me tonight.' She giggled.

Jack topped up all the wine glasses. 'Plenty where that came from.'

'There's a whole cellar,' Niamh said, 'a cellar within a cellar, oodles of the stuff from their vineyard in the south of France. I'm like a kid in a sweet shop down there.'

Jack laughed. 'Cheap plonk really.'

'It's not so cheap if you buy it in a restaurant.'

'Ahh, but we make it, we don't buy it. As the little birdie says, cheap, cheap, cheap.'

I looked at the wine label. There was a French name on it that I didn't recognise, but the logo on the label looked familiar. 'Is this . . . ' I wasn't sure how to phrase it, 'your business?'

'Among other things,' Niamh said. 'F and J enterprises are very well connected.'

'I guess we were once upon a time, but now life is simpler, now we are happy.' Jack sighed contentedly.

'À table, people, à table!' Frank piped up in his best French. The guests moved towards the dining room and I followed.

'Sit wherever you want.'

There was a long oak table that contrasted with the bright Delft-inspired crockery that sat on top. Candlelight flickered, and the low hum of jazz music burbled in the background. I sat between Jack and Tim and opposite Niamh, but Killian was firmly in my view, sitting to her right. I tried so hard not to look at him. I felt if I started I wouldn't be able to stop. I turned my attention to the university student beside me.

'So, Tim, are you from Hy Brasil?'

'No. Me and a friend moved out here about a year ago. We rent a house on the other side of the island.'

'You do live here then?'

'Well, we are staying here,' he replied, somewhat evasively.

'Okay.'

I must have smirked because he started apologising. 'Sorry, we moved here because of the surf. We're working on an app, we've been flat out for the last year, we've a little sweatshop

The Enchanted Island

going, but we're almost there with it. It's all top secret, you know yourself.'

I knew all about secrets. I nodded, interested, and dying to ask more questions.

'You make it sound like you're working on some blog, Tim,' Niamh butted in. 'Tim has pioneered games and apps, they're not some small-fry geeks.'

He laughed. 'Yeah, we're big geeks, huge geeks.'

'I'm a bit of a gaming geek myself,' I confessed, 'or at least I was. I've given it up the last few years but I used to be really good. I've three older brothers, and games were one of the few things that I could absolutely annihilate them all at.'

'No way.'

'Yeah.' I laughed, remembering early teenage years lost to Resident Evil 3 and 4. 'I think I'd more patience than them and I was always good at the puzzle solving.'

He straightened up and leaned into me. 'Seriously? You're good at puzzle solving?'

I nodded.

'Don't leave without me getting your number. Back at the house we're stuck on this game from 2005, we've been at it for weeks. We don't want to google it, but we could do with some coaching.'

'What's the game?'

'Resident Evil 4.'

My chest swelled with pride, I smugly crossed and uncrossed my legs, then patted Tim's knee. 'That's not a

139

problem, I happen to be the 2005 17 Clontarf Road, North County Dublin champion of Resident Evil 4.'

'Seventeen Clontarf Road?' He looked at me, confused.

'My home address. We had a very competitive household.'

'Well, I'll set you a challenge then.' He grinned, delighted, showing a chipped front tooth. I wondered if it was a surfing injury.

'I've noticed the internet signal is really good here, too. I was surprised.'

He nodded. 'Wait and see – your phone will never drop out, and the internet connection is so speedy. We should really start a whole online community here, get developers and programmers out by the dozen.'

The whole table laughed.

'That would never happen,' Niamh said. 'They'd never let that happen.'

'They?' I looked around, clearly missing out on some insider joke. I could literally feel a shadow creep across the table, and I watched as Jack's eyes flicked from Frank to Niamh, nervously.

'Oh, they, them, the powers that be, whoever ...' Niamh spoke in a shrill voice and drained her glass.

I turned to her. 'Are you a native islander?'

She nodded, smiling, and leaned into me conspiratorially. 'I am, but I'm only back a few months. I came to straighten myself out, to get some balance. I'm going through a divorce.' She had whispered the word divorce, but she was smiling so widely I could only guess that it was a jolly one.

The Enchanted Island

'I probably should have married one of my own kind, another islander, like my parents wanted me to, but Dave was sexy as all hell. We settled in Cork. He still is sexy. He's just got that swagger, you know?'

'Niamh is the island baker,' Jack said. 'That chocolate cake you brought, Maeve, that's one of hers.'

Niamh positively glowed with pride.

'Wow, so you're responsible for this.' I patted my expanding stomach.

'You can afford to put on a few pounds.' She chuckled. 'I didn't mean to become the baker, it just kind of happened. I've always cooked, but since coming back I've been working out my divorce through cakes. Cooking is very cathartic, and in a strange way the island and the cooking is healing me.'

I nodded, pretending I knew what she was talking about. I've never been much in the kitchen.

'I think of happy memories and I pour all that emotion into my cooking. Every egg cracked, every ounce weighed, all of it brings me huge happiness and relief. I'm beginning to understand our marriage and what happened to us. There were a million little things against us; sometimes love isn't enough. That chocolate cake you bought, when I was baking it, I was thinking of a trip Dave and I took to Paris. We were so in love. We drank champagne with strawberries on a picnic on the Seine, watching Parisians sunbathe. We kissed on the Lover's Bridge, and locked hands like our lives depended on it. I'd never had that before, that love. I poured the memory into the cake. You should taste little bubbles on your tongue with the icing and feel the romance.'

I smiled. Their romance sounded so mind-boggling. I didn't think real people outside of movies and books had experiences like that, but then again, how would I know? I'd never been in love. All the guys I'd dated since college, and there was a list, a long one, saw me bolting for the door when things might have been moving to the next romantic level. I'd see a flicker in his eye, a look that I felt could be leading somewhere that I didn't want to go: to cozy nights in, sharing spring rolls, signing up for ten-mile runs together and feigning interest in his preferred football team. And I'd sprint into the arms of a guy who would never have a flicker in his eye for me, who wasn't capable of it. *Like Carl*, I thought, as I sipped my wine, knowing that getting close to someone, really close, terrified me.

'I'm planning on cooking every cake I know how to, and then I think I'm going to feel better and the island is going to straighten me out and tell me what to do with the rest of my life.'

'No pressure.'

'Nope, none.'

'Maeve, you're from Dublin?' Killian's soft voice flowed across the table to me. I felt the hairs prickle at the back of my neck. Slowly I lifted my eyes and met his gaze. He was smiling. Warm and inviting. He seemed so happy.

I gulped loudly and felt my skin tingle as all the blood in my body rushed to my face. 'Yes. I'm just visiting Hy Brasil –'

'You might be here for a while,' Frank interrupted.

'Maybe, I'm not sure.' My voice was shaking. I'd have kicked myself under the table if I could have. 'Are you a local?' I glanced shyly over at him.

He grinned. 'I was born here, but I was brought up in Galway. My family moved off the island when I was young.'

'But you had to come back and take a look for yourself,' Jack butted in, eagerly playing chaperone.

'I did. My parents told me nothing about this place and I was so curious. I've been travelling for the last ten years and it occurred to me how ridiculous it was that I'd never been here. So I came for a couple of weeks about a year ago.' He laughed. 'I've been drawn back to the mothership.'

The island, the mythical lady. 'People do seem very attached to the place.'

'Attached.' He gave a loud laugh. 'That's a good way of putting it, it's like people have got these magnets in their heads, and at a certain point she flicks the switch and we're pulled back, we've no say on the matter.'

'Well, now, not everyone comes back.' Frank appeared with a large salad bowl and a tray of brown bread. 'Some pear and walnut salad, just a little bite before the main.'

'Love it.' Jack jumped up to help him.

'Not everyone comes back,' Frank repeated, sitting at the top of the table and grabbing his wine glass. 'My mam and all that gang.'

The table nodded.

'Your mam left?' I asked.

'Yeah, there were about forty people, I think, who upped sticks and left and went to America. It was a mass exodus at the time. Quite a big deal on this small place.'

'Were they just looking for a better life?' For me that was the obvious move, get off the island, and go to where life was. America would have been such an exciting prospect.

'You know, I'm not so sure, I think it would be easy to assume that, but I've dug around . . .'

'You love a bit of genealogical digging.' Jack laughed.

Frank nodded. 'I do, I really do, but I don't think it was as clear cut as all that. I don't think it was a straightforward emigration. I suspect that something happened on the island, and they couldn't live here anymore.'

'Like what?' Niamh asked.

'Well, you know the rumours.' Frank smiled and rolled his eyes. 'But there are some letters, I have them in my study, and there's something a bit off. I have suspicions that things weren't clear cut.'

'Rumours?' I couldn't help myself.

'Ghosts, goblins and Banshees wailing from every corner of this island,' Niamh said. 'Watch out, Maeve, they'll come and get you next.'

The noise, I thought, should I ask them about that terrible noise? And then the death, that fellow Jimmy, should I ask or am I just getting too macabre? What if he'd been a friend of theirs? No point bringing in talk of Banshees to his memory. No, best to stay quiet.

The Enchanted Island

'Look, it's interesting, and I will keep on digging. It's a pet project of mine, the history of this place, the present, and maybe even the future.' He nodded at his wine glass and raised it ceremoniously to the table. 'To our future.'

I joined in happily. The bridge. The glorious future that the bridge would bring. I took a long sip of my wine and peered over the top of my glass at ridey Killian. Maybe there was a future on the island after all.

14

After dinner, Jack lit a fire and everyone moved into the sitting room. I felt like I was at a very adult party when Frank offered glasses of brandy. I'd only drunk brandy once before, aged fifteen; my brother Murray, wild as a bag of cats, dared me to gulp back as much as possible from Mam's cooking brandy, which was only used a few times a year to top up the Christmas pudding. I can never resist a dare, even if it did mean getting as sick as a small hospital afterwards, while Murray doubled over with laughter. I gave Frank a little head shake when he swirled a glass in front of me, but appreciated the gesture.

There was a beautiful painting of the sea on the wall, an oil painting, and you could see lumps and brush strokes speckled on it like it was the surface of some faraway planet. It made me think of the artist wielding his brush like a weapon, poking and smoothing, his mind swimming in the ocean of his creation, rarely coming up for air.

The Enchanted Island

'It's nice, isn't it?'

I jumped. Killian was standing behind my shoulder.

'Lovely, yeah.'

'Frank did it.'

I turned around to him. He was holding a red wine glass in his hand, smiling at the picture, looking relaxed and comfortable. I was standing close enough to smell him, no aftershave, but a fresh scent, like the sea in the painting.

He laughed. 'I don't know how he does it, he does pottery as well, the plates on the table at dinner, all the stuff you see around the house are his. I couldn't paint to save my life, although I was pretty good at finger painting at school.'

I put my hand to my chest in fake shock. 'What? And you only reveal this now?'

'It's not something I like to brag about, I keep it to myself – there'd be groupies and I just don't have time to keep up with the fan club.'

'All those people going through your bins?'

'It's embarrassing, but it's the price you have to pay for talent. It's a curse really.'

I smiled widely at him. He was funny. I hadn't expected him to be cute *and* funny.

He grinned crookedly back at me, and I marvelled at the cheery freckles across the top of his forehead and the bridge of his nose. 'I teach nine- and ten-year-olds and every Friday afternoon we have art class. It's the worst day of the week for me. I hardly sleep Thursday nights. I tried to turn it into an extra sports class – sports I can do – but they won't let me get away with it. They're a riot. I even did a couple of tutorials on YouTube to try and get up to scratch but the kids see right through me every time, it's all, "Mr McCarthy, can we do pottery next week?" I'm colour blind too. Sure, I've no hope. Do you paint?'

I laughed. 'No, no artistic leanings whatsoever. I do have a brother who is a tattoo artist.' I rolled my eyes at that. 'He's gone very pretentious altogether since he opened up a tattoo studio in Dublin.'

'Saving one life at a time?'

'That kind of thing, yeah. He really does believe that when he inks *carpe diem* or some bollocks on a teenager's wrist that he's changing their lives.'

'Maybe if it was in Sanskrit.'

That made me giggle into my glass. 'That's exactly the kind of thing he'd say.'

'Are there many in your family?'

'Three brothers, I'm the youngest.'

He shook his head sympathetically. 'I feel your pain, I really do, when the odds are stacked against you, there's nowhere to run. I have four sisters, I'm second from the end, but the youngest one is worse than the other three. When I was small they had stickers all over the house, *No boys allowed*. Sure, there was only me and Da. They'd dress me up like a girl, handbag and all, and then I'd be let play with their toys. For years I didn't know that boys wore shirts, I thought everyone wore blouses. Sure I shouldn't be telling you this. You'll think I'm a crossdresser or something.'

I spat my wine a little, laughing. 'Ah, stop, that's too funny. I totally get it though – I was brought up one of the boys, the same but different. They used to send me through the slap machine to toughen me up.'

'That was nice of them.'

'Part of the training, I guess.'

He shook his head. 'Those teenage years.'

'So terrible. Do you know how smelly three boys are? It's just in them, this *stench*.'

His coppery curls wobbled slightly when he laughed, which made me grin. 'Ah, look, a bit of boy smell is nothing compared to cans and cans of Impulse and bottles of nail polish. There'd be, like, a fog hanging over the house. I still get headaches when I even think about the smell.' His eyes twinkled at the memory. 'The bathroom was like an exorcism had taken place in a beauty salon. Sure, I had nothing but a bar of soap. I had my first shave with a Ladyshave.'

I found myself drawing nearer to him, an intimate circle of just the two of us. 'Do you think we'll ever get over the scars?'

He raised an eyebrow at me, and I smiled encouragingly. 'Unlikely – I know all the words to the Spice Girls songs. That's not something you can forget overnight.'

'It was Metallica in my house, they played on a loop for three years.'

'Sure we're lucky to have come out alive and hanging onto our own genders.'

I laughed and laughed. Usually when I'm talking to a guy who I'm hoping will feature in the opening credits of my soap opera life, I'm very focused on a few key flirtation rules. I'll always remember to angle my body towards him, so he knows I'm available but not overly so; to run my fingers through my hair, always a good flirty move; to draw attention to my mouth, that's easy when you have a drink in your hand; and to lean over and touch him in some way. That can be trickier, I'm not so good at casually running my fingers across a guy's hand, I always feel slightly medical doing it, like I'm a nurse on a ward offering comfort. But it was so strange: I was able to talk to Killian like he was a normal person and not a potential end-of-night kiss, even though he was so sexy. Like, *very* sexy. And then it occurred to me that since I wasn't flirting, I mustn't fancy him. Although I did seem to be feeling a certain stirring towards him, a kind of pull ... But I hadn't even remembered to pout, so I couldn't be interested in him, right?

'Do your sisters live in Galway?'

He nodded. 'Two of them do, another one is in Boston, and one in Limerick. It's funny, I didn't want a bar of them when I was younger and now I'm on Skype all the time with them. I see my folks a good bit too, which is great because now that I'm older, I can appreciate them a bit more, I don't just think they're a pair of old dinosaurs.'

'I just moved back in with my mam,' I confessed. I would never normally have admitted this failing, but because I didn't fancy Killian it was okay, I could tell him stuff. 'Being close to family, in my family, is a bit overrated.'

He looked a little sheepish. 'So you're not married or anything?'

The Enchanted Island

He was asking *the* question. Was he interested in me? I paused. 'Nope, I'm single. I kind of fell out with my flatmate.' I felt my innards pinch. 'I have to say it's nice to get away from living with Mam, she's gone very overbearing since I've moved back, it's only been a week but she's really been on my case.'

'She still thinks you're a teenager.'

I nodded, knowing that wasn't the full story. It was funny, a bit of distance was making me question a few things. I was beginning to think that I had been acting like a teenager. I was always mad at her for not reaching out to me, but I never reached out to her. I never initiated nice conversations. I never gave her credit for how tough her life must be since Dad died, I'd only ever thought about how hard my life had been. That was pretty typical teenage behaviour, wasn't it? To be completely self-absorbed. And there was a slim chance that that behaviour hadn't stopped with Mam, and maybe Sasha had had a point when she kicked me out. Maybe I should dye my hair pink, get my belly button pierced, roll up my skirts indecently short and be done with it.

'I never thought I'd be happy to be living in a caravan in the pouring rain on a godforsaken island with nothing going on, but it's okay I suppose.'

I watched as his face fell and wondered what I'd said.

'You don't think much of Hy Brasil, so?'

I shrugged. And then I remembered some of the moments I'd had, and some of the raw uncomplicated beauty I'd seen, and I knew I had been quick to judge. 'Do you know what? I think it's growing on me, I really do. And the food's great.'

His face lit up. 'It is, isn't it?' There was something about his face, about his eyelashes and the crinkly smile lines in the corners of his eyes that made him look completely honest, that he couldn't tell a lie if he tried.

There was a shrieking noise from the corner, where Jack was crouched at a stereo pointing a remote control angrily. He swivelled back to the room, his face red. 'This bloody thing, can anyone work it?'

Killian laughed and moved over to him, and it gave me the opportunity to discreetly check him out again. Trying to be as subtle as possible so no one would see what I was doing, I admired his broad shoulders and long, strong legs.

Some terrible howling music came out of the stereo, like puppies being strangled, then faded into a more plinkity plonk tune.

'What is that?' I whispered to Tim, who had been resting on the arm of an armchair nearby.

'Saoirse's new album.'

'Jesus.'

He bit his lip. 'I know.'

Saoirse was this enigmatic and surprisingly spooky Irish singer. She seemed to have been around for decades. Her music had always been that Celtic ballad style, lady screaming into the wind and a few uilleann pipes diddly-eyeing in the background. Her voice would normally give you goosebumps, and you'd want to listen to it again and again to find out what it is about it that's so mesmerising, but you just can't put your finger on it.

The Enchanted Island

She used to have this long curly blonde hair, Rapunzel-like, and wore a lot of crushed velvet and long necklaces with trinkets dangling from them; you know the type. You'd be pretty sure if you went to her house it'd smell of incense and there would be wind chimes and Indian talismans looped around curtain rails. She was really big all over the world about twenty years ago. Her music was still released but she hadn't been spotted in public in donkey's. Her videos now were all either landscape shots of waves dramatically crashing onto cliffs, or animated figurines doing an Irish jig. She still sells, though. She's always listed in the top five richest women in Ireland.

'This doesn't sound like her stuff. Where's the lilting ballad?'

'I think she's gone all experimental.'

It sounded like someone was playing the tin whistle out of tune underwater. I cringed. 'Are the lads fans?'

Tim tugged on his ears. 'I dunno, but she lives on the island. Have you seen that fabulous house on Mount Culann? Abhaile? That's hers. Maybe they're just trying to support a local artist. Jesus, though, I might have to ask them to turn it off before my ears start to bleed.'

That fortress at the top of the mount, with the spectacular view. Saoirse lived there? I was surprised. Well, if I'm honest, I'd never given any thought to where she may or not be, but if I was one of the top five richest women in Ireland, I wouldn't be living in Ireland. I'd be cruising past it on my yacht on my way to sunnier climates, a Mediterranean diet and white linen sofas.

'Will you be here a while, Maeve?'

Killian was back by my side. I liked the way he said my name, it sounded velvety and smooth.

'With music like this, who'd go anywhere?'

He smiled at me with a lovely open face, searching my eyes for something else – what, I wasn't sure.

'I meant the island.'

I blushed. 'I'm not sure, I thought it would only be a short stop but it's almost been a week already.'

'It'd be great if you were here for a while.'

Our eyes locked. It felt like there was a promise. A moment. A secret arrow pointing towards us. Did I imagine it?

'You'll be here long enough to fall in love with this place.'

'You never know.' I smiled and I wondered if he could be right.

15

The day after the dinner party I spotted Sean Fitzpatrick, or at least I assumed it was Sean Fitzpatrick. My daily excursion past the twitching curtains, sneers and glares finally yielded some success.

Kind of.

He was there, I saw him. Fishing, my arse. He was sitting at the kitchen table drinking a mug of what I assumed was tea. I was so excited to see him, I practically jumped through the closed window. I forgot that maybe he wasn't going to be as excited to see me. He may have been avoiding me after all. Didn't stop me though, like wee Willie Winkie I rapped at the window.

'Sean, Sean, it's me. I'm here.'

He saw me. He couldn't miss me. He twirled around in his chair and waved his arms in a shooing motion. What did I think would happen? That he'd happily invite me in to look at his fishing haul?

'Sean, can we have a chat?'

'Feck off, feck right off.' He jumped up out of his seat like there was a dodgy spring poking into him. His cheeks were flushed pink. His shock of white hair looked like the end of a broom. He flew towards the window, nervously scanning behind me as if he was looking for someone else. He quickly pulled across some flower-patterned curtains. He shouted so loudly that the glass in the window frame trembled. '*Feck off!*'

I was delighted though, really I was. He was here. I could banish the terrifying, cold-sweat midnight thoughts that kept creeping into my mind about getting my hands on a rowboat and scouring the sea shore like a disgruntled pirate. He was ignoring me, which was fine. I had suffered through enough teenage discos not to take offence at being ignored by men. He was here and this was progress. I would get him. I would be stubborn, tenacious and annoying and I would get in front of him. Watch out, Sean.

I scribbled a note and popped it under his door.

Flooded with relief, I stopped a few yards from Sean's house to rummage through my bag for my phone. I searched and I searched, wallet, makeup, half packet of mints, four hair ties, Chapstick, scrunched pages of I don't know what, but no phone. No phone. An image flashed up in front of me: the phone on my pillow. I could hardly believe it. I'd left it behind. The last time I stepped outside without a phone attached to me would have to have been a time when dinosaurs roamed the earth. It did not happen, ever. This was so

The Enchanted Island

unlike me. Was this some type of early-onset Alzheimer's? And then I realised that when I'd left the caravan, I hadn't automatically plugged headphones in, which is what I had done the last seven mornings on my walk to Sean's. It struck me as odd for a couple of reasons, but mainly because I must have walked over here in silence and it hadn't even registered. Silence is something I try to avoid because of the noises in my head, but my thoughts couldn't have been pinging back and forth otherwise I'd have noticed.

But silence be damned. Back at the caravan, I lovingly pounced on my phone and triumphantly rang Harry, letting him know that I had made contact with Sean and we had started negotiations. *Feck off* was a type of negotiation, I supposed. I sounded very business-like on the phone, really all over it, confident and competent until Harry dropped the clanger.

'So he'll sign today?'

'He said he needed some time to mull a few things over.' A little white lie never hurt anyone.

'Tomorrow, so. I'll give Dan a call, let him know it's under control. Good work, Maeve.'

Well, I wasn't going to disagree with him when he was complimenting me, was I?

I twisted my phone in my hand and thought about calling Sasha again. We hadn't ever gone this long without speaking. I hated it.

'Hi Sash, I just called to say hi. Em, I'd love to talk to you, I hope everything is okay there. I'm going to get that money to you really soon. Did George move in? How is it living with a smelly man? Jocks on the floor and football on TV? Okay, bye.'

Uh oh. I shouldn't have said that about George. I was trying to make a joke but it wasn't funny. Sasha will just think that I'm being a bitch about him. Was I being a bitch about him? George was fine, boring but fine; I always felt like there was a more exciting greased-up Latin lover or English toff or game-playing rogue type out there for Sasha. Like the guys she used to date. She briefly dated this Norwegian guy, Bjorn, who had white eyelashes and white-blond hair in a perfect bob. He looked a bit like a serial killer, but a handsome one you'd happily shag, and his hair smelled of apples. His English was terrible. He'd taught himself off the TV, and all he seemed to watch was *CSI* or *Law and Order*, so he had these phrases like, 'Justice will be served', 'We will hunt down the accused', 'Minor lacerations to the upper torso'. It wasn't much to build a relationship on, I suppose. But he lived in this great party house, and every weekend the sitting room was cleared out, decks appeared and some European DJ danced in one spot for forty-eight hours, sliding his hands over records, while we all got plastered and fell over around him.

Bjorn cheated on Sasha with some Nordic beauty, all porcelain skin and piercing blue eyes. She found out on social media, there were photos of them wrapping their legs around each other in a club. And then what seemed like hourly updates of the two of them kissing all over Dublin. It was horrible. She was devastated, but she wasn't mourning him, it was more the public humiliation that was killing her. We sat in

The Enchanted Island

for weeks, we made voodoo dolls of him, googled curse words in Norwegian and sent him abusive texts, drank a vineyard dry and ate our body weight in nachos. George wouldn't do that to her. He's more of a solid type of guy. Straight up. The only things he posts on social media are comments on rugby games. She knows where she stands with him.

Most of the time I love social media, but other times, like when Sasha was being subjected to toothy grins and love hearts of the guy she had just been kissing, I think it's cruel and I'd like to throw every phone and laptop out the window and tell people that they need to start again.

To take my mind off not hearing from Sasha, I flicked onto Carl's Instagram. He'd been at The Meat Cafe the night before and snapped a picture of his steak; he didn't tag his dinner companion though. How annoying. Now I would just fixate over whether or not Rebecca Sheils had been sharing his dish with him. Maybe I'll IM him. What would I say? I needed Sasha to help me out. She was always good at directing me.

I felt a bit deflated by it all. So I did something that I knew would make me feel better: a spot of online stalking.

I googled *Killian McCarthy Hy Brasil*. Nothing. I googled *Killian McCarthy Hy Brasil teacher*. Nothing. I googled *Killian McCarthy Hy Brasil teacher sexy*. You don't want to know what came up there. I googled *Killian McCarthy facebook twitter instagram*. Nothing. It was infuriating. How can a person have no online presence? I mean I get it, I know there's this hipster movement about living off the grid and stroking your beard in protest to apps, but I don't buy that at all. I'm sure those people are logging on under pseudonyms. Killian didn't seem like that though. Was it possible that he just wasn't online because he didn't want to be? I sighed to myself. If that was the case, he was a whole other breed of man.

Hazel popped up online. Good. Contact with the outside world.

> *How's it going?*
> *Baaaaaaaad*
> *?*
> *3 people got let go Friday – 2 from accounts, Marnie and Patricia, and Aidan out of facilities.*
> *No, what the hell?*
> *Yes. It's so horrible here. Everyone is so nervous. There's been no announcement or anything, we were all just pinned to our desks. Good thing you weren't here.*
> *It's awful.*
> *I know – what's happening there?*
> *Nothing. Still chasing the signature.*
> *That guy Dan was in here today.*
> *With Harry?*
> *Yep in his office for a good two hours, they looked super nervous about something.*
> *I wonder what?*
> *I'm going for a wine with Harry's PA Wednesday, I'll see if she knows anything.*
> *Good work.*

16

I was sitting on a wall outside what I presumed was the community hall: a large square building at the top of Main Street. Niamh had invited me to her aerobics class. I thought I'd give it a whirl. I was so bored – after I did my daily hike to Sean's house, tapping on the windows, peering through cracks in the drawn curtains, I didn't know what else to do with myself. I was frustrated and a bit of exercise might help. I am a fully paid-up gym member in Dublin, not that I went. I mean I did sometimes, but it was all so severe and sweaty. Attending the spin class was like landing on the beaches of Normandy in World War Two. There were terrified whoops, and triumphant 'Go get 'em!' squeals, heart racing and an enormous amount of adrenalin. A girl collapsed off her bike once and the instructor kept pedalling. 'Don't let your heart rate drop!' she screamed at us as we left the injured behind. It was dog eat dog. There was always a queue for the scales in the change room, everyone eyeing each other up and down, checking out abs or lack of them. If you didn't get the number you liked on the scales, you could just pop into the sauna for another bit. The fights for the hairdryers were like something out of a bad romcom, half-dressed girls wide-eyed and screaming at each other for ownership. If I went, I normally brought my own, and my own straighteners, and eliminated the possibility of nearly losing an eye.

I had no hair straighteners with me today but I did have a nice gym outfit on, which I'd brought with me from Dublin: three-quarter-length black lycra pants with neon orange ribbing and an orange vest top, with a push-up sports bra underneath. It was a warm evening. I had a hoody in my bag but hadn't needed it on my walk over. I watched as a heavily pregnant woman, around the same age as me, walked slowly on the other side of the street. There's something about that pregnant plod, slow and laboured, that looks so painful. Her belly was so distended she had to have been carrying twins. There was nothing about her that shouted pregnancy bloom. I bet she couldn't wait for it to be over.

'Woo hoo!' Niamh was grinning at me. She was cycling and waving with one hand, wearing a green tracksuit. She threw her bike against the wall and as she came closer to me I was enveloped by the smell of a tangy lemon zest. 'Oh good, you look all set.'

I smiled and flexed my arm muscles.

'Sorry I'm late, some of my chickens got out, I had to round them up.'

The Enchanted Island

'You keep chickens?'

'Accidentally – they all just arrived. About a week after I landed back here, they started to appear at my gate, clucking around, and leaving these beautiful golden eggs. There were two dozen eggs there before I knew it. What else could I do but bake?'

'They just turned up?'

'Who'd believe it? The island sorts you out, every time. She wants me to bake. I'll bake.'

I couldn't help myself. 'Would you have said that if a load of drug dealers arrived at your gate with a shipload of crystal meth for you?'

She exploded with laughter. 'Now that would never happen.'

I decided to see if Niamh could help me get in front of Sean Fitzpatrick. 'There's someone on the island I need to talk to. For my work.'

She cocked an eyebrow at me. 'Dan's will?'

I looked at my shoes. 'Kind of, in a roundabout way, I suppose. But this person doesn't want to talk to me and I was wondering if maybe you knew him, you might be able to introduce me?'

'Who is it?'

'Sean Fitzpatrick.' I don't know why, but I pointed in the direction of his house, just in case the island was littered with Sean Fitzpatricks, I suppose.

'Why do you need him?'

'I just, em . . . do.' Now would be the time to come out with some brilliant lie, some well thought out, cleverly devised storyline, but no, I drew a blank. I've never been able to lie. I felt my face flush and knew that I was seconds away from breaking into a sweat.

She looked at me a little suspiciously, and I immediately felt guilty. 'I don't know him,' she said. 'He's an auld fella, isn't he? Maybe ask some of the older people on the island, they might be able to help you? Or just call round to his house?'

'I've tried that, he doesn't want to talk to me.'

'Really?' She paused. 'He's avoiding you?'

I nodded.

'An introduction won't do much then, will it?'

'I'm not sure.'

She looked hard at me, and I knew she wanted to quiz me. 'If he doesn't want to talk to you, he's not going to talk to you. But you seem pretty fearless, Maeve, I wouldn't imagine someone saying no to you intimidates you.'

I smiled at her. 'I don't think anyone has called me fearless in a long time, it's kind of nice to hear. Thanks anyway.' I would need a better approach. I had to think of something, and soon.

We watched a trickle of ladies (definitely ladies, aged fifty-plus) walk through the town hall's double oak doors. All mature, and all dressed in bright sweat pants, some carrying water bottles, chatting amicably. They weren't as old as the decrepit islanders who had been so rude to me, and I wondered if they'd be friendlier.

Niamh ushered me through the doors. 'This class is great fun but it can be a bit full on. You look like you can handle it.'

The Enchanted Island

'I go to the gym in Dublin. I'm pretty fit,' I said a little bit smugly. I guess it wasn't strictly a lie. I do go to the gym, more to use the sauna or collapse in the pool than actually work out. Same same.

'What do you think of Killian? I could sense a bit of chemistry there. I'm never wrong,' she said matter of factly.

I could feel myself blushing. 'He seems really nice. But you know I'm just visiting this place, I'm not going to be hanging around.'

'I'm not suggesting you get married. What about a bit of fun? We all need fun.' She retied her hair into a tighter ponytail.

I smiled. I got a lovely warm bubbly feeling when I heard his name. It had been on a loop in my head, like a song I couldn't shake. The memory of his face, his smiley green eyes, made me feel a little bit moony inside. I didn't really know what to do about it. We would probably be a terrible mismatch, a country mouse chewing on hay and a city mouse in a waistcoat and high heels.

We moved into the hall, a bright, airy space with bouncy wooden floorboards. The instructor had her back to us, and was bent over a very early 1980s-looking ghetto blaster. She was wearing a lilac leotard over her tights. You couldn't buy something that lilac if you went looking in a hundred shops. I was nervous of the camel-toe reveal. Some Calvin Harris dance song started to pump out. She flipped up and started dipping her hips to the rhythm. The room was forming orderly lines. I could feel the music through the floorboards.

Niamh and I positioned ourselves near the back of the room, Niamh busily waving hello to everyone, and much to my surprise a lot of the women smiled and waved a friendly hello to me too. I grinned ecstatically. The instructor flipped around. It was Maura the hairdresser.

'Ladies, are you ready?' she screamed at the top of her lungs. She had full makeup on, lilac eye shadow too. The troops started to march on the spot in anticipation.

'I'm not going to go easy on you today, ladies. Today, I am going to make you sweat.'

I laughed quietly to myself. I was definitely the youngest person in the room; if I broke a sweat I'd be surprised. I really didn't think that Lilac Leotard was going to make anyone sweat.

'Okay, let's go.'

And I knew. I knew in seconds I was out of my depth. It started with the stretching. These women who had at least thirty years on me were bending and shaping their bodies like they were melted rubber. Their arms stretched back for an eternity, their legs kicked easily into the air at ninety-degree angles. Their pelvises popped and swung effortlessly. I looked at Niamh, who was also moving like she was on rollers.

And then the workout really started.

I'll save myself the embarrassment, but let's just say that, five minutes in, I wanted to throw up, and fifteen minutes in, I ran to the bathroom, and I did.

A little green around the gills, I resumed my position with wobbly legs, and marvelled at how the ladies zoomed around as if they were pepped up on jumping beans. Granted, some looked a little flushed, and there were a few slightly sweaty armpits, but overall they were lunging, planking and leaping with such ease and grace, and such tremendous strength, I was awestruck. This would put my class in Dublin to shame.

Maura was hopping around up front, her makeup still perfectly in place, encouraging everyone. 'Don't forget to breathe. Good lunging, Bridie, don't forget that pelvic floor, pull it in.'

I tried to keep up as best I could, but I was five steps behind at all times. I was squatting when they were doing burpees, jumping when the rest of the class were boxing. I was a disgrace.

I praised the Lord an hour later when Adele came on the ghetto blaster and the class started to wind down. Maura led everyone through breathing exercises and a series of calming techniques. There were a lot of happy sighs in the room, and a massive sigh of relief from me.

Niamh looked a little apologetic. 'I know it can be a tricky class.'

'That's putting it mildly.' I knew my face was a dark red. Even my hands had swollen slightly. My mouth tasted salty – that couldn't be normal, could it? Can you sweat in your mouth?

'Don't worry, we'll get you up to speed. In a few weeks you'll be doing the crab like Aine over there.' Aine looked like she was made of Play-Doh. 'There's Pilates on Wednesday and Thursday and a dance class on a Friday. I'll sign you up for them.'

I nodded in agreement and mild shock. I had to. How could I not? I had to at least try to get as fit as these older women. Also it would give me something to do on the island, for as long as I was here it could help fill my very empty diary.

'The best part is yet to come,' she whispered conspiratorially to me.

'Are we right, ladies?' a grey-haired woman, who just a few minutes earlier had had her nose pushed up to her right knee, shouted out to the room. Everyone seemed to know where they were going, and there was an excited whir.

I shook my head. 'Oh, Niamh, please I can't. I can't do any more exercise.'

She looked at me, eyes shining, and clapped her hands in delight. 'It's time for cake. After class we all go to Tansey's for some cake.'

'One of yours?'

'Yes, I supply the cakes to half the island. And I think they have some of the carrot cake left. That one is filled with the memory of painting our first house together, there's extra frosting on it. It was a happy time.'

Well, *that* I could do. I looked at the happy flushed faces around me, and beamed back at them. There was a lovely sense of camaraderie and friendship that only back-breaking exercise and the promise of really good cake could give. I was delighted to be part of this group. I knew it would be tough but worth it.

17

The hostile villager waved a chainsaw in the air. I kicked her in the gut and watched her collapse with a groan and a thud as the rabid dogs ran in to take a bite of her.

'Can I get another Diet Coke?' I hit pause and stretched out my aching fingers. I could feel the calluses forming on my thumbs. There was a stress pain shooting across my shoulders, and I was sweating, but the adrenalin was racing around my body and felt magnificent. Resident Evil 4, your mistress is back to conquer you.

Tim collapsed onto the cream couch beside me and passed a cold can. I popped it and melted into the fizzy goodness.

This was my third visit in a row to Surf HQ. I was happily filling my evenings here, trying to keep myself busy to distract from the quiet days. I was at a loss over Sean Fitzpatrick; other than pounding down his door a few times a day, I didn't know what else to do. How could I get him to talk to me? I was frustrated and annoyed and felt absolutely helpless. What was I even doing on the island if I couldn't get his signature? How long was I going to stay here? And what was I going to do with myself, play video games indefinitely and try to avoid Harry's phone calls? It was madness. At least playing Resident Evil gave me something to do. And I liked Surf HQ. It was like a student house, but the best kind of student house, where the students had money and never had to go to lectures. Tim and Shane had a happy camaraderie that only the best of friends in their early twenties can have and understand. They loved each other in a shoulder-punching, drunk, slightly misty-eyed way.

I had yet to meet Shane sober. He sat bleary-eyed or giggly on a giant bean bag, either staring at the TV or towards the spectacular view they had of the ocean. To be fair, I think I hit him on his down time; by all accounts he worked through the night, surfed in the morning and got wasted in the afternoon. There was no mention of sleep. Tim had the business savvy. He was responsible for knocking on doors and for having knocked on the right door to get this project funded. He'd told the venture capitalists that they were not going to have any updates, or quarterly reviews of how the project was progressing, that they were going to take one full year and present them with the finished product. It was not negotiable. I knew by the way he was talking that Tim and Shane must be really good. No company in their right mind would give two kids who looked like they'd parked their skateboards next to their Lego kits free rein on a project for twelve months.

Tim reminded me of my brother Patrick, he was soft and gentle with a good head on his shoulders. Even though he was older than me, he'd always felt like my younger brother; there was something heart-achingly vulnerable about him, and Tim had that same quality.

Surf HQ was on the south-eastern side of the island beside Inch Beach, where Tim and Shane surfed every morning. The house was furnished straight off the pages of an IKEA brochure, clean lines, modern steel chairs with floral cushions, and an array of tea lights that the boys looked at with amusement. They had a TV and sound system that would rival any state-of-the-art cinema in the world. It was eardrum-blasting fantastic. They had a never-ending supply of artisanal beers and grass. And it was here that I was kicking arse all over again at Resident Evil 4.

There are some skills you never lose.

The problem with gaming too much is that you start to see life in a series of levels, power kicks and spinning blades. Reality becomes pretty disappointing when you realise you can't somersault and destroy zombies with lasers shooting from your eyes. It was one of the reasons I'd stopped gaming, that and the fact that occasionally I like to leave the house.

It was funny. Tim and I chatted a lot, but neither of us were upfront about work and the projects that had brought us to the island. We were both keeping secrets. But after I had spent what I deemed to be an adequate amount of evenings lounging on their sofa, I felt I could approach an island conversation with him. After all, we were both outsiders in a peculiar place. I think I was trying to find an ally in Tim, someone to help me make sense of the nonsense.

'What do you mean "weird"?'

'This place, like, it's weird isn't it?'

He shrugged. 'I guess, a little.'

'I mean, there's no contact with the outside world.'

'Of course there is.' He waved his iPhone at me.

'No. I mean –' What did I mean? I was struggling. Weird? Weird was as good as I could get to describe this place. 'You know some nights there's a patrol? On my first night here, Dan and I got kicked out of the pub and I had to stay in my van.'

'Yeah, it's the old people. They have torches and luminous vests. They're like police or something. Who cares, right?'

Me, I thought, *I'm pretty sure I care.* 'Don't you wonder why they're doing that?'

'No. If they want to walk around, let them walk around.'

'Have you heard that noise, the shriek? The first night I was here, I've never heard anything like it, it was bone chilling.'

He nodded, his eyes glistened a little, looking more interested. 'We've heard that a few times too. The locals say it's the wind.'

'Do you believe them?'

He ran his fingers across his chin, which was sprouting the tiniest bit of stubble; I guessed it had been there for days with only the patchiest of growth. 'I hadn't thought about it. Why wouldn't it be the wind?'

'Because I've never heard wind like that. I've never been terrified of the wind.'

The Enchanted Island

He bent over the glass coffee table, grabbed a cigarette paper and started sprinkling tobacco and grass inside, leaving a trail of what looked like mouse droppings behind, before expertly twisting and folding.

'I don't know. It's a cool place though, don't you think it's cool?'

'It's pretty beautiful.'

'Ah man.' He sparked up the joint and took a slow drag from it. 'This is the best we've ever had it. This is the dream for us. We surf, we work, and we grow the best grass in the greenhouse out the back. This is heaven.'

'You're not curious?' I eyed him happily smoking his joint and figured that he probably wasn't. 'You know, the day after that noise, I saw a gathering of people on Lissna Tra. They were waiting for something, or someone, to come in. What was that?'

Tim's eyes had started to glass over. He offered me the joint, which I refused like I did every time. I don't like drugs. I don't like losing a grip on my reality.

'I think it's weird. Weird as hell.' Shane piped up, practically smothered by the red corduroy bean bag.

'You do?' I turned enthusiastically to him, and then wondered what kind of sense he'd make; his cheeks were rosy and his eyelids had swollen over his pink squinty eyes. He had been quietly sipping on a beer, staring at my gaming achievements with a stunned expression on his face that I'd like to think was awe but was probably just drunk-slash-slightly-drug-induced.

'The people can be so weird, right?'

I nodded.

'Remember that old guy, Tim, when we got here first?'

Tim giggled. 'The island welcoming committee. Some auld fella came out and wanted to know all about what we were doing, and how long we'd be here. We couldn't tell him much, confidentiality agreements and all that. I think once he knew we'd just be here in the house or maybe in the pub, he wasn't too bothered. We told him we'd be leaving after twelve months too.'

'Was it Sergeant O'Donnell?'

'Maybe. I don't really remember.'

'It was. That was him.' Shane waved his beer bottle slightly. 'He creeped me out. He kept pushing, "What's your app? Why are you here? Is it anything to do with the island?" Remember, Tim, remember? We told him we needed somewhere quiet to work. That we were computer geeks, we wouldn't be bothering anyone. He was like the mafia. Do you remember he said something really weird, it was like, if this affects the island there are higher forces at work that will work against you? Man, it was like he'd watched too much *Star Trek*, it was like this weird nonsensical threat.'

Higher forces. He had said the exact same thing to me. Maybe that was his intimidation catchphrase. *Get off the island before the higher forces get you.*

'Yeah, I remember. I mean we're paranoid enough about the secrecy of the work. You know, we won't even store things in the cloud.'

'Do you know how often the cloud gets hacked?' Shane added.

The Enchanted Island

I pursed my lips and gave my head a little shake. I had never given any thought to the cloud or hacking.

'Let's just say *a lot*.' Shane snuggled back into his bean bag.

'Anyway, we don't really have anything to do with anyone here, like any of the older people. Have you noticed the way they always get served first? Like no matter where you are, everyone stands back so they never have to queue.'

I shrugged my shoulders, remembering the old ballet dancer in the coffee shop and how the middle-aged man had jumped to attention so she could skip the queue.

'Good manners, I guess.'

'I don't know if it's that simple. I saw an old guy stop a man on Main Street and demand he get off his bike and give it to him.'

'Really?' I felt my eyebrows crease in confusion. 'Maybe they knew each other?'

'Nah, it was, "Of course, take my bike, it would be an honour," almost bowing to him crap.'

'That's strange.'

We all nodded and sat in silence.

'It's like they run this place.' Tim paused for a moment, and I remembered that that was exactly what Dan had said. 'It's okay, we've nothing to do with them. They don't bother us. The only one we've had dealings with was O'Donnell. He came back a few weeks after we'd settled in, I was down on Inch Beach, I'd set up a camera to record the tides. Jesus, he went ape. I showed him how it worked; he kept saying that it wasn't permissible, as if I needed his permission.' Tim inhaled again, smiling slightly. 'Bullshit.'

'And then what happened?' I said, slightly on edge, waiting for the big reveal, some type of revenge act by Sergeant O'Donnell.

'Nothing.'

'Nothing?'

'Yeah, we didn't really see him again, I don't think. At least he didn't call out.' He shook his head dismissively.

'Nothing.' I didn't buy it. I just didn't feel like O'Donnell would give in that easily. He saw equipment, he felt threatened and he did nothing about it. 'Think hard – was there anything strange?'

They looked at me, puzzled. 'Give it up, Miss Marple,' Tim said.

'He knows you're only here for another few months, maybe he's willing to let you go in peace.' I spoke quietly, almost to myself. 'But your work? Does it impact the island?'

'Impact?' Tim furrowed his brow at me. I could tell he was concentrating hard through the haze of smoke.

'I know you can't tell me, but is what you're doing going to change the island at all?'

'No, but I suppose you never know. If our project is successful, which –' he wagged his head from side to side, '– it's looking like it has that possibility, then the island will be known. People will know about this place.'

I shivered. 'Does O'Donnell know this?'

'He couldn't.' He laughed. 'Unless the house is bugged.'

Shane shifted uneasily in his bean bag. 'Man, don't say that kind of thing, you know I get paranoid from this stuff.'

The Enchanted Island

We laughed. Maybe I was the one being paranoid. Maybe I just had too much time on my hands. Maybe I was gaming too much and stepping too far into a fictional world. But I couldn't shake the feeling that there was a lot more to this place than 'a happy little spot'. There was something a lot more sinister at play.

18

The following evening I was out for a walk. I had a dance class at six, and while I thought I was maybe getting a little bit fitter, I found if I went for a walk beforehand, my muscles kind of warmed up a little and I didn't feel as likely to puke/collapse/have a stroke during the class. That Maura was mean. It wasn't immediately apparent from her array of pastel leotards, but there was a streak in her that I'd only previously seen in war movies. Her shouts were so loud they must have been heard on the mainland.

Earlier that day, I had casually asked three people if they knew Sean Fitzpatrick. I had strolled up to the cash register at The Shop with a packet of animal-shaped jellies, and a sliced pan, coughed, nervously bit my lip and barked at the shop owner: 'Sean Fitzpatrick?'

He had jumped back slightly and stared at me. Then told me he knew the name but didn't know the man. He was a better liar than me.

The Enchanted Island

The barman in Mulligans had just looked past me when I said the name, didn't even waste his breath on pretend politeness. And another old man who was wrapped around his phone like a lovesick teenager just outside of Mulligan's told me to 'be gone' and waved his hands like he was exorcising an evil ghost. I needed a better strategy.

Harry was now officially stalking me, in twenty-four hours he had called me four times. Not to mention text messages.

Do you have any news?
Have you got the signature?
Where is Sean Fitzpatrick?
Have you got the signature?

Eh, not in the twenty minutes since your last text message, Harry.

I could hear the anxiety in his voice, the frenzy. I had been forced to remind him of the conversation we had had back in his office what was beginning to feel like a lifetime ago but in fact was only two weeks back, when he had said that it might take a while. He apologised and backed off. For a whole half an hour.

Dan didn't show much more restraint – every time my phone beeped, I wanted to smash it. I was so mad at myself, too, and my inner demons were screaming at me. This was a simple job, this was so straightforward and yet I seemed to be failing at it. Why couldn't I figure this out? Was there another way? If there was, right now I couldn't see it.

Jack had gone all misty-eyed when he'd told me the island gives you what you want. I wanted a signature. *Hand it over, missus*, I thought as I walked.

I spied Abhaile from the foot of Mount Culann. Now that I knew Saoirse was there, creating her spooky music, it held even more interest. The big gates out the front were at least twelve feet high and completely intimidating. I didn't expect her blonde curls to appear around the gate as she shouted down at me for tea, but I did wonder if anyone got invited around. Surely Saoirse has staff, butlers and the like buttling around inside, but it all felt so secretive. Even though she's a global megastar I'm sure she'd still like to go for a drink in the pub now and again – I would. Why was she just hidden in her house all the time? Maybe she wasn't even there. And how come nobody was cashing in on her? I'd expect to see tourist buses sliding by. The Shop didn't even sell her CDs – if you ask me, that's what I would call a missed opportunity.

I saw some people cutting turf. I have never cut turf. I have no idea how to do it. As far as I'm concerned, you heat a house by turning on a switch. But I know people do cut turf, they make lattice incisions on the earth and shape bricks out of compressed bog, dry them and bring the bricks indoors for a few months before winter arrives. It's back-breaking work, literally crippling, I'd put it on a par with breaking stones on a chain gang without the gospel singing. I could see isolated groups, shovels in hand and baskets at their feet. I noticed that it was all old people doing it, not a youngster in sight.

The Enchanted Island

Shovels swung rhythmically up and down. Large baskets filled with turf bricks were being transported by donkeys. I had to do a double take when I saw a donkey's legs wobble, and a man bend down to lighten the donkey's load, swinging the turf basket over his shoulder as easily as if he was moving cotton wool. There was some bionic force going on with these old people that I'd only previously seen on strongest men competitions on TV, where a big, burly, fake-tanned man in a vest moves a truck with his teeth. These weren't burly men, these were rakish old men, with wrinkles and concave cheeks, lugging baskets of turf around, not a string vest or an oiled-up muscle in sight.

Mam's voice echoed in my head: *It's rude to stare.* I averted my eyes and hurried past even though I wanted to stop and point and shout, take out my phone and video these people. Post it all over social media with a *WTF?* caption. But no, I would look away and pretend that these strong old people were completely normal. I grimaced. It was amazing how Mam's voice could annoy me even in my imagination.

My walk turned into a slight trot, and I ran down the road towards the sea. The day was clear. The sun had broken through the clouds. I still had some time before my class. There were more green fields, more waist-high stone walls, and more sheep grazing. The wind whipped my hair into a candy-floss cone, but it was fresh. A cliff face dropped in front of me, and the road swiftly turned to the left. Huge birds glided over the edge and hung aimlessly, catching the air, moving with it, trusting the elements, not fighting them. The very edge seemed alive. I could hear the sea now, crashing tunelessly, a noisy garage filled with amateur drummers bashing away to their hearts' content.

I went off the path just to peep over the edge. I let my runners plod into the spongy field. I had to see what was there. The sheerness of the cliff took my breath away. The abruptness, the finality of it. The slate-coloured wall that almost looked smooth to touch rose a few hundred feet out of the angry ocean, majestically and defiantly mocking the ocean's attempts to knock it, to erode it. The cliff was magnificent. I was mesmerised. I had never seen such stark beauty, never felt such a part of the elements, never felt so alive, so vibrant, so happy. I let out a roar, a wild, exultant roar, threw my arms apart and my hands wide to the sky. It was a feeling of freedom I hadn't known before. I felt exhilarated. I roared like a lion, with fire in my lungs.

'Can you keep it down over there?' a man's voice carried on the wind.

I spun around. I couldn't see anyone. 'Hello?'

'To your left.'

I turned quickly.

'Your other left.'

I couldn't help myself – I started to laugh, whipping around. There was Killian sitting cross-legged on a mat under a tree, facing the ocean, waving at me.

'What in the name of God . . . ?' I stomped over to him, a little embarrassed about the roaring, but then figured he should be embarrassed too; he was sitting under a tree, not doing anything. Anyone could see him, what if he got snapped? It would be mortifying.

As I got closer to him, he shifted over on his mat and patted a spot beside him.

'Really?' I asked.

'Why not?' He grinned so widely it would have been impossible to say no. With the elegance of a baby elephant I sat down next to him. There was that smell, that freshness from him, so vital. He turned towards me and, still smiling, said, 'Hello there.'

'Hi.' I smiled back. I watched his eyes follow my hand as I pushed a strand of hair behind my ear. And he looked at me with an intensity that made the iris in his eyes quiver. I felt something warm and at the same time desperate fill my body. His eyes moved to my lips and back to my eyes. I felt tangled.

'Having a bit of a roar . . . ?' He cleared his throat as he spoke, as if attempting to recharge himself.

I put my hands to my face, embarrassed, and laughed into them, the sound discharging the electricity between us. 'Ah you know, nothing like a roar into the ocean of a Friday.' I swayed into him a little bit to bump him. 'Anyway, what are you doing here? Having a sit of a Friday?'

'This.' He threw his two arms out and took a deep breath. 'Isn't it . . . . ?' His words dissolved into fresh air and blew away.

It was. It *was*. It was life. It was so breathtakingly beautiful it caused an ache in my chest. I wanted to run into it and away from it at the same time. The sheer vastness of it, the ocean that stretched into infinity, the sky blanketing it – this was nature. But not like I had ever seen it before, or thought of it before. This was an overpowering force. Never before had I felt so inconsequential. In the city, I was always a cog in a machine, I got on the bus, I paid for my ticket, we drove down the congested streets, I was part of the heartbeat. But here, here I was invading. I was the alien. I wasn't even a pinprick on the island's radar, I was an afterthought. It was unnerving.

I looked at Killian. He clearly didn't think the same way as me, his face was moulded into an expression of bliss. He looked so happy.

'It's like we're on a magic carpet, and a wave is going to slide under us and whisk us away to never-never land.'

'You're already there.'

'I don't know. This scares me.' I was almost talking in a whisper, I didn't know if he could hear me.

'This is you,' he said very loudly.

'You mean like nature and fresh air and stuff? It's funny, when I got here I thought there was no life on the island, that life belongs to a city, but this . . . I was completely wrong. I've never experienced anything so alive. I can see why people think they're lucky to be here. Really I can.' I paused. 'This makes me feel small and intimidated.'

He smiled at me, and shrugged slightly. 'I heard that roar. You get it.'

'What's a roar between friends?'

And then we were silent again, watching, scanning, and breathing. All was calm, but still my heart was beating out

The Enchanted Island

of my chest. Time passed, I've no idea how long. The clouds jumped across the sky and the temperature dropped slightly.

I felt Killian's shoulder gently push mine. 'You okay?'

I nodded.

'It can be a bit overwhelming, this spot.'

'What are you doing here anyway?' I didn't really need to ask, I could see why anyone would come here. It would be like riding a rollercoaster that terrifies you again and again. It would be impossible to resist the thrill of it.

'I come here for this, and I tune out and tune in.'

'Meditate?'

He smiled.

'Well, I didn't have you down as the hippy type.' I'd never met anyone who meditated before, definitely not handsome school teachers on a rugged island. I thought only movie stars talked about meditation, or people who did a lot of that hot, sweaty yoga.

'I'm not. Well, maybe I am. I'm not any kind of type, I'm just this, I guess, but I empty my head here. I free my thoughts and let them escape into the wind.'

'You can do that?'

'Yeah.'

'Just pour your head out? So there are no thoughts bouncing around?' I asked enviously.

'You know you control your own thoughts? It's up to you what you allow to bounce around.'

I paused for a moment, thinking about what he had just said. It had never occurred to me that I could control my own

185

thoughts. All those voices and worries and concerns, I just thought they were there, that they existed independently of me. I never actually realised that I put them there. Or that I could take them out.

'I control my own thoughts.'

He lifted his index finger and tapped it gently between my eyebrows. 'You can calm that busy mind, you know?'

'Does it feel good?' I knew the answer. It would feel liberating and amazing to clear your head.

'Yeah.'

The cold started to kick in and a shiver crept up on me.

'Are you cold? Here.' And Lord almighty, if he didn't unzip his hoody and, in the manner of a gallant gentleman, throw it over my shoulders. Like I was a helpless woman and he was a manly man. And it felt wonderful; it was still warm and I slipped my arms into it and let his heat envelop me.

'I'll let you borrow my spot here whenever you want. Come meditate.'

'I don't know how. Is there a book?'

'You'll be right, just sit and breathe and be still.'

'Easier said than done.' I grinned at him. Normally if I caught someone meditating and if that someone suggested that I be still, I'd have laughed all the way to the nearest bar and downed a few shots of vodka, cackling with some girlfriends about it all. But it was Killian suggesting it to me, and he wasn't just someone, he was *someone*.

'I do it with the kids at school.'

'Really?'

The Enchanted Island

'Yeah, everyone on the island meditates in their own way – not everyone calls it meditation, but that's what they're doing. You can see it with people here, the trance that they're in, the happy state, everyone learns it at a young age, how to empty out your mind, and let goodness in.'

'I would never have thought . . .'

'I know. It's just one of those things.' He shrugged.

'I wouldn't even know where to start.'

'Just breathe, and sometimes you can use visualisation techniques, like whatever relaxes you, or try and picture emptying out your head . . .'

'Into a giant cargo ship.'

He laughed. We sat in silence for a few minutes, and I saw cartoon pictures of my head tipping out and words spilling into the ocean. And I wondered how long we needed to sit there for it to officially be meditation. Who decides what was long enough – time for a cup of tea?

'It's probably time to go, can't have you freezing up here,' Killian said finally.

Great stuff, good call, Killian. I got up with a bit of a trip, feeling a little delighted with myself that I had now officially meditated. I might even casually drop it onto a tweet: *Just in from a life-changing meditation experience. Feeling Zen ;)*

Killian rolled up his mat and put it under his arm.

We found ourselves on the road and slowly started walking back towards the village.

'I'm on my way to a dance class.'

'I'll walk you there. I've heard Maura is a bit of a hard taskmaster.'

I shook my head. 'You have no idea. I normally keep an exercise app on my phone that counts calories, but I couldn't even begin to categorise Maura's class, other than *taking a beating*.'

'Is there an app for meditation?' Killian grinned at me.

'Probably – there's an app for everything under the sun. Don't you know about apps?' I frowned.

'Ah, come on now, Maeve, I'm not completely clueless.' He turned to me and crossed his eyes.

'Okay, well, I don't know, you know, I don't know what you know or don't . . .' What I wanted to ask was, *Are you a complete hick who has no idea of the outside world, and fast cars and pool parties? Or are you in fact a worldly man, who has chosen to live on an unworldly island?* Either way, I couldn't really make sense of him.

'I know what I know.'

'That sounds terribly philosophical and kind of pretend deep.' I threw my hand to my head in pretend exasperation.

He gave a loud laugh. 'I use apps, Maeve, I keep track of my running, I get some recipes, and, you know – normal.'

I shook my head and maybe a bit too loudly protested, 'No. It's not normal, you're not on Facebook or Instagram or Twitter. You have no online profile.'

He stopped walking. The town was yards away from us now; the footpath had risen out of the roadway.

'You know, I'm right here. If you want to find out something about me, you could just ask, you don't need to google me.' He frowned slightly and shook his head.

'I didn't mean that I'd been looking you up, well, I did but –' I felt my cheeks go bright pink.

'I'm right here, Maeve.' He held his hands out wide, still frowning.

'It's just, it's what I know, it's what I do. I google.' All in a fluster, I took off his hoody and bundled it back into his arms.

'Thanks for the hoody, we're just here. I should run. I'm a bit late. Maura will probably make me run a marathon to catch up with the others.'

I spun around and started to trot towards the town hall, aware that I was fleeing Killian, fleeing an embarrassing conversation like an idiot. I turned on my heel and shouted back to him, 'You can ask me things too, if you want.'

He stretched out a long arm and waved it, I was relieved to see he was smiling, and hollered back to me, 'You bet I will. I won't be googling you.'

19

Do you have any idea what it's like waking up to the sound of silence? It is deafening. The next day I woke to nothing but my own thoughts pinging around my head. *Is Killian weird because he meditates? Or is it kind of attractive? Is he some odd hermit type? Why haven't I heard from Sasha? Where is Sean Fitzpatrick? Why is Harry so interested in the island?* It was exhausting and confronting. Other than tracking down Sean Fitzpatrick, I had nothing to do except think, and my thoughts overran themselves, noisy and chaotic.

To make matters worse, I had gotten an IM from Carl at two in the morning. He'd obviously been out partying on Friday night.

Where are you, babe?

I had seen it and hadn't responded, which showed tremendous strength of character on my part. The irony was not lost on me, though. It is so typical that the second there was a sniff, just the slightest suggestion of potential interest from another man, Carl popped up. I didn't know how to answer him and I wasn't sure I wanted to. There was something about being on the island that was giving me a bit of perspective and literal distance on a few things, and Carl was one of them. What was I doing with him? Like, *really* – what was I doing?

I felt icky about everything that morning. It was so quiet it was impossible to turn my head off. I blared the radio but still my head spun. I needed noise, I needed cars and pedestrian crossings; it was so strange to be somewhere where there are no traffic lights.

Normally when I feel like this, displaced and upset, which happens often after a night with Carl or a giant credit card bill arrives, I shop. I find great comfort in the fluorescent lighting in shops, the warm recycled air, the displays, the colours, the variety. It calms me down immediately. I love the music that I hum along to, usually out of tune. I love the smiles of the sales assistants, with their flawless makeup and shiny lipstick, greeting me warmly like a long-lost friend. I love the moment of purchase, when the sales assistant wraps up your new top in delicate, crinkly tissue paper. I wish everything came in tissue paper. It gives me goosebumps even thinking about the pleasure I get from it. I knew that would clear my head. There was no point doing online shopping, it would be unbearable waiting for the boat to come in with my new jeans/cardigan/shoes.

Surely there was something to buy here, there must be some shopping. Wasn't there an itchy wool shop? I could pay them a visit.

I flicked onto Facebook.

> **Annie O'Reilly** *just now*
> *Just been crucified at the gym. Love crossfit.*
> **Orla Finnan** *9 minutes ago*
> *I am so grateful to have so many wonderful friends in my life. Sending everyone hugs.*
> **Patrick O'Brien**
> *Severe gastro, anyone know a cure?*
> **Elizabeth English**
> *On my way to Berlin, stay shining, sunshine*

I sent Patrick a quick IM. Gastro in Morocco can't be good – I hope he's okay. I sent Sasha another text, one that I was sure she'd have to respond to:

> *I defo think Sara has the best figure on* The Bachelor

Sara had the worst figure, she has boobs like inflatable soccer balls floating on her collar bones. There was no way Sash couldn't respond to that.

Shop. I would shop. I pulled on my skinny jeans and a grey batwing sweater, and my staple black military-style jacket that really wasn't warm or waterproof enough. It was such a pity that I had to team every outfit with wellies but it was next to impossible to plod across that field in anything other than knee-high boots without slipping down a mudslide.

The Enchanted Island

The shop window was full of sheep teddy bears, pictures of sheep, a woolly jumper worn by a mannequin that looked like she had a sheep on her head and an array of folded Aran sweaters with thick cable-knit stitching. The door jingled like a cow bell as I entered. The shop smelled like wet wool, which smells like a wet dog. I sneezed immediately.

There was a shout from the back, a man's voice: 'Bless you!'

I couldn't see anyone. Woollen jumpers were stacked high on tables, looking like a mini Manhattan skyline, threatening to topple. The walls were lined with higgledy-piggledy shelves, filled to the brim with colourful woolly items all on the verge of collapsing on me, the one and only shopper. There was no music playing, no pop beats for me to drum my fingers to, but still I told myself it was a shop, there were bound to be some gorgeous undiscovered little delights here. I shook out a cream Aran knit. It looked like it had come directly off the sheep's back. You could tell by the stitching that this was all hand done; the craftsmanship was beautiful. As my fingertips traced the fabric they started to feel itchy. I folded it and gently placed it on top of the pile. I moved around the shop, picking up cardigans and jumpers admiring the work on them.

There was a clicking sound coming from the back of the shop. An old man, white-haired, head down and wearing an Aran waistcoat with large brown buttons was seated at a desk, knitting. I don't think I had ever seen a man knit before. There were balls of wool in a wicker basket beside him, and he was tugging on one gently with one hand.

'Hello.' I waved cheerily at him.

He looked up with a smile, and then his eyes registered who it was and his face immediately hardened. He spat out a greeting: 'Howerya.'

That made me mad. Here I was, a potential customer, a willing, obliging cashed-up customer, and he couldn't even give me a smile. I'd kill him with kindness.

I beamed at him. 'What a lovely shop. Do you knit everything?'

'Aye, most of it.' There was a flicker of pride that raced across his face. His chest swelled a good inch. His eyes flicked to a mobile phone near him. He looked like he was itching to get at it. Was he planning on notifying someone of my arrival or was I just paranoid?

'I'm looking for a nice cardigan, something stylish.' Even as I said the word I knew I was probably barking up the wrong tree here. Comfortable, practical and warm, that's what these jumpers represented.

He pointed a needle to a pile to the left of the shop. 'Cardigans are there.'

Charming. I pulled out a few. There was a chunky cream one that I thought might look nice on.

'Is there a mirror?' I hollered back to him.

He sighed, rested his knitting on his chair and slid behind a doorway. There was a crash, bang and a wallop before he reappeared carrying a very ornate and heavy-looking floor-length mirror. I dropped the cardigan and ran to him.

'Let me help you with that.'

The Enchanted Island

I put my hands on it. It was a dead weight, a solid mass. Something that I would expect to see three hulking removal men in muscle tops with shaved heads and love heart tattoos bending their knees and heaving over.

'Go on, would you, I got it.' And he did. He moved like a ballet dancer across the shop floor, gently and easily propping the mirror against a side wall.

'You do have it,' I said, a little bit shocked, watching him as he straightened his waistcoat and returned to his knitting.

I picked up the cardigan and pulled it over my batwing jumper. The overall look was bulky but I could tell the cardigan was in another league of comfort, and so cosy I felt like I was wearing a hug. It was a bit shapeless, hanging down over my bum, but that'd be great for walking around, my jeans wouldn't get soaking wet all the time. I felt a little surge of adrenalin as I twirled in front of the mirror.

I spied some dark green anoraks and pulled one out from its hiding place. I unfolded it and waved it in front of myself. Covered in buttons and zips, it definitely wasn't the most attractive jacket I'd ever seen.

'Is this waterproof?'

'Aye.' He didn't even look up from his clicking needles.

Sold to the city girl attempting to carry off island chic. I was delighted when I left the shop. My purchases had cost thirty euro, unbelievably cheap for an anorak and a hand-knitted jumper. I swung my bag around and felt an unmistakable surge of adrenalin. I felt great, I wasn't consumed by all those thoughts anymore. Shopping was good for the soul; I don't care what anyone says.

I was looking into the window of the furniture, baby clothes and wellies shop, genuinely contemplating buying a second pair of wellies, which would be unnecessary, but I just felt like spending more money. My thoughts were interrupted when the shadow of a man ran past my reflection. I pirouetted and caught a glimpse of the back of his head as he ducked down a side lane. Sean Fitzpatrick. Out in the wild, running like an endangered species from a spear-wielding warrior. I couldn't help thinking the knitting man had texted him. *Well, watch out, Sean, I am going to hunt you down.*

I took off like a welly-footed gazelle in too-tight jeans. I caught sight of him taking a left onto a back road – he had to know I was chasing him. I kept running. He was way ahead of me and seemed to have stretched the distance. He looked back. And I ran faster.

I heard my feet pounding and felt a burning on the soles. I could see him ahead of me, but he was moving so fast. I picked up my pace, stretching my legs, putting a force behind my stride, breathing heavily. He seemed to have the wind behind him, pushing him uphill. I'm not saying I'm an amazing runner, but I'm okay. I can normally make a decent attempt at a sprint for the finish line, but this man had decades on me and was smashing any PB I could imagine making. I watched as his white head became a pinprick in the distance.

I gave up. I couldn't catch him. I bellowed out, 'Sean!' Not that I expected him to hear me, but figured it was worth a

The Enchanted Island

shot. I put my hands on my thighs and bent over, waiting for my wheezes to subside.

I had just chased an old man up the road and he had outrun me. What was happening? When the heat in my lungs cooled, I started to run again, at a much more leisurely pace this time, half speedwalk, half slow jog. Fuelled by a desire not to be outdone by an old man, I kept moving in the direction of his house, which I assumed was where he was running to, although it probably wasn't the cleverest place to run to if you were trying to escape someone who regularly sought you at your house. I kept going, determined to reach him, to finally corner him, to force him to sign if I had to. I practically threw myself at his front door. My fists pounded angrily on it as I puffed out his name like a winded dragon.

'Feck off,' a muffled voice said from inside the house.

My heart froze as a curtain to the right of the door slid open and a sharp nose appeared in the gap.

'Sean, please talk to me.'

'No. I've nothing to say to you,' he shouted through the glass.

'Please, please, two minutes.'

'No, no. I'm signing nothing.' He shook his head furiously. 'Feck right off.' He closed the curtains and his beak nose disappeared.

I felt my inner resolve crumple like a piece of paper. What was I going to do? I couldn't give up. At the very least I had to talk with him, I had to find out why he was so resistant to signing.

20

Jack opened the door with a massive smile. 'Maeve, what a lovely surprise.' He ushered me inside, kind of shooing me in like you would cattle.

'I was passing,' I lied, and then I felt terrible about lying. Jack was so nice; why would I lie to him? 'Well, no, that's not true. I wasn't passing, but I just thought I'd drop by and say hello.' What I wanted to say was that I fancied some company and was feeling a bit lonely, but I thought I'd just sound desperate and vulnerable and needy. I found Sundays lonely days, everyone was always busy with family and lovers – it was a tough day to be single. Besides, I loved Jack's company, he was such fun, just being around him made me feel vibrant. I had been feeling sad about Sasha. This was the longest I had ever gone without speaking to her.

'Great, great, let's have a coffee.'

'I hope you don't mind, I'm a bit unannounced.'

The Enchanted Island

We went to the kitchen and half perched on a bar stool was Killian. I froze. He quickly stood to attention and nervously wiped his hands down the front of his jeans. He looked around the room sheepishly and grinned. 'Maeve.'

'Killian.' I felt myself smile, and a warm feeling crept over me. I was still trying to remember where I knew him from. Everything about him was so familiar.

He looked at his wristwatch. 'It's such a pity, I have to go. I said I'd help at school choir practice.' And he smiled at me. 'Jack, thanks for the chat and the coffee.'

'You should stay.' And if I wasn't mistaken, Jack glanced towards me, in a you-should-stay-and-chat-to-Maeve way.

'I can't, the kids. Someone has to instil a moral compass into them,' Killian said, laughing, and ran his fingers through the top of his soft curls. 'Nice to see you again, Maeve.' He swung his jacket on and started to walk out. Then he turned and this time his cheeks were pink. 'We were going to go down to Tansey's tomorrow night for a drink, it can be a bit of craic there on a Monday, random I know for a Monday, but it is. Do you fancy coming down?'

I hesitated. I definitely wasn't expecting that offer.

'There's a few of us, like.' He furrowed his brow and bit hard on his lip.

'Yeah, great.' I nodded. 'Sounds like a bit of a party.'

'Right, we'll be there around eight I'd say.' He turned to leave. 'Right so.'

'Right so,' I said quietly under my breath.

Jack gave a little 'mmm' and his eyes popped out of his head with excitement. He turned his back and started making coffee. When we heard the front door slam, he spun around.

'He's really nice, you know. Don't you think he's really nice? And so handsome, he has that real rugged Irishman look. You could see him on a Guinness ad.'

'He's nice, he's definitely nice.'

'Single.' He said in that singsong voice.

'Mmm.' I tried to make exactly the same sound he had made. He clocked it and we both burst out laughing.

'You could ask him out? Look at you, you're a stunner, he'd jump.' He nodded expectantly at me.

'I've never asked a guy out.'

'Why not? It's not the Middle Ages, you know. Anyway, you don't seem like the type of person who cares about what other people think. I'd say if you wanted to, you would just do it.'

I was a bit taken aback. Was that how he saw me? As someone who didn't care about what other people think? Not the person who posts selfies and craves online attention then, but someone else? More like the someone I used to be. I could hear Sasha's voice bouncing around my head: *You never used to care what anyone else thought.*

I shrugged, unsure how to answer. 'Is Frank around?'

A coffee with foamy milk slid into my hand and a plate of biscuits accompanied it.

'He's down in his dungeon, working.'

The Enchanted Island

Frank was mucking around with mud and clay and creating wonderful pieces, examples of which were littered around the house: ornate dishes, lamps, bowls. His inspiration came from the island, that was obvious, the colours and carefully painted designs were mirrors of the sea and the landscape of Hy Brasil: moody greys and greens, peaceful, tranquil and really beautiful. Jack said they were coveted. What had started off as a hobby was now an artisan business and the pieces sold online for hundreds, and were shipped all over the world.

I got the impression that Frank and Jack didn't need the money, but Frank really liked the thought of his lamps or bowls sitting on a coffee table in Brooklyn or fixed to a wall in Yorkshire. The orders just trickled in, and they responded with no particular sense of urgency or desire to create a business, it had just happened.

'Jack, can I ask you about the island?' I bit into a crumbly biscuit that was to die for. 'About the island being split in two. Dan said something about the elders and then everyone else. I mean elders sounds a bit sci-fi, but . . .'

Jack nodded. 'I know, it is really. It's not spoken about, like, there's no Berlin Wall between us but there's a split in that we don't mix very much. But that's okay, I mean, how many of your neighbours do you know in Dublin?'

I shook my head. There was mad Mary downstairs, who carried a doll in her handbag, and a really hot man next door, who Sasha and I had decided was recently divorced – he had that look of history about him – who wore sharp suits and drove a gorgeous car. The only reason I even knew of his existence was because he was good-looking. And then I felt a pain across my chest. I didn't live there anymore. That wasn't my home anymore.

'So we coexist.' He shrugged, indicating that this was the most natural thing in the world.

'Is there –'. I didn't quite know how to phrase it, I didn't really know what I wanted to ask either, '– is there something up with them? The elders?'

He arched an eyebrow at me. 'In what way?'

'Dan seems to think that they're protecting a way of life.' *A way of life that I might be about to destroy.* 'But that they see their way of life as special, unique to them?' I fought with myself – would I say the word? Oh go on, I would. 'Magical?'

Jack seemed unconcerned. 'It is, this place is special, unique and magical. They protect the island and the island protects them. At least that's how I think they see it.'

What about the noise? The patrol? What about me being hit on the head? That weird crowd at the beach waiting for something to come ashore? The woman in labour hopping onto a boat? What about the seaweed – now that seemed pretty magical. Was it true what the Boat Man had said to me on the first day, that they kept secrets? Were the elders keeping a secret? I wondered if this secret was going to be tied to the island.

'There's a feeling,' he continued, 'at least the way Frank and I see it, that the island is all a careful balance, the right amount of people, of weather, food, animals. It's a little bit Yin–Yang. It's all very Zen, darling.'

The Enchanted Island

'Really?'

'We believe we are our own ecosystem here. Practically self-sufficient – if we could brew our own Guinness, we'd be set.' He grinned at me. 'Haven't you noticed the elements here? They're at their crudest, their most basic and extreme.'

'In Ireland?'

'Yes, it's like a Bermuda Triangle, but it's an area that's gone under the radar because it's just so obscure and hard to get to, no one's bothered with it. And because it's inhabited too. But apparently, yeah, it's all happening around us. Electrodes and magnets are tugging away at our atmosphere.'

'Wow, that is interesting.'

'Absolutely.' He nodded enthusiastically. 'It's like we're under a glasshouse here.'

'Frank said the same thing to me before.'

He laughed. 'I probably stole that little analogy from him, but there is a feeling that if you upset the balance too much, you could destroy the whole place.'

'Upset?' Like building a bridge, removing tonnes of seaweed, fiddling with the island's ecosystem?

'The magnets, the negatives and the positives, they all work together.'

'It is an interesting place,' I said, suddenly feeling nervous. Would Jack be a fan of the bridge? Would I be upsetting his life too?

'You know, if you're interested in the island, Frank has a little shrine to it in his study.'

'A shrine?'

'Well, not exactly a shrine, but he's interested in the history of this place, you know, because of his mam. He has lots of old letters, and maps and quirky little things. I'll give him a shout and get him to show you around.'

'That would be amazing, I'd love that.' I *would* love that, I was getting more and more interested in this unusual place as the days were going by. 'Don't disturb him, though. Maybe I could come around some other time?'

'Come for morning tea on Tuesday.'

21

Was I an addict?

Maybe.

Was I okay with that?

Definitely.

Dan had said the treatment might wear off after a few months, but one week in, I swear I could see dimpling. Small pockmarks like acne-scars were bubbling underneath the skin on my thighs. I was not happy. But at least I knew what to do.

Like a thief in the night – in fact, exactly a thief, nothing *like* about it – I snuck out to Dan's with a black bag stuffed into my pocket. I knew he was still in Dublin, and I had texted him to ask if it was okay for me to go out and get some more, so I wasn't strictly a thief, but I still felt like a cat burglar, all tippy toes, swag bag and black polo necks.

I went back to the spot I had been to with Dan. It was late afternoon, not night time, it was a grey day like many others

I had experienced on Hy Brasil, a light mist of rain spritzing me. I peered over the ledge that he had done the Houdini act on. Under normal circumstances I would probably have second-guessed jumping to the bottom ledge – it was probably six feet down, not that far – but I didn't know how secure it was, and while I'm strong, I don't quite have the ability to hang off the side of a cliff by my fingertips. But Dan was heavier than me and he had done it without any hesitation, and besides, desperate thighs call for desperate measures.

I leaped and landed with a small thud, perfectly safe. There in front of me was the seaweed, magically tangled and wrapped around itself, stuck to the cliff face. In the manner of a crack addict wrestling her dealer for one last fix, I grabbed, scooped and scrimmaged. I'm not going to deny the air of desperation, the lawlessness, the panic and the wild frenzy that overcame me as I threw myself into the task. Glorious seaweed that would smooth and evenly plaster out the bumps that nature had so cruelly bestowed on me.

If I'd stopped for a second I would have smelled the storm coming, that mugginess in the air, the slightly burnt scent that appears right before the thunder advances. I was so consumed with my lucky bag, I didn't even notice the wind pick up, or the clouds slowly cover over like a dark shadow, or that the rain was starting. The bag was three-quarters full, which was way, way, way, too much for one person, but I had decided to try to give myself a full-body wrap this time. In the manner of a mad scientist, I was even going to put it on my hair, just to see.

The Enchanted Island

Giddy with excitement, I tied a knot in the top of the bag, and that's when I noticed just how bad the storm was. The rain was causing small rivers to trickle down the side of the cliff, the mossy ledge that I was standing on had become a small swamp. My wellies were sucked back into the mulch when I tried to pluck them out.

I should go.

I was soaked through, and suddenly felt very cold. I wrapped my fingers into a tiny furrow to get some leverage to pull myself up, but when I put the tiniest bit of weight on it, it crumbled, coming away like dust. I tried again with a second groove in the cliff and the same thing happened, and the same with a third. Was the rain doing this? I grabbed the bag and threw it over my shoulder. I was going to hurl it up onto the ground. I took a deep breath and watched it flip as I released it onto the ledge above. It landed with a soft plop and I willed it to stay put.

The rain was torrential, like a giant was dumping buckets of water over my head. Water crashed down on top of me. The cliff face was slippy, but I knew if I could just get one firm grip I'd be able to heave myself up to the top. I felt my jaw shaping into a stubborn square; I was determined to make this move work. I scanned the cliff face, and slightly left of my reach was a branch. It was large and looked to be well embedded in the rock. I could reach it if I moved to the very edge of the ledge and balanced on one foot. It looked tricky more than dangerous. I could do it, though. I knew how to take calculated risks.

I shuffled to the edge and peered down, something I shouldn't have done. It was probably a thirty-foot drop; I could see the waves swirling cantankerously below, the foam conjuring up images of teeth and a Venus fly trap. Nervously I moved my body into the cliff face, clinging with open palms. I placed my cheek on it, wet and slimy, and took a few calming breaths. I would be fine. I slid as far left as I could, as close to the branch as possible. I'd have to jump, maybe half a foot, and I'd be extending from my right foot. If I missed the grip, I'd be landing back on one foot, which was never ideal – it would leave me wobbly and unbalanced, susceptible to falling. But I could do it. I knew I could do it. The rain and the wind raced at me, spinning around me, taunting me.

I should have brought a rope or at least some better shoes. I hadn't told anyone where I was. This was really stupid of me. I was unprepared to take on the elements of the island. But I would; she wouldn't get the better of me. And then I caught myself – was I turning into one of them? One of the islanders? Picking a fight with an island? Or was the island picking a fight with me? I would have laughed if I hadn't been so scared.

I extended my arm, took a deep breath, bent my knees, closed my eyes and jumped.

Gloriously, I caught it. My foot found a furrow and I balanced my weight as I swung my right arm up to the surface. My elbow hooked the ledge and I heaved my torso onto solid ground. My wellies scrambled for a grip, I took one final push off the ledge and catapulted myself onto the grass. I lay face

The Enchanted Island

down in the mud, hugging the soggy stability of it. I flipped myself over and let the rain wash my face clean.

'You won't beat me,' I shouted into the rain.

I smiled to myself, feeling victorious, and more than a little stupid for putting myself into that situation, and also for shouting into the rain. I slid to my knees, and watched in amazement as the rain subsided, reverting to its original delicate mist. The black clouds deflated like party balloons and rays of sunshine started to penetrate. The wind was vacuumed up, replaced by a warm, summery breeze. In a matter of seconds, it became a summer's day.

Had my timing been that terrible? If I'd waited a few more minutes, would the rock have dried off and my ascent been easy? Or had the rain only stopped because I was off the ledge? That didn't make sense, not at all. I sounded paranoid. It was a coincidence. I should have waited for the storm to subside. I was safe now, it was over. My bag of seaweed was intact; I shook the puddles of rain off it, and slung it casually over my shoulder.

Knowing that I looked like a mud creature from the deep, and was likely to scare any children I might meet on my journey, I headed back to the caravan to take a shower and have a tall milky cup of tea.

22

'Killian, you're here early.'

He rose to his feet and beamed at me. He ran the palms of his hands down the front of his jeans and then shot his right hand into mine. I took it, it was so formal and weird, but then a kiss on the cheek might have been stranger. We didn't know each other, after all.

'I am. I didn't want you to get here first and be on your own. I know a lot of people don't like being in a pub on their own. Especially girls.'

'Thanks, that's nice of you.'

He blushed. 'No bother at all.' He was wearing a navy shirt and dark denim jeans. He looked like he'd just stepped out of the shower, clean and fresh, his hair wavy and soft and his skin bright. Was he using the seaweed too?

'Have a seat. I didn't know if you'd want a stool or a chair, or there's the couch of course, although that's not as comfy as you might think.'

The Enchanted Island

Dotted around the table was a mismatch of stools and chairs – tall, short, cushioned, collapsible, like a mad hatter's tea party.

I smiled. 'This is grand.' I grabbed the nearest stool, and wheezed in pain as I sat down. I had come after Maura's dance class and had stretched my muscles into another realm of pain. I was stiff and creaky and exhausted. I rummaged in my handbag for my wallet to get some drinks in. I deserved one.

'I'm up, don't worry about it. I was going anyway.' There was a full pint of Guinness on the table, which had to have been his. He started to walk towards the bar, and turned back. 'Sorry, Maeve, what'll it be?'

'A white wine will be grand, whatever they have, thanks.'

At the table on my own, I felt really nervous. Where were the other people? Didn't he say there'd be a few of them? I'd dressed for the pub: blue jeans, black top and cream cardigan. My hair was brushed out and I had minimum makeup on, pale lipstick and nude eye shadow. Normally for a night out I would have gotten a blow-dry, but I didn't think I could handle another Dolly do from Maura's. Maybe they were coming later; it was just eight o'clock, there was plenty of time. The pub was quiet. There were a few barflies soberly sipping on pints, and maybe three small groups of people huddled around tables. There was an eighties pop tune playing quietly, and my foot started to tap to the beat; at least I think it was the beat and not my nerves.

Killian put a glass of wine in front of me and sat on the couch opposite.

'There's a few others coming in.' He picked up his Guinness, made a cheers gesture to me, then took a sip. He had a lovely bow-shaped mouth I noticed, soft.

I don't know why I felt relieved about others coming in, but there was something about Killian that unnerved me. One part of me wanted to rip him open and find out everything about him, but another part of me just wanted to close him up like a jar of olives and step away. I think he scared me, not in a serial killer way but in a way that I felt like if I got to know him, if I did rip him open, I might like him a lot. Maybe too much. And so we sat in silence, and I gulped back half a glass of very bitter wine and looked anxiously around the bar, trying to decide what I should say, where I should start, where we should start. Our eyes met and something flicked across his face and goosebumps raced up and down my arms. And everything I'd thought I did or didn't want to do, any plans I might have had, skipped right on out the door.

His face lit up with a giant smile and I felt a buzz of excitement. I shot an elephant-sized smile back at him, and just like that a little bubble appeared and we waded into it. It was me and Killian, and the rest of the place was just orbiting around us. We were sitting still, right now, in this moment, dazzling each other with grins.

'So . . .' He looked into my eyes and I had to look away because I felt such an intensely joyous feeling I wasn't sure where to look.

'Yeah,' I managed to cough in his direction.

The Enchanted Island

'You look really great, by the way.' He said this quietly, for my ears only. 'Lovely.'

'This old thing, would you stop.' I batted the compliment away, never good at taking one in person, much more comfortable online.

'Have you had a nice couple of days?'

'Okay, I guess, nothing too exciting.'

And then we sat in silence, which would normally be excruciating except it wasn't because it was filled with us throwing little glances at each other and grinning like two big eejits.

'Is your work going okay?' Killian looked so earnest, like he'd offer to help me out if he could.

'It's fine.' I really didn't want to talk about my job. I wanted to brush that whole topic under the carpet and tread all over it. 'So, how long have you been back here since your hiatus?'

'About a year.'

'You don't miss the mainland, and all that other stuff?'

He shook his head. 'I know what you mean, the other stuff, but I spent two years teaching in Seoul in Korea. I lived in this tiny flat, it was like a spaceship, everything was so contained and neat. It drove me mad.' He grinned at me. 'Have you been to Asia?'

I shook my head.

'There's people everywhere, you can't breathe for the people. And you can't escape technology; there isn't a surface that isn't a touch screen. It's very futuristic but all these things that are supposed to make your life easier, they just complicated it for me. I was choked up by the end. I was dying to pack it in. All I wanted to do was to go somewhere I could breathe for a while. It was a great experience, though, don't get me wrong.'

'You love it here?'

'I do.' He looked serious for a moment. 'It was a big decision to come back to Ireland, I never thought I'd end up here. I just wanted to see where I'd been born, and where my parents had come from. I think it might have been to do with turning thirty, too. I was only coming for a look. That was a year ago.'

'Why did you stay?'

'I fell in love with the place immediately, and then it was strange – I was here about a week, just touring around, and was in here having a pint one night, and I mention to Stevo that I'm a teacher . . . next thing the school principal is in, before I know it, I've moved into a cottage on the school grounds and I've a class of curly-haired youngsters looking up at me. Everything just slotted into place.'

The island gives you your heart's desire. 'Like a game of Tetris.'

'Exactly, and it's really been a great year. Hy Brasil had generations of my family here. It just seems to be in my DNA.'

He took a long drink of Guinness and sucked back a creamy moustache with his bottom lip.

'Was it hard for your parents to leave?'

He shook his head. 'Mam had had a couple of still births after I was born, and I think she wanted a change of scene. They both did.'

The Enchanted Island

'Makes sense. It would be a funny place to bring up kids anyway.' I shook my head.

'It would be heaven to be a kid here,' he said, disagreeing with me. 'The freedom the lads have that I'm teaching is just brilliant. They're so smart because they have so much time to just develop themselves, there's no one looking over their shoulders telling them what they can or can't do, they're safe here. That's worth anything. They're great kids. Have you seen them down on the rocks dancing and singing? Ahh.' He threw his head back with glee. 'Ten years of age and they've got a little band going, tin whistles, fiddles, and a couple of them have hard shoes and they dance on the rocks because of the noise they can tap out. The craic they're having, singing and dancing. It's like a wild party of ten-year-olds every afternoon.'

'You sound jealous,' I said, teasing.

'Only of their musical ability. Everyone here can sing or play something. If I'd been brought up here, I'd bet I'd be able to.'

'But then you mightn't have had ten years off travelling the world. Can you speak Korean?' I leaned forwards; our fingertips were inches from each other and I could nearly feel the zing sparking between us.

'A bit. I can order a beer and ramen noodles.'

'Surely that's all you need to get by?'

'You'll get far anyway. The kids were great there though; I'd a good laugh with them. During the year they had watched *Dead Poets' Society*, they watched so many movies to improve their English, and on my last day they stood up on their desks and said, "Oh captain, my captain."' He threw his head back and roared with laughter, a big belly laugh. 'Oh sorry, every time I think of it, I just die laughing. It was the funniest thing, and obviously I'm not that good a teacher because it was very, "Ahh cappytain, my cappytain."'

I took a sip of wine and watched him with admiration; he was so sure of himself, so confident.

He suddenly looked concerned. 'Is the wine all right?'

'Grand, yeah. Did I just do a face or something?'

'You looked a little bit shivery there,' he said.

'The first glass sometimes isn't the smoothest.'

'But the eighth goes down a dream.' He chuckled.

I wanted to know everything about him, but I didn't know where to start. *Who are you? What makes you? What do you feel?* I wondered if he liked puff pastry, the way it crumbles on your lips and falls onto your clothes; hot tea that slides down your throat and warms your belly; I wondered if he liked to read a book in the sun; if he pondered the big questions or didn't think about them at all; if he hated jumping into a cold bed and loved burnt sausages. I wanted to know everything. I wanted to unwrap him.

And a little part of me, the part of me that I was scared to open, was more than a little bit terrified. What would I uncover in him, let alone me? What would be the inevitable flaw? The chink in the suitable-man armour? At what point would the inevitable let-down come? What would it be? Wife? Kids? Gay past? STD? Penchant for threesomes?

'Am I interrupting?' Tim stood over us, tall like a willow tree. I felt like I'd walked out of the cinema in the middle of the day, shocked by daylight and slightly shrivelled by salty popcorn.

'Tim.' Killian jumped like he'd received an electric shock. He stood up and hopped from foot to foot. 'Have a seat. Let me get you a drink, good to see you. Maeve is here,' he babbled without taking a breath.

Tim looked slightly confused and pulled up a cushioned chair. 'I'll have a Guinness, thanks.'

Killian looked at me excitedly. 'Same again, Maeve?'

I fixed my eyes on his and felt a warm glow release from me again, then remembered my manners. 'No, I'm up. You sit, it's my round.'

'Nonsense, I'm already standing.'

I stood up, widened my eyes and stuck my hands out as if to say, *Well, would you look at that.* I grabbed my wallet and hightailed it, shouting over my shoulder, 'Two Guinness, yeah?'

I took stock at the bar, straightening my cardigan and trying to centre myself. What was that? What was that conversation? I don't know if I'd ever spoken like that to anyone. Or been spoken to like that, it was so intense and liberating at the same time. I put my hand to my cheek, aware that I was probably red-faced, and smiled, secretly, into my open palm. I had a small tornado whipping around my stomach.

I ordered the drinks off the ruddy-faced barman. I stepped back, waiting for the Guinness to settle, watching the cream and black merge, then separate. I had worked as a lounge girl in the Goat Pub when I was sixteen. My brother Murray got the job for me, he was working behind the bar there and all the other lounge girls fancied him. It was mortifying, they'd try to befriend me to get his number. I think he eventually kissed all of them. Murray did the rounds. But more importantly, I learned how to carry four drinks at once. Three was easy.

I approached the table expectantly, waiting for Killian to jump, to smile at me again, to give me that look of earnest anticipation. I felt my chest tighten in excitement. But that didn't happen. They were deep in conversation, to the point that I was practically ignored as I hovered over them. I made a guttural sound in my throat, and clinked the glasses together. They looked up at me, their faces pinched, brows furrowed anxiously.

'Is everything okay?' I knew immediately it wasn't. I sat down and carefully placed the drinks on the table, balancing each on a Heineken beer mat.

'It's Shane. He was in an accident today.'

'Is he okay?' I looked at Tim and noticed his pale face and the dark circles around his eyes.

'Yeah, he should be grand. Just a bit shook, you know.' He took a long sip of Guinness. 'Me too, I guess.'

'You probably need a brandy.' I smiled at him. 'A brandy cures everything.'

He smiled and sighed heavily at the same time. 'It was just so strange, we were surfing where we always surf, same rip, same tide, we've literally done it hundreds of times, and you know –' he looked at Killian, '– we know the formats –' he looked to me, '– we know the weather. That's part of what we're working on; we have the most up-to-date feeds from satellites. I've studied meteorology and we know the weather and the currents before they even happen. But when we got out there today, there was something else at play.'

He shook his head. 'Now I sound crazy, now I sound like one of your spooky elders.' I noticed a tremor in his hand. 'It *was* spooky, though. It was – God, maybe I've gone mad, but it was angry.'

Himself and Shane had headed out to the same spot they did most mornings, a dry enclave facing Dunlaven's Rock. The cliff face had eroded to form a staircase perched on a landing of smooth rocks that the sea caught with a gentle ripple on arrival. Every morning they straddled their boards and rode out like warriors ready to wrestle. Normally the current took them to one of three places where they glided and raced and danced with the ocean. They'd happily spend a couple of hours there, shouting back and forth to each other, taking in the morning light. They were greeted by the birds hovering close by, ducking and diving for breakfast, and there was a family of seals that they'd nicknamed the Murphys that they'd watch soak up the heat of the sun, when there was sun, which Tim said was a lot of the time.

They'd headed out as normal that morning. The weather was still as forecast. The foam swirled calmly on the rocks as they scooted down the staircase. They were excited; they were always excited to surf. They let the waves carry them out, and paddled with the current.

They were getting close to Lettermore's Cove, the very spot where they'd surfed the day before. They were side by side and bobbing like rubber ducks in the bath, waiting for the waves to curl, for the chase to begin. They were chatting about a TV show they'd watched the night before, and some theory Shane had on the word 'hoodwinked' originating from a team of mechanics. They were laughing. It was fun. Then Tim noticed that the birds weren't circling like they normally were, in fact the sky was completely empty, and the Murphys weren't barking and basking happily. He pointed the absences out to Shane, but he didn't think anything of it. The sea was calm, like a glacial lake; they were ten minutes in and there wasn't even a ripple. This hadn't been forecast. The surf was supposed to be perfect. They felt disturbed by it, their program had never been wrong, they were worried. Had they miscalculated? And then a blackness, that's the only way Tim could describe it: he said it was like someone had spilled a pot of black ink into the sky. It dribbled out, stretching like a claw over them. And seconds later, they were in pitch black. There was no moon to illuminate them. It was all cloaked in darkness. They shouted back and forth to one another, but couldn't see anything. They agreed to stay put, stay where they were and keep talking, keep making sounds. They huddled closer, and tried to find one another's hands, to cling on tightly.

Tim was terrified. The air was so thin he couldn't breathe. Then the noise started. The shriek. An inhuman wail. He heard it as clear as if he'd pushed play on his iPod: 'Leave!' Then the sea started to rock, and they released each other and clung to their boards, while the wind whipped up and blew angrily at them. Tim wrapped his arms around the board, clinging on for his life. He squeezed his eyes shut, and screamed. He said he felt madness in him, a type of hysteria; he couldn't explain it. Then, as quickly as it had started, the rocking stopped. He opened his eyes. It was bright, the sun was out. He was alone. He couldn't see Shane. Panicked and adrenalin-fuelled, he started paddling wildly, shouting for him. He saw the shine of Shane's wetsuit – he was lying on the rocks like a discarded doll, where the Murphys normally were, but he was lifeless.

'Well, I thought he was dead.' Tim looked soberly at me and then back to Killian. 'But as I got closer I could see he was breathing. He came to pretty quickly. He even managed to hop up the steps.' He laughed half-heartedly.

'Jesus,' was all I could manage. This was the craziest story I'd ever heard. I looked to Killian, who somehow didn't seem as shocked as I did.

'Any broken bones? Is he okay?' Killian drained the end of his Guinness.

Tim nodded. 'He might have cracked a rib, sprained an ankle. The boat comes early tomorrow morning, so we're going to head to the hospital.'

We all nodded, that seemed like the wisest thing to do.

'The really strange part is, he doesn't remember any of it, not the sky turning black, not the noise. Nothing.'

'What time did this happen?' Killian said.

'Around six.'

'I was up jogging around then, I didn't see anything strange at all.' He sounded suspicious and there was a slight edge to his voice. Did he not believe the story? But why would Tim make it up?

'And you know what else?' Tim said excitedly now. 'None of it has shown up on our systems. No satellite memory of it, no blip on the radar, nothing – the morning was recorded as a perfect morning.'

'Tim, don't take this the wrong way, but I know you guys like your mushrooms . . .' Killian trailed off.

Tim looked serious now. 'I thought of that too. But it just doesn't happen like that. Anyway, it was six in the morning.'

'But Shane doesn't remember anything, he didn't see anything?'

He shook his head. 'No, he wants to leave now. This is major.' He drained his pint. 'Go again?' He looked to me and then Killian. We both nodded, and he went to the bar.

Killian looked at me and half-smiled. 'Don't do drugs.'

'Really? You think that's what this was?'

'These guys are great, I love them, but they grow their own marijuana plants, they have a mushroom field that's constantly in season.' He shrugged. 'I'm just saying.'

'The noise,' I said. 'That shriek, that unholy noise, I've heard it. I know the sound he's talking about. I don't do drugs. What the hell is it?'

'The wind.'

The Enchanted Island

'It's not the wind.' I felt angry with him. We'd just had this great conversation, so why wouldn't he tell me the truth? Why was he so quick to dismiss Tim's story? 'What the hell goes on here, Killian?'

He said nothing, just closed his eyes.

'For God's sake.' I didn't mean to sound so irate but I was; no one around here gave a straight answer. It was all wink wink, nudge nudge, you know yourself. Except I didn't know myself, I didn't know anything. And now Shane was hurt, and I knew he wasn't an islander, he wasn't an original, and I had been hit on the head by a rock, and I wasn't an islander either.

Tim slid the drinks onto the table and I stewed at Killian. Our lovely bubble popped.

'If you leave, what happens to your project?' I asked Tim.

'I don't know, it's a mess. Number one is that Shane gets better though, maybe we can pick up the project after. I don't know. It's just happened.'

'The noise, Tim.' I felt myself glare at Killian. 'That's the noise I talked about before, the one I heard the first night I was here, last Monday week.' I huffed, spitting out the last word.

Tim nodded. 'I didn't hear that one. Didn't that auld fella die though, straight after?'

'Yeah, what was his name? Jimmy the Yinkee.' And then I felt an icy chill, the hairs on the back of my hand stood to attention. Was he saying what I think he was saying? 'You don't . . . ? You're not . . . ?'

'Maeve, you've got me thinking of things I hadn't thought about before. You're the one who said the island is weird. It is.'

'But . . . ?'

'The Banshee.'

'That's ridiculous.' I laughed. 'She's an ancient myth, a rural myth. Come on, we're long past the age of listening to the wind for news of a death. Seriously?'

'There was something supernatural in that water today. I can't explain it. What the hell else is going on here?'

'What, you think the Banshee lives here? Have you gone mad?' Killian grinned at both of us.

'Don't worry, I'm not mad.' I laughed into my drink. 'The Banshee. Come on.'

But as I said it, I felt that icy chill race across my spine again. Was it possible that there was something supernatural here? Could there be a type of magic that the islanders seemed to think exists here? No. Come on.

Tim finished his pint and, seeing that our drinks were practically untouched, stood up. 'I'm getting another one. I've finally stopped shaking. There's something going on here and I'm scared. I don't like it. I'm an outsider and I don't belong here – neither do you, Maeve. I hate feeling like this, I'm outta my skin.'

I bit my lip. 'I've a job to do.'

'How long will it be until you're next? Maybe next time it won't just be a cracked rib and a sprained ankle.'

Or a bruised head.

I didn't get a moment alone with Killian for the rest of the night. Jack and Niamh arrived, full of laughs and completely parched, gasping for a drink. I wished everyone else would just disappear so Killian and I could have talked some more. He seemed like such an honest guy, I couldn't imagine that he wouldn't speak the truth. But he was so dismissive of Tim. Was he keeping a secret too? I slipped a few smiles at him when I felt no one was looking, and he'd grin back, but it didn't feel like it was my grin anymore. The moment had passed and I started to think that maybe I'd imagined it all. Maybe he was like that with everyone.

23

The next day I called into Frank and Jack's for morning tea. Frank's study was magnificent. The walls were oak lined. There were beautiful leather-bound books stacked neatly on floor-to-ceiling shelves. Two dark green suede armchairs sat side by side in front of a stone fireplace. There was a huge cow hide stretched lazily on the floor. The place was masculine, dark and comfortable. Frank moved to his large mahogany desk. He pulled hesitantly on his moustache, looking a little sheepish.

'It's a bit opulent, I know.'

'It's amazing. This room is amazing. Do you just lounge in front of this fire and have a gorgeous red wine and sigh happily to yourself? That's all I'd do here, sigh happily.'

He nodded, and quietly said, 'I do sometimes.'

He gestured for me to sit. I did. I collapsed into one of the chairs, and immediately felt like I could doze off. But I was

The Enchanted Island

excited to see what Frank had on the island, the history, the people, and to see if he had any theories on the magical element of the place. And I wanted to know what he thought about Tim and the accident. I had spoken to Tim earlier that morning; he was at a hospital on the mainland. Shane was doing well – they'd bandaged him up and were sending him back to heal. I still felt I couldn't dismiss their story as easily as Killian had.

There was such an aura of calm about Frank. I'd say nothing bothered him. He reminded me of a dad in a Disney movie. The one that makes pancakes in the morning, and tucks his kids into bed with a kiss on the forehead – gentle and strong and could teach you wise lessons about life.

Frank opened and shut a few drawers in his desk.

'You heard about the boys surfing?'

'It's such a dangerous sport, that one. Looks like fun but it's risky.' He looked up at me and smiled.

'You heard about the sky changing colour and –'

He cut me off: 'Those boys smoke too much.'

'You don't think . . .' I didn't know what he might think, but it was worth a shot.

'Think that their story is true? Oh come on, Maeve. I heard Tim thinks it's the Banshee.' Frank laughed.

'That noise though, I've heard it.'

'The wind, this place is full of gales and mini hurricanes.' He smiled warmly at me. 'Oh, to be young and stoned again, wouldn't life be wonderful?'

He removed a wad of documents from the drawer and closed it. 'It's all a bit piecemeal. A bit of a jigsaw that's been through the wash and gotten mangled. There's maps, some documents and letters. What I'm really interested in is around the time my mam left here, 1937. All those families leaving at once and going all the way to the US – I want to know why and was there some type of catalyst, but I can't figure it out.' His head was buried deep in the papers. 'There mightn't be anything to it, they might just have all decided that they couldn't stand it here anymore, but why all at once? For a place with no immigration, that was a big ballsy move.'

'Is there a local historian? Is there someone you can ask about it?'

'You are a doer, aren't you? You like to get things done. I can spot one.'

I smirked, knowing that I had been found out.

He continued: 'I think maybe you're looking at the local historian. I've tried, but people don't want to talk about the past here, and then I just feel like the arsehole American looking for my ancestors. I've never gotten very far.' He pulled out a box that looked like an old biscuit tin and held it in the air. 'Now this stuff is special. This is the gold. Letters. Love letters. They're written from John to Cathy, they date from around 1938, just before the Second World War. She –' he walked over to me and sat in the chair opposite, '– had left Hy Brasil same time as my mam, went to Missouri. He stayed here. She was friends with Mam, which is how she ended up with the letters, but they're something else. They're just beautiful.'

'I've got goosebumps. Can I see them?'

The Enchanted Island

He handed me the well-scuffed, well-used tin. There was a faded drawing of a cat on the front.

'I kept the original box.'

I nodded, understanding that was necessary. To house love letters in anything but their original home would be a disservice to them. I popped it open. There were sheets of thin paper, piled in, almost like baking paper, their creases still visible. The words were tightly written in a blue ink, front and back. I picked up the first sheet. It was delicate, almost fragile.

> *Cathy a stór*
>
> *I dreamt of you last night. We were walking through Flynn's fields and the grass was up past our knees. It was night time, but we were lit by the moon – it was a navy twilight. Your hand was in mine, our fingers laced together, and we hopped through the field, laughing. I haven't stopped smiling since I woke. You were here with me. I can still feel the heat of your hand. I can hear you laugh. Seamus put me on the cutting at work, you know I hate that, but I didn't care, I thought about your hand in my hand all day and I smiled. I think he thought I was half cracked. And maybe I am.*
>
> *I won't let me think about you leaving, about that day, I can't ever think that kiss was our last kiss. I think of our first kiss instead, your face next to mine was as bright as all the stars twinkling in the sky. It was the beginning, sure, it was only the start of us, of the happiest I've ever been. I know you're not physically here beside me, but it's as if you are. I see you everywhere. I hear you laughing and joking, I see*

you flicking your hair and sashaying through the town like you haven't a care in the world.

I don't want you to be crying in America, I want you to be happy. I'll get money together to come to you. Wait for me my love. I adore you.

Le grá

John

'Wow.' That was about all I could muster. I felt nervous, intrusive and spellbound all at the same time. One part of me wanted to close the tin and never open it again, to leave Cathy and John alone. And another part of me wanted to devour the letters, to spill the pages out, absorb the words, merge with the emotions. To fall in love with Cathy and John.

I looked over to Frank. 'Are they all like this?'

He nodded. 'I won't . . .' He paused. 'I'll let you read them.'

'I don't know if I want to. I mean, I do and I don't. Does that make sense?'

'I know. It's the privacy thing, like you're reading someone's diary. But Jack and I have already read them. They're both probably long dead by now – maybe this way they live on.'

I would never have thought of it like that. See? Disney-dad wise.

'Read them,' he said softly.

'What other treasures do you have here?'

He patted some pages on his lap. 'Maps, some photocopied pages where the island has appeared in books; there's not much, not really. They think the name comes from some wayward Portuguese ship that got lost and then shipwrecked here.'

'Seriously? Like Brazil?'

'Without the heat.' He laughed. 'Before they landed here, people on the mainland knew of an island. They could see it, but they thought it was spooked, because of that constant grey mist hanging over the sea between us and because the weather is so bad. It seemed to them that it would appear and disappear. So a legend grew that it was only visible every seven years. And young men would have competitions to row out and if they touched the soil, they said they'd live forever, you know the type of thing. But you know what the seas are like here, there was tragedy after tragedy. So, eventually they stopped. But the island has been inhabited for centuries. I can't find any evidence to say where the first settlers came from or when they arrived, but I suspect that it was one of the islands on St Brendan's Voyage back in about 600 BC.'

I did a quick history class scan in my head. St Brendan was one of Ireland's most famous saints. His voyage which was a quest for paradise is legendary, he's even thought to have discovered America before Christopher Columbus did.

'So way, way back.' I laughed. This place hadn't changed that much since then; the only difference was a few shops and people wearing Gore-Tex jackets instead of animal skins.

'Way back before the iPhone, if you can imagine such a time,' he joked. 'Anyway, there are several versions of his voyage in Latin and Irish dating back to a couple of hundred years after. They're so old it's hard to rely on them, but he was definitely here, there's evidence in the texts and also that he possibly found what he was looking for. The Irish versions of the story have him looking for Tír na nÓg.'

'The land of youth?' I wanted to laugh. The Land of Youth is a nightclub in Dublin where all the underage kids get in because no one checks ID on the door.

'Yes, well, he did find his island of paradise apparently, but because it was so long ago and not documented properly, no one has been able to find it since.'

'So you think he travelled through here?'

He nodded.

'You think this could be paradise, don't you?'

He nodded again.

I burst into a fit of giggles. 'Don't you think the weather would be better?'

'I know, I know.' He batted the air with his hands. 'I'd at least expect some coconuts and monkey butlers.'

'At the very least.'

He started flicking through some more papers. 'There was a monastery here at some point, too, maybe around the eighth or ninth century. There's a ruin of a –' he coughed, clearing his throat dramatically, '– you'll have to excuse my Irish, a *clochán*. It was like a pod, an old beehive hut for Christian monks. It's right where the ruin of the church is, have you seen that?'

I had, I had walked through there.

'That's from the ninth century? My God, the place is ancient.'

The Enchanted Island

'I know.' He sighed. 'Remote, isolated and ancient. And isn't it amazing how there's no written history of the place? A place that clearly has a rich history.'

I raised my eyebrows at him. 'More secrets?'

'I'd say so, yes.'

'That superstition about the island appearing and living forever, is that where the island gets its magical mystique?'

He shrugged. 'Maybe. Who knows with these things?'

Clutching the tin to my chest, I left Jack and Frank's a few hours later, full to the brim with sandwiches, mini quiches and salmon en croute. I had promised to guard it with my life, and I would. The truth was I wanted to be alone with the letters. I didn't want to share my experience of reading them. I think Frank understood that, in his wise, Disney-dad way.

24

'Update me, Maeve,' Harry said a few hours later. I knew exactly what he was doing. He was sliding back on his worn leather chair, swinging idly on it, arm thrown over the back and his phone nestled to his ear. He'd have a number of files strewn on his desk, and if the conversation didn't go well, his body would close up: he'd bring his shoulders together and crouch over those files like he had a stomach ache.

'Harry, this place is weird.' I was in the caravan with my feet up on the couch, tired out, having walked the three miles back from Frank and Jack's. *The Bold and the Beautiful* was on mute on the telly and I had a cup of tea in my hand. The tin of love letters waiting to be read was on the table. Really, I was in a pretty good spot.

'Yes, you keep saying that. You're not giving me anything.'

Let the crouching commence.

The Enchanted Island

'Where's the bloody signature, Maeve?'

'I – I'm having a few difficulties with Sean Fitzpatrick.' I know I sounded flabbergasted. I felt flabbergasted. I had chased him, he had told me to feck off, he didn't return my calls, my notes, my texts. I was frustrated and annoyed, but I didn't actually know what to do. It was ridiculous.

He took a deep breath and coughed slightly, attempting to keep his cool. 'So what have you been up to?'

'I've mapped the site, I've taken photos. I'm in a good spot, except –'

'For the signature,' he butted in. I could literally hear the swear words pinging around Harry's head. 'Maeve, this seems to be going on far too long . . .'

Had he just called to give me a bollocking?

'Harry, when we spoke initially you mentioned that you thought the island was protected. What did you mean?'

He made a noise that indicated he was close to the foetal position.

'I can't help thinking if I get to the bottom of whatever is going on here, then maybe I'll understand why Sean Fitzpatrick is so reluctant to sign.'

'I get it, you're in a tricky situation. Look, do you need help? Do you need me to come?' I heard him swallow nervously.

'Honestly, Harry, I don't know what you'd do that I'm not doing. Give me another week and let's see how things look then.' I couldn't let Harry come here. I couldn't look like I'd lost control of this project, and I didn't know what I was doing. I would look like an absolute failure. This was my big break. I had to make it work.

I hung up and I curled into the foetal position myself. What the hell was I going to do? What would Maeve the grown-up do? Click her fingers and put on some red lipstick? She might make an action list. So that's what I did or at least tried to, but I didn't get much further than *Talk to the old bearded woman in the coffee shop*. She was probably what a private investigator (which I was somehow morphing into) might call a hot contact.

I threw on my mucky green wellies, Aran cardigan and green anorak, pausing to pull my hair up into a top knot, and off I went.

Twenty minutes later I was admiring the jaunty daisies sitting in milk bottles on cheery blue gingham tablecloths. The place looked like a smile, and there she was. Old Nora Batty herself, beard neatly clipped, and a navy apron tied tightly around her middle. I spied her from the window, happily wiping down the counter and singing to herself. I still wasn't sure if my approach was going to be hard and aggressive, or smiley passive–aggressive as I swung the door open.

Tinkle tinkle, time to meet your match, lady.

''Tis yourself.' She looked up and defiantly stuck her chin out at me. The radio was choking out some Rhianna song about whips and chains, which didn't seem quite appropriate for a showdown.

'Hello.' *Nice*, I thought, *smooth, friendly, normal, nothing to see here*. 'I thought I'd treat myself to another one of those delicious fruit scones.' I gestured pleasantly at the plate of crumbly goodness. I was being so friendly she wouldn't know what had hit her when I started the attack.

'Tea with that?' She smiled at me; it seemed genuine but maybe she was a game player too. I was so bad at reading people, I missed all the so-called signs.

I loitered at the counter, pretending to be transfixed by the cake display. 'Do you make these scones yourself?'

'I do, aye.' She slid out the plate with the tumbling scones. 'Many of the ingredients are sourced on the island, that's why they taste so good.'

'Fresh,' I said approvingly.

She nodded with a smile and the wrinkles bunched up around her eyes.

'Was there a funeral for Jimmy the Yinkee? I haven't seen a graveyard on the island,' I said, trying to butter her up for some Sean Fitzpatrick information.

'No.' She poured boiling water into a small tin teapot. 'No body, no funeral. Always the way.'

'Oh, I didn't realise there wasn't a body.'

She sighed to herself. 'Never is around here, with a drowning.'

'I hadn't –' And then I realised I hadn't thought at all. I'd never asked how Jimmy the Yinkee died. 'Was it at Lissna Tra? I saw a crowd gathered there afterwards.'

'Aye, they'd have been there to pay their respects before the wake. In the hope that he'd wash in. They often don't though.' She pushed the tea and scone across the counter to me.

'That's sad.'

'No. That's the way it is. It's not sad, that's life. He was as old as billy-o. Time to go.'

Pretty philosophical, I thought, considering she was no spring chicken herself.

'Two euro, thanks.' She held her hand out expectantly.

As I rummaged for gold in my wallet, I glanced at her shyly. 'I hear the fish are biting. Sean Fitzpatrick must be having a great time out there.' I'd play the ignoramus; she wouldn't know that I'd already chased him up the street with not a fish in sight.

A thin smile formed on her lips. 'Fishing? Is that where you think he is? He wouldn't know a fish if it came up and bit him, he's the worst fisherman on this island.'

My breathing started to quicken. 'Where is he then?'

She paused and smiled at me, drumming the coins in her hand. 'He was in earlier, bought his lunch off me.'

'He was?' I nearly fell backwards.

'Aye. He's off to his sister's to fix the roof of her cowshed.' Her eyelids dropped to half-mast, and she started to shuffle away from me. 'He'll be there all day, I'd imagine, her roof is in a terrible state.'

I felt my heart beat faster. I could ambush him. *Play it cool*, I thought, *play it cool*.

I smeared butter on my scone. 'His sister, she's the one at Miller's Point?' I replied nonchalantly, chancing my arm like a faux local.

'No.' She spun back. 'She's the one near Skellig Rock, the house right at the edge of the cliff.'

That was a good five-mile walk from here. I could do it. It would be completely worth it if I could get him to talk to me. I clenched my fist with excitement. He'd have to talk to me.

I swallowed the scone in two bites, anxious to get going. I slung my handbag over my shoulder, waved goodbye to the Beard, whose head was buried, concentrating on her phone, and took off as fast as my wellied feet would carry me.

I pounded down Main Street, my feet and heart beating out a similar rhythm. I swung my arms, and sang every Spice Girls song I could remember. I had forgotten my phone again, but that was okay. I was okay. I was on a mission, and I had a five-mile walk to work out how it would play out.

It took me over an hour, and there were no short cuts. The road was relatively flat most of the way. I traipsed by sodden green fields and white-washed cottages and met umpteen sheep who poked their noses over the stone walls to say hello. I passed a few people on bikes, mainly old codgers, who whizzed by, grinning, until they saw me and then they'd flatten their faces into a frown. One white-haired man flew past me, texting and cycling at the same time, and while I wondered if that was legal I was admittedly very impressed with how tricky it would be to hold the handlebars and type.

I enjoyed the walk, it didn't rain and the air was fresh, and I started to wonder if I was morphing into one of those women I had sneered at: the fresh-air types, sturdy boots and ruddy cheeks, always eating sandwiches and sipping tea from flasks outdoors. I doubted it, but I was loving the air, and weirdly the silence was lovely and peaceful too. I was enjoying the outdoors and even becoming immune to the smell of sheep shit. Wonders will never cease!

Finally I could see Skellig Rock from the road. I knew that Shane and Tim surfed here, although the sea looked rough. The pathway snaked to the left, with no clear entrance onto the cove nearby. You probably had to hop a wall. I was sure there were steps down to the beach somewhere. The Beard had said the house was near the cliff edge, so I kept walking, disappointed that the pathway seemed to be bringing me more inland and further from the coast. I could see a building up ahead, but there didn't seem to be a clear path to it. I hopped over a stone wall, and my pace quickened in spite of the rugged terrain. The building started to take shape. It wasn't a house, so it must have been the cowshed, and sure enough, there were cows in the field I was wobbling through, and some very large cow pats. I strained my eyes – I couldn't see anyone on the roof, but that didn't mean he wasn't there. Feeling giddy, I almost ran. There were large cement walls and a maroon roof. The heavy wooden door was unlocked and creaked open as I pushed. I stuck my head inside to make sure he wasn't there, eating his sandwiches. It didn't look like anyone was here. With gleeful expectation, I stepped into the very dark and stinky shed.

'Hello?' I couldn't see anything. There were no windows. My right hand was still resting on the door. 'Sean?'

As quick as lightning, someone pushed me – I felt firm hands on my shoulders and then a powerful shove threw me onto the floor of the cowshed. I spun on the cement and watched as the door shut behind me.

The Enchanted Island

I heard the sound of a lock sliding. And then a voice, old, deep and female, shouted, 'Go home!'

I got up and threw myself at the door, bashing my fists against it. 'Let me out! Let me out!'

Silence. She was gone.

There was a chink of light between the door and the wall. My eyes adjusted to the darkness. I could see that there was no handle on the door. Why would there be? It's not like cows need to let themselves out. I wasn't scared, in spite of the lack of light, and being trapped, I was angry, and there was a fire in my belly. I was not going to take this lying down. I had been set up. The elders weren't going to get one over on me. No way.

My hands traced the door. I wondered if I could jimmy the lock open from this side, but I'd need a tool, something long. The hinges on the door were wobbly. They'd probably come off quicker than trying to pick a lock, but I'd still need something to take the screws out. I held my handbag up to the light and rummaged, cursing the fact that I didn't have my phone. I popped a Polo mint that had taken refuge at the bottom among some crumbs and tissues into my mouth, and breathed a sigh of relief when I plucked out a nail file. I sat down on the floor near the bottom hinge and, with great patience and channelling Nancy Drew, I began the slow process of flicking the screw to the left. Slowly, slowly, it started to budge. I knew I'd get the door off eventually, my summers on building sites had served me well. I started to think about what the hell was going on here. Obviously this was no accident. I had been sent to a very remote part of the island by the Beard. And that door hadn't locked itself. Maybe they planned on coming by in a while and sliding the lock open. The first screw fell out and hit the ground with a chime. Well, I'd be long gone by then.

An hour and four screws later, the door was hanging off one large hinge at the top. With great satisfaction I released a mighty shout and kicked it. It squeaked and moaned and cracked open at an angle, and with a huge push I had more than enough room to step out into the daylight. Blinking, I grabbed my bag and took off like Usain Bolt. I knew exactly where I wanted to go.

Right before I burst through the door of the coffee shop, I composed myself. I knew I had a temper, and I knew right now I was more than capable of unleashing a demon. Deep breaths, I told myself, deep breaths.

The bell tinkled, announcing my arrival. I deliberately didn't wipe my wellies, knowing that they were covered in cow manure. The Beard looked up from the till and as I watched the shock register on her face, I knew she had set this whole thing up. She quickly composed herself and cleared her throat.

'You're back.'

'I am, yeah.' I walked up to her defiantly. I put my hands down at the till and leaned across the counter to her. I looked

The Enchanted Island

her straight in the eye. 'I thought I might get another scone, to take away.'

I watched a pink speckle stretch across her cheeks. She stepped back. 'Grand so.'

I flicked my tongue across my lips. 'I'd a great chat with Sean out at the cowshed.'

She froze.

'Everything is going according to plan. He was thrilled to see me.' I broke into a full-toothed smile as she passed me a brown paper bag with a scone inside. My eyes narrowed. 'Gorgeous, I love these. Two euros, isn't it?'

She nodded and slid a wizened hand towards me.

'I might just run to the bathroom before I go.'

She pointed to the left of the counter. 'Through there.'

I grinned at her.

As I locked the bathroom door behind me, my whole body started to shake with rage, with fear – I wasn't sure. Before I could change my mind or question my plan, I quickly grabbed every toilet roll in there and rammed each one down the toilet bowl. *Do it, do it, do it.* And I did. I pushed the button. I flushed. And then, I flushed again. And I watched the water start to seep up through the bowl and slowly cover the lid and drip down the sides. It was a small victory, in no ways equal to a potential kidnapping situation, but at least these people knew I wouldn't just roll over and *go home.*

I happily waved goodbye to the Beard, and headed back to the caravan, looking forward to kicking off my wellies, eating my scone and snoozing on the couch. But before I gave myself over to relaxation I decided I was going to text Sean Fitzpatrick again. Call it frustration, stubbornness or just my inability to lose at anything. I would not hit a wall with this man, I would march through it. I would tell him the offer had doubled, and that he had two days to get back to me.

25

I banged hard on the door. No one was answering. I peered through the letterbox and shouted. Where were they? I banged again, even louder this time. I heard a shuffle.

'Hello? It's Maeve.'

A mumble: 'It's okay, it's Maeve. I'm going to let her in.'

The door opened a crack and Tim's hand reached out, grabbed my shoulder and quickly pulled me through.

'Ow,' I said in a slightly exaggerated voice. I rubbed my shoulder. 'What was that about?'

Tim was wild-looking. His eyes were popping out of his head, his jaw was clenched and he was taking short breaths through his teeth like a weightlifter. He had a filthy T-shirt on him and a pair of tracksuit bottoms that looked to be sizes too big for him. He was anxiously rubbing his hands together.

'Tim, are you okay?'

'We're just –' He paused and ran his hand across his forehead. 'Man, we're freaked. Come on in.'

I followed him through to the sitting room, which looked like an Icelandic volcanic ash cloud. I waved my arms and coughed, trying to clear some air to feed my lungs. I walked over to the glass doors to let some fresh air in. I noticed they were triple-locked. I played around and sprang them open. Glorious air.

'Have you lost it? How much are you smoking? When did you turn into these weird recluses?'

'Should she be doing that?' Shane looked anxiously at Tim. He was sprawled on the couch, his left arm in a sling, his right arm cradling a beer. He was pale, which only made his red eyes stand out more.

'Shane, this place is suffocating,' I said. 'How are you feeling? You don't look too good.'

'I'm okay, I've got some good painkillers.' He smiled. 'Should be back up and going in a bit.'

'What's happening here?' The house was a mess, like more of a mess than two straight guys living together normally made – it was chaotic. It had turned into a squat. There were papers and notepads strewn everywhere, empty bottles, chocolate wrappers, dirty mugs, plates; there were duvets on the floor.

I sat on an armchair, having brushed some papers away, waiting for an explanation.

Tim was quietly pacing the floorboards. 'We've shut up the rest of the house. We're kind of sleeping, eating, living down here now.'

The Enchanted Island

'Why?'

'There's been activity, especially at night. We're freaked out.'

'What do you mean "activity"?'

'Noises, man, like you wouldn't believe. A shrieking noise, a howling – we've been hearing it all the time. And there was clawing on Shane's bedroom window, like someone from outside was trying to get in, but there was no one there. It was like an animal.'

'Was it an animal?'

'No.' He sat down opposite me and put his hands on his knees, trying to calm himself. 'It's like this place is haunted.'

I nodded. Tim had lost it. He looked crazy, he was talking crazy. He was clearly paranoid. Jack and Killian were right, these boys did way too many drugs.

'Shane, what do you think?'

'That guy O'Donnell has been round a bit.' Shane's voice sounded scratchy. 'He came the first time to see if I was okay, like whatever.' He rolled his eyes. 'As if he cares. It was just an excuse to poke around. Second time he came, he told us that we might be better off leaving, said that we had upset the island, as if the island is a person. Said there were things we didn't understand about this place and that he knew our work was going to disrupt it.'

It all sounded a bit familiar.

'The thing is, he couldn't possibly know what our work is, no one on the island knows.' Tim looked worried. 'At least I hadn't thought so, but since his last friendly drop-in, the computer screens keep flicking, and there's a hum – can you hear it? A noise coming from the server. I think we've been bugged. I'm searching but I can't find it. It's driving me crazy.'

I couldn't hear anything, but I could see they'd lost it. They were demented.

'What do you think is happening?' I asked.

'I think we may have to get off this island.' Tim looked at me soberly.

'That's a bit drastic, isn't it? What about your project?'

'It just doesn't seem worth it.' He put his head in his hands. 'We can't live like this.'

What had happened? They had lived here happily for ten months, no one had bothered them, and now they were literally on the verge of breakdowns. They were terrified.

'You're being bullied. You're being bullied by O'Donnell,' I announced triumphantly. 'I bet he's behind it. You should confront him.'

'He's not the one clawing at the window, Maeve; he's not the one howling.' Tim shuddered slightly.

I frowned, looking at all the Rizlas and tobacco on the coffee table. This seemed like classic drug paranoia, but still I was torn. Why now?

'Your work? If you leave now, will you be able to complete it?'

'No, probably not. We might be able to work off the mainland for six months, change some of our findings, alter it; it won't be nearly as good . . .'

'But it's a surf app; surely you can operate from anywhere?'

I watched as Tim chewed on his bottom lip and his eyes flicked quickly to Shane. 'It is, it was. But the idea has gotten more complicated since we've been here. We've made some findings.' He paused. 'Let's just say we've uncovered things about the island accidentally and they're a lot more interesting than our surf app.'

'What do you mean?'

He laced his fingers together and started to crack his knuckles. 'This place is fascinating – a team of scientists need to come out here and explore. It's a geographical anomaly. I don't know how they've kept it under the radar this long.'

'Maybe they've bullied everyone else away too?'

He stood up. 'We're so close to completion – three more months. This could be a platform for us for the rest of our lives. We leave now, we might never get an opportunity like this again.'

'What about you, Shane?'

He scratched at his head anxiously. 'I'm scared shitless. I think if I could get out and surf again, I'd want to stay, but I can't, and I don't think there are ghosts howling at us. I think there's wind and I think we're scared.'

I couldn't understand why there was no fight in them, why they were willing to just let this happen. Good thing there was always a bit of Mike Tyson in me. 'I'll go with you to O'Donnell.'

'And say what?' Tim was sitting down again; he was up and down like a yo-yo. 'You think he's howling outside our house?'

'No,' I said, remembering lessons from childhood on how best to confront a bully that did not involve sticking their head down a toilet. 'But let him know that we know he's involved. Tell him you're not moving. Why would you?'

Tim shrugged, then nodded compliantly. 'I guess we could.'

'It couldn't hurt. You need to stay here and finish your work. What's the worst that could happen?'

On the walk from Surf HQ to the village, Tim and I were laughing. We had turned from slightly apprehensive and a bit jittery, to a pair of boisterous teenagers, nudging each other, making fart noises, and squealing with laughter. It had to have been the nerves. The nerves and the Diet Coke I'd smashed back in three seconds in preparation for our big confrontation. We had decided to take on O'Donnell in the manner of Turner and Hooch: Tim would remain stoic and puppy-eyed in the background promising not to drool and I would fire questions at O'Donnell in a New York accent.

Our cunning ruse was to make a complaint to O'Donnell about someone trespassing at Surf HQ. Why I would be making this complaint, considering I didn't live there, we weren't too sure. But while Tim was in better spirits and decidedly more animated than I'd seen him in a while, I kind of knew he wasn't up to any kind of confrontation – he needed support. And from my brief meeting with O'Donnell, I doubted he had a moment when he wasn't ready for a fight, so I would take the lead.

The Enchanted Island

As we approached the small cottage on the opposite side of the street from Tansey's that served as the Garda station, Tim's giddiness subsided and his face went ashen. I gave him a smile that I hoped was reassuring, but I'm guessing by the frown that I felt creep across my forehead it was more of a grimace.

The door was open, and so I marched right in, assuming that Tim was behind me. I felt a little shiver of excitement crossing the threshold. I was finally going to get to poke around one of these gingerbread houses. My eyes scanned my surroundings: boringly functional. The cottage had been converted, the back knocked down and a large unimaginative extension stretched out the back. The floor was tiled with a grey slate, and across the expanse of the room was a large plywood counter framed by pigeon boxes of passport forms, driving licences (ironic considering there were no cars on the island) and ID forms. There were cheap framed photographs of seascapes lining the walls.

O'Donnell was sitting on a red plastic chair with his feet up and a movie on the TV in front of him. I could hear the whirr of the DVD player. By the way his shoulders rose and fell, I knew he was asleep. How you could sleep through *Catch Me if You Can* I'll never know. It confirmed everything I thought about O'Donnell: he was a fool of a man. Empowered by this realisation, I turned back to grin excitedly at Tim.

Where was he? Not behind me in the manner of a loyal German shepherd, but cowering out the front, lurking in the doorway. I took the two steps back to him, grabbed him by the hand, and gave him a stern talking to with my eyes. *Even if you're not tough, you've got to play tough.*

I stepped back up to the counter and cleared my throat. Startled by my cough, O'Donnell's black-soled shoes slipped off the table and caused his body to jolt back to life. He pulled his knitted sweater down around his middle. I watched his eyes narrow in recognition as he slowly stood and walked towards us. Behind him I noticed Leonardo DiCaprio getting into a pickle. I wanted to shout at him to push pause, you don't want to miss what comes next, but no, I wouldn't. That would learn him.

He leaned firmly on the plywood and it heaved an asthmatic breath right back at him. His fists were red and dimpled. He took a breath and rose up to a considerable height, indisputably a big man, maybe even a beast of a man. I fought the inner voice that was beginning to cower and stoop and get scared. Let him speak first, I thought, not trusting whether or not my vocal cords would warble. I smiled at him, my best child-star smile.

'How can I help yis?'

'Thank you, sergeant. We're here –' I turned my frightening grin to Tim, who was studying the floor with intensity, '– because there have been some unusual occurrences at Surf HQ.'

'Unusual?' He feigned a look of disinterest, but I knew his game.

'Yes, we believe there could be trespassers on the property, there have been a number of noises . . .' I trailed off; his blue-eyed stare was unnerving. 'There was an attempted entry at one of the bedroom windows.'

'A breaking and entering?'

'No, no breaking or entering.' I cleared my throat again. 'Just some scratching at the window.'

'Like the branches of a tree?'

I nodded, and frantically looked back at Tim for some support. He was nervously pulling on the strings of his blue hoody, transfixed by a spot on the wall behind O'Donnell's head.

'Has anything been taken from the property?'

'Well, Shane thinks that his computer might have been bugged.'

O'Donnell shrugged and sighed heavily. 'You know it's an offence to waste police time?'

'What are the noises? The shriek? That maddening shriek, what is it? I know you know what I'm talking about.' My voice had slipped into school-teacher mode, demanding, abrupt and slightly shouty.

He folded his arms across his chest. 'You don't live at the premises in question. If this gentleman here behind you would like to make a complaint about his dwelling, I can talk to him, but all you're doing is interfering in something you know nothing about.' His face started to prickle with different shades of pink and he shifted from one foot to another. He was getting annoyed.

'Go on, Tim, tell him.'

Somehow Tim had managed to shuffle backwards and was inches from the door. I felt my jaw clench in frustration at him and exhaled in anger.

'Tim.'

He shook his head, mumbled something about everything being fine, took a step back and left the building.

I growled in annoyance. What was I supposed to do? I stormed out and grabbed him, physically grabbed him by the hoody and pushed him inside. 'Make a statement.'

He looked terrified. What was he seeing that I wasn't?

'It's okay,' I whispered to him. 'Really, it's okay.'

With my encouragement, my poking and prodding, he started to talk, or rather mumble. He mumbled on and on about technical viruses on their computers, how their software made it next to impossible to be infected but everything was pointing to just that, an infection. How they kept hearing noises, that there was scratching at the window, they felt there was a presence in the house, that they were being watched. As he talked, I watched O'Donnell's mouth stretch into a line. He stopped taking notes and tapped his pen on the counter. And I listened to what Tim was saying. I heard what O'Donnell was hearing and suddenly realised how crazy it sounded: scratches at a window; impenetrable software; a presence? I had to stop him before he mentioned the surfing incident, before he completely lost all credibility.

'Maybe that's enough, Tim.' I squeezed his hand.

But he didn't stop, he wouldn't. I had created a monster.

'And that noise, that screeching, I'm pretty sure that was the Banshee. The Banshee lives on this island and you know, and you're protecting her.' Tim jabbed the air with his index finger and I saw him as O'Donnell must be seeing him. He

The Enchanted Island

had dark circles under his eyes. His face was flushed and there was a moustache of perspiration on his top lip. His clothes were filthy and his hair wild. The chip in his tooth, which had looked endearing, now just made him look homeless. Spouting off about the Banshee wasn't lending anything to his credibility. This was a mistake.

'Now look . . .' O'Donnell replaced the lid on his pen in a gesture that said game over. 'The people on the island have been very good to you. We've asked no questions about your business, we've let you proceed and live here with no issues, and now you come to me saying these things, making a mockery of our hospitality. If you don't want to be here, you know where you can go.'

'Ha! You'd like us to leave, wouldn't you?' Tim was no longer mumbling – Tim was shouting. 'You know we've almost completed our project, you know if we leave now we have nothing. That's what you'd like, isn't it, for us to leave and have nothing, so no one will ever know about this place!'

O'Donnell looked at me. 'I think you better take your friend home before he gets himself into trouble, before things get really heated around here.'

I nodded, for once agreeing with him. I had been wrong, this was not the way to find out what was going on. I yanked Tim's elbow and shuffled him out, as he continued to rant on about the Banshee.

26

The next day I got a text from Carl.

Where are you, babe? You free tonight? Cx

It occurred to me that I hadn't posted on social media in days. That was probably why Carl was looking for a hook-up – I am never offline. I hadn't posted a selfie in almost two weeks. I just didn't know what I would post, and for the first time maybe ever I didn't know *why* I would post. I didn't feel like sharing my pretend perfect thoughts and life with 524 people who I really didn't know other than through their pretend lives. It just felt a bit fake. My hand hovered over the screen and I wondered what I would write.

Chasing old men down streets in wellies.
Seriously considering meditation, no seriously.
Have met Superman's granddad.

The Enchanted Island

Have escaped an attempted imprisonment situation. How was your day?

I put the phone back on the coffee table and opened up the tin with the letters. Feeling nervous and excited, I folded back the pages, and got comfortable on the couch.

Cathy a stór

They're preparing the town hall for the start of summer dance. I remember seeing you there last year like it was yesterday, but sometimes yesterday can be hazy – I remember it like it is now. I can close my eyes and remember now.

Half the island was there. It was nice for everyone to get together for fun, to laugh. Everyone was in their good clothes, the women with their hair curled and blusher smeared on their cheeks. They wore brooches and earrings that caught the reflection of the glitter ball; peacocks, Oxo had called them, and I'd laughed. The men too, were in jackets and clean shirts, their hair was slicked back on their heads and you could see the comb marks through to their scalp. There was a smell of soap and powder in the air.

And then everything stopped. The glitter ball stopped twirling, the noise stopped chattering, the band stopped playing, the steam froze off the cups of tea, the lights went out. I couldn't breathe. I felt my heart leave me, shoot across the room and jump around you, exuberant, joyful, screeching with delight. But I was stuck, the blood drained out of me and I wondered if I'd vomit. You were a vision in a red dress, your dark hair forming a halo around your heart-shaped face. Your long lashes fluttered to touch your cheeks and then your eyes opened and looked in my direction. Your mouth slipped into a knowing smile. And that was it. I didn't have a clear thought, if I had it would have been that this is the girl I'm going to marry. Instead my head was broken. I was overcome with emotion, I wanted to sweep you into my arms and run away with you, plant delicate kisses on your cheeks, breathe you in, know the feel of your hand in mine, know how it might feel for your hair to brush my face, or how I might feel if I made you laugh. I knew then what I know now, that I could love you forever.

Le grá

John

I was all aquiver. I put the letter down beside me and closed my eyes, savouring the emotions. They were rich and deep and unsettling. I was unnerved by the rawness of it. He was looking at her like she was a painting, studying her eyelashes, the shape of her face. He knew everything in an instant. How could anyone experience such emotions? Maybe it's because that was the moment he fell in love? Maybe that's what love feels like, what real love looked like, not an emoticon and a chance of a hook-up, and, God, it was beautiful.

I hoped there was a happy ending; I hoped they lived happily ever after.

The Enchanted Island

A text message beeped through. Could it be Sean Fitzpatrick?

So the offer has doubled

It had to be Sean-of-the-no-fishing Fitzpatrick. How to play this, I wondered, feeling tempted to jump up and down with delight. This must be how it would feel to get the first bleeps from big-eyed aliens in outer space. *Houston, we have made contact.*

Yes. Let's meet to talk through?

Oops, I'd better clear the doubling of the offer with Dan, although with the amount of money he was set to make, I was sure it would be okay. I stared numbly at my phone, transfixed, willing it to beep. I didn't have to wait long.

OK. Lissna Tra at 4 o'clock

Giddy up. I had a date, of sorts. My initial elation was quickly crushed. What if this was another set-up? I know I played tough, but I didn't want to get ambushed again. What if there was a whole group of the white-haired posse waiting to launch a knitting-needle attack at me? But what could I do? I had to go. I could imagine a puzzled private investigator coming out to the island to investigate my disappearance weeks from now and everyone shaking their heads at my photo: 'Nope, I've never seen her before, maybe she was on another island?' They'd erase all traces of me, it would be a giant island conspiracy, like the moon landing. I was nervous.

What followed after a rock to the head and a temporary imprisonment? I had to leave a trail of breadcrumbs to prove my existence. I sent Hazel a text.

> *In case anyone is looking for me, I'm meeting Sean Fitzpatrick at 4 on Lissna Tra.*
> What?
> *I know. Don't ask, just don't delete this text until you hear from me again. Sorry for being weird.*
> OK

I took a quick pit stop at Tansey's for some delicious quiche. I had the unnerving experience of literally being shoved out of the way at the bar while ordering. An old man with sharp limbs barked his order over mine and stabbed me in the arm with his elbow: the pointy bit. I was a bit shocked but not that surprised, the white-haired contingent really did dominate this place.

I was constantly amazed at how good everything tasted. I wasn't too happy but also not that surprised about the fact that I'd gone up a notch on my belt. I was walking everywhere and hopping like a possessed witch doctor around Maura's classes, all flailing arms and sweaty face, but I was eating like a ravenous contestant at a hot-dog-eating competition. I was a bottomless pit, but I was getting such enjoyment out of food that I had no desire to stop.

It took me about forty minutes to walk to Lissna Tra. I hummed a collection of Katy Perry hits to distract myself from the nervous energy that was eating away at my stomach.

This would be fine, this would be fine. Sean Fitzpatrick had been avoiding me, but he'd never done anything to harm me.

If this was a genuine meeting, and not a geriatric attack, the game would almost be over. Checkmate Sean Fitzpatrick. I could head back to Dublin tomorrow. As that thought crept into my mind, it collided with the feeling that I didn't want to leave, a feeling of sadness. I couldn't explain it other than to say I felt momentarily confused, and a bit hazy. *Just keep on walking*, I thought, *just get this signature, kung fu any old people that might be looking for a fight, talk to Harry and then think about leaving. Remember the seaweed, remember the bridge, remember your life in Dublin.*

I sighed at the very thought of my life in Dublin: my fight with Sasha, my home with Mam, my credit card life. *Shake it off, think about it later, focus on the signature.*

I took the fork to the right and my pace quickened with the downwards slant of the road. I pulled my jacket tight across my shoulders, imagining eyes watching me from every angle. Lissna Tra had large grey rocks bookending a half a mile of white sand. The sea was dark and choppy, white foam crashing against the shoreline. The wind had picked up and the waves were peaking like sinister shark fins. It was deserted. I checked my watch – bang on four.

I walked down to the sand, hands on hips, and took some deep breaths of clean sea air. I spun around, my eyes madly scanning my surroundings for any pale skin, beak nose or ear hair.

'Maeve.'

I heard a shout. I couldn't see anyone.

'Sean?'

'Maeve.' A flash of skin appeared from behind a rock at the back of the beach and then quickly disappeared. A hand. I walked to a waist-high rock and peered over. Cowering behind it, a navy hat pulled down over his ears, a green jacket pulled up to them, was Sean Fitzpatrick.

'Quick, get in,' he spat at me, waving his hand urgently.

'What?' I stood and stared.

'Quick, before anyone sees you.'

A case of espionage. I clambered over the rock and slid down the other side. I plonked down beside him on the sand, wondering if I should offer him a hand or a hug. He was well protected behind the rock, it would have been impossible to spot him from outside.

'Hello, Sean,' I said, feeling incredibly awkward. If he hadn't been three hundred years old it could nearly have been romantic and not like being bundled into a car boot with an old, stale cigarette-smelling stranger, who had yellow teeth and curly white hairs poking out of his nose.

'Were you seen?' His eyes darted from side to side like a pinball.

'Are there others here?'

'I didn't tell anyone.'

'Good, good.'

'So, were you seen?'

'If you didn't tell anyone, who would see me? The birds, the fish, a sand critter?'

The Enchanted Island

'Shh, yer awful loud.' He held a finger to his lip, shushing me like a school teacher.

'Who's going to hear me?' I said quietly, sensing another case of paranoia, although Sean Fitzpatrick didn't look the stoner type.

'Just shush.'

I pursed my lips.

'So the Yankee is doubling his offer?'

I nodded.

'I'm not interested. That's it now, you can go home to Dublin. I'm not selling.' Spittle formed at the corner of his mouth and I looked away.

I didn't believe him. Now that I knew this wasn't an ambush, why drag me out here behind a rock? Why even bother meeting me if he wasn't interested? Why did Dan think he would sign, when clearly he won't?

'That's a terrible pity,' I said, pretending to look morose.

'It is, but that's it, that's the way it is.' He nodded abruptly, like hammering home a nail with his forehead.

'We'll just build the bridge off someone else's land then. It's a pity for you to miss out on the money.' Even I was amazed at my passive–aggressive negotiation skills.

'What?' He straightened up and lifted his drooping eyelids in surprise. 'There's nowhere else to build it from, it's my land or nowhere.'

'That's not true: we can go off a number of spots on the eastern side of the island. Dan thought this would be a good opportunity for you, given your situation.' I let that hang in the air between us, and attempted to look sympathetic and knowledgeable about his situation.

He tugged on his earlobe anxiously. 'Well, I didn't know this, I didn't know this at all. I thought it was me or no one.'

I shrugged.

'Well this . . . this is difficult now, you see.' There was a deep line between his eyebrows which was getting deeper by the second. 'There are people here who don't want me to sell, you see, who don't want a bridge, but they're not exactly going to give me the money I need. And I don't give a shite about a bridge, a bridge would be grand. Change things, you know. We're stuck in our ways here, we need to change.

'I've travelled, you know, I haven't been here me whole life. There's things here that are different.' He pointed his index finger in the air fiercely. 'That aren't right. And just because we're cut off from everyone they think they can do what they want. They've had it their way for a long time, and they've made mistakes.'

They? The elders? I didn't want to interrupt, he was debating it out loud. But there was definitely a chink of hope here.

He wrapped his arms around himself. He was shivering slightly. 'Jesus though, what they'd do to me?'

'Do you need more time, Sean?'

He nodded. 'Give me a few more days.'

I smiled. 'No problems. Just don't disappear on me, keep talking to me.'

He grinned thinly.

'Sean, why are we hiding behind a rock?' This is not World War Two, I was not a member of the French Resistance in a fetching beret and cunning moustache disguise. It was Hy Brasil, and now I had sand on my jeans and most definitely in my knickers, which was no fun, ever.

'I can't be seen talking to you. If I do this, I have to make sure I've got everything covered, and if we're seen they might get to me first, and there'd be no deal, ever. I need to work it out, I need more time.' He lifted his knuckle to his mouth and bit down on it, then blinked hard, there seemed to be tears welling up in his eyes.

'Okay,' I said, nervous that I might make an old man cry. 'Send me a text when you're ready to sign.' I didn't put a timeline on it, and I wondered if, subconsciously, I hadn't given him one because I didn't want to leave – not yet, anyway.

27

The knock at the door startled me. It was Sunday morning and I was in my pyjamas with a cup of very hot tea in front of me. I'd started reading more of John's letters, getting whisked away by his beautiful words. I folded the letter I held and put it back into the tin.

I swung the door open. 'Killian, hi.' I immediately crossed my arms, unsure if it was a defence mechanism or if I didn't want him to see my flannelette pyjamas with small pink monkeys dancing on them.

'Sorry, I would have phoned but I don't have your number.' He sheepishly waved his phone in the air, green eyes blinking at me, his curls standing a little bit on end. He looked fresh-faced and clean.

'That's okay, is everything all right? Tim and Shane? Do you want to come in?' I asked reluctantly, not quite sure I wanted him in my tin cell. He didn't seem to care though;

The Enchanted Island

he stepped right on in, and immediately started to remove his army-style jacket. His tall frame filled the place up.

'I'll just stay a minute.' He sat down comfortably on the couch.

I grinned to myself at his forthrightness. 'Tea?'

'Sure go on, I will.'

'So how are you?' I flicked the kettle and got two mugs out, a fresh one for me.

I watched as he straightened his stripy jumper, pulling out the wrinkles, and looked around the caravan.

'Grand, yeah. So this is where Dan put you?'

'My own little Hilton hotel. Fancy pants, isn't it?'

'I can see why Hy Brasil has been a bit tough for you, being in a caravan and all.'

'Ah, it's fine. I'm no princess you know, and it's dry.' The kettle clicked off, and I poured the boiled water.

He smiled. 'Ah, sure I know you're not a princess, those brothers would have beaten that out of you, but still for a girl . . .' His voice tapered off and he looked genuinely concerned, which made me feel a little bit gooey inside.

'Honestly it's fine, I've got the internet, TV.' I set the two cups down on the table. 'Tea. Who needs anything else?'

He raised a cup at me. 'Cheers.'

My phone rang. It was Dan. I looked at Killian apologetically.

'Work away.' He nodded at me encouragingly.

'No, it's fine, I'll just mute it.'

Seconds later my phone buzzed with a text. Dan.

'I'll just ...' I said, quickly tracing my fingers over the screen.

I'm on my way back to the island. See you soon.

'Busy?'

I sighed. 'No, I'm really not.'

He inhaled deeply, and I watched the colour rise in his cheeks. He furrowed his brow a little bit. 'So I was going to see if you wanted to get a bite to eat some evening? Maybe on Wednesday?'

A date. He was asking me out. I felt all a-flutter and suddenly a little bit nervous. I bit my lip.

'Yeah, that would be lovely.' I have never been asked out on a date in person. My date requests have only ever come in text or IM form. It felt really nice and chivalrous that he'd crossed over a muddy field and knocked on my door. It *was* very nice, very Jane Austen and old-fashioned.

His shoulders relaxed and he grinned. 'Ah, that's great, I didn't know, you know, if you'd want to or not.'

I smiled back at him. I did want to. I did. I really did.

'There's a pizza place at the back of Main Street that we could go to, if you like pizza?' He looked at me earnestly.

'I love pizza,' I said. 'Wait. There's a restaurant here?' How had I missed another opportunity for eating? I was surprised, given my appetite, that I hadn't bashed the door in demanding to sample everything on the menu. 'I didn't know there was a pizza place here.'

The Enchanted Island

'I wondered that, I mean, I wondered how well you knew the place really, if that's why you don't like it so much. I –' He stopped and his eyes widened and he burst into an ecstatic grin. He looked like a kid who had just heard Santa's bells on the roof, delighted and a little bit terrified. 'What are you doing today? Let me show you something?'

'I don't have any plans.'

He clapped his hands, and then ran his eyes over me. 'You might want to change out of those monkey pyjamas. They're great and everything but you'd probably get a bit cold.'

I buried my head, mortified. I had completely forgotten what I was wearing. 'I'll just run and get changed.'

He nodded. 'Maybe nothing fancy, we might get a bit mucky.'

'Brilliant,' I said and I meant it.

'We're still on for dinner though, like, we'll do this today, but we've still got dinner to look forward to.' He seemed almost worried.

'Yes. A double whammy.' I scampered off. 'I won't be long,' I shouted from the bedroom, surveying my limited clothing selection and feeling completely overwhelmed with giddiness at the thought of spending a day with the lovely Killian. Because there was no time to get ready for this date, to obsess over what to wear, what to talk about, how to behave, I had no option other than to be *me*.

I presented myself in my Aran cardigan and green anorak, my hair tied in a braid, light makeup, a spritz of perfume and my trusty green wellies. This was a dating first.

Killian looked at me wide-eyed, almost starstruck. He smiled so broadly I thought his mouth would slip off his face. 'You look . . . beautiful.'

For a second I even believed him.

I gathered my handbag, and my hand hovered over my phone but I decided not to take it with me. I didn't need it. Everything else could wait.

'Let's go.'

Outside the sun was peeping through the clouds and there were speckles of blue sky threatening to reveal themselves. It just might turn into a nice day. Killian stared from me to his bike and back again. It was black and ancient but sturdy-looking.

'You don't have a bike, do you?' He started to push it through the field and as we approached the road he stopped and settled himself onto the saddle.

I shook my head.

'Hop on the crossbar.'

I didn't hesitate, not for one second. I slid myself on sideways, allowing my legs to dangle, and firmly grasped the inside of the handlebars. We wobbled and started to giggle. I leaned back slightly into his chest and he moved towards me, his long arms encasing me protectively. His cheek was so close to mine I could almost feel the graze of his stubble. He gripped the handlebars and rang the bell.

'Watch out, here we come.' He pushed off and we rocked from side to side. Slowly we moved, balancing precariously, finding our rhythm.

'You okay?' he asked into my cheek.

'Yes, yes!' I shouted into the wind.

Gradually, we picked up speed. Killian knew every lump in the road, he slowed and warned me to brace every time a pothole approached. When he picked up speed, we darted downhill and I felt like the wheels would come off and we would start flying. We hopped over the bumps, and took off when the hills gave way. We screamed with delight, and whooped and exclaimed as if we were on the highest, fastest rollercoaster at the fun fair. It was exhilarating. A complete adrenalin rush. My cheeks hurt from smiling, and I don't know if I'd ever laughed so loudly.

Killian had been pedalling uphill for a bit, and he was huffing. We slowed down and came to a full stop.

'We're here.'

'Woo hoo,' I cheered as I came off the crossbar. I swung back to him. 'That was the best craic ever. I'm going to have such a sore bum but, God, it was worth it.'

He propped the bike against a stone wall and stretched his arms to the sky then shook his legs out. 'No more biscuits for you, Miss O'Brien, or we'll never make it back.' He grinned.

'Would you stop? Sure, you'd hardly have known I was on that bike at all. You need to get to the gym, mister, work up those muscles.'

He raised an eyebrow at me and nodded his head towards an open field. 'C'mon.'

And off we trekked through a soggy field, which led to another soggy field, which led to a near confrontation with a cow, which eventually led to a cliff face with a sheer drop into the ocean. Killian ushered me down a few steps where the slate stone of the cliff top smoothed out. Killian started to walk out onto it, but I wasn't confident I wouldn't twist an ankle, so I moved slowly. He stretched back and took my hand. My fingers curled around his and, even if I had fallen over there and then, I think I would have kept smiling.

'Here we are.' There was a hole in the cliff about a foot wide. Killian knelt down beside it and looked inside, then back up at me, his face glistening. 'Look.'

I copied him, sticking my face into the hole, and stared into the wild ocean below. The sea swirled and crashed underneath, the noises echoed around my ears. Suddenly a large wave crashed in and the force of it gushed upwards like a fountain. The wave spouted towards me through the hole, like smoke from the chimney of a steam train and I got soaked by freezing cold water. The shock of it pushed me over and I fell on my back in peals of laughter. Killian jumped over to me, his face inches from mine.

'You okay?'

'I never expected that.' I laughed breathlessly. 'That was amazing.'

'It's a blowhole. It's brilliant, isn't it?' He beamed at me proudly. 'I knew you'd love it.'

'Let me do it again.' I got to my feet and pushed him out of the way.

And that's how the afternoon went, taking turns at the blowhole, laughing and daring each other not to jump

The Enchanted Island

away when the hole exploded. I don't think I've ever had so much fun.

Hours later my face hurt from smiling as I heaved myself back onto the crossbar and snuggled into Killian's chest like there was a little groove there made just for me. We freewheeled most of the journey home, to many squeals of delight from me as we hopped and jiggled on the road.

Killian leaned in and gave me a big hug outside the caravan. I was hoping for a kiss; I wanted to reach up and grab his face and kiss the living daylights out of him, but I held off. Instead I melted into his chest, and nuzzled my nose into his neck for a nanosecond, drinking him in.

'Dinner Wednesday?'

'No blowhole?' I murmured.

'Just pizza, see you there at seven.'

We smiled like eejits and I watched as he stepped through the muddy field.

28

It was late Monday evening and I was having dinner in Tansey's with Frank and Jack. My daily allowance was now officially being spent in Tansey's kitchen, with an occasional interlude at The Shop for a cake. I was piling on the pounds. I had completely taken my eye off the ball but with no scales I was able to kid myself that everything was fine. Nothing to see here, I was still a size 10. And if I happened to slip into a comfortable size 12 pair of jeans, it was the label's weird sizing issues and not my problem.

We had feasted on the fish pie. It tasted so good, it had collectively shocked us into silence. I collapsed back into the couch and wondered if it would be wildly inappropriate to pop open the button on my jeans before it popped itself. I'd had two glasses of white wine and was swirling around my third and feeling quite a bit tipsy, but nowhere near as tipsy as Frank. He had turned into the jolliest drunk on glass number four, flushed pink and smiling and slightly swaying on his stool. It had been a lovely evening that I didn't think could get any better, until a voice started to crackle in the far corner of the pub. It was almost like a cow braying, one note that filled the place. An immediate hush fell on the crowd. Heads nodded approvingly. I watched as a few people closed their eyes and began to sway.

I turned to Jack. He pursed his lips and shook his head, like an altar boy scared to be caught chatting by the priest.

And then a beautiful lilting voice emerged. A man sang in Irish. I couldn't understand a word but the haunting emotion of the song had angels dancing up my spine. It was breathtaking. I closed my eyes and felt like I was back at that viewing point, Miller's Point, with Killian, but this time the ocean actually did rise to meet me and I stepped onto it and rode the waves and slipped out to sea, lost in the moment. I felt peaceful and euphoric at the same time.

There wasn't just one song, there were maybe four or five, each more beautiful than the last. They left me light-headed. This big beautiful voice was coming from a small figure at a table of five people, all rocking back and forth. The songs ended and the room waited expectantly.

'Jaysus, Johnny, that was awful powerful,' Stevo the barman said. Another voice shouted back at him: 'We'll have to liven the place up so, Stevo.'

Out of nowhere, as if they had been hiding in the far corners of handbags, under stools and behind pint glasses, appeared a collection of musical instruments: tin whistle, fiddle, bodhran drum, the melodeon, all clicked into waiting fingers, feeling out their familiar grooves. And suddenly the roof was lifting off the place and the floor collapsing as the music took hold. Cheeks burst with smiles and every knee was being patted to the rhythm. A session had started.

I was surprised at the involuntary movement of my own feet as they tapped wildly up and down, keeping pace. A loud, whooping noise erupted and a table of people stood, grabbed each other's elbows, and started swinging one another around. They squealed with delight, energised and free. And then I was up. Someone hooked their elbow around the crook of my arm and suddenly I was spinning around the room, whirling and twirling and laughing and, not wanting to break the chain, I grabbed Jack, who grabbed Frank and we danced and spun and laughed.

It was the best fun, and I didn't once stop to take a photo or even to reapply my lipstick. I didn't care what I looked like or how other people saw me. It was wonderful. After a few more lilting ballads it came to a stop eventually, and the exhausted dancers filed up to the bar for some thirst quenching refreshments.

My cheeks hurt from smiling, as a happy trio we collapsed into another bottle of wine.

'Such fun,' I exclaimed to the beaming faces before me. Jack and Frank nodded in agreement.

'Do you guys have any plans to move anywhere?' I asked breathlessly.

Frank looked at me, confused, and said, 'Where did that come from? Who would leave this?'

The Enchanted Island

'I don't know, you just – I mean . . .' with the music still ringing in my ear, I probably hadn't chosen the best time to ask this question. I really didn't want to offend. 'You're two men of the world, you're well travelled, you seem well off . . . is this place really where you want to be, like not just for a holiday or a weekend break, but for good?'

I watched as Jack's jaw clenched. 'We still travel, you know. We're not anchored to Hy Brasil.' His voice sounded tight.

'I didn't mean to offend, oh God.' I leaned across the table, cupping my face in my hands. 'It's just, the island doesn't have a lot of things that, I don't know, a city can offer. Theatre, movies, movie popcorn, McDonald's, cars – like, there are no cars here. I can't get used to that, none, no cars.'

They flashed a look at each other, and Frank smiled warmly at Jack then leaned across the table so we were practically nose to nose. 'The island saved us, Maeve. Well, saved me.'

I nestled back into the couch, wondering if this was going to be another story about fresh air and dandelions and finding spiritual fulfilment.

Jack inched his stool closer to Frank and patted his knee. 'There's no need, Frank, she doesn't need to know.'

Frank's eyebrows dropped an inch, and in a stern voice he said, 'Why not, Jack? I've nothing to hide.'

Jack's face went red. He looked very uncomfortable and glanced quickly at me. 'No offence, Maeve, but there's no need to explain everything, Frank.'

I interrupted, waving my hands in a gesture of surrender. 'It's okay, you don't need to tell me anything. I don't want to cause a domestic, especially between the happiest couple I know.'

Frank shifted on his stool, and in a clear, clipped voice that most definitely told Jack where he stood, said, 'I'm not embarrassed, Jack, it's a happy story. Maeve is our friend.'

Jack shrank backwards and crossed his arms over his middle, looking decidedly unhappy. He sighed heavily as Frank started to talk.

'About ten years ago I was diagnosed with an incredibly rare kidney disease. We'd been living hard, fast lives then, we were based in New York but flew all over the world for our business. We didn't see each other, we never slept, we were living furiously. I can't say I was surprised I got sick – it had crept up on me. I'd been feeling unwell for quite a while, but I never had time to go to the doctor. How ridiculous, when you think about it. Then the diagnosis came in, and – look, it's clichéd, but it caused us to take stock. To reassess everything.'

He smiled over at Jack and gave his hand a squeeze. Jack's eyes were glistening. Frank poured some more wine and sighed happily.

'Jesus, Frank, are you okay? What happened?'

'The prognosis was terminal. I was given a year, maybe a bit longer. It was very difficult.' He stared lovingly at Jack. 'In many ways it was harder on Jack than me.'

Jack shook his head. 'Nonsense, my love, so long as you are by my side, nothing is hard.'

Frank paused again and stared into the distance.

The Enchanted Island

'You can't stop there,' I exclaimed, 'you can't just say a year to live and stop talking. This isn't some TV movie. What the hell happened?'

Frank laughed out loud, a big open-mouthed laugh. 'I bet you always read the last page in a book first.'

'Obviously. If I die before I finish it, at least I'll know what happened.'

'Okay, so yes, I went through every treatment under the sun, you name it, I was never a candidate for a transplant for a number of reasons and my shot, my percentage for recovery was this.' He held up his thumb and forefinger with only the slightest sliver of light shining through. 'So I made a call; we made a call. I wasn't going to do it anymore, I was going to die my own way, without wires and chemicals carousing through me. We had renovated our place here a few years before, but never given it too much thought, and it was when I was deciding on where to go – where to die, effectively – that I knew it had to be here.' He chuckled. 'God, I'm a depressing dinner companion, aren't I?'

I shook my head, more than a little shocked. 'But, Frank, that was ten years ago.'

'And look at me now.' He splayed his palms outwards and wiggled his fingers. 'Jazz hands.'

'You made a full recovery?'

He nodded. 'I am in fantastic health, I need to shift a few pounds but otherwise, my blood pressure, cholesterol, everything is top notch. And my kidneys function just like they should. The disease has gone. Poof.'

'What . . . how?'

He raised his arms in the air as if giving praise. 'Hy Brasil.'

'Hy Brasil?' I repeated, confused.

'Well, that's my theory. There's something magical about this place. The other theory, our doctor's theory, was more to do with me relaxing and enjoying life for the first time in a long time. But when have you ever heard of a terminal patient making a recovery because he relaxed? It doesn't happen.'

'You're saying you believe the island cured you?' I leaned back into the couch to let that statement settle in. 'How? The rain? The food? I mean, this pie was pretty good.'

'A combination of everything.' Frank nodded, a look of satisfaction on his face.

'Well, that's a bit of an exaggeration,' Jack piped up.

'You don't buy it, Jack?'

'Magic. I mean, come on, you're drunk, darling.' Jack placed his hand on Franks knee trying to quieten him down. 'We should probably get going.'

Frank threw him a glance that would put icicles on a snowman. He rolled his shoulders towards me and in a tiny voice whispered, 'Look around you, Maeve, no one gets sick here, ever.'

I thought about the fact that there was no chemist on the island and that The Shop didn't even stock cough sweets. And with all the old people, I hadn't seen one person walking with a cane, in fact, everyone was unusually robust. And I thought about myself, and how good I felt since I'd come here; in spite of being constantly caught in the rain I hadn't once coughed or needed to take anything. I was sleeping better than I had in years. And the seaweed, the seaweed that might cure cellulite – I was living, walking proof of that. Could there be other cures on the island? Could this be a place of healing?

'This is big stuff, what you're saying. This is big. Do people know? Does everyone talk about this? I mean, is this a thing?'

'He's drunk, Maeve, he's drunk, don't mind him,' Jack piped up.

Frank nodded, ignoring Jack. 'We don't go around talking about this.' He winked at me and for a moment I felt special, and then I remembered the bridge, the whole reason I was on the island.

'But you can't keep this to yourself. Other people need this.' I felt something in the pit of my stomach. Dad. Memories of Dad flooded my head: Dad screaming at the rugby on the television, cursing at the ref; pushing me on a swing; sliding extra money into my hand for a trip into town. Dad smiling, swinging his arm across Mam's shoulder and throwing his head back and laughing. My dad. I had loved him so much. Could the island have saved him? The bridge should have been built sooner. Everyone should be here. If this was a place of healing, if there was even the tiniest bit of truth to what Frank was saying, the floodgates should open. Hy Brasil could bring great solace and hope to people.

Frank shook his head. 'This place has a delicate balance, Maeve. If you upset it with too many people, put too much of a strain on the natural resources, it doesn't work anymore.'

'How do you know that? You can't know that, not for sure. You're just assuming – until you do it, until you try it, you don't know that.'

'Most islanders here believe that.'

'Believe, but don't know,' I spat. 'You just stumbled across this place. Why should you be the only lucky ones?' I could feel hot tears building up in my eyes. I never cried, never. And here I was about to blub. It was Dad. What if he'd been here? Could he have been cured from the cancer that ravaged him, that stole him from us? That stole Mam from us too? Could the island have saved our family? Frank was terminal and he made a recovery. I was devastated; it was as if I had failed Dad. Could he still be alive? It was too much. I didn't know what to feel.

'You're right, you're right.' Frank spoke softly. 'We've also thought because I have a connection to the island through my mam, that I have her genes, it might have contributed. But really, Maeve, we don't know.'

'We need to tell people about this, we need to open this place up. There needs to be wellness centres all over the island.' If there was even the tiniest bit of truth here, it couldn't be kept a secret. No one should be denied good health or at least a chance of it when there seemed to be no chance.

Jack's face had paled. 'That's not how it works, Maeve, you open it up, it closes down. This ends. There's a balance that needs to be maintained.' He sounded angry, at me or Frank, I wasn't sure. He shook his head, and the determination in his voice scared me a little. He seemed to swallow back his anger. 'Time to go home, Frank, come on.'

The Enchanted Island

'I don't understand.'

'Opening up the island may not help anyone else,' Frank said. 'Nature is a delicate balance, and it definitely won't help the people already on the island.'

Meekly, I replied, 'Like you two?'

Frank nodded.

'You think if it opens up, it ends?'

'And whoever is benefiting from it won't benefit anymore.'

'Like Frank.' My hand hovered around my drink, but I felt too numb to lift it. 'The surf boys . . . Their project touches on this, doesn't it?'

'We think they might have come across something.'

And they're being terrified off the place, because they might be getting close to cracking the island open.

'We need to go.' Jack stood abruptly. 'You need to get to bed, Frank, you're looking a little too well oiled. He'll snore the house down. The sheep in the next field won't sleep a wink because of him.'

I watched Jack's face relax back into the one I knew, happy Jack.

Frank beamed as he put on a brown leather jacket that looked like it was borrowed from Indiana Jones. 'How did I get so lucky to find you?'

'God was smiling on you that day.'

A look of utter contentment and bliss passed between them, and a stillness encircled them, radiating happiness.

'Come on, ye auld drunk, let's get you home.'

29

I didn't sleep a wink that night. I'd snuggle down into my duvet, happy and calm, and within seconds start flapping my legs and burrowing furiously into the pit of my mattress. I could hardly believe what I'd been told. I sat bolt upright and threw the duvet onto the floor, and glanced at my phone: 2.34. I didn't even know who I would call to talk to about this, not that anyone would be awake. It felt completely unbelievable. Frank was implying that there *was* something miraculous about the island. I told myself he was drunk, maybe there wasn't any truth to it. But then I'd remember Jack's reaction and reconsider. He had tried very hard to shut the conversation down, to stop Frank opening up to me. He did not want me to know, which made me think that there was something to know. Frank's story was like something from a previous century, a religious experience, except that it was current. If there was any truth to this, how was it a secret?

The Enchanted Island

And yet there were so many things that could be explored here that might help people. If seaweed could cure cellulite, what could other things on the island do? If there was something miraculous here, in the soil, in the air, in the food, these islanders didn't deserve to keep it to themselves. A couple of hundred people might benefit now, but that was nothing when there was a world of sick people who needed help.

I couldn't sleep. There was no point staying in bed. I got up and wandered into the caravan and flicked the telly on. But it was no good. I couldn't rest. I couldn't find a calmness. I was angry – angry at everyone for keeping this secret. What if Dad had been here? A wave of rage moved from my toes, encased my stomach and froze my lungs. I felt the urge to hit out, to grab something and smash it. I had the rage of the Incredible Hulk, looking to pulverise anything in my path with my giant cartoon fists. I scoured the kitchen, and my hand reached for a plate. I felt overwhelmed and powerless. I thought my head would explode.

Just breathe.

What good was breathing going to do?

You can control your own thoughts.

My own thoughts were helter skelter.

Try it.

'Right so,' I shouted defiantly into the night air, 'I will.' *That'll show you, imaginary voice in my head.*

If I had been a dragon there would have been fire pumping out of my nose. But I breathed, and I tried not to think of the fire but instead of cool, icy liquid. Breathe it in and breathe it out, and try not to drown in it.

I filled myself with silence with each icy breath. In and out. Or at least I tried to, and after a few minutes of breathing like a deranged underwater monster, I started to calm down. The facts were before me. I didn't even know if it was true, after all it had been a conversation with a drunk man in a pub. And no, I couldn't have saved Dad. I saw his face flash in front of my eyes and I smiled to him, at the memory of him and all the good and great and imperfect things he was. And I took a long deep breath in and every inch of me recognised how much I missed him, and it was good to remember him and to feel his absence. Another breath and I felt peaceful. I opened my eyes.

It's amazing what a little breathing and self-control can do. Killian had a point. I felt good. Weirdly, I felt happy.

There were music videos on the telly. Some 1980s rock band in white leather trousers smashing their long hair at each other's guitars. I turned it up and swished my own hair back and forth. I was wide awake now. No point in even thinking about sleeping.

My eyes fell on the tin of love letters. I was savouring each one, but now was as good a time as any to read on.

> *Cathy a stór*
>
> *You're gone a year now. A full year – 365 days without my love. I wonder if I am becoming a shadow in your mind and if you can't see me clearly anymore? When there was no*

The Enchanted Island

letter last month that's what I thought, I was as mad with the world as anything, I was like Kevin's bull, flaring up at everyone. I thought the worst, and I know it's terrible to say because I am sad that your mother was unwell but I was glad your silence wasn't because you'd forgotten me. I'm a terrible person to think that, but I couldn't stand it if you'd forgotten me. I haven't forgotten you, but I wonder sometimes if you've changed, if that's an old you I'm remembering and you're different now. When you said you had your hair cut I wanted to scream out, I know I'm an eejit, but I want you to stay the way you were, sitting on the wall, swinging your legs, and laughing. When I go past that wall I always nod my head to you – I see you there clear as day. I miss your face, the smell of you, I miss what we don't have, what we may never have.

Le grá

John

Oh God, these letters were so sad. So beautiful and sad, and romantic and happy. They made me feel sick and weak and giddy at the same time and not just a little bit jealous. I couldn't even imagine someone pining after me, or me being so in love with them that I was tormented by their absence, and that I'd say hello to the ghost of the memory of them. I thought about the smiley faces that Carl used to send me and it was so unbelievably laughable that I was okay with that. Not even okay, but *flattered* by a wink, and the effort it must have taken him to push a few buttons. It was pathetic. Why had I thought that that was okay? I wondered if that was what all love felt like, or just for the lucky ones. Did everyone feel as deeply as John and Cathy? I wondered if that was how Mam and Dad were? They'd always seemed so happy, so content with each other. I remembered that they used to go for a walk around the neighbourhood most evenings. Dad would always hold Mam's jacket out for her and she'd slide her arms in, and off they'd go, holding hands. Even though we were their kids, in many ways we were outside the two of them, excluded from their very deep love. There must have been hundreds and thousands of intimate moments that made up their marriage, but I could only remember a few: the jacket, the talking, the hand holding, the dancing. Poor Mam.

I picked up my phone to send her a text, so as not to wake her. She wouldn't get it until morning.

Hi Mam, hoping I'll be home soon. We'll go for a nice dinner in town. Missing you x

I should reach out to her more, I should be a nicer daughter. It wouldn't kill me to send a few texts. I felt guilty about not being good to her. I know she wasn't a TV mother, with open conversations and hilarious one-liners, but she was my mam, and she loved me completely, even if she did slap my hand away from biscuits.

I folded over the letter, placed it back in the tin and took a deep breath. I was rationing them out.

I leafed through a book Frank had given me about the west of Ireland. Hy Brasil was mentioned. There was a claim that during the famine in the 1840s no one on the island

The Enchanted Island

had died, which again I thought might have lent credence to its magical status. This little spot lost no one, when every other town, village and island in the country lost a third of its population. How did they explain that at the time? The island must have been self-sufficient, not reliant on the potato crop. Still, disease was rampant – it was strange. Was this something to do with the miraculous cures Frank had talked about? Even back then? Or did no one ever travel to the mainland, were they completely isolated? This place was getting more and more unusual and I'd only scratched the surface. What I was really surprised at was how it had remained so untouched; were the islanders that good at keeping a secret, or did they genuinely not know what was going on? Was it just the elders who held the keys to the place?

I must have fallen asleep over the pages of the book, because the next thing I knew the caravan was shaking with knocking on the door, and I was wiping away drool from my cheek. Startled and more than a little dishevelled, I opened the door. It was Dan. He had a waxed coat on, zipped up to his chin. Rain droplets were sprinkled on his shoulders, his wellies were caked in mud and he balanced a hand on the wall to take them off.

'Good to see you, Dan, come in,' I said, wiping the sleep out of my eyes. My phone told me it was 9.13. I really had dozed off.

I automatically went to the kitchenette and started making tea.

'So, we're getting close?' Dan had swung his jacket onto the back of the couch and plonked himself down.

I nodded and stared into the tea.

'What do you reckon? Do you think he'll sign today?'

I clinked the cups over to the coffee table.

'It would be great if we got it by the weekend.'

I sat down on the far end of the couch 'Have a chocolate bikkie.' I ripped the packet open and let some spill out onto the table, thinking how Mam would be all in a tizzy at the thought of crumbs and the impropriety of it all. I expected her to pop up from behind the fridge, screaming: 'What? No doily?'

'How's Harry?' I asked.

Dan rolled his eyes. 'You know Fingers-in-pies Holmes: it's like there's a black, white and grey area, and Harry dances all over the grey.'

I didn't say anything, hoping he'd elaborate.

'He's keen we get this deal signed and move on to the next stage of the project.'

What was Harry's involvement here really? Was it possible that he was involved in the *project*?

'Have you and Harry worked together before?' I flipped my voice up high and girly, and let the question twirl in the air above us, like I was just making polite conversation, like I didn't really care what the answer was.

'We've been involved in a number of projects over the years. We opened a chain of gyms in the US; they went under though. But we have a chain of sunbed studios across the west coast,

The Enchanted Island

a couple of nail salons in the Caymans. Harry and I go way back.' Dan nodded as he spoke, delighted that I seemed to be taking an interest in him. 'Nothing as big as seaweed though.'

It seemed very unusual for a partner in a major law firm in Dublin to have businesses in the US and the Cayman Islands. Weren't the Cayman Islands a massive tax haven for uber rich people who chewed on pineapples and wore panama hats and linen suits all day? Why would Harry have a nail salon there? I smelled something, and it wasn't just Dan's feet.

'Is Harry involved in the seaweed?' I sounded edgy and a little bit shrill, a little too excited to get an answer.

Dan changed the conversation immediately. 'So, Sean?'

I should have played it cooler. I smiled at him victoriously. 'So, yeah, I met with Sean three days ago and he's thinking it over. He'll sign. I swear he'll sign.'

Dan nodded, and blew on his tea before taking a sip. 'Soon? I've got people breathing down my neck.'

'I think so, em . . . I promised him something, well, it kind of . . . with negotiations and . . .' *Oh God, just blurt it out.* 'I told him you'd doubled the offer.'

He looked unperturbed. 'Grand. To get this project under way I'd probably triple it at this stage.'

'Oh, that's okay?' I said, probably sounding a little shocked. 'Great so, and the other thing, well, the thing is, he seems scared, Dan.'

Dan's face fell. I watched his cheeks wobble slightly, and his eyes turned serious, almost sad. He sighed. 'Poor fecker.'

'The elders?'

'Yeah. You know he's one of them too?'

Sean Fitzpatrick was an elder? I hadn't expected that, although of course he was ancient. He was one of them. And he was scared of them. Scared of his own people. That must feel strange.

'It's tricky. And he knows what they're capable of.' There was a loud crunch as Dan bit into a chocolate digestive.

'It sounds like they're kind of a committee?'

'Ah, no, they aren't, like, a governing body. It goes generations and families back, it's the old island families. The elder members of it.'

'So there's a lot of them?'

'Ah, yeah. At least a hundred, anyway.'

That's about a fifth of the island, and then you include their families ... No wonder they seemed to have so much power here.

'Is O'Donnell the leader?'

'That old fart? No. There's no leader, it's not like that. He's more of a middleman, he goes between both sides of the island, but ultimately he's one of them.' Dan shook his head, and I wondered if he knew, if he really knew, the lay of the land.

'So they want to protect the island?'

'They think they're preserving it. They're relics, the lot of them.'

'I heard something, Dan,' I said cautiously, 'about the island having certain healing properties other than seaweed.' I studied his face intently, watching for a flicker, anything. 'I mean, it's probably nothing.'

Slowly he nodded. 'Sure just look around you, there's no doctor here. You'd be hard pressed to get a tub of Sudocrem.'

'Is there something here?'

'Good genes? Honestly I don't know, and I don't care. I care about the seaweed, and we know that that works.' He may have been brought up here, but he'd never questioned it. He didn't know that there might be something bigger here – then again there might not.

'Is that what the elders are trying to preserve?'

He didn't answer me but he did that face I'd seen him do before: he looked completely dismissive of them, as if they had nothing to preserve. Nothing worthwhile. And I caught myself wondering, for the very first time since I'd arrived on the island, why I didn't feel dismissive of them; instead I wondered if maybe they had a point. Maybe these old people might be on to something; by clinging to their way of life they were preserving their morals and traditions, their family history. Everyone said they were happy; maybe they were just trying their best to keep that happiness in one place. In that sense, the island was worth preserving, I could see that now.

'What could happen to Sean Fitzpatrick, Dan?'

He shrugged. 'Not sure, but he knows they would stop at nothing.'

And having been hit on the head by a rock and been a victim of an attempted imprisonment, I believed him.

30

There was very little to give away that the cottage I was standing outside was an Italian restaurant. It looked no different to all the other cottages: whitewashed front, two windows onto the street, a slightly recessed door that was painted red. But there was a tiny sign screwed into the wall at the side of the doorway – ALFONSO'S ITALIAN RESTAURANT – and an overwhelming stink of garlic. Bingo.

There were little gremlins doing somersaults in my belly, I was so excited and nervous. I was off on a date with a guy I really liked and who, I was pretty sure, liked me too. This was new territory. I had a buzzy sense of anticipation but also felt weirdly calm – this felt like we already knew each other, it wasn't a test date, it was a real date, a next-step date. I was wearing a black dress, which was probably complete overkill but I wanted to look like I'd made an effort, and like I knew this was a real date. I also had matching underwear

The Enchanted Island

on, which never happened, and was probably the only set I had on the island with me, which was purely accidental. It was yellow with little rosebuds and didn't scream sex like something red and frilly might have, but it was all I had. I didn't know if there would be a chance to show off the rosebuds, but I wanted to be prepared, so I had shaved, moisturised and plucked. I had also allowed Maura to get her hands on my locks – and she had given my hair a healthy shine, and it smelled great. I kicked my wellies off at the side of Alfonso's (a first on a date) and slipped into a pair of black heels.

Killian was already there. He looked like he had made an effort too: hair gelled back, curls smoothed out, black jumper on. This really was a date, a real one, for grown-ups. He stood when he saw me, and I wanted to run right into him and bombard him with kisses, but I held back, calming the rush of hormones that were exploding under my skin. He leaned in and gave me two cheek kisses, and his hand slipped over the small of my back and kind of hovered there, making me feel like I was drowning.

I pulled a wicker chair into the table, which had a red tablecloth and a large wax candle that reminded me of church. There were two other couples, some Italian violin music, dim lighting and garlic bulbs hanging from the ceiling. It was perfect.

Killian and I grinned at each other.

He spoke out of the corner of his mouth: 'Alfonso has gone a bit overboard on the sunbeds.'

I swung my head around. An orange-coloured man with blinding white teeth and bouffant hair as black as night was coming towards our table.

'Howerya, Tommy.' Killian raised an eyebrow in greeting as menus were placed in our hands.

'It's Alfonso here, Killian. Atmosphere, you know?'

'Got ya.' Killian nodded and slipped a smirk at me and I thought I'd die laughing.

After we'd ordered some wine and Alfonso had spun back to the kitchen, Killian leaned across the table.

'Tommy lives three houses down from me. I don't think he's ever been to Italy.'

'He's putting on a good show, though. He's probably got *The Sopranos* box set.'

He laughed. 'Have you been to Italy?'

I shook my head. Turns out Killian had, he'd been pretty much everywhere. I blitzed him with questions, and as I ticked off the countries he had travelled to on my hands, I eventually ran out of fingers.

He shrugged modestly. 'It's one of the perks of being a teacher, you can travel and work really easily, that and I've never minded backpacking, I'm good on a small budget and dodgy buses, that kind of thing doesn't bother me.'

'I've been nowhere. Two-week holidays in Spain, a couple of trips to France, shopping expeditions to London. I've never seemed to have the money to travel. It hasn't seemed that important to me, which is ridiculous really – of course it's important.'

The Enchanted Island

'It's only as important as you make it. I love it, but I don't think travelling makes you a better person or anything, I probably just have more photos on my memory stick.'

I doubted that, thinking of the number of pictures I'd plastered all over social media.

'Well, look at you now, in the epicentre of it all.'

'Finally I can scratch Hy Brasil off my bucket list.'

We grinned and that happy feeling bubbled through me again. And then I went and popped it.

'Will you stay here?'

It was a loaded question and we both knew it. His expression immediately turned solemn.

'It was never my plan, but I like it here so much.'

'With time off for good behaviour?' I tried to lighten the mood a little bit, annoyed at myself for asking the big question so early. Why couldn't I just shut up?

'I got tired of travelling, and big cities, and I feel so centred here. There's your hippy-dippy crap, yeah? That was always my plan anyway.' He exhaled heavily, and stared deep into my eyes.

Boom. There it was. It was said and it wasn't said.

'Well . . .' I couldn't manage anything else. All other words were stuck somewhere in my oesophagus. I knew what he was trying to say. I nodded. I held my breath and smiled at him, hoping he knew that I knew.

We devoured a garlic-fuelled meal: garlic mushrooms, garlic bread, salami pizza with garlic salt. We threw back red wine. And we talked. It was as if I had prepared a list of questions – not as if: I actually had them in my head, though I hadn't written anything down, that would just be weird – and they spilled out of me. And I think he had done the same. We were unwrapping each other. Getting down to the essence of one another. All the while stealing little glances, swapping intimate smiles, letting the world revolve and move on around us. We didn't care what was happening outside of us.

My head was full of shooting stars when he kissed me. Up against a wall, no less, the side wall of Alfonso's, where I had stumbled, a little bit pissed, looking for my wellies.

'After all that garlic I must stink.' His eyelashes were almost touching mine.

I laughed. 'Is that what they call whispering sweet nothings?'

His lips lingered on mine, soft and warm, and as he pulled his head away I pushed myself into him for another kiss.

It was brilliant. And I didn't care that we both stank of garlic and I was holding a pair of wellies in my hand, that I had a green waterproof anorak on, nor that the rain had started falling on us, destroying my sleek locks. I threw my arms around his neck and pulled him closer to me. He pressed himself against me, and I felt the hardness of his thighs and the flatness of his stomach. And suddenly my clothes, his clothes, everything between us was a burden that needed to be removed immediately. I was overcome with desire; I had to feel his skin against mine. He buried his face in my neck, breathing heavily, I threw my head back and wrapped my leg around him, encasing him, bringing him closer to me.

The Enchanted Island

'We have to get out of here.'

'The caravan, five-minute walk.'

'I bet we could run it in three.'

We made it in two. I felt dizzy and light as I took the two steps into the bedroom, leading Killian inside. He spun me around and pulled me to him, looking deep into my eyes, his chest heaving. I was swamped by lust. I ran my hands around his waist, fingering his belt and deliberately plucking his shirt from it so I could finally touch his skin. I ran my palm up his back, his glorious, smooth-skinned back. Within half a second we were both naked and had fallen onto the bed, rolling around, holding each other.

'Condom,' I managed to spit out.

He lifted his head from my neck. 'Oh no.'

'What?'

'I've no – I didn't bring one.'

'Oh . . . okay.' This was different. This was unexpected. 'You didn't . . . ?'

'I didn't think we'd get to this point. I didn't want you to think that was what I was after.' He gave that adorable lopsided grin and I thought I would levitate with desire. Instead I made a noise like you would make if you saw a basket of kittens.

He bit his lip and laughed, shaking his head. 'I have some back at my house.'

'That's an hour's walk away.' I laughed too – in fact, I roared. It was hilarious. Two willing, able-bodied naked people gagging to have sex with each other and we couldn't. He leaned over and kissed me.

'We have plenty of time.'

He stood up. 'I'm going to get a glass of water, you want one?' He walked out – his lovely long legs and his pert bum and fabulous broad shoulders – like he had been walking naked around this caravan his whole life.

I snuggled under the duvet, smiling to myself. I remembered moments like this with Carl. When he would pop out to the loo, I would scramble to reapply my makeup, to look flawless in bed. I didn't need to do that with Killian, he liked me for me. It felt glorious and I was happy.

He slid under the duvet with me, and raised his arm and I curled into him, laying my head on his chest. We started to chat and laugh about nothing and everything, like we had been chatting like this our whole lives and we had our whole lives to keep on chatting.

31

'Maeve, Maeve,' a shrill voice called. I knew who it was, I just didn't want to spin around.

Again, she shouted, this time louder: 'Maeve!'

I couldn't ignore her, I was only a few feet away. I turned and walked back, waving half-heartedly. 'Maura, hi.'

She was standing in the doorway of her salon (or as she called it, her 'saloon') pointing a makeup brush at me.

'Sure you're not up to anything. Come in, I need you.' She grabbed me by the shoulders and pulled me so close I thought I'd gag on her heavy perfume, Poison.

'Well, I was just . . .' I pointed up the street. I had been on my way out to Dan's. He hadn't stopped calling me all day, like a needy boyfriend, we had to have a face-to-face so I could tell him to give me a break. My own face was glowing and my body aching after my glorious non-sexual night with Killian. I had fallen asleep cocooned by him, encased safely in his arms, swallowed up in the happy moment, until his alarm went off and he bounced out of bed for school.

Like a hurricane in a snow globe, Maura pushed me into the salon and slid a chair under me.

'I just got a new shipment of makeup. Summer colours, and I'm not familiar with the tones, I need a guinea pig.'

It was the way she said 'pig', the way the word fell gleefully out of her mouth, that I knew I was in for it. I put my hands on the armrests and tried to stand up, gazing longingly at the door. I could just run. Although I knew Maura's speed and strength would out-manoeuvre me in seconds. She pushed me back down.

'I don't have time, Maura, I have to see Dan about his will.'

'Don't mind him.'

'I have an appointment,' I lied.

'You'll be late, it's grand.'

I knew I was being bullied and I should probably start a Twitter hashtag campaign immediately about the injustice of all this, but instead I gave in.

'I'll make a tea, there's a few biscuits in the back too.' Maura tottered off.

'How long will this take?' I shouted after her.

'Twenty minutes at the very most.'

I looked at my reflection in the mirror. Normally I'd be checking under my eyes for mascara cobwebs and pinching my cheeks for a blush check. But I wasn't wearing any makeup. I knew that the wind and rain on the walk to Dan's would have turned me into the Joker from *Batman*, so I was bare-faced.

The Enchanted Island

I noticed that my eyelash extensions had started to fall out, making my eyes look uneven. I started to pluck away at the remaining few, correcting the balance. My eyebrows were filling out, my skin was pale but dewy from all the rain, and my cheeks had a natural pink glow. It was strange, looking at myself bare-faced, a state that I would only ever normally be in the middle of the night after my night creams wore off, or first thing in the morning before the beauty battle started. It was only ever an in-between state, but I looked – I wasn't sure how I looked, I never saw myself like this. And then it struck me: I looked happy. I wasn't pulling or preening or viewing myself as others saw me, I wasn't pouting or arching. I just was. And it suited me. I looked happy. I didn't care that I hadn't moisturised and that Maura was about to run her fingers over my face, that she'd know, that she'd judge me. I didn't care. I smiled, and I saw that my reflection was beautiful.

I looked away, embarrassed, immediately thinking I was wrong. *But I'm not beautiful*, I thought. *That's not me.* I peeped through my eyelashes. *I am. I definitely am.* I felt a surge of emotions I couldn't explain. I wanted to cry. *Maybe I'm okay. Maybe I look okay, more than okay. Maybe I am beautiful.* I gulped back a sob that was suddenly threatening to overpower me. What was this? Why was I feeling like this? I was stripped of all the stuff, that barrier of makeup and creams. And I was okay, in fact I was better than okay – I was great. Sasha was right when she'd shouted at me, screaming that I needed to lose all the stuff, to go back to me. She was right. Sasha was right. I just hadn't known it all those weeks ago. And it wasn't just about how I looked, it was about me. All this time alone, walking in nature, exercising, eating, enjoying myself with lovely people – and Killian – all of this, on this strange island, was bringing me back to me. My shoulders shuddered with a sob that I quickly breathed back, blinking my eyes. I laughed to myself. Oprah would have a field day.

'Ta da!' Like a magician's assistant, Maura displayed a tray of pots and powders in colours that belonged in a children's nursery: bright blues, yellows, greens, oranges.

'Wow.' I reined myself in quickly, turning my head from the mirror and focusing on the makeup. I sat up straight and took a long breath. 'It's like a rainbow.'

She clapped her hands in delight. 'That's the name of the collection, Summer Rainbows. I did an online tutorial about how to blend rainbow stripes on the eyes. I really want to try it out.'

'Okay, let's go for it.' I grinned. Why not? Maybe this might be fun. Maybe not caring about what other people thought might feel really good.

Four cups of tea and three hours later I emerged looking like an Irish Harajuku girl, wearing coral-pink lipstick, my hair in a swishy ponytail decorated with diamantes. My skin was now caked in a sun shimmer foundation that was so dark it looked like my face had been born in India, while my neck and chest were one hundred per cent Irish. Maura had hugged me, told me I was gorgeous and as a thank-you promised to do my hair for free next time.

The Enchanted Island

I was slightly dazed as I ambled up Main Street, and was having difficulty seeing clearly underneath my electric blue false eyelashes. It was eight o'clock, probably too late to go to Dan's. The evening had a twilight feel to it, a purple hue that stretched forever, clinging to the sky. It was warm but I could sense that in minutes the temperature would drop as night descended. I sat myself on a stone wall sheltered by a tree and pulled my phone out.

'Hazel, can you talk?'

'Just got the boys to bed, they've been asking for you.'

'It's been too long; I'm dying to see them.'

'Brian has opened a bottle of wine, heaven. How are you going?'

'Fine. I've met this fantastic guy.' I felt myself blushing.

'What? That's the last thing I expected to hear from you.'

'I know, it's completely caught me off-guard, he's so nice, and lovely, and smiley. He smiles all the time.'

'Who is he?'

'A school teacher, he's not even on Facebook.'

'Can you send me a picture?'

'I don't have any.'

'This is new.'

'I know, he's different.'

'How's the other stuff going?'

'Yeah, I'm close, I think. Did you find anything out?'

'Oh yes, I did, something stinks about this whole thing. Harry's PA is quite secretive, she's very loyal, so it's difficult to put the pieces together. Turns out Dan and Harry have a company, Savannah Holdings.'

'Yes, Dan just told me they have operations in the US and the Cayman Islands.'

'I mean, there's nothing shady about it, Harry can do what he wants with his own money, and Dan is listed as a client of the firm, it's all above board. But his PA accidentally left a client account cheque book on her desk the other day, and I had the quickest flick through the stubs. It was very *Miami Vice* of me – I had literally half a second. Anyway, Harry is writing cheques like they're going out of fashion.'

'Couldn't that be related to the redundancies and the company being in trouble?'

'Yeah, but that's client money, it's not supposed to be used for anything other than client transactions.'

'He might have had some.'

'Of course, it's just he has written a lot of cheques. It's not a normal amount. You know, Maeve, that client money just rests in the firm's account, we only hold on to it when marriages split up or when properties are sold, or after a death, before the money gets distributed out to all parties, or when a company is bought. It's not our money; it still belongs to the client. The only reason a cheque needs to be written is when it's given back to the client or distributed to whomever is owed the amount when their case is closed. He's been writing a lot of cheques and we haven't been closing a lot of cases these last few weeks.'

'You sound really suspicious.'

'I am. I saw cheques made out to Savannah Holdings – a lot of them.'

I was stunned. 'From the client checking account?' I asked, just to be sure, to be sure.

'Yes. If Harry is using the client cheque book for anything other than paying clients back their own money, it's highly illegal. It's stealing. I would be so mad if Harry was up to something and the rest of the company was paying for it.'

We chatted a bit more, but it stuck in my head. I hung up, sliding my phone back into my bag. If Hazel was right, Harry wouldn't just be disbarred, he'd be sent to prison. He'd be practically camouflaged, with his orange tan blending with an orange jumpsuit. She'd need a lot more evidence, though, and she'd have to be careful who she spoke to. She was getting into dangerous territory.

From underneath my shady pine I noticed some old people parading down Main Street, their white heads bobbing like beacons. There were some of the caped crusaders too, wrapping their knitted shawls around their shoulders. They walked briskly, with intent. I watched as they purposefully marched into the town hall, two by two, as though waiting for a flood. Could it be bingo? Although they didn't look the bingo type; I couldn't see any of these crotchety old ones getting excited about two little ducks and the chance to win a casserole dish. And yet something was going on in there. A dance? A good time waltz? What did old people do anyways? And then I saw that heavily pregnant woman. The one who seriously looked like a baby was going to roll out from under her dress at any moment. I could see the woman's cheeks puffing in exhaustion, exasperation or labour, I didn't know. She was being helped up the steps by two very frail old men, but I knew that appearances were deceptive and while they might look like a strong gust of wind would blow them over, they could probably do one-armed push-ups. She stopped momentarily at the top of the steps to rub the small of her back before waddling inside. The large oak doors shut behind her and the street went quiet.

Well, I couldn't resist, could I?

I crept up to the window to the right of the doors and, realising I was still very visible from the street, stole down the side of the building. I grabbed a flower pot and hopped on top of it, trampling some yellow pansies. I placed my hands on the window ledge and carefully peered through the glass.

Well, it definitely wasn't bingo. It was a meeting. The hall that was normally Maura's aerobics torture den was filled with neat rows of chairs. There were maybe a hundred people, all white-haired except for the balding contingent, and one lady whose hair was Lucille Ball red. I wondered if it was Maura's handiwork. I could see the Beard from the coffee shop, the barman from Tansey's ... I recognised quite a few faces. Shawls were pulled tightly across the women's shoulders, while the men were in an array of tweed jackets, or shiny well-worn suits with jumpers underneath. They looked very solemn. There was a lot of head shaking. I watched one man repeatedly bring his hand to his eyes and another was wringing his cap in his hands so fiercely I thought he might tear it in two. All eyes were transfixed on the front of the room.

I couldn't hear anything other than a low mumble. Someone was speaking, but it was difficult to see. I shifted my weight and felt the flower pot wobble. I strained and regained my balance. It was O'Donnell speaking. He stood tall at the front of the room, chest puffed out proudly, an Aran sweater pulled across his belly. He didn't look upset like the rest of them. The pregnant lady was sitting beside him, her hands covering her face, and she looked to be swaying slightly. O'Donnell took a step backwards, and she stood up, heavily, and started talking to the room. She stared at the floor, never raising her eyes to look at her audience. Big fat tears streamed down her face. She didn't speak for very long, and when she was done she awkwardly took her seat. As she did, about a third of the people in the room raised their hands, slowly, almost nervously. I watched a tear trickle down the face of one old woman whose hands had stayed firmly in her lap. O'Donnell waved his index finger, seemingly counting the hands. He nodded abruptly, and firmly closed his mouth. Whatever they were doing was done.

The vote was taken, but no one looked happy. I could see now that the pregnant woman was sobbing, deep gut-wrenching sobs. Her shoulders were shaking, her hands came free and she seemed to be saying thank you over and over again. Were they tears of happiness? They didn't look like it. No one looked happy. What was happening? Was this a community vote, were they all clubbing together to buy her a new pram? Why the tears then? Why did everyone look so upset?

Then a man stood up on the far side of the hall, he looked mad. He was waving his fists, his face turning red. I wished I could hear what he was saying. He stamped his feet. He sliced the air with his fingers splayed like the leaves of a palm tree. I wasn't sure, I couldn't be sure, but I thought maybe he was saying, 'Enough, enough.' But no one was paying any attention to him, people had started buttoning up their jackets and readjusting their caps. All except for one man. Sean Fitzpatrick. I could see his face watching the upset man intently and nodding slightly. His mouth was hanging open and he leaned forwards as if he wanted to get up and join the shout, but something was holding him back.

Silently, the geriatric parade started to file out, some stopping at the angry man and patting him on the shoulder. O'Donnell helped him with his jacket, nodding and shrugging. I could see the rage slipping from the old man's face, and something else registered – defeat. I wondered what he had lost.

32

Harry had called me four times and it was only ten o'clock in the morning. How do you tell your boss to piss off?

He was laying the pressure on me, threatening to come down to talk to Sean Fitzpatrick himself. I put a stop to that. There was no way Sean would sign with Harry's bully-boy tactics. I told him I'd get to Sean today, that I'd speak with him and report back. It was the only thing I could say to get Harry off the line. The thing was, I didn't want to speak to Sean. I didn't want to put pressure on him. Whatever he was going to do would have to be his decision – I couldn't force him to do something that was clearly such a struggle for him, and I didn't want to. If he signed, he was going against his people. Why would he? Money, I supposed, but would money be enough to justify being an outcast in your home?

But then I thought about the potential of the island and its healing properties, if that's what it had. It needed to be explored, it had to be opened up for teams of scientists to uncover whatever was happening here. Everyone deserves a chance at good health. This island could offer so much more than a cure for cellulite.

So, as it had nearly been a week since I'd met with Sean, I decided it would be okay to send him a text message, unobtrusive and friendly.

> *Hi Sean, just checking in, hope everything is going okay with you. If you need to talk about anything let me know.*

Good and vague. That would do.

My phone buzzed.

> *Thursday next week, lunch, I'll come to you.*

Well, I hadn't expected that. I wondered if he'd arrive with a selection of cold cuts and some foie gras, crackers and a chilled bottle of white and we could picnic on the eight inches of mud outside my caravan. Or if he'd sneak around the back with his flat cap pulled down over his ears and tap on the window like a woodpecker. Either way, it was on. Thursday was six days away. I took a deep breath. This island adventure could be over in six days. If he signed, I'd stuff the documents into my bag and hightail it back to Dublin. I'd slap them down on Harry's desk, and I'd take Sasha out for a meal in that organic restaurant that gives its tomatoes first names. I'd get a flat share with someone and get out of Mam's house and, most importantly, the island might open up and whatever was here might be able to work its magic out there. I could see it all shaping up, my Dublin life in front of my eyes, the nights out, my vast wardrobe, my tremendous, non-welly shoe collection, posing for photos, always looking perfect, primped and primed.

Then I felt a stress pain pop in my stomach. I hadn't missed my Dublin life. In fact, I realised that I was relieved to be away from it. I wasn't constantly seeing myself as other people saw me. I wasn't worried about people's perceptions of my hair, my legs, my cleavage. I wasn't contorting my body to take the perfect selfie and totting up the number of likes on Instagram. I didn't care about my designer or lack of designer wardrobe and I definitely didn't care about my next Botox appointment. I couldn't believe that I'd taken Sasha's card to have that stuff pumped into my face. And for what? To have a perfect photograph. Was I really that shallow? The last few weeks had been liberating – I had literally released myself from the shackles of my constructed life. And yet I was planning on racing back to it. Why would I do that? Why would I go back to that fake life?

I felt a pang at the thought of leaving wet and wild Hy Brasil. I couldn't deny that it had gotten under my skin. The silence that I'd initially found so eerie was now peaceful. I felt calmer because of it, the constant conversations in my head had quietened. I felt a happiness in myself I hadn't known in a long time. Was this because of the island? Was it because I had met Killian?

Killian.

Would it be so easy to say goodbye to him? I felt my eyes sting with tears at the thought of him fading from me; his smiley face and the magic way he looked at me with such hope in his eyes. How could I say goodbye to him? I loved the stillness that enveloped us, the protective bubble that swirled around just the two of us. We were full of toothy smiles and deep breaths. I loved the crinkle at the corner of his eyes when he smiled. The heat of his hand as it folded on mine. The very warmth of him, his very *self*. How could I leave that? And yet we didn't know each other, we didn't have pages of history, but there was something deep inside me that felt we could have a future. Could I say goodbye?

Maybe Sean wouldn't sign. Maybe I'd be forced to stay here longer – it could be weeks yet, weeks and weeks. I felt better already.

I reached for my tin of letters.

> *Cathy a stór*
> *We're shearing sheep. I can hardly believe it's that time again. Young Mickey Kelly helped me, he's gone sweet on Rosemary, you can see it in his face. He raced after her, tripping up, to show her a baby calf. She laughs at him but there's a smile there too. The days are getting longer and the sun seems to dance in the sky all day and night now.*
> *Patrick Flynn died last week. He was the first of the new way. I am not sure it is a better way, but Da is. He says it'll keep the island right. Keep it and us the way we're supposed*

> to be. I suppose we'll get used to it but the keening at the wake was awful raw. Maybe it's better you're not here for that.
>
> I wish I could see you in your new dress, twirling at the dance. Sometimes I close my eyes and try to see what you can see – it must be awful different to what we have here. At least you know what we have here, you don't have to go imagining like me.
>
> I thought we'd be married by now, we'd be setting up our home here on Hy Brasil. It breaks my heart that that can't happen.
>
> Will I ever see you again?
>
> Le grá
>
> John

It made me sad. Why couldn't he see her again?

I felt compelled to follow up my own love story, to not let it disappear. Spurred on by John, I sent Killian a text

> *Dinner tonight? My place, watch out, I'm cooking.*

It's funny. I would never have sent a text like that to Carl. Firstly I would have consulted with about five friends about the right or wrong way to word it, and I know the idea of me cooking dinner would have been shot down immediately. I could nearly hear the objections ringing in my ears.

'He should be taking you out to dinner.'

'Make him pay.'

'You can't cook for him until you've had the conversation.'

'Too forward, you're too pushy.'

'He'll never respond to that.'

But I didn't feel like I needed to ask for advice with Killian. I didn't care what anyone else thought. And sure enough a text flew back seconds later.

Great stuff. But why don't you come here to the bachelor pad?

OK but I'll bring food if you bring wine.

I smiled at my phone, fizzling with excitement. That was the thing, whenever I thought about him, which was pretty much all the time, I couldn't stop smiling. I was a big goofy grinning idiot. I felt like there had been something rattling around in me, an empty feeling, and then Killian with his melty voice and sexy eyes had filled up the missing bits, and the rattle stopped. Just like that. Now my smiles were on the very edge of me, literally bursting out of me.

And then I decided to do something that a few weeks ago would never have even occurred to me as an option. I deleted Carl. Took out his number from my phone, his WhatsApp, Facebook, Twitter. I erased him. Poof. Gone. Just like that.

I hoped Killian and I would have a sleepover. I felt nervous at the thought of having sex with him, but I wanted to, every inch of my womanly loins was straining to have sex with him. I got goosebumps at the thought of running my hand across his flat tummy, feeling his skin against mine, tracing the line of hair from his belly button. Oh God, I'd have to put those thoughts away if I was even going to think about getting dinner started. Dinner. What was I thinking? What would I possibly cook?

The Enchanted Island

Mam's chicken and broccoli dish. I loved that, but I could only half remember the recipe. I'd give her a call. I automatically tensed as I scrolled for her number, starting to prepare a counterattack for her inevitable comments about my hair, friends, clothes, job. I took a deep breath.

'Maeve, I thought you'd never call.'

The phone works both ways, Mam. But I didn't say that, I would be the model of restraint. 'Sorry, Mam, I should have called earlier.'

'Oh okay, how are you getting on? Paula from next door was in yesterday. Phillip has just got a job in the US with a big property company. He was two years behind you at school.'

I literally held my tongue not to scream back at her. I was a cool, poised grown-up now. 'Isn't that wonderful news.'

'Murray did some surf thing last weekend, he's on YouTube, loads of people watched it apparently. I had a look but then my computer went haywire on me. Patrick's on the mend in Morocco, Amy is looking after him, he'll be grand.'

'Mam, remember your gorgeous chicken and broccoli dish? I'm going to cook it tonight. Am I supposed to use mayonnaise in the sauce – I can't remember – and was there curry powder?'

'Yes, a teaspoon of curry powder for every two people, and you should probably use the low-fat mayonnaise, Maeve, you know you have a tendency to pile the weight on and it's just so fattening.'

I swallowed, closed my eyes briefly, and took a deep breath. 'Thanks, Mam.' I was going to hang up and then I didn't,

I decided to say something that I hadn't said in a very long time. 'I love you, Mam. I really do.'

There was silence down the line. Virtual tumbleweeds.

'I . . . I . . . well, thank you.' Her voice suddenly sounded dry, every word catching heavily.

'That's okay. Talk to you later.' And I hung up.

And then I sent Sasha a text. I sent her the text I probably should have sent her a month ago.

> *I am sorry I have been such a bad friend to you. I'm sorry I took your credit card, that was a miserable thing for me to do to you. I can't believe I did it. I have transferred all the money into your account. I hope you can forgive me. Xxx*

I didn't know if I would hear back from her, I knew I would do my best to restore our friendship but maybe I had crossed a line, maybe I had gone too far, maybe we could never go back to where we had been. She had been right all along about me, that I had built up this barrier of protection around myself and it made me hurt other people. She really knows me, the real me. A true friend like that is a rare find. I missed her and her wise ways. I wanted to share all that had been happening to me with her, to fill her in on Killian, to let her know that I got it, that I think I got it. That I was sorry I had been such an arsehole about George. He was her guy; it didn't matter what I thought about him, I needed to respect them as a couple. It was nothing to do with me. I had been an overgrown teenager. I could see that now.

The Enchanted Island

I opened up my online bank account and transferred the money across. Because I'd been living on Harry's allowance since I'd been here, and I hadn't paid any rent, my balance was looking tremendously healthy. I actually felt a little flutter, like a wealthy Milkybar Kid: 'I'm rich, gold bars are on me.' This was the best I had seen my account looking ever. Two pay cheques had gone in – the perk of being paid fortnightly – and I hadn't even made a dent in the first one. I'm normally on my hands and knees clawing at the ground for scraps by payday, yet I hadn't even noticed these two whizz past.

My finger hovered over the mouse. I knew I was a few clicks away from some gorgeous new purchases, a silk blouse, a new jacket, some shorts to show off my cellulite-free legs. I clicked on my credit card, and transferred money across. I think it was the first time I paid off more than the minimum amount. I felt my chest swell momentarily with pride.

I was growing up, and it felt good.

About time.

My phone buzzed.

> *Thank you, Maeve. When you get back from the wild west let's go out and get really drunk. I miss you. And Sara has the worst boobs, what were you thinking?*

First there was sex, then there was chicken and broccoli and then there was more sex. And then Killian and I stumbled out to the kitchen ravenous once again for even more chicken and broccoli. I wore one of his T-shirts and a pair of knickers, and Killian was bare-chested, but had pulled a pair of combat trousers on. He started to reheat dinner for the second time and opened a bottle of wine for the first time. My body held a lingering delicious ache, and I sighed contentedly.

'I'll cook next time.' He pulled out two glasses and filled them up. 'I do a mean lasagne.'

'Great, I'll hold you to it. Now come on, before we get distracted again, give me a tour of the bachelor pad.'

He draped his arms around me, pressing his legs against the back of mine, forcing me to walk. 'It's this way to the bedroom,' he said in a lazy drawl.

'I've seen the bedroom, show me the rest of the place.'

The house was bigger than I'd expected. The floors were tiled, the walls freshly painted, but there was a distinct lack of decorative flair: no pictures, no plants half dying, no corner units housing books.

I cocked an eyebrow at him. 'Minimalist?'

'Or just a bit lazy. I'll get to it.'

We walked into the sitting room and I understood what the house was all about: the view. The ocean was practically kissing the floor-to-ceiling window that formed the back wall. There was an L-shaped sofa and a giant TV and a music system. Killian moved to the window and slid it open. He stood on decking that looked like it could drop into the water at any moment. I ran over and joined him excitedly, feeling the air whip around my legs. I danced on the spot. The sky

The Enchanted Island

was the colour of blackberries as night began to fall, stars blinking in the evening light. I felt a surge of happiness, like I could reach up and stir them, like anything was possible under their guidance.

'I can see why you'd want to live here.'

'But there's no shops,' he said, mimicking my voice.

'Shut up.'

'It's pretty nice for a teacher's cottage, isn't it?'

'I know. Like, what a view and it came with the job. Kind of ridiculously good.'

'Pretty dreamy, I can see why you were happy to take it.'

We moved back to the couch, collapsing onto it, practically on top of each other, as if we needed each other's body heat to exist.

'Killian, I know you love this place, but have you ever found it a bit unfriendly and strange?'

He shook his head, his nose inches from mine. 'I know people can be unfriendly here, but I've never experienced it. I guess it's because I was born here – in a way, I'm one of them.'

'Have your parents talked about the island to you?'

'No, not at all. I didn't even know I was born here until a couple of years ago. They never talk about it. They've never been back in nearly thirty years.'

'That's weird.'

'Yeah, but Mam had those stillbirths. I don't think she wanted the memories.'

I wondered what he knew, if he knew anything. He'd only been born here; Dan had lived here until he was eighteen and

I don't believe he knew what was going on. But Killian might, he'd lived here for a year now and he was a curious type. Was that long enough to figure it out?

I realised we were both holding on to secrets. I hadn't told him about Dan or the bridge. It wasn't that I was worried about Harry swearing me to confidentiality, it was that I was worried about Killian's reaction. How would he really feel about a bridge opening up the island? He was so Zen and calm and peaceful about this place. This was his nirvana. Was I going to shatter it? How would he feel about me then? Would he look at me the way he looked at me now?

He stood up. 'I'll get the wine, and give dinner a stir.'

'Good idea. Quick question, when you were travelling and seeing the world, did you get sick at all?'

He slapped his stomach. 'Ah, man, I've got an iron stomach, I escaped all of it. All the lads I was travelling with got the works, Delhi belly, you name it. But not me.' He grinned and I watched him walk away.

Perhaps being born on the island gives you good genes and some kind of immunity to illness.

'Killian,' I shouted after him, 'what happens on the island?'

I watched as his broad shoulders tensed. He didn't turn around. 'Something is happening here that isn't normal. I've seen some things. I have some theories, but . . .' He trailed off.

'Why are the old people so strong? Why does no one get sick? Who are the elders? Like, who are they really? I have crazy thoughts. I think this place is like planet Krypton, breeding all these ancient supermen in flat caps. I've seen

The Enchanted Island

things that are nearly not human. I hear things and everyone seems to have a bit of a theory, but no one knows the full story, or if they do, they're not telling me. And it's driving me mad. I want to know. What goes on here?'

He finally turned around, his eyebrows furrowed. He was holding his cards close to his chest too. And it worried me. How can you find yourself slipping and sliding into someone's heart when there's an obstacle before you?

He looked at me so intensely, so full of truth and honesty and hope, that I could have forgiven him anything, even if he'd known all the time that this was Krypton.

'I'll tell you what I know, I promise I will, I really will. But do you mind if I don't just now? Do you mind if we just have this before we get into that? I really like you, Maeve, and I didn't expect you.' He came back to me and ran the back of his hand across my cheek in the most delicate and tender of ways.

'I didn't expect you either.'

33

It was the night patrol. I was sure of it. I rememberd Tim telling me about the torches and luminous vests, and peeped out from behind the curtain. Sure enough, I could see streams of light racing across the field out the front of the caravan, like a soundless dance. I almost expected O'Donnell's face to pop up. Boo! There was no noise, though: that incredible shrieking that had spooked me wasn't accompanying the patrol.

I wished I hadn't told Killian to go home. We had been bed hopping for the last two nights, his house, the caravan, but he couldn't sleep a wink with me up against him. I suspected I snored the place down but he was too nice to say anything, because I had no problem sleeping. He, on the other hand, was exhausted, and was carrying little purple suitcases under his eyes. He needed a good night's sleep to be able to control his classroom of renegade nine- and ten-year-olds, so I had sent him home – after some loving, obviously.

The Enchanted Island

I could feel myself whirling around in a tornado with him. I was completely mesmerised by him. On the one hand, I wanted to let go, let myself spiral into him, to breathe him in and jump. To fall into the abyss, to take that risk, to allow myself to be truly exposed and vulnerable, to crack myself open. But I was terrified. What would happen? Would he get to know me and not like me? Would I end up a shell of a person like Mam, empty and rattling? Or divorced, baking and running after chickens like Niamh? I was on an edge, like the cliff at Miller's Point, and I could take that leap, or run behind the tree for cover.

I picked up my phone and called someone I would never have considered calling for advice just a few weeks before.

'Maeve, that's twice in one week, is something wrong?'

'No, Mam, I just wanted to talk to you.'

'Uh, okay. How was your chicken dish?' She sounded softer than normal, which was good because I was nervous. We'd never even come close to broaching the subject I wanted to talk about.

'It was delicious, I was delighted with it. I, em . . . I cooked it for someone.' I paused, this felt monumental, I'd never spoken to Mam about boyfriends. 'I've met a really lovely guy here, Mam.'

She paused. 'Oh, well that's a surprise, I didn't see that coming.'

'No, neither did I, he kind of came out of the blue, and the thing is –' I could hear a shake in my voice, '– I'm scared.'

There was a silence, both of us probably shocked by my honesty, my uncharacteristic show of vulnerability. I gathered my words.

'He's wonderful and amazing, and I think I could love him, Mam, I really do, but what if he doesn't love me back, or what if he leaves me, or hurts me?' And the next bit I just blurted out, even though I didn't mean to. 'What if he dies, Mam?'

There was nothing but air on the line.

'Oh, Mam, I'm sorry, I didn't mean to say about him dying, I just –'

'It's okay, I know where you're coming from, you look at me and you think, *I don't want that to happen to me.*'

'No, I didn't say that.'

There was silence. I was just about to talk again when she broke it.

'Ah.' She sniffed. 'You're in love.' She sighed down the phone.

'I dunno. Maybe I am. But why do I feel so scared? I thought love was supposed to make you happy.' My breathing was so rapid I'd have to reach for a brown paper bag soon.

'That's what it's all about, that's what love is. An almighty leap of faith.' I could hear a sad smile in her voice. 'You put yourself out there and you hope. And all of those things are possible – he might hurt you, reject you, leave you – but he might love you back too, and everything in the world is worth that.'

There was a long silence. I wanted to hang up and erase this conversation. I didn't want to upset her.

'Oh, Mam,' I sobbed gently down the phone.

'It's okay.' She took a deep breath. 'Maeve, you may not think it, but I'm the luckiest woman in the world. Yes, my heart broke when your dad passed away. But we had the greatest love, and even if we'd had half that time, even if we'd only had a day together, I'd do it again. It's worth it, all the pain is worth it. When you love someone and they love you back everything that ever was makes sense. There is no happiness like it. When your soul gets wrapped up in theirs, you are locked into each other for an eternity, death doesn't matter, separation doesn't matter, love transcends all that.'

The tears were stinging my eyes.

'Now if this boy has caught your heart, he must be something else. What's his name?'

'Killian, and he is, he is something else.'

'Oh Maeve, I'm so proud of you for letting yourself go like this.'

It was all about unleashing, I realised, throwing everything away and falling. Letting go of myself.

'Well, I'm trying, Mam, but it's hard, you know.'

She was quiet for a moment, before she softly responded, 'I know. I really do.'

'He's great though, really, really great.' I laughed, giddy again at the very thought of him.

'He sounds it, Maeve, he sounds great. Now what are you doing on the phone to me? Go get him! I'm looking forward to meeting him, we'll have him for dinner when you're back. We'll get the boys round, make a night of it.' And she sounded excited and happy. 'My darling girl, now go get that lovely boy, if he has a brain cell in his head he's already madly in love with you, how could he not be? You're our Miss Maevo.'

I hung up the phone and stared into the abyss, stunned. I had never had a conversation like that with Mam in my life. Never. She was amazing and wise and smart, and so insightful, she would leave the Dalai Lama out shivering in the cold. Had she always been like that and I'd never seen it? I smiled, proud of her and proud of me too, for talking about the big stuff, and it had gone really well. No one had slammed a door or screamed. There had been no tantrums. It had been lovely.

Another flash of light crossed my thin curtain. I peeped out the window again and saw shadows carrying torches in the distance. There was no urgency about their walk – it looked to be more of a midnight stroll, lazy almost. They wore heavy jackets and caps, but I could make out some white strands of hair springing out. Why did these people not dye their hair? They'd take years off. They'd pass for a spring chicken of eighty with some warm hues or auburn streaks. Not to mention a bit of fake tan.

Very quietly, almost like a cow lowing, they were calling someone's name. I pressed my ear to the cold glass of the window, listening so hard I nearly burst an eardrum with the strain.

Blackie. They were calling for Blackie. Who was he? A dog? It sounded like a dog's name, some chocolate-eyed Labrador. If they were just looking for a dog, I should go out and help. I told myself they were only a bunch of old people,

The Enchanted Island

out searching for a dog at night. Completely normal, in fact, rather civic-minded of them. But gnawing away at me was that evil voice of distrust: things were never what they seemed here, and I should be worried. I should be scared. I drowned that voice out with a gulp of cold tea. Dan wasn't here this time to hold me back, I was big, bold and brave enough to find out what was going on.

As I buttoned up my jacket, my fingers shook slightly. *For God's sake, Maeve, these people are old, they're looking for a dog. There's nothing to worry about.* I slid into my wellies and made sure to lock the caravan door behind me. I ran across the field, my heart thumping, racing up the road to catch the lights. The air was damp and my wellies splashed into puddles.

'Excuse me.' My voice sounded muffled and weak. 'Excuse me.' Better that time, said with a lot more conviction.

A white-faced old woman spun around and shone a torch directly into my eyes. I could feel my irises singe. Her mouth flew open, but no sound came out.

I covered my eyes with my hand and dipped my head into my chest. 'Are you looking for a lost dog? Can I help?'

She screamed. She screamed at me. She suddenly found her voice and it was a scream, loud and angry. The noise of it caused me to step back in shock. Still blinded by her light, I could only see shadows on the periphery float towards us as other people approached.

'What the hell is going on here?' A man's voice. I couldn't make out his face, just his girth.

'Who is she?' The woman had stopped screaming and was pointing an accusatory finger at me, like I was the devil incarnate.

'I just offered to help you find your dog,' I pleaded to the jury, who were slowly coming into view. All old, men and women, most looking at me angrily.

'Have you lost yer dog, May?'

'No, I have not. I don't know what shite this young one is on about.'

'Blackie?' My voice rose in pitch and I sounded like I was about to burst into song.

She shook her head in confusion. 'My dog is Toby. He's at home by the fire.'

The rest of the circle started to shuffle their wellied feet, muttering between themselves.

'What's going on here? We'll never find him if everyone has stopped to natter.' O'Donnell burst through the group and gave me a look that would curl hair. 'You should be going home, Miss O'Brien.'

I looked at the ground, tipping the toe of my wellie into a puddle and swirling it around. 'I thought I could help you find Blackie.'

'This is none of your business. Go home.' His voice was stern.

Go home. Get off our island.

'Well, if there's a dog missing, it really is my business as a good neighbour and animal lover,' I said meekly, and then hated myself for feeling intimidated by this brute of a man.

He flashed his teeth at me, like a dog snarling, and shouted, 'Go home!'

The woman called May spoke up: 'Why does she keep talking about a dog?'

'Maybe her dog is gone?' A man's voice.

'Ah, no, have you lost your dog?'

'I thought you were looking for a dog?' I said, trying to straighten things out.

O'Donnell took a step in front of the group, his massive belly shielding them from me. He flicked out his arm in a salute and pointed towards the village. 'Get!' he shouted, like I was an errant lamb.

Maybe I would. It was wet anyway, and a bit cold. 'Well, I just thought I'd ask, I don't see why you'd get so annoyed at someone trying to help, for God's sake.' I was putting up a front. His shout had startled me, my heart had leaped out of my body and any remaining organs had spilled into my wellies. I started to back away, nervously. 'Good luck with your search.' I deliberately straightened my back, standing as tall as I could and slowly, as leisurely as I could, I walked away. *You see, O'Donnell? You didn't get to me, not one bit.* Good thing he couldn't see my face, and my quivering chin.

I threw myself onto the couch and into a packet of biscuits, and got back to my letters. Cathy loved John, you could feel it in his words, his responses. But their worlds had drifted. She was becoming a city girl, she had been talking about dances and shoes, ribbons in her hair. She was being pulled away by the lights. I understood her. I found it harder to understand John; he pined for her so completely yet he wouldn't go to her. He wouldn't chase her down. Was he a bit like me and scared of what falling in love might mean? Scared of being hurt? Scared of rejection? But reading these letters, all I wanted him to do was hop on that white horse and live happily ever after. He could have gone to her. Why didn't he? Then I stopped myself. These things work both ways, she could have come back for him. She could have given up the bright lights and run into his arms. Maybe life was just getting in the way for them. In movies and books life gets tied up in a neat bow. If this was a movie they'd reunite somewhere romantic with twinkly lights, get married, have chubby-cheeked babies and live happily ever after. But real life doesn't work like that, because real people are complicated and proud and arrogant and ignorant. And maybe sometimes love isn't enough. I gulped nervously, thinking of me and Killian. It was ironic, I was being unashamedly romantic about John and Cathy and yet feeling cautious about romance in my own life.

> *Cathy*
>
> *Has it been twenty years? It seems such a long time since I last wrote to you. I am not even sure if this letter will find you, or where you live now. After a while I thought there was no sense in writing anymore. It just reminded me of how much of a failure I was, of how I couldn't muster up the courage to leave, and I never wanted to hold you back. I wanted to see you take America by storm, to leave the*

The Enchanted Island

past behind you, and I hope you have. I hope you've left a blaze of glory in your trail.

I love you. Is it wrong to say that now after all this time? I say it because it makes me feel so good inside. It's the truth. There's no off switch for me. I know you would want my life to be filled with happiness, and it is, my love. Other women have stood in front of me but they just pale in comparison to you. I still have you with me, you see? I carry you in my heart. There's no room for anyone else. It makes me happy to still love you so much.

I wonder if you think of me, or of the island or of all that has been before. But know that time makes no difference to my love for you. I wish you every happiness – know that you are loved.

You are forever my sweetheart.

Le grá

John

That was it. The last letter. He still loved her. She had received it, and she'd kept it all these years, she'd kept all of them, which means she must have treasured them. Treasured their love. It was a bit like what Mam had said to me, that love transcended time and grief and absence, that real love is that powerful. And that it's all worth the risk, it's worth the fall. I felt happy and sad at the same time when I curled under the covers and started to slip off into my dreams.

An hour later that shriek, the bone-shattering shrillness of it, had me sitting up straight in my bed, icy cold and scared, a shiver racing through me. The noise was inhuman, it rattled my very core. I pulled my knees to my chest and buried my face in them. What is it with this island? I was half scared to death. I wished Killian was here beside me. I hated hearing this on my own.

34

My meeting with Sean was two days away and I hadn't seen or heard from Tim in a while. I wanted to see how himself and Shane were, if things had settled down or if they were going to pack up and leave. I nearly expected to see suitcases at the doorstep when I arrived. I didn't, but I did see Jack's bike resting up against the white wall. I am so shallow, I thought immediately of his scones and then found my heart racing just a little when I imagined biting into one with cream and strawberry jam.

I buzzed the door, and when Shane swung it open, I instantly knew things were brighter – he smiled hello and his face looked healthy and relaxed. I leaned across and gave him a kiss on the cheek. He smelled fresh, minty.

'You look great, how do you feel?'

'Fantastic. I'm a new man.' He stepped back to let me through. 'Jack's in the back with Tim.'

'No sling? No bruises?'

He grinned and ran a hand through his hair. 'I'm as good as new, maybe better than new. The doctor on the mainland can't believe my recovery.'

Neither could I. Just a few days ago he was pale and sickly, hugging a sore arm and a few bruised ribs, but now he didn't even look remotely ill and, interestingly, he looked sober. Was this the island's mysterious healing powers at work once again?

Jack and Tim were in the very clean, light-filled sitting room where the windows were wide open. Tim looked smart, wearing a clean collared T-shirt and khaki combat trousers. The place looked nothing like the den of iniquity I'd previously visited. They were sipping on cups of coffee. Jack's scones were on the coffee table. It took every inch of restraint I had not to pounce on them. Shane announced me and Jack immediately jumped up, racing to give me a double cheek kiss.

'Sit, sit, sit. There's more coffee in the pot, isn't there, Tim?'

Tim dutifully hopped to it, pouring me a large mug, and retrieved a plate from the dishwasher for a scone.

Rizla papers. That's what was missing. There were no papers anywhere, and no tobacco crumbs floating on smooth surfaces.

'Don't take this the wrong way, Tim, but what happened? It's like the place had a makeover and you and you –' I looked at Shane, '– had makeovers too.'

Tim blushed a little. 'We just cleaned up.'

The Enchanted Island

'No, it's more than that. The last time I was here this place was like a madhouse, you were both acting like inmates. What the hell happened?' I hadn't seen a transformation as good as this since a *Beauty and the Geek* episode when one of the Geeks ended up with a modelling contract. I collapsed onto the couch and reached for a scone.

'Well, after we met with the guard – sorry about that, by the way.'

I nodded; apology for being a bungling idiot accepted.

'Myself and Shane had a big conversation about the business, what to do, what not to do. Anyways, long story short, we both feel like we've invested too much to blow it now. And we thought what if we were just being paranoid about the wailing and the scratching at the window, and the bugged computer, like everyone else seems to think we were? But figured if we gave up the smokes for a bit, that might help straighten our heads out. So we have, and it's helped to get us thinking again and we've been working double the hours. We might even finish sooner than we thought.'

'Okay. So are you saying the wailing and the scratching has all miraculously stopped? There's no Banshee howling at your window?'

He nodded, and I thought I might fall off the couch in shock.

'What? So all that was paranoia?'

'Maybe.'

'Or maybe our chat with O'Donnell did achieve something. Maybe he took notice?' This hardly made sense to me, that they could be teetering so close to the edge and then get sucked back. Not that I wasn't happy for them, of course I was. It just seemed unusual.

'What do you think, Jack?' I turned to my left and noticed that Jack seemed to have shrunk slightly, his shoulders were low and his neck had recoiled into them.

'I'm just hearing about this now. I hope it's the right decision.' He bit his lip nervously. 'I hope there are no repercussions.'

'The elders, right?' Tim piped up. 'Jack was just filling me in on them, and how we should be careful.'

'Really?' I laughed. 'You're normally so dismissive of them.'

Jack looked pale. 'Well, this project directly affects the island. They won't be happy. I would just be careful.'

'We think we have another two months work here, that's it. If we stay clean and sober, we can do it. We just need to plough through.' Shane looked steely and focused. In fact he looked the model of sobriety, a cover boy for *Men's Health Magazine*. This guy could split the atom if he could stay away from the smokes for long enough.

Jack started to scratch at his leg. He seemed edgy.

I put my hand on his knee and whispered, 'Are you okay?'

He nodded a little too quickly.

'You seem a bit preoccupied.'

He shook his head and said loudly, 'Let's all go to the pub tomorrow night to celebrate.'

This was a good idea. Who didn't love a pub celebration?

'I'll ask Killian.' I felt a million hot needles prick my neck and face as I said his name.

Tim looked to Shane. 'I don't know if we can afford to take a night off.'

I nearly exploded laughing at this almost military level of discipline.

'Such focus, gentlemen.' Jack laughed a little shrilly. 'It can't be all work and no play, come on now. We'll all get rip-roaring drunk and have a grand old time of it.'

'We could go for one.' Shane grinned and Tim nodded in agreement.

'Tansey's?' I said, as if there were a host of other options available to us.

35

In Dublin I had seen my phone as an extension of me, a shiny limb that was the gateway to my social life. I loved it hugely and protectively the way people love their cats or their cars. The many hundreds of photos on it were like a jigsaw that pieced together my life, or rather the life I liked to show the world: my busy, hectic, *fun* social life, full of smiles and sparkles. That life seemed so far away now, just like my phone had gotten further and further away from me in the last few weeks. Literally – I had gone out umpteen times and forgotten it. I didn't feel the need to check up on who was doing what. It didn't matter. My phone was less and less important. And as of today, I officially hated it. Harry and Dan would not leave me alone. If it wasn't Harry, it was Dan; if not Dan, then Harry. I wanted to throw the phone down the toilet and listen to the two of them drown each other out.

'Has he signed?' Harry screamed, all pretence of civility long gone.

'Thursday, I've told you I'm seeing him on Thursday.'

'Why won't he sign today?'

'I don't know, it's only two days away. I think if we put more pressure on him, he'll crumble.'

'Maybe we need him to crumble. Maybe you need to use some force on him?' I could hear him pacing in his office, picking things up and throwing them down again.

'Harry, are you saying I should threaten him?'

He paused. 'You need to do whatever it takes.'

I sighed; this was really getting out of hand. 'Thursday, Harry, he'll sign on Thursday.'

'I could come down, I'll be there tomorrow.'

I could just picture Harry in his Gucci slippers looking for a vodka martini and a gluten-free pasta dish in Tansey's.

'No, Harry. Please give me until Thursday.'

He'd hang up and twenty minutes later he'd call again and we'd have the exact same conversation.

Dan would ring, having just come off the phone with Harry, wanting to know if he should go find Sean and sort him out. Dan was trickier to control than Harry – he was only a few miles away, and he was like a pot about to boil over. With him, I was calm and soothing.

'It's all under control, Dan. It's in the bag. It'll be signed, sealed and delivered on Thursday.'

The thing was, I didn't want to put any more pressure on Sean than he was already under. He was clearly deeply involved in the island. He knew that by signing his land over and agreeing to the bridge he was going to change things dramatically. I didn't know Sean Fitzpatrick well, but I felt like it would be unethical of me, and morally wrong, to interfere in his decision. And I know that I'm the last person in the world to talk about morals and ethics after what I did to Sasha, but it was as if I couldn't see straight before and now I could. Now I knew what was right and wrong. And I knew that the right thing for me to do was to stand back from Sean Fitzpatrick and let him decide. Also, if Sean made this decision on his own and decided to sign, then it wasn't my fault. Whatever happened to the island wouldn't be my doing. If there was a balance, some equilibrium that was likely to be upset because of the shift in nature a bridge would cause, I didn't want to be responsible for the consequences. I didn't want to feel like I could have been responsible for interfering in Hy Brasil in some way. Although maybe that was a bit dramatic, maybe there would be no collapse, maybe things would go on as they always had, just there would be a bridge to the mainland.

No, I knew in my heart of hearts that wasn't true. The minute that bridge opened, this place would shatter. Japanese tourists with selfie sticks would be taking photos of the men hauling turf and plastering them all over social media as modern-day freak shows. They'd hold novelty surfing competitions off the west coast of the island. There'd be an Ibis hotel overlooking Lissna Tra, and a Wetherspoons pub offering five beers for twenty euros that would host stag parties with naked grooms waking up in a field surrounded by sheep. The roads would be tarmaced, there'd be traffic lights and cars. I couldn't imagine the sound of a car or the smell of one zooming up Main Street. All I'd thought about when I had arrived was how I craved cars and nightclubs and bright lights and noise, how I had judged the island to be lacking in the essence of life because there wasn't a twenty-four-hour kebab shop. But now I was pretty sure I was wrong about that. Not every corner of the globe needs noise – sometimes silence is quite wonderful.

Frank was rummaging in a drawer. Papers were scrunching up as he packed piles of loose pages on top of one another on his big oak desk.

'I have it here somewhere.' His head fell in deeper, his hair masking his face. 'Ta dah!' He flapped a photograph. 'I knew it was here.' He smiled happily and sat down on a leather ottoman near where I was comfortably nestled in a large armchair.

I gazed at the photograph, a perfect square, curling at the edges. The colours looked fake, they were a shade too bright and they didn't mesh naturally with each other. Two elderly women stared into the camera, beaming. They were both holding ice-cream cones. The lady on the left was wearing a floral purple dress, cinched at the waist, and a string of pearls, oozing glamour. The other had her hair set in tight auburn curls, and wore a red blouse that contrasted starkly against the bright blue sea behind them. I flipped it over.

Me and Cait, Coney Island, 1972.

I looked at Frank and raised my eyebrows.

'That's my ma.' He pointed to the lady with the auburn curls. 'And that's Cathy.'

'Cathy and John? That Cathy?'

He nodded, and I brought the photograph up close so my nose was almost touching it. Examining her face, I felt like I knew her from John's letters. She was an attractive woman, but I doubted she'd ever been the Helen of Troy that John had described. Although I suppose when you really love someone they are the most beautiful person in the world.

'Cait is the Irish name for Cathy, Ma always knew her as Cait.'

I put the photograph on my lap. 'Coney Island is New York, isn't it? Cathy never came back, did she?' I knew she hadn't, she had been pulled further away from him. And look at her with that string of pearls sitting proudly around her neck, she wanted what she'd never have gotten here in Hy Brasil: the high heels and nightlife. And it looks like she got it.

Frank shook his head. 'No, she never came back.'

'What happened to her?'

Frank sighed heavily and crinkled his mouth into a lopsided smile. 'You know, I met her. I don't remember her, but she used to come to our house when I was a kid. Mam told me I used to climb up onto her lap.' He moved over and sat in a high-backed chair opposite me. 'She married young, a rich car dealer, but apparently it wasn't a happy marriage. He used to hit her; they never had any children. She died about a year after that photo was taken. Car crash.'

'No. Take that back. No,' I spat. I wanted to put my hands over my ears and unhear what he'd just said. This was so sad. All this time I had seen myself in Cathy, I had understood her and her choices, and this is what had happened, a string of pearls and a black eye. No. 'This is horrible, Frank. I feel so terribly sad.'

'I hope John found happiness.'

'God, me too.' We sat in silence for a few moments. 'You felt it too, didn't you? The love they had for each other.'

'Absolutely, but sometimes love isn't enough. If Jack was here he'd probably do a little dance and shout at me. He's such a romantic. Jack believes that love conquers everything. There's nothing he wouldn't do in the name of love.'

'And you?'

'I'm a realist. Don't get me wrong, I love Jack fiercely, with my whole self, as he does me.' He smiled to himself. 'But I don't think that love is a magic dust that makes everything okay. I think life can be hard, and having love helps, but for some people it might not be enough.'

'When you were sick, did love play a part in saving you?' I gazed at the two women in the photograph, captured a million miles from where they'd first met.

'My wonderful, camp, over-the-top, emotional roller-coaster, beautiful Jack definitely had a part to play.' He smiled from ear to ear. 'But the living here is good, you can see that now, it's healthy. Love helps, it makes everything sweeter but I don't think it made me better.' He paused. 'You seem different from when you first arrived. You've slipped into island life very easily.'

I nodded, suddenly feeling an urge to tell Frank about the bridge and what I was really doing on the island. It was as if I was at the end of glugging a bottle of truth serum and all I wanted to do was spill my guts onto the table and confess, confess, confess.

'Frank, I need to tell you something . . .' Could I just blurt it out? He'd hate me. This lovely, warm Disney dad would never speak to me again.

'I'm all ears,' he said and cupped his hands behind his ears.

I shook my head. 'No, it doesn't matter. It's not important.' I changed the subject. 'You know in the letter, John talks about the new way of doing things? What does he mean?'

'I'm not sure, but I'm pretty confident that it is something to do with the mass emigration, because this new way came in at the same time.'

I leaned forward in my seat, excited. 'They have to be connected.'

'Without a doubt,' he said, seriously.

'But what is it? What is the new way?'

'If we knew that . . .' He raised his palms to the ceiling.

'Is there more? Do you know more?'

'Bits and bobs, nothing concrete. Sometimes it's hard to get the truth out of people.'

I swallowed hard. It was as if he knew I hadn't been straight with him. In a flash I hated myself for being so deceitful. Maybe I could tell him tonight at Tansey's; maybe he'd understand, he might even be happy about a bridge.

'Are you coming to Tansey's tonight?' My voice sounded scratchy. 'Jack was really keen that we all have a big night.'

I'd tell him tonight. I'd get him on his own and tell him the truth.

36

The noise. Just as I hit Main Street, it raced up and slammed straight into me. I choked with the shock; my throat closed up and I clawed at my mouth for air. I braced myself and broke into a run, holding my jacket around my chin, trying to focus on my breathing, air racing in and out of my teeth as I huffed up Main Street. The haunting shriek sounded devastatingly sad and the hairs on the back of my neck stood straight up like soldiers as I raced towards Tansey's. There was no one else on the street, no one else outrunning the spooky sound of the island.

I burst through the doors, relieved that I wasn't facing that sound alone. Turf was burning on the fire, and the smell crackled through the air. I took a deep breath, levelling myself out, and leaned against the wall to support my shaking legs. You couldn't hear the shriek in here. It was amazing, all these people acting like there was nothing going on.

The Enchanted Island

The pub was busy, definitely the busiest I'd seen it – the chat was loud and the wailing was drowned out. I saw Tim, walking back from the bar with a glass of Coke in his hand, his sandy hair standing on end. I grabbed his arm.

'You okay, Maeve? You look like you've seen a ghost.'

'Come outside with me, that noise is going again.'

I watched his face contort with anxiety, his eyes narrowing and his neck retracting into his shoulders. He nodded.

Slowly we walked out the door, with me clutching his elbow for support.

It had stopped.

Silence. A dull roar from the pub behind us, but the island was in silence.

'I swear I heard it. I just ran up the street.'

'I believe you.' Tim turned his head as if he could see a noise, waiting for it to jump out from behind one of the shops.

'It's stopped.' I could hardly believe it. I held my hands up in complete confusion. 'What the hell goes on here?'

Tim laughed unexpectedly, a loud belly laugh, and in a deadpan voice responded, 'Who knows? This place is crazy.'

Like synchronised swimmers, we turned on our heels and pushed the doors open: nothing to see, folks, move along. Tim crossed the room quickly, and I saw Killian.

Our eyes locked. I smiled. I felt this cord in my chest pulling me to him. He was beaming as he zoomed up to me. He paused for half a second, his face an inch from mine, and whispered, 'Hi', before he softly kissed my lips. I could have left there and then, grabbed him by the hand and taken him back to my lair for more kisses, soft and warm, deep and sexy. It would be agony if I wasn't going to be able to run my hands all over him, if I was going to have to spend the night making conversation with other people, when all I wanted was to curl up naked next to him, entwining my legs around his, feeling the weight of his chest on mine, smiling into his eyes. The next few hours would be excruciating.

My lips brushed his ear as I whispered, 'How long until we can get out of here?'

He laughed and put his arm firmly around my waist, proudly displaying me to the bar, to the world, as his girl. I loved it.

'I heard that noise again just now,' I said, almost forgetting the terror of a few moments ago.

'Oh yeah?' He leaned the tip of his nose onto mine, almost touching, and grinned. 'You spooked?'

I shook my head. 'Not now.' And it was true, I wasn't. With Killian holding me tightly, I wasn't scared of anything, the only emotion I felt was happy. Happy and more than a little sexually charged.

He bustled me down the back of the pub to where Jack, Frank, Niamh, Shane and Tim had taken their seats around a table.

'Ah, the happy couple,' Frank shouted, clearing a space for us. I blushed but I clearly didn't mind, as I kept grinning. Did somebody say cat and cream?

We sat on two low stools. Killian's thigh pressed firmly against mine and I could actually feel an electric charge running between us. Frank poured me a glass of wine. I would try to pull him aside tonight and tell him about the bridge. I nearly wanted to ask for his advice on it, he was level-headed and worldly, surely he could see both angles?

Jack reached across the table and swung his glass wildly, his eyes frantic, face flushed. 'Here's cheers.'

There was clinking and laughing as we all brought our glasses together. I took stock of how lucky I was to have met these lovely people, and how gracious they had been to invite me into their little family of misfits.

'And to Niamh, we are going to miss you.' Frank smiled at her.

'What?' I asked.

Niamh looked positively serene. 'Today I made a pavlova, as crisp and fresh as the layers of netting on my wedding dress, and I knew it was my last cake, because I felt so happy. I've mourned my marriage. I'm ready to go back into the world.'

Jack clinked glasses again. 'Cheers to you, Niamh. We'll miss you terribly.'

'What'll you do with your chickens?' Shane asked.

'They found me, so I suspect they'll go wandering and find someone else who needs them.'

Frank started to tell a funny story about a time he and Jack had accidentally taken part in a gay pride parade in New York. There were feather boas, sparkles and a tiny pair of shorts involved. The drinks were slipping back easily.

A steady stream of old people wearing black armbands was making its way to the back of the bar.

'What's going on?' I asked Tim, nodding in their direction.

'A wake. Some old guy died.'

Most of them looked familiar to me now: the man from the turf fields, and the woman from the coffee shop. Their translucent skin fell in pleats on their faces and their eyes were sometimes pink and watery, cheeks occasionally hollowed, but all straight-backed and agile. They perched on bar stools and moved with ease around the pub, no creaks, no aches and no pains. They were a collection of well-oiled tin men. I wondered if Sean Fitzpatrick was there. If I spotted him, I would ignore him – I'd be seeing him soon enough – or maybe give him a subtle wink, nothing to draw attention to myself. There were a lot of smiles and back patting; for a wake, it didn't seem too morose. I wondered if the body was there, laid out on a table for everyone to stand over and share one last drink with, or was it like with Jimmy the Yinkee, a drowning, so no body? That gave me the shudders. I hopped up, excusing myself from the group, telling them we needed a few packets of crisps, and made my way to the bar. Stevo was busily flipping Guinness taps like they were a game of dominoes. He bobbed his chin to the ceiling, indicating I was good to shout my order through to him.

'Five packets of cheese and onion crisps, thanks.'

He bent down and grabbed a few bags with his left hand, correcting the end of a pint with his right.

I leaned over the counter, sliding a ten-euro note with me, and as quietly as I could, while still trying to be heard over the noisy chatter, said, 'Who died?'

The Enchanted Island

He slammed some change back on the polished oak and without even stopping to look at me called back, 'Connors, Blackie Connors.'

The breath was pulled out of me. Blackie. The night patrol, that's who they had been looking for. So they must have been trying to find him, but perhaps had found him too late. My hand stretched across the bar and grasped Stevo by the wrist.

'What happened to him?'

He turned his head swiftly to me, momentarily confused by my gesture. 'Drowned.' He shook me off and busily moved to the other side of the bar.

I've been here a month, and there's been two drownings of two old men – would you call that an unhappy coincidence? I looked at the elders smiling, laughing, staring into their drinks and nodding conspiratorially together, and I felt a madness wash over me. This was all wrong. There was something very wrong going on.

I felt slightly out of myself, like my body was a shell and I had momentarily slipped its edges. The noise, the clattering roar seeped into me; their rosy cheeks, bulging eyeballs, wide mouths, heads thrown back in laughter, all of them laughing. A cold fear was creeping up on me; I knew then, absolutely, that there was something fundamentally wrong with this island. Something wasn't right. Who were these people? What was going on?

I went back to the table, quietly sitting down. Killian immediately laced his fingers through mine. And somehow the heat of his hand drew me back into myself. I squeezed his hand and desperately wanted to pull him away to quiz him about the island, to find out what he knew, what he really knew. No more pussyfooting around. It was time for a straight conversation. I looked at my new friends and wondered what they knew, what secrets they were keeping. But they seemed so innocent of anything untoward. Shane was talking about a new, entirely computer-generated, action movie that he had adored. Frank and Tim were up in arms about it, calling it a disgrace, a cartoon, a poor substitute for cinema greats. There was finger pointing and passionate arguments being made, it was all good-natured fun.

When I thought no one was looking, I leaned into Killian's ear. 'I need to talk to you.'

It must have been in my tone, or maybe my face was strained, because he looked immediately concerned. 'You okay?'

I nodded.

He ran his hand up and down my back reassuringly, and somehow he managed to move closer to me.

'Where is my errant love?' Frank slapped the table and laughed, looking around the room.

'Jack went to the loo, didn't he? Been gone a while – dodgy tummy. Ha!' Shane smiled as he drained his glass. 'Sure, it's my shout, I'll go to the bar and I'll catch him on the way back and he can help me with the drinks.'

Firmly clasping Killian's hand, I leaned into Frank. I trusted him; I knew I could trust him. 'The wake at the back of the bar, it's for Blackie Connors. Did you know him?'

The Enchanted Island

'Didn't he live over near Dan? Was a sheep farmer?' His face was impassive, unreadable.

'He drowned.' I watched him for a flicker of recognition, a clue, anything that might give me an insight into the island.

'That's sad.'

'That's the second drowning in the month that I've been here.' Either rubber rings need to be handed around by some hot lifeguards or some high fencing needed to be built.

'These waters are treacherous.'

Especially at night, especially when you're being chased by a group of people.

I felt Killian tug at my arm. He stood up, pulling me with him.

'We're just going to go outside for some air.'

Frank clapped his hands together with glee. 'Oh, the young lovers, off you go for some air.' He smiled. 'If my lover hadn't fallen down the toilet, we might go for some air too.'

I stood with my back against the side wall of Tansey's. It was coated with a film of rain but I didn't care. Killian stood in front of me, earnestly studying me. I think he was looking for a clear case of undiagnosed madness.

He raised his hand gently to my face and cupped it lightly. 'What's the matter? Are you okay?'

'No, Killian, I'm not. There's something going on here. I don't know what. Those old people, I think – I think they might have killed that man. Two drownings in a month, on this tiny place.' I'd said it. I'd said it out loud.

Killian took a step back. I watched his mouth open and then close again, like a stunned goldfish.

'Tell me, Killian, tell me what you know,' I said in my best Judge Judy voice.

He bit his lip and dropped his chin into his chest. 'I don't want to lie to you, Maeve.'

'Then don't.' I looped my finger around his belt and pulled him to me. I stretched up to him and kissed his mouth, breathing him into me. He devoured me in return, passionately pressing himself against me, kissing me with urgency, as if this was our last moment.

'When you know what I know . . .' he panted, his forehead touching mine, 'it's not right, Maeve, I'm not saying it's right. It just is the way it is here.'

I kissed him again. I couldn't imagine anything he'd say to me would make a difference to how I felt about him. 'Tell me.'

My heart was beating so wildly I thought for a moment I could hear it. I *could* hear it – a rhythmic pounding which for a second was disguised by our heavy breathing. Then it came closer. We relaxed from our embrace, our arms still around each other but our heads apart. It was footsteps: someone was running towards us at a frightening pace.

Killian peered into the night, calling into the shadows, 'Is everything okay?'

'No, Jesus. There's a fire, there's a fire,' the night spoke back. 'Down at Lissna Quail, the white house.'

Surf HQ.

The Enchanted Island

We leaped apart. Killian started to run down the street towards the house, screaming back at the man, 'Tim and Shane, they're inside, tell them. Now.'

I ran after Killian.

37

It was the smell that hit me first. The smoke filled my lungs as I ran towards the house and I struggled to catch my breath. The charcoal smoke curled up my nose and caused my eyes to stream. And then the roar of the fire exploded in my eardrums. The heat billowed towards me like a volcanic fever. The entire house was alight. The fire was strangling the walls, and the silhouette of blackened window frames appeared through the inferno. Golden flames raged as they tore into the shadows. The fire poured out of the house like an angry monster, spreading its tentacles, higher, deeper, faster. It licked the night sky as if trying to quench its thirst.

Killian and I stopped fast, swaying in shock. I watched Killian bend in two as if he'd been punched in the stomach. He heaved, his whole body lurched forwards and he threw his hands in front of him to regain his balance. I hooked my elbows under his arms and pulled him back. He straightened up, his face a picture of pure terror. I realised I was screaming, but my voice was drowned out by the fire.

We scanned the garden and surrounding area automatically. Five seconds, thirty seconds, thirty minutes – I have no idea how long we stood there. We were the first ones here. I knew the boys were in the pub, but they'd be moments behind us. I knew there shouldn't be anyone in the house, but I wasn't sure, I couldn't think straight. I looked at Killian, sure he was thinking the same thing. We ran to the edge of the fire, as close as we could to make sure the place was empty, shouting and roaring to carry our voices over the hell in front of us. A shadow flicked past the side of the house, and I grabbed Killian's arm, signalling to the left. We chased the shadow around to the back. In the smoke and the confusion it seemed almost impossible that there was the figure of a man standing as still as a statue, staring up at the sparks releasing into the night sky. We threw ourselves at him, our hands feeling him before our eyes could see. He jumped back, as if awoken from a daze.

Jack. It was Jack.

He didn't see us, he looked past us, he looked all around us, searching for something, his eyes wild and feverish. I saw the cuffs on his jumper were singed, as if he'd been up close to the fire. Killian placed an arm at Jack's chest and moved him away, shuffling him towards the front of the house, away from the fire. I ran ahead of them.

The pub had emptied out, the cast and crew of Tansey's standing like wounded foot soldiers in the shadow of a battlefield. Someone brandished a bucket, but it was laughable, a tiny bucket, minute in the face of this mountainous rage. Other people were racing back and forth, one man's voice louder than everyone else's, commanding authority: O'Donnell. He was barking orders, attempting to rally the troops, to take control back and to tame the fire. He pointed and marched and pushed people out of their state of shock; like bees they took off in separate directions, returning with more buckets and a couple of garden hoses. He bullied them into lines and within moments there were teardrops being thrown from buckets into the tornado of flames.

I ran from person to person, looking for Tim and Shane. Confusion muddled my brain. If Jack was here, could Tim and Shane have been in the house somehow? Could they have popped home for something? Was there any way they were inside that house? How long had I been outside with Killian? I spun from face to face, desperately seeking them out, hysterically shouting their names. I put my hands on a man's shoulders and turned him towards me. It was Frank, his eyes popped in shock and his mouth hanging open, but he registered who I was immediately, and opened his arms, drawing me in for a hug. I could feel his heart hammering in his chest.

I shouted, 'Tim? Shane?'

He pointed at two figures crouched on the road. I fell towards them, embracing them.

'You're okay. You're okay.' I was crying hysterically, tears spilling down my cheeks, sobs drowning my lungs; it was next to impossible to breathe. I gagged and coughed.

The Enchanted Island

They were both crying too, on their hands and knees, folded over by the sheer destructive force of the fire. We rolled back into a sitting position. Shane's hands covered his face as his body convulsed. Tim wiped his eyes and took a deep breath. We sat for an eternity or a brief second. O'Donnell's shouts became the only noise over the deafening blaze. *Get up*, I thought. *We need to help.* We seemed to gather ourselves and clambered to our feet. We slotted into a line: Killian had taken position at the top of one line, racing at the edges of the fire with buckets, sloshing water. I watched him bravely tackle the flames with my heart in my mouth. *Stay safe, my love.*

Time stretched on. The passion of the fire ebbed. Hour after hour we passed basins and buckets between us. But we didn't put it out; it ran in circles until it had nowhere else to run. Its arms had stretched as far as they could; there was nothing else for it to cling on to. Everything close by that it could have destroyed was gone.

My limbs ached as the adrenalin slowly eased out of my body and was replaced by a numbing pain. Finally, as daylight cracked through the dark shell of the night, the heavens opened and glorious rain covered our weary selves like a welcome blanket. We sighed in relief.

My head pounded as I moved away from the line for a bottle of water and a moment's rest. Killian was sitting on a wall, his hands on his knees, looking exhausted. He waved at me. I grabbed a bottle of water from a bag and gulped it back, stepping over tired islanders. I sat beside him and rested my head on his shoulder. We both stared at the smouldering remains before us. The roof had fallen in. The skeletal limbs of the house still clung together, tingling at the edges, waiting to collapse. Black-singed rubble carpeted the house. It was destroyed, and everything inside it would be too.

Wordlessly we passed the bottle of water between us, sipping it, quenching our thirst. Killian put his arm across my shoulders and squeezed me tightly; he brought his face down to mine and kissed me.

'At least no one was hurt.' He smiled.

'Thank God the boys were in the pub.'

'You did great out there, you must be knackered.'

I felt a little twinge of pride, but shrugged it off. 'No more than you.' The stone wall was digging into me. I squirmed, trying to get more comfortable.

'Why don't you go home and get some sleep? The rain's going to take care of most of this now.'

He was right. The embers were dying down, the smoke simmering from the earth, the anger subsided. 'Where are the others?'

'Tim and Shane are still hard at it.'

I could see the ferocity with which they were passing the buckets to each other hadn't waned. They were caught up in the intensity of the moment, maybe clinging to the vague hope that they might be able to salvage some of their belongings. It would be impossible – there was nothing but ash. Their project, their hardware, all of their hard work over the last year, had gone up in smoke. There would be nothing to show their investors, all that work had been for nothing.

The Enchanted Island

Just as they had decided to stay to complete the work, this had happened.

'I'll take them back to mine eventually. Let them sleep.'

'Jack? Frank?'

'They left about an hour ago.' Killian looked at me, his face serious. 'What was Jack doing here?'

'I dunno, he must have gone outside for some air or something.' I was so exhausted I wouldn't have understood a basic *Home and Away* plotline. I could hardly see, and if I blinked for too long, I was sure my eyes would close over and I'd fall asleep in the comfort of a damp field.

'I wonder how it started. It could have been faulty wiring, one of the computers could have overheated. The guys had a bunch of technical equipment in there.'

'We're not going to figure it out now.' I squeezed his knee, a sudden wave of sleepiness enveloping me. 'I'm going to go, I feel like I'll just about make it back to the caravan before I collapse.' I slid off the wall, my body heavy with exhaustion. 'Don't stay here much longer, get the boys home and get some sleep. It mightn't look so bleak in the morning.' Although I doubted that, it was like a bomb site: dark, smouldering and devastated.

I could still hear O'Donnell's relentless shouts echoing through the sheets of rain as I fell into my bed, too tired to take my clothes off. I welcomed the heavy weight of sleep as it arrived and allowed me to slip into oblivion.

38

As I showered and washed away the stench of smoke and the filthy black soot, feeling every inch a chimney sweep, all I could think of was Jack. What was he doing at Surf HQ? Killian and I were the first people on the scene, but there he was with singed clothes and a catatonic look on his face. As much as I tried to shake it off, I couldn't. I played back the evening. We had been in the pub; Jack had gone to the loo. When exactly? How long had he disappeared for? How long was it from when he went to the loo to when Killian and I got to the fire? Was it possible for him to have gotten down to Surf HQ in that time?

My shoulders ached. I stretched and strained every muscle in my body, trying to relax the tension that had overpowered me. I needed a shirtless, greased-up Swedish masseur to work out the knots in my muscles, stat. Instead I sat down to a cup of tea and some toast and sent Killian a text. I didn't want to call; although it was midday, I suspected they would all be asleep.

It's funny how something bad unites people. Last night in the pub, the elders had sat at the back of the bar, hosting their own party, but a few short hours later we had come together as a team of fire fighters. Every islander had been there. I'd seen Dan pass buckets to Maura and Frank. And O'Donnell, a man I had felt wasn't capable of anything other than blowing hot air, had meticulously organised and conducted the masses into a well-orchestrated machine. Even I hadn't felt like an outsider last night – I had felt like an islander.

I wanted to see how it looked in the cold light of day and to see if anyone was still down at Surf HQ, if there was more work to be done. Dressed in my baggy jeans and runners, I set off in the midday drizzle, thankful for once that the air was damp.

It was a depressing scene; the carcass of the house wobbled, now an empty shell. Where there was once green grass, there were just muddy footprints. The air smelled like a week-old barbecue, smoky and stale. There were a few people like me, sightseers kicking our muddied feet around the smouldering debris, not sure what to do with ourselves, still somehow caught up in the panic of the night before. I shuffled around to the back of the house, the point where Killian and I had found Jack, and stood where he had stood. I had a full view of the remains of the house. It was sad.

I could see someone moving around inside. That couldn't be safe. With trepidation, I moved forwards. I poked my head through the charred bones of a window, nervously scanning above me for something to fall dramatically on my head. There, in what used to be the sitting room, hunkered down, staring intently at the floor, was Tim. My heart melted at the sight of his broken face. I called out to him softly. 'Tim.'

He looked up, his eyes red and his face covered in charcoal dust.

I waved at him, signalling for him to leave. 'You shouldn't be here, it's not safe.'

'I know, I just . . .' He sighed and stood up, carefully tiptoeing his way out of the door. He stood beside me, turning his back to the house, and glared out at the ocean, shaking his head.

'Is there anything worth saving?' I don't know why I asked that, it was obvious there wasn't.

'No. It's all gone.' His mouth was pursed in anger.

'At least no one was hurt.' Isn't that what people always say? And it's true, it's very true.

'O'Donnell was here earlier, had a poke around. You know what he thinks?' His nostrils flared, and I watched as his fists balled up in a rage. 'Arson. The gas pipe in the kitchen was cut. Hacked, he said, someone had gone at it with a knife. Wouldn't take long, he said, for that to fill up the kitchen, and boom, the place would go up like a rocket.'

Fear snaked over me. I stayed silent, watching him punch at the air in frustration.

'This place. I wish we'd never come here. It's over, it's all over. What a waste.'

I found my voice. 'Does O'Donnell know who did it?'

He let out an angry laugh. 'Even if he did, as if he'd tell me. I'm not one of them. If it was one of them – and let's face it, it probably was – nothing will ever happen.'

I agreed.

'They win. All our work was just a waste of time. They were humouring us. We were never going to get off the ground.'

'You think?'

'All those warnings, all that bullshit about the island getting what it wants. I see it now. We would have put this place on the map. They wouldn't stand for it.'

We ambled along together and finally stopped at a small stone wall. I hopped up onto it and swung my legs, surveying the masses of rubble before us. Tim joined me, kicking his heels off the stones.

'We were on to something, you know.'

'Really?'

'When we started, the plan was to just build a regular surf app, with weather and tides. We work with these engineers who have prototypes for boards that will seriously revolutionise surfing. Part of our role was to measure surfable wave faces, to establish patterns of wave curves and report our findings back to be incorporated into the boards.'

I squinted at him. 'I thought you guys were just computer nerds?'

'We are. But we're also scientists; Shane has a PhD in oceanography.' He paused, his face angry. 'We took things easy here for the first couple of months. Life was good, we surfed, we smoked, we hardly did any work, but then we knuckled down and got into it. Honestly, it was all coming pretty easy to us. And we'd started looking at a few other things that we found interesting. We're geeky guys, we like this stuff. We found a type of coral here off Skellig Rock that I haven't seen before, which I suspect is unique to here, and there's a frog with fanged teeth that, I'm no expert, but I think is a hybrid of a frog native to Papua New Guinea.'

And the seaweed with its magical properties. And then I realised how I hadn't thought about the seaweed in a long time. I had been so excited about it, and now it just didn't seem that important anymore.

'There were just a couple of things that made Shane and I question this place, from a scientific perspective. So we started having a poke around, but we're not experts, all we've done is surface-level stuff.'

'What did you find?'

He sighed. 'There are really high levels of radon gas here.'

'What's that?'

'It's a naturally occurring gas that forms when uranium in the earth's soil decays. There are low levels of it everywhere, it's in water, soil, the air; like I said, it's natural. In some places when it occurs naturally in water springs, it can be used as a therapy for cancers, and it's supposed to be able to play a part in curing arthritis. It's a form of radiation.'

'Like nuclear radiation?'

He paused and looked at me. 'Depending on the levels, it's highly radioactive. High levels of radon gas can cause cancers, not cure them.'

'Okay, so what does that have to do with Hy Brasil?'

'The levels on the island are incredibly high. Literally through the roof.'

'What does that mean?'

'It's not normal. Honestly, everyone on this island should be dead.' He cleared his throat. 'There's nowhere like this on the planet. We were just tipping the iceberg – we'd need a full team of scientists to look at this place. All we really have now are hunches.'

'What kind of hunches?'

'Whatever way the land here is calibrated, the weather, the people, it's like they've created an original ecosystem within this circle –'

'Have you seen the old people here, the strength of them?' I interrupted him.

'I know. That's part of it, a little utopian society that has evolved independently under a microclimate.'

'But you don't know anything for sure?'

'It's a hunch. We suspect that over many, many thousands of years there may have been a genetic mutation in an islander – going way back. And they adapted and evolved to this environment and these high levels of radon gas. All you need is one who breeds and then his descendants will have a beneficial mutation. Then it's possible the ageing effects of free radicals and other environmental hazards that harm normal people are not only diminished, but they may even enhance these descendants.'

'Wow, that sounds like . . .' Like what? I didn't know.

'It's evolutionary, it happens in nature.'

'I know the families here go back generations and generations; a lot of them have never left the island.'

He nodded. 'It's possible that the radioactive environment has given way to an evolutionary adaptation. It does happen in animals. It is a possibility. We had findings that we were planning on sharing, samples, cuttings, hard evidence that we were going to get analysed, to find out what's actually going on here. But, poof –' he looked back at the charred remains, '– it's all gone up in smoke.'

We sat in silence for a few moments while I let what he had said digest.

'That day that you and Shane were surfing, and he got hurt, that was nothing to do with radioactivity, was it? How can you explain that?'

'I can't. I don't know what that was. Maybe it was the weather, I don't know.'

'When we were with O'Donnell you started spouting off about the Banshee. What was that about?'

He raised his eyebrows at me. 'I lost it a bit there, but I was just so frustrated. Obviously I don't think it was the Banshee, but as a scientist, when something unbelievable happens and you can't find a reasonable and rational explanation, it's frustrating.'

'What about drugs, would that not be an explanation?'

'Maybe.' He kicked his feet out, scuffing the heels of his runners on the wall. 'We're leaving today. Killian is getting a boat to take us to the mainland this afternoon.'

The Enchanted Island

'So soon?'

'What's the point in hanging around? We can't salvage anything. Why stay to watch people lie to our faces, pretend they don't know who did it? I couldn't stand it.'

I looked away. Was I one of those people? Did I know the truth?

'I get it, I just . . . I don't want you to go.'

He put his hands on my shoulders, firmly grasping me. His eyes stared at me with a great intensity. 'You need to leave here too. These people are dangerous. You're not one of them. Your story about a will, no one's buying it. Everyone knows you're here for something else. How long until they find out? Get off the island now, Maeve. Come with us today.'

I was breathing fast. I couldn't. I couldn't leave Killian, I couldn't just run away. 'I know what you're saying. But I'm nearly finished up here. I've one more day; I'll be right behind you. We'll have a pint in Dublin and laugh about all this.'

His face was hard. He would leave the island broken, his spirit shattered. He had been a victim of something dark and sinister and it had leaked into his carefree soul. This wasn't right.

'We're getting the boat at four.'

🍃

A few hours later, we were standing on the boat ramp where a month earlier I had arrived. A small rowboat with an ancient-looking motor was bobbing in the water, impatiently waiting for its passengers.

Killian's hoody was swimming on Shane. He looked like a kid in his dad's clothes, baggy sleeves tumbling down on his wrists. He was wearing a pair of jeans that I recognised as Killian's too; the belt must have been pulled very tightly around his waist. Tim had a tiny backpack on his shoulders, probably filled with a few more bits and bobs of Killian's to get them through the next day or two on the mainland, before they got back to Dublin.

Killian had deep bags under his eyes. 'There's a friend of mine in Knocknamee, Hugh. Himself and his missus will put the lads up. He'll pick us up on the other side. I'll stay there tonight and probably tomorrow night too and come back Friday morning.'

I pulled him to me for a quick kiss, aware that Tim and Shane were hovering. As quietly as I could, I whispered to him, 'We need to talk.'

'I know. Friday.'

We broke off and I turned to Tim and Shane, swinging my arms to them for a quick hug. 'Good luck.'

Shane nodded solemnly. 'I'm glad we're getting off here, we've just got to put it behind us. Onwards and upwards mate, yeah?' He slapped Tim on the shoulders.

'We'll see you for a drink in Dublin, Maeve. We could meet up for a pint in Kehoe's next Saturday? Send me a text when you're back.'

The Enchanted Island

Killian flashed me a look of confusion. There was so much I wanted to say to him, but this wasn't the time. I just watched as all three hopped into the boat and waved them off. Killian slid the rope off the mooring and pushed them away.

'Safe trip,' I shouted after them, hugging my arm to my waist.

39

I was exhausted. It was as if there were weights strapped to my legs and arms. My body ached with tiredness. I know Maura would say that I was due a workout, and that would sort me – a good stretch and some hardcore sweating and I'd feel good again. But seriously, I couldn't even imagine raising my arm as high as my shoulder without collapsing in a tired heap. I sprawled on the couch, resisting the urge to close my eyes and slip into a deep sleep. Sean Fitzpatrick was on his way over. This was it.

He might sign, he might not. Either way, this would come to a conclusion. This was the moment I had been waiting for. This was why I had been sent here, after all. My job. My career. I needed to remind myself of why I had been put here in the first place: I had been given a chance to finally stand out in the office.

There was a tap on the window at the back of the caravan. I should have guessed Sean wouldn't arrive the conventional

The Enchanted Island

way, through a door like a normal person. I rolled myself off the couch and pushed the window open and was greeted by a flat cap pulled so low that only Sean's beak-like nose gave his identity away.

'Come around the front, I'll open the door.'

Seconds later he was running his fingers through his hair, his flat cap tucked into his trouser pocket, about to sit himself on the couch.

'I'm as jumpy as I don't know what.' And just to illustrate his point he sat and hopped up again as if an electric charge had zapped him.

'Why don't we have some tea and settle ourselves?' Moving my tired limbs to the kettle, I pushed and shoved some cups and tins around the kitchen looking for biscuits. There weren't any. I could hardly believe it, but then I ran my hand across my waist and I could. I'd stopped wearing my belt on my jeans, I didn't need it anymore, but also I didn't need the constant reminder of the notches on it.

'Will he give me more money?' Sean was pacing the few feet that he could in the caravan.

I popped two mugs of tea onto the table and sat on the couch, hoping he would join me. He was making me anxious, walking back and forth.

'He might. What were you thinking?'

'I'll do it for a hundred and eighty thousand. That's enough for me to get off the island for good. He can have the house, he can have the whole lot, I'm going to leave.'

I pulled out my phone to text Dan. I knew he'd be waiting by his phone to hear from me anyway, but if I called him he'd want to speak to Sean and it could all fall apart. My phone buzzed back.

Tell him he has a deal.

I nodded at Sean. He didn't look relieved or happy, he might have even looked a little sad. I didn't know how I felt either. This was it. Mission accomplished. I had done it. A month of running in circles chasing an old man around an island had finally paid off. I should feel relieved and happy, I supposed, but truthfully I think that I too felt a little bit sad.

'Sit down, Sean, have a cup of tea.'

He fell back onto the couch and picked up a mug, looking into it solemnly. 'I suppose we should be celebrating, this should be champagne.'

'Well, here's cheers.' I moved my mug to his and clinked them, thinking how much I would love a glass of champagne, no – make that a bottle. 'I've got the papers here.' I slid the document out of a file that had been on the table. A few magazines and papers fell with it. I handed Sean a pen and pointed to the spot on the document for his signature. I watched as he peered into the pile of papers on the floor. He stood up, then bent and stretched his hand into them, his fingers playing through the pages. He pinched the corner of a letter that had been poking out and pulled it towards himself. It was one of the Cathy letters. I must have forgotten to give it back

The Enchanted Island

to Frank, it must have gotten tangled up in the magazines and newspapers.'

He froze. He looked at me, his face ashen. The letter hung between us like a white flag of surrender.

'Do you know this letter, Sean?'

He stumbled back to the couch looking like he had gone ten rounds in a kick-boxing ring. His body crumpled, he hung his head between his knees, his breathing was coming in short, sharp grunts. Slowly he lifted his head to me, wide-eyed with shock.

'Know it? I wrote it.'

I saw stars before my eyes, black speckled dots creeping into my peripheral vision. My head started to spin. I put my palms flat on the couch beside me, convinced I was about to fall off.

'You're John?'

He let out a laugh, staring at the letter in his hand. 'Cait wanted us to sound American. I couldn't be Irish Sean there, I'd have to take my English name – John.' He traced his fingers over the words, caressing the inky swirls. 'How do you have this?'

'Frank. His mother was friends with Cait; she left her these letters.'

He flinched.

'He was looking into the history of the island; he thought your letters might hold some clue. He wasn't prying, Sean, he wasn't interfering. He thought that John, John from the letters, would be long dead by now.'

He raised an eyebrow at me, and shook his head. 'I should be, I should be long gone.'

'The letters are beautiful.'

His eyes filled with tears. 'I loved her. Oh dear Jesus, I loved her. I'd never met anyone like Cait before, she was feisty.' He threw his head back, laughing at the memory. 'She was a spitfire, no one could tell her what to do. For a young girl, you know – she was sixteen when she left – she had a temper like a wild bull. She'd tell everyone where to go. She made me laugh something awful.'

I nodded, enjoying how his face had illuminated, his cheeks bursting with a smile.

'We fell in love over a summer, that's all we had really, a summer. But sometimes when it's meant to be, when it's destined, the time you have together doesn't matter. You can have an eternity in a day. That's what we had, we had forever in a summer.'

A stillness washed over him and he looked lovingly at the letter in his hand.

'She left?' I prompted him. I wanted to know more about what happened.

I watched his face harden. 'Not willingly, mind. None of them left willingly. They had to go. Overpopulation, that's what they said. Me da, he was one of the ringleaders, him and his cronies. They decided what was best for the island. To maintain the magic of the island.'

'Magic?'

The Enchanted Island

'Well, that's what we call it. That's the name we give to the goings on that we don't understand on the island. Don't tell me you haven't noticed how strange this place is?' He sighed. 'Back then, things happened to show that the island couldn't sustain its properties with the population growth. People would have to leave.' He stretched his arm out and wobbled his hand from left to right. 'The island has to be so-so. Too many people and it doesn't work anymore, but just the right amount and it's paradise.' He snorted through his nose. 'If you call living to one hundred and twenty paradise.'

'Longevity?' I was stunned. That's what this was all about. That's the secret the elders have been working so hard to keep. That's why they shut out the rest of the world: to preserve their wrinkly old selves. This whole place was a glasshouse after all, breeding a type of super-centenarian. But at what cost? The book Frank had given me flashed before me, that story about nobody from Hy Brasil dying during the famine times, but that was nearly two hundred years ago. Had it always been this way?

'That's what this is all about?' I tried to remain composed, but I could hardly believe my ears. One hundred and twenty years old. That was obscene.

'In part. I probably shouldn't be talking to you, but you know, I'm so tired of all of this, it's not right, it's not natural.' Sean looked shattered, so old and so tired.

'How long has this been going on for?'

'Since there's been grass on the fields.'

'Is it everyone on the island? Will everyone here live that long?'

'It used to be like that. The older families, like mine, the ones that have been here for generations, well, we just go on and on and on.' He sighed heavily, and shook his head. 'But things here are changing. It used to be that no one left. You wouldn't go to the mainland, let alone weekend trips to London. You wouldn't leave the land, you see. So we knew what was what, and who was where they should be. You have to live here, see? You can't come and go and you have to be born here. It has to be your everyday, the spirit of the island; well, she has to be in you. And then you'll see one hundred and twenty as fit as a gymnast.' He took a long slurp of tea and nodded at me approvingly. 'You make a good cup.'

I smiled, hoping he wasn't about to go off topic.

His face hardened. 'But at what price? The older I've gotten – I'm ninety-five, you know – the more I've wondered, is it worth it? Are you really living if these seven miles, this slate rock, these mud-filled fields, are all you know? I've always wondered if this greed in us old folk, these old families, to live these long lives, has imprisoned everyone here.'

He looked so sad. I realised that the delay in signing wasn't necessarily to do with Sean being worried about the actions of the elders. He had been wrestling with his own conscience. He had been asking himself some big questions.

'The rest of the world is hopping on planes and sinking their toes in sunny waters, and eating with chopsticks and speaking other languages, and we all just stay here, clocking up our extra years.' He pounded on his chest like a silverback. 'For me, it isn't worth it anymore. Who are we to play God? We decide who lives and who stays.'

I started to interrupt, still struggling to comprehend everything he was saying.

'We can't keep it a secret any longer anyway,' he continued. 'Every corner of this planet is opened up and peered upon now, we're not kept hidden from the mainland by a mist any longer. This place is finished. It's all over.'

I knew he'd made up his mind. He was going to sign. I was relieved and anxious at the same time.

'The people who left, who went to America, how did they decide who left?' I shifted to the edge of the couch, trying my best to remain patient, trying to tease the answers out of him.

'They volunteered, most of them; some were pushed. The thing is, they had to go and it was better that they went together as families. Certain families were pushed more than others, ones that weren't liked so much, you know.'

A popularity contest.

'There were a lot of hearts broken that day. Not just mine. It was like a hell. A hell to make a paradise. It never made any sense to me.'

'So those people – Frank's ma, Cait – they were banished?'

He nodded. 'In a sense, yes. In those days no one ever came back from America, it was too far, too expensive, it wasn't like today. I couldn't go to the shore the day they left. The rain fell something terrible, it was like Mother Nature knew, she was crying for us. The howls of people never to look on one another again. There was a cruelty to this place, a selfishness in the people. It was as if everyone's hearts turned to stone that day. The island has never been the same since. It used to be great, not anymore.'

He shook his head and looked into the distance. 'We said it could never happen again. There was too much pain that day.'

I could hardly even digest what he had told me. It was like a bad reality TV show where people got kicked off the island, but for real, not for a prize of a monster truck and a magazine spread.

'So they came up with the offerings, me da and some of the others.' He spat the words out. 'Offerings! Make me laugh. More like murders.'

'The town hall meeting, the voting, is that . . . ?'

He looked at me, as if he'd forgotten I was there. I shouldn't have opened my mouth. 'How did you know?'

'A hunch maybe, I don't know. I saw something from the window last Tuesday.'

'Blackie, the poor shite. They voted him gone. He had to top himself, give himself back to the island. So Vicky Ryan could have her baby. She made her case to the group, why she should be let have her baby on the island, let her baby grow up here and live long. She made her case.'

'It sounds so clinical. If you don't win your case . . . ?'

'You could try to get to the mainland, but then your baby isn't an islander, or you try again.' His face hardened. 'You see, the balance? He was one hundred and eighteen, it was time he went. Only he didn't want to go.' He laughed to himself. 'Good man, Blackie. He did a runner, hid out on the island at Carrig Cross, but they found him eventually, of course they did. He kicked and screamed all the way to Lissna Tra, but they got him into the boat eventually, and he jumped. He did that part himself.'

'It's horrible.' It was the appropriate response, but it didn't even slightly resonate with what I was feeling. I was shocked, sickened and disgusted that something like this could go on. And yet the penny was dropping, things were lining up, reality was grim and upsetting. I wondered if Jimmy the Yinkee went willingly, or all those before him. 'They as good as pushed him,' I said more to myself than to Sean. 'It's murder.'

'It is and it isn't. If this hadn't happened he'd have been dead at seventy, or eighty years of age, like everyone else; this way he lives another forty years. He just had to go quietly at the end. That's the price. Sure, I remember me da at one hundred and eighteen, lugging rocks from the quarry on his back. He'd never set foot on the mainland, born here, died here. Like most of the men here he fished, and he never learned to swim. He was the one came up with the drownings.'

Lissna Tra, the people standing on the shore line after Jimmy the Yinkee died, they weren't waiting for someone to come in, they were making sure that no one came back.

And then a thought occurred to me: What happened if you didn't jump? If you refused to go?

'Sean, if you didn't jump off the boat, would you live forever?'

He raised an eyebrow at me. 'There's a few that won't go, that are as old as billy-o. The rule is one hundred and twenty, or closest to it. There's a small group that have managed to avoid it somehow, they're clocking up the years, not showing any signs but they're knocking off everyone around that age now, so they'll have to be next.'

'What happens if they don't? You said things happened that showed the island couldn't sustain everyone. What did you mean?'

He looked sad. 'The babies are born dead. The balance you see? The old for the new.'

'My God. This place is like a hell.' I was numb, I could hardly believe what I was hearing. I remembered Killian saying his mother had suffered a number of stillbirths on the island.

He looked at the cup in his hands. 'That's how we know when things are in balance or not. Sometimes after a while if no one has offered to jump for a long time the island will cause a ruckus, she'll kick off in anger, and there'll be disaster after disaster. The sea will rise, the floods, you name it. This island is a cruel and beautiful mistress.'

He wasn't really speaking to me anymore, he was ranting, almost lost, wrapped up in his own train of thoughts. His eyes had a faraway look to them.

'The thing is, if you're one of us, you have to agree to it. There's no other way. If you want to keep on living, you have to eventually give yourself up. You have to.'

'Do people not die naturally?'

The Enchanted Island

'What do you mean, naturally? Of illness or sickness, that kind of natural? Nothing natural about that. No, don't be daft. There's no sickness here, there's great health, everyone is sprightly and strong. Don't tell me you haven't noticed? There have been a few accidents over the years, there's great relief when that happens, it's always followed by a bumper year for the babies. There's huge happiness then, the decision is taken from us. Hasn't been an accident here in a long time.'

I kept thinking of my dad. 'Can people be healed here?'

'Maybe one or two, but you couldn't open it up. It wouldn't work, the island would retaliate.' He put his hands on his face. 'The babies.'

'But one or two?' I thought of Frank and his miraculous recovery. Maybe he was right, he had been one of the lucky ones. Somehow he had slipped through the net.

Sean nodded. 'Maybe.'

'How does it all work? What's going on here?'

He shrugged. 'Do you think we know? We have lots of theories, lots of ideas, but everyone is too scared to go digging for the real answers in case it upsets the apple cart. We all work very hard at staying invisible.'

'What do you think?'

He shook his head. 'This island has been here since time began. There's a rumour that St Brendan found it on his voyage back in 600 BC.'

I nodded. Frank had mentioned this.

'Not long after, some monks tried to settle here, sure who wouldn't? St Brendan had called it paradise. Thing is, they couldn't stay, there's a mention of their time here in some ancient scribes; they were driven out, they weren't wanted here. The noise, you see. She didn't want them here. It's her island. A priest came again in the tenth century and set up a church, it took him two years to build it. It took her one night to knock it down. Have you not found it strange that there's no church on the island today?'

I hadn't really noticed, but now that he mentioned it, it was strange. Every mouse hole in Ireland has a church, but there was nothing religious on the island.

'I think the Banshee lives here. I think this is her home. I think she lets us stay here because we keep the island a secret and in return she gives us happiness and longevity. But she doesn't want religion here. She keeps it out.'

My jaw was officially on the ground. 'You know this . . .' I whispered, struggling to find my voice.

He looked straight at me, his face serious as he spoke. 'Sure, what would I know, I'm only an old man. I'm probably senile at this stage.'

I could hardly breathe. 'The noise,' I managed to splutter, 'I've heard the noise.'

He nodded. 'Followed by a death?'

Jimmy the Yinkee. Blackie. I thought about the boys with the surfing accident. They had heard a noise and then Shane had had that accident.

'I heard it the night before last, too.'

He cocked an eyebrow at me. 'There's no one scheduled. Who was with you when you heard it?'

The Enchanted Island

'Just me.'

'You need to get off the island. She's trying to stop you.'

What, was I on a hit list? Some Banshee's hit list? This was too much information for me to process.

'She's trying to stop this deal going through. She doesn't want a bridge.' He laughed. 'I'll bet you one hundred and eighty thousand euro this deal won't go through.' He almost looked complacent. 'I'll sign whatever you want, but this deal won't happen. There'll be no bridge. We can try, though.' He pumped his fists in the air. 'Goddammit, we can try.'

He flattened the letter out in his hands, pressing it between his palms. 'I was so young when I wrote these. I thought I could change things. I tried to go to her, I tried to get to America, but my da stopped me, I was scared to do wrong by him. He was a stern man. But this island madness, it needs to end. I'm signing these documents for me, for Cait, for all who have gone before and will come in the future. This is no way to live. Let's try our best. I'm going to leave, I've had enough. I don't want to live to one hundred and twenty. I'm ninety-five. I want to die in my own bed, my own way.'

'Where will you go?'

'The money will help; I've friends in Clare I can stay with for a while. I want to travel. I want to go to America, to see the Empire State Building, to look on the things that Cait would have seen, to imagine that she's walking beside me.'

'Sean, when I read the letters, I – can I ask? Have you had a happy life? Have you been happy since Cait left?'

'Aye.' He smiled. 'I've had a great life. I've had so much happiness and love in my life, I have been lucky. My father was right in one way, the island has given me immense happiness. But this last year I've realised it's at the cost of too much. Us old people, we're playing God here, it's not right. But yes, I've been happy. But I'm so full of regret too; I wish I'd been brave enough to leave this place, to stand up to my father, to go to Cait. I never married. There was no point, when you have a true love, your one true love, no one else will ever hold a candle to her.' He smiled happily, and it made me think of what Mam had said about Dad, how love transcends grief and time and it's worth it all. 'I know Cait married. I'm glad she did. And I'm glad she travelled.'

I wanted to cry. He still loved her, all these years later. Sean may not have been a car dealer, some big money man, but he was a good man. It would have been easy for me to say that Cait made a mistake, that she should never have gone, but the choice was taken from her, the choice was taken from both of them. I suddenly felt so sad about the imperfections of life.

He looked at the letter again. 'Can I keep this?'

I nodded. 'Of course, it's yours, and Frank has the rest of them. I'm sure you can have them.'

'Aye, I might pay him a visit.'

He leaned over the table and picked up the pen and hastily scribbled his name on the dotted line.

With steely determination in his voice, he said, 'Build the bridge, and open this place up. End this madness. And, Maeve, get off this island as fast as you can.'

40

Harry's phone went straight to voicemail.

'It's me, he's signed.'

I cradled the phone in my hands, staring at it as if it had answers. Sean had left half an hour before, and I hadn't moved an inch. I was trying to digest everything he had said, holding it all in my head, not letting a single word slip. If what he was saying was correct, the island was like something from mythology. A fable. Was that really how I was going to explain it? As a fable? A fairytale? Except it wasn't a fairy tale, it was a nightmare. There were ghouls and goblins behind every corner in the form of murderous old people protected by some cloak of farcical justice. The thing was, I believed Sean. I believed that he believed what he was saying was true. But it couldn't be true – could it? The rational part of me felt that Tim's explanation held more weight. But there were holes in that too.

I guess old age is possible, like really old age; I remembered reading about a place in Japan where people live into their hundreds. But there was no power or force shielding them from the elements, it was more to do with raw fish and simple living. What Sean was suggesting was other-worldly. The thing was, I kind of did believe him, having lived here all these weeks. I had seen the strangest things that I couldn't make sense of. Was it possible that there was no logical sense to it? Or had these people just managed to create a madness themselves? There was great health here, I could see it.

But babies born dead ... I shuddered. Was that just coincidental? Was that something that had frightened them into this idea of balance? How would I ever know the truth?

And just as I thought that, Killian popped into my head. I needed to talk with him. He was a man who had sought out balance, who had deliberately stayed on the island for balance. Niamh had come looking for balance too, but she had left. I wondered if she couldn't stomach the place, didn't want to pay the price for happiness here? I felt a pain in the corners of my heart, and my eyes started to sting as tears prickled. Had Killian known about this stuff and never told me? This was too big a secret. This wasn't like me keeping the bridge a secret, this was much bigger. It was like I'd just found out he was married with kids. It felt *wrong*. Had I been completely misled? I thought there was something different about him because he wasn't online, he wasn't updating his status or tweeting about his dinner; he was living life, not showing it. No, I couldn't believe that he would mislead me deliberately, he just wasn't like that.

The Enchanted Island

I exhaled and dialled Dan's number, which went through to voicemail too.

'Dan, he signed. I amended the final figure, so I'll need your initials on the document, but it's all done. And Dan, he told me about the island, all about it.'

I figured he knew. He must – Dan was born here, after all. Although interestingly he wasn't choosing to live here, he wasn't looking for balance and longevity. Dan was chasing money. Maybe he'd worked out his own balance, had weighed up what he really wanted and decided on a fast life, instead of a long one.

What did Killian want?

What did I want?

Right at that moment, it was a Big Mac meal and a large Coke. I wanted to sit on plastic seats, and listen to the hum of fluorescent lights. I wanted to cough bus fumes and ram earbuds down my ear canal and listen to heavy rap music on a train. I wanted to slide down a busy pavement in the rain, jostling my feet impatiently behind a slow walker, and burst into the doors of a shopping mall. I wanted to play Guitar Hero with my brothers and shake my hair out. I wanted to give Mam a hug.

I wanted to get off the island, away from this madness; I didn't want to be a part of this anymore.

I was relieved. That was it. That was what I wanted.

I rang the doorbell twice. Frank looked tired; he was wearing a pair of navy silk pyjamas, and brown leather slippers. He didn't look surprised to see me, it was almost as if I was expected.

We shuffled into the kitchen and he started to make me a coffee.

'Jack's still sleeping.' I listened for a hint of something in his voice, but he was impossible to read.

I sat on a bar stool, and glanced at the magnificent view. The sea was a dark green spiked with white frosting, swirling incessantly. It stretched into infinity; we were merely a dot, a minor obstacle on its course.

'I was down at Surf HQ yesterday.'

He groaned. 'How was it looking?'

'Terrible. It's all destroyed, nothing is salvageable.'

He sighed sadly and put the coffee on the counter. He sat on a bar stool beside me, suddenly looking older. 'It's a miracle no one was hurt.' He splashed some milk into his cup.

'Tim was down there, going through the rubble. He's pretty mad.'

'Wouldn't you be?'

'They left yesterday afternoon. There was no point in them hanging around.'

'I suppose there isn't.'

'All their work is destroyed. It's a terrible waste.'

Frank brought his hands together, resting the tips of his fingers on his lips. 'Everyone is safe, though. That's the important thing. There was no real damage done.'

The Enchanted Island

Was he trying to justify what had happened?

'Except for their possessions, their work, the house?'

He stayed silent.

Oh, bloody hell; I was just going to come out with it. Frank wasn't going to lead me anywhere with these questions.

'Jack was there, Frank. When Killian and I got down to the house, Jack had been there long before us.' I spoke carefully, and I watched for his response.

He nodded. He knew.

'We were the first people on the scene. Jack was supposed to be in the pub, he was supposed to be in the loo.'

Frank was so incredibly still. It was hard to tell if he was even breathing.

'The gas pipe in the kitchen had been deliberately cut.'

He slipped his fingers across his face and silently traced the outline of his moustache on his top lip. 'No one was hurt.' He bit his lip and his chin quivered slightly. 'He loves me, Maeve.'

I sighed. 'But, Frank, there would have been another way.'

He placed his hands flat on the counter and looked deep into my eyes. 'Look at how he planned it: he made sure we were all at the pub, no one was there. That house is detached, a fire would never spread. No one was hurt.'

'All their work.'

'It could have destroyed this place.' He shook his head. 'Jack was just trying to protect me, to protect my health.'

I nodded. 'He would do anything for you.'

'He loves me, Maeve.'

'Well, he got his wish for now anyway – they left the island.'

'I'm so sorry to see them go.' His eyes looked moist, like he might cry.

A few moments passed before he spoke again. 'This island has been the best-kept secret forever. Jack was just trying to keep it that way. It might be hard for you to understand, but there was no malice in it.'

I wasn't sure how to answer that; arson felt pretty malicious. I finished my coffee. 'I'm leaving tomorrow, Frank, I wanted to say goodbye and to thank you for everything.'

He put an arm around me and whispered into my ear, 'Don't be cross with Jack. We all make mistakes.'

He walked me to the door. Always a gentleman, even when someone is accusing his love of being an arsonist. 'Come back and visit,' he said cheerfully.

'I'm not sure I'll be welcomed back here, and I'm not sure I want to come back,' I said, thinking of everything Sean had said to me. 'Maybe I'll see you in Dublin?'

He smiled at me sadly. 'Maybe.'

41

My phone chirped at me. Hazel.

'I got the signature. Hazel, it's over.'

'Oh my God, you haven't heard.'

'Heard what?'

'Have you been talking to anyone from the office?'

'No. What's going on? Oh no, have you been fired?'

'No. But there was huge drama here this morning: Harry was arrested.'

'What the hell are you talking about?'

'You wouldn't believe it, there must have been six police here, they came flying in at around ten this morning. They headed straight for Harry's office; even if he'd wanted to run he wouldn't have been able to. They brought him out in handcuffs. Marched him straight out of the building.'

'No. What? What did he do?'

'He was shouting the whole ways down the stairs – "This is ridiculous, do you not know who I am? This is my firm, for crying out loud!"'

'No! Hazel, what did he do? Why was he arrested?'

'Client money. He *has* been using client money to fund the company he has with that guy on the island, Savannah Trading.'

'Dan.'

'Yes. Their whole business is completely illegal. Harry has been stealing money from the client account of Holmes and Friedman for years and using it to fund projects for Savannah Trading. Millions and millions of euro.'

'Oh my God.'

'I know.'

'Jesus, Hazel, I just got the signature. What does this mean? Did I just do something illegal? Am I wrapped up in this somehow? I can't go to prison, I didn't know this was wrong.'

'I never thought of that. But you were just doing what your boss asked. I'm sure you're fine. Don't worry. But honestly I don't even know if there'll be a firm in the morning. I don't know if we'll have jobs. Everyone is running around here like headless chickens, there's TV cameras out the front. Harry is going to be on the evening news. What clients will stay with the firm now?'

'What's Friedman doing?'

'He's going to make a statement in a bit; I think he's just calling clients, trying to smooth down feathers.'

'I wonder if Dan knew?'

'He must have; the police will be looking for him.'

'What will happen now?'

'I don't know.'

'Maybe I can find him. I'll call you later.'

I raced out of the caravan and into a wall of wind. I lowered my head and battled through. It was like trying to run in the wrong direction on a travelator. I felt my heart thumping in my ears as endorphins ricocheted around my body. I had to talk to Dan. My feet pounded out on the road as I extended my stride, throwing myself towards the far end of the island to find Dan, all the time wondering about what Sean had said. Thinking about how he had spoken with such inevitability. Yes, he had signed, but he bet every penny on the deal not going through, on somehow the force of the island, the power of her, being able to stop it. Her cloak of secrecy could extend as far as she needed it to.

The front door was swinging open on its hinges, flapping wildly in the gale. I ran in, calling for Dan. My shoulders bounced off the walls as I moved from room to room; it was as if the floor was rocking underneath me. I could hardly hold my own balance, I felt seasick. My shouts echoed around the house. He was gone. There was no one here.

The boat ramp.

It was the only way off the island. He might still be there. I ran like my life depended on it. I emptied my lungs of oxygen and let the wind carry me. And as I got closer I saw him, or at least I thought it might be him, a small boat bobbing furiously offshore. A silhouette of oars flailing and bending into the breeze.

I ran to the edge of the ramp and screamed his name into the wind.

He was hunched over the oars, wriggling to maintain his balance, a small case at his feet. He was close enough to hear me. His red face turned and he looked bewildered.

'Dan, have you heard about Harry?'

'Arrested, yeah. I've gotta get out of here, Maeve, before they find me.' He wrestled with an oar as it punched him in the stomach. The waves were taking him out, he was drifting away.

'Where will you go?'

'Back to LA. I'll get some lawyer to work this out.'

'What about the bridge?' I could hear the despair in my voice, the pleading whine.

He shook his head. 'I've gotta try and stay out of prison. There's no money for the bridge now. I've got bigger fish to fry.'

The crest of a wave lifted his tiny rowboat and he rode out on it.

That was it then. No bridge. No chance of opening up the island. For now anyway. It also meant no seaweed. I shrugged that off; just a short time ago that had felt so important, a cure for cellulite. Now it was insignificant, almost laughable compared to the real power of the island. How had I ever thought a cure for cellulite was necessary or important? The island was so much more than a cosmetic cure.

The Enchanted Island

I watched as the sea pinged Dan back and forth. He leaped and dipped until finally he became a faraway shadow.

I made my way over to a stone wall, and leaned against it, watching the shadow. I reached into my pocket for my phone, and quickly dialled.

'Sean, it's Maeve. It's a non-starter. Dan and Harry Holmes were embezzling money from the company. It's illegal. They've been caught. There's no money for a bridge.'

There was a silence down the line.

'Sean? Sean, are you there? Did you hear what I just said?'

And then, most unexpectedly, laughter filled my ears: a deep raspy chuckle.

'What did I say? I bet all the money.' His voice was triumphant. 'Ha! She's done it again. The power of this place, hey? I knew it.'

'You did.'

'Well, what odds. I'm not staying anyway, that's for sure. I've had enough of this island. She's not for me anymore.'

'You're going to go? But you needed that money.'

'I have enough. I'll just cancel the Rolls-Royce in New York. I'll be grand.' He laughed away to himself. 'She never ceases to amaze me. Good luck to you, Maeve.'

'And to you, Sean, it's been a pleasure. I hope your travels are really special.'

I hung up and I closed my eyes for a second to send him positive vibes. To wish him bucketloads of fun and shenanigans in the US, to dance and live and party like only a 95-year-old in the prime of his health can.

My phone vibrated in my hand, a Dublin city number.

'Maeve O'Brien?' A man's voice that I didn't recognise, gravelly.

'Yes,' I answered tentatively.

'Paddy Friedman, of Holmes and Friedman.' As if I needed an introduction to who Paddy Friedman was. I immediately stood to attention, stepping away from the wall.

'Mr Friedman?'

'You may have heard that Harry Holmes has been arrested for inappropriate use of client funds. I want you to know that I had no dealings with this, and I am cooperating fully with the police and their investigation.'

'Okay.' I swallowed.

'I also believe that you are on a special project that Mr Holmes commissioned independently, and I am greatly sorry that he abused your trust and position in the company to send you off on a wild goose chase for his own benefit. Again, Maeve, I was not aware of this and I deeply apologise.'

'That's okay.'

'It's incredibly unprofessional. I'd like you to get back to Dublin as soon as you can, and I'll compensate you for your time on Hy Brasil. Needless to say, Maeve, your position is safe in the company for as long as you want it to be.'

'Oh, I thought there were redundancies and –' I blurted without thinking.

'No, no. We've just brought on a new client, Gresham Holdings, we'll just be operating as Friedman Solicitors from here on in, but everyone has job security.'

The Enchanted Island

Gresham Holdings. That was Antonia's father. She had saved the day.

'Wow, okay. That's great news. I'll come back tomorrow, there's a boat.'

'Excellent, Maeve, please call into my office, and again I apologise, and thank you for your work to date.'

I was stunned. My job was safe, I would be compensated, but I was leaving. It was over.

42

Killian was asleep on the couch. His head was propped up on an armrest, a book resting on his chest. He looked so peaceful. His lips broke apart as he exhaled. His front door had been open and I'd walked my muddied boots onto his slate floor, not pausing for the half-second it would take to remove them. I needed to speak to him now. I stood over him, aware that I was treading a very fine serial-killer line, hovering over a sleeping lover.

Calling his name softly, I started to pluck at the copper curls on the top of his head. I knew, looking at him there, dreaming calmly, that I had given him my heart. That I had completely fallen in love with him. That I had opened up and would never be stitched back up the same way again. I was truly, madly, deeply in love. And it was terrifying and wonderful at the same time. I understood the overwhelming force of love, the transcending emotion that should overcome everything in its purity.

His eyelids flickered and slowly opened. He gave a lazy smile. 'What are you doing here, beautiful?' His voice sounded dry.

My heart was racing. 'I . . . I needed to talk to you.'

Would I be able to forgive him for keeping this secret from me? Would he be able to explain himself? And then suddenly all I wanted to know was did he love me too?

He made a sleepy noise and inched up the couch. He placed his hand on my hip and pulled me towards him, while stretching his neck for a kiss. 'Such a nice surprise. C'mere.'

I fell into him, unable to resist his green eyes and sleepy drawl, forgetting that I was mad at him, that I needed to quiz him, that my brain was fried with questions. Instead I needed him. I needed his kiss like I needed air. I slid onto the couch beside him and wrapped my body around him, burying my face into his, kissing his mouth, snaking my legs around his, holding him tightly, clinging to him like he was my lifeline.

He pulled away and looked down at me. 'Are you okay, baby?'

I had started to cry. I could feel the wet tears rolling down my cheeks. What was wrong with me? I was so confused. I knew I loved him but everything was such a mess, it was crumbling all around me and I felt so vulnerable. My little bubble was so close to shattering.

He kissed the top of my head and rolled me down onto his chest, rocking me delicately, shushing me. 'It's okay, love, you're with me.'

We stayed like that for a long time, me curled into a foetal position, Killian stroking my hair and comforting me for reasons he didn't know.

When I came up for air, I brushed my hair from my face and stared into his eyes. 'Sorry, I didn't mean to go completely mental on you.'

He chuckled. 'Are you all right?'

I nodded. I sat up straight and composed myself. There must have been something about my demeanour, because Killian sat up too, and he looked worried.

'I haven't been straight with you, Killian, about why I'm on Hy Brasil.'

I watched as his jaw clenched and his mouth hardened into a tight line.

'I never expected to meet someone like you. I never expected to fall in love.' The words came slowly and carefully. I had said it first. I had probably broken all kinds of dating rules, but I couldn't pretend to know what the rules were now. I knew I had to tell him I loved him. I was jumping, I was free falling. *I'm doing it, Mam! I'm doing it, Dad!* I kept my head down, staring intently at my hands, I couldn't look at him.

'I was never here to work on Dan's will. I was here to get a signature from Sean Fitzpatrick. Dan was planning on buying his place to use as a site for a bridge to the mainland.'

'A bridge?' Killian coughed the words out.

'Dan was planning on exporting seaweed off his land and needed a bridge to secure a safe passage to the mainland. There was going to be tonnes and tonnes of it.'

'What?'

My voice was rising. 'Sean signed, and while he was with me, he told me all about the island.' And as calmly as I possibly could, I repeated what Sean had said to me. I tried not to exaggerate or let my own opinion slip in, which was difficult, considering how full of opinions I was.

Killian didn't make a sound.

'Did you know any of this?' I turned to look at him.

He had paled and was breathing heavily. 'Did you believe him?'

'Yeah, well, I believe that he believes it. Anyway, why ask me if I believe him? Tell me, did you know this?'

He nodded. 'Some of it, yeah. Some of it I'd picked up – people will talk freely enough to me because I was born here. I'm one of them. But I didn't think you'd believe me. You know – how do I start that conversation? – and I didn't know if we had a future, if you even needed to get involved in all this.'

'And now?'

'Now all I can do is think about you, and I'm so mad at myself that you had to get roped into this place.

'The problem is that it's not like this is written in a science book – that there's a definitive answer about what goes on here. No one seems to understand it fully. But I had suspected what Sean said about the babies. I had wondered about it for a while. It's always back to back, a death and birth. They don't really hide it. There isn't normally a non-islander around. I think this is how the island operates.'

'It's not normal, Killian, none of this is normal.'

He shrugged and the gesture annoyed me immediately. 'Whatever is in front of you is normal. This is normal to these people.'

'How come nobody else knows about this place?'

'Births and deaths go unrecorded here, they always have, so people can try and poke around but they won't get very far, and you've seen how the locals are, no one talks to outsiders. I'm surprised Sean opened up to you. You must have made an impression on him.'

It was because I had the letter, I thought. Otherwise he would never have told me.

'I don't believe him about the Banshee, I don't think that's true. But there's something else about the island though, it's almost immune to external influence, it's as if there's a protective shield around it.' His eyes were staring at me with an unnerving intensity.

I stood up and started to pace the room. 'I don't know what you mean.'

'I knew the boys' work wouldn't get off the ground. I would have put any money on that. I knew something would happen to stop it.'

'The fire?'

'A fire, a break-in, something. Over the years apparently there have been opportunities to boost Hy Brasil, to shout it out to the world through tourism, or there was an oil company, there's oil everywhere here apparently, but as soon as it comes to crunch point, something will happen. Something always happens. Hy Brasil will stay under the mist.'

'How?'

'I don't know. And that's what I'm trying to say to you, no one knows. But you have to look at this place as protected, and know that it will survive long after you and I are gone.'

'So the bridge?'

'It will never happen.'

'And you just accept this?'

'You can't fight it, it's the natural way here.'

Quietly I whispered, 'You never told me.'

He stood up and walked across the room to me, his hands hanging limply at his side. 'I don't have any evidence, it's just hunches. Would you have believed me?'

'No, but that's beside the point,' I huffed.

'I promise from here on in to tell you everything.' He grinned. 'So this morning I had two sausages on toast for breakfast and a cup of tea – you sure you want to know everything?'

'We might just stick to the important stuff like if there's anything else supernatural in your life or if, like, you live under the sea, or anything like that.' I grinned at him, cursing him for being so cute that I couldn't stay mad at him for long. 'So you don't believe it's the Banshee pulling strings here, that's fine, but what's the noise, Killian, what's the bloody noise that I've been hearing, the one that creeps me out of my skin? Sean Fitzpatrick thinks because I heard it, it was a warning and I need to get off the island quickly. What did I hear?'

'I don't know.'

'Are you lying?'

'No, no lies, remember?' He sat down on the edge of the sofa. 'What does it sound like?'

'Horrible.'

'Do it. Go on, make the noise.'

'You'll laugh.'

He shook his head.

'Okay.' And I proceeded to imitate the crazy, spooky sound that I'd heard. The one that gave me goosebumps and that shook me to my core. Only I didn't sound like that, I just sounded a bit screechy, a bit screamy, a bit crazy.

Killian was biting his lip, trying not to laugh. He said nothing, but waved a finger in the air at me, and walked over to the sound system. He pushed a few buttons, and with a wide grin turned to me. 'Just an idea, did it sound like this?'

And there it was. The shrieking wails. I wanted to find a table to cower under. My gut was thrown into involuntary spasms. I pointed at him. 'That's it.'

'Saoirse's new music.'

'What?'

He was laughing. 'It's terrible, I know.'

'But I heard this sound outside, it was everywhere.'

'When she's working, her house is up so high on Mount Culann, the wind can catch the sound and blow it around the island. It was grand when she was into all the lilting ballads, but this new stuff is just awful.'

I nodded, but I wasn't sure. Sean had lived here much longer than Killian, he knew the island a lot better. If he suspected the Banshee, why would I disagree with him? Was that just an impossible idea? But then again, the island existed in a realm of impossibility. Everything I had seen had stretched my parameters of reality. It wasn't that big a leap to make from where I was to believe in a supernatural force. Or maybe the answer was scientific, closer to Tim's explanation of high levels of radiation on the island that allowed for these healing properties to blossom in nature. I didn't know. But if I'm honest, as much as I wanted to be part of a cure for sickness, I was happy not to be a part of Hy Brasil. It was a magical place, however you define magic. There was a luminous bliss to the islanders, most were deliriously happy, there was no illness, there was longevity and there was music in the air. It was a type of paradise that had not been touched by the hard pressures of the outside world. They had bargained with nature and, while I didn't understand their actions, it wasn't my place to attempt to destroy their world. It was worth keeping a secret. And I vowed to myself that when I left, I wouldn't breathe a word of it to anyone. I would keep the island's secrets.

I looked at Killian's hopeful face. He was dying to end this mystery, to tie it up in a neat bow, to explain it all with some bad music, because, for him, the other explanation was unthinkable.

I smiled at him. 'Come on, do you want to go for a walk? Get some fresh air? We'll both feel better after listening to that.'

We hiked up to Miller's Point, not talking very much, letting it all sink in. Breathing in the air that was dampening at the edges as the light turned to dusk. I swung my arms and let my limbs stretch out, feeling the vastness of the sky, the sea, all of it around me. Killian seemed lost in the moment too; a hint of a smile played on his lips. He looked happy.

We settled under the great tree that I had found him meditating beneath. That felt like a lifetime ago. I rested my back against the trunk and splayed my legs out in front of me. It was a blissful spot. We cuddled into each other, enjoying the great expanse of the grey-blue ocean before us. The sky was turning a peachy-orange as the sun began its descent.

Killian took my hand in his and laced his fingers through mine. 'I love you too.'

I felt like I would explode with love, that fireworks would burst out of me, shoot up into the sky and form a love heart with a bow shooting through it. *Did you hear that, world? He loves me. I jumped and he caught me. I am safe with him.* And Mam was right, it was bliss, pure bliss to love and be loved. I smiled happily.

'You know I have to leave tomorrow.'

'I know.'

'Will we – what will happen?'

'I'll Facebook you.'

I looked at him and burst out laughing. 'You will in your arse.'

'I don't know, Maeve, we'll figure something out.'

Is that what Cait said to Sean?

'Sometimes love isn't enough,' I said sadly.

'And sometimes it's too much. Look at what Jack did for Frank. He'd do anything to protect him.'

The Enchanted Island

'I'm not going to burn anything for you.'

'You won't have to.'

I knew it was going to be hard for me to ask, I knew we were at such an early, delicate stage, we were the flicker of a candle that needs to be protected before we could blaze.

'I can't ask you to give it up, Killian. But I know I can't live here.'

'I know that too.'

'It wouldn't just be giving up the island, it would be giving up living into your hundreds.'

He stopped me. 'I've only had a year here, I don't know that that option would still be open to me. It might, but I don't know.'

'Still . . . I couldn't ask you to.'

He moved close to me and put his forehead on mine. 'It wouldn't be living if you weren't by my side, if I didn't get to live life with you. What's the point of living into my hundreds without you? I choose you every time, Maeve.'

We sat and watched as the sun set and the sky's dusky twilight met with the ocean. I understood completely what people had said when I arrived on Hy Brasil. That it is a type of paradise. That the island wants you to be happy.

The island gives you your heart's desire.

Acknowledgements

I have been lucky enough to be surrounded by some great minds and awesome cheerleaders during this process. A big thank you to the outstanding team at Simon and Schuster Australia, particularly Roberta Ivers and Larissa Edwards who managed to brainstorm the hell out of this book with me. Your clear thinking and guidance got me somersaulting to the finish line. Thanks also to Kylie Mason, Laura Senkewitz, Anna O'Grady and the entire sales and marketing team at Simon and Schuster, it takes a village . . .

Thanks to Jacinta di Mase, my agent extraordinaire for stalwart advice and direction.

Thank you Steven Branston for scientific guidance.

Deep gratitude for my sisters Niamh and Cathy, and brother Shane, for their unending support. They are much more than my first and last readers and unpaid editors – they are the people I turn to when I have 'a bit of an idea' for a story, followed by an exhaustive discussions. And to Mum and Bren, it has been wonderful sharing this experience with you.

If the Island of Hy Brasil sounds familiar, it exists in folklore and has been explored as a possible site for the lost city of Atlantis, and as a home of an advanced civilization, among many other legendary tales. I have borrowed from Irish folklore and myths for this story and any discrepancies are my own.

I received such an overwhelming response and unbelievable support for my first book, *Reluctantly Charmed*, from amazing friends and family, not to mention the many readers, booksellers and book bloggers who review with such consideration, time and thoughtfulness. All of you have contributed to this incredible journey for me, more than you can ever know, and I am beyond grateful.

To my wonderful Joe, and Cian, you bring sparkles to the chaos.

Ellie O'Neill

About the author

Ellie O'Neill is a born and bred Dubliner who worked in advertising for years and came to Australia on a long romantic holiday (what does a girl have to do to get a second date?). Six years later she is an Australian citizen, and lives in Geelong with her (still romantic) partner Joe, son Cian and a mini human growing in her belly (as yet unnamed and unknown). *The Enchanted Island* is her second novel.

www.ellieoneill.com.au

Book club questions

1. Maeve's first job was working on building sites with her father. What was your first job? Do you remember it fondly?

2. Maeve talks about her transition from hardhat-wearing tomboy to girly girl who considers Botox a genuine emergency – have you been through a similar transformation in your own life?

3. What were your thoughts on Maeve 'borrowing' Sasha's credit card? Did she deserve to be kicked out of the flat?

4. At first sight, Maeve is less than impressed with her 'accommodation' on Hy Brasil. When have you stayed in some less-than-stellar lodgings? How did you cope?

5. Initially Maeve is addicted to social media and the thrill of posting selfies, but ultimately she questions it and

wonders about its actual value in her life. How do you feel about social media, and when do you think it crosses a line? Do you feel that society today is too 'plugged in' to their smartphones in general?

6. Maeve makes reference to 'famine walls' – built during the Great Famine in Ireland in the 1840s. What do you know about the Great Famine – its causes, contributing factors, and toll? Why was it so devastating?

7. When Maeve first climbs to the top of Mount Culann, she is struck by the stark beauty surrounding her. When have you felt overwhelmed by a natural landscape?

8. Maeve finds release from the thoughts buzzing around in her mind by indulging in retail therapy, whereas Killian prefers meditation. What are your strategies for quieting a busy mind?

9. Ireland is a land and culture steeped in tradition and mythology – the Banshee and Tír na nÓg are two legends mentioned in the novel. What are some other common Irish or Celtic myths? Do you know how they are viewed in modern Ireland?

10. Sean Fitzpatrick asks the question, 'Are you really living if these seven miles, this slate rock, these mud-filled fields are all you know? I've always wondered if this greed in us

Book club questions

old folk, these old families, to live these long lives, has imprisoned everyone here?' What do you think about Sean's dilemma?

11. If you were faced with the same decision as Maeve – to open the island up to outsiders and potentially benefit the health of thousands, or to keep the island's healing powers a secret – what would you do?

12. How did you feel about Jack's actions at the end of the novel? Did he do the right thing to guarantee Frank's continued good health, or was he reckless?

13. At the end of the novel, Maeve and Killian seem destined to part ways for a time. Do you think that their relationship will survive, or is it likely to become a tragic story like that of Sean Fitzpatrick and his sweetheart Cathy?

14. It's left unclear whether or not the island is protected by a magical force, or whether something more scientifically plausible is at play. What do you think?

Also by Ellie O'Neill

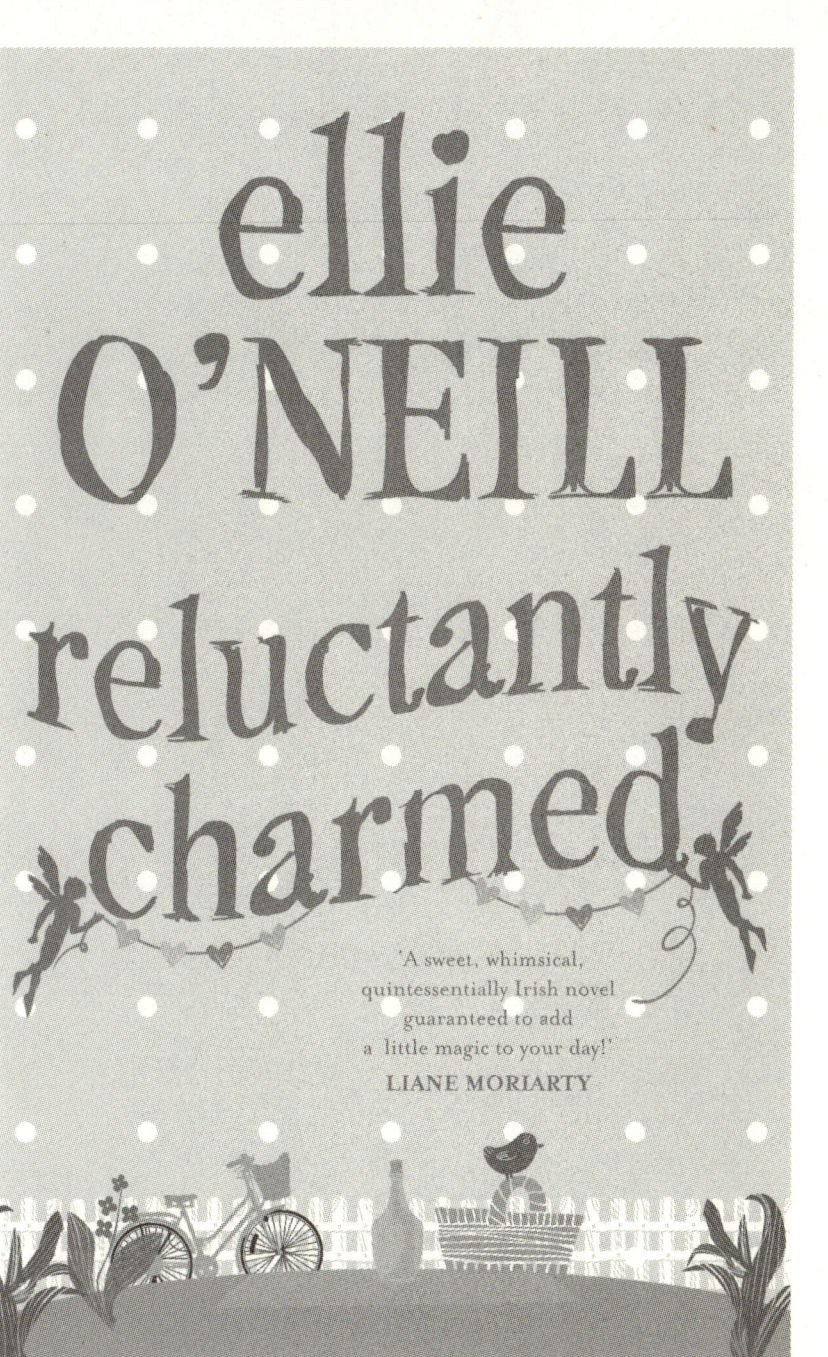

ellie O'NEILL
reluctantly charmed

'A sweet, whimsical, quintessentially Irish novel guaranteed to add a little magic to your day!'
LIANE MORIARTY